Rasputin's Prodigy

Book 3, The Hidden Amongst Us

By

Michael Louis Weinberger

Copyright 2014 Michael Louis Weinberger

1

Published by Purple Mountain Publishing

International Standard Book Number: 978-0-9837683-6-4

Edited by Dan Hankison

Cover Art and Formatting: Bill Kutcher: www.pbase.com/ibill

Printed in the United States of America

First Edition

Dedications

This book is dedicated to my family for all their love, support, encouragement and belief in me.

Prologue

Pokrovskoye, Siberia. 1905

At first it was only an ominous cloud of snow and mist that rose in the distance and offered any indication to the villagers that something was amiss. Life in such a barren and desolate area was difficult enough without the need to contend with the bands of marauders that would occasionally try to raid the village; however, such danger was a reality that every village in Russia had to contend with from time to time. All work ceased as people watched and listened while the cold haze grew closer and closer until the thunderous sound of the hoof beats sent ominous vibrations through every man, woman and child within the immediate surroundings. Terror gripped the villagers as they realized the white plume in the distance came from riders who charged toward their tiny village of Pokrovskoye from along the Tura River. The frozen Siberian settlement immediately came to life as the men ran for their homes only to emerge moments later brandishing well-worn farming implements, spears and clubs. The women of the village gathered up the children and headed to the largest of the erected shelters, which also happened to be the village church, in order to huddle in protected numbers against whatever violence the riders may bring with them. The villagers did not possess the modern rifles that the horsemen would wield nor could their farming tools hope to match the immensely sharp Shashka swords that were fastened to each of the oncoming rider's belts; however, what they did possess was a fierceness and toughness that life in the frozen wastelands had developed within each of them. That, they knew, would make them a match for any trained soldier.

Eight riders emerged from the mist followed by an ornately designed coach whose craftsmanship was remarkable. Gently sloping curves of meticulously crafted burled wood that had been

4

sanded and polished to such a fine degree that the structure looked like carved marble. Following the coach was another group of eight riders and the entire escort raced forward with such precision that it almost seemed as though all the horses were tethered together and moving as a single unit.

The escort slowed to a trot as it entered the village and headed directly to the area where the villagers had taken up their positions in front of their church. The rider in the lead slowed his horse to a walk and the rest of the escort followed suit as a very large villager stepped to the front of the defiant townspeople.

White bursts of heated breath plumed from the nostrils of each stallion, soldier and villager as the escort continued to ease forward toward the church. When the lead rider was no less than thirty feet from the mob he raised a hand in command for the escort to come to a halt, looked from the mob to the building they stood in front of, noticed the modest three barbed cross that adorned the rooftop of the building, then returned his gaze to the men standing defiantly before him.

Slowly the lead rider dismounted, dusted the snow off of his formal uniform and heavy winter coat before taking a couple of slow steps toward the villagers.

Speaking in an authoritative voice that boomed through the town, the lead rider said, "My name is Nikolai Galitzin and I am the Commander of the Tsar's personal guard."

Worried glances flashed among the men of the village for a fleeting moment, but their countenances quickly returned to stony resolve as their grips tightened around the makeshift weapons they held.

The villager who had stepped in front of the rest spoke in a deep rasp as he addressed the Commander, "Why are you here Commander?"

The Commander regarded the man briefly then responded. "My charges have come to see the *Starets* that lives in this village."

"And who would your charges be, exactly?" The large man faced the soldier with such confidence that it almost appeared as if he wished to provoke a confrontation.

"We are here on official business of the Tsar. I would suggest you assist us in…"

The Commander was cut off by the villager, "that didn't answer my question."

One of the soldiers still mounted on horseback drew his Shashka. Immediately, the Commander whirled and bellowed an order for the man to sheath his sword. Thoroughly chastened by the Commander's verbal onslaught, the soldier hesitantly saluted and sheathed his weapon all the while averting his eyes in embarrassment from the mob in front of him.

Turning back to the villager, who had raised a spear and jutted the point less than six inches in front of the Commander's face, the Commander said in a calm voice, "Forgive my men, they are becoming more and more high strung in these uncertain times. Please my friend, we are only here to see the *Starets* and have no other interests in your village or your people."

The stare the lead villager shot back at the Commander was a strange combination of mistrust and anger, but the rest of the mob seemed to relax ever so slightly as soon as the Commander had finished speaking. Then the burly peasant relaxed his arms and let his spear drop from the throat of the Commander.

"Your horses…and men, will be in need of water and food after your long ride, yes?"

Frowning, the Commander studied the man as if waiting for him to say more. Then in a moment of clarity he said, "Ah! Yes, of course they will, and I would imagine you and yours have the goods available for purchase during our brief stay in your village?"

"Indeed." As their leader spoke all of the defiant faces on the men standing before the escort quickly turned to smiles.

"Am I safe to assume we have a reason to stay in the village? The person we seek is, in fact, here?"

There was a loud creak and snap of locks and latches before the doors of the modest church slowly began to swing open and the luminescence of candlelight within flickered in the darkness of the open doorway. All eyes turned to the church as a tall man, clad entirely in black, slowly strode from the inside of the church until he had moved fully into the light of day. The man was not overly muscled but looked powerful in stature, had long brown hair parted down the middle and wore a full beard that extended several inches past his chin. The black garb he wore comprised the religious vestments of the Russian Orthodoxy; however, the black leather boots he wore were more akin to those of military origin. What was most striking, and most disturbing, about this new arrival was the raptor-like intensity of his very dark eyes. So intense and piercing was his gaze that the Commander only realized that he had taken an involuntary step backward after pulling his own eyes away from the man's glare.

Standing stiffly at the top of the small flight of steps that led into the church, with his hands clasped behind him, the man examined the escort for a moment before he quietly spoke.

"I believe that I am the one for whom you are looking." He then turned to the villagers, "tend to their horses and their needs my friends, they are expected."

The man in black then turned to face the doorway of the church and beckoned to someone who could not be seen from the darkness inside. Almost immediately the women and children of the village began to pour out and descend the steps. The men set their makeshift weapons down and began to disperse toward their homes or shops while some of the children made their way to the riders still astride upon their mounts. A few of the children held small wildflowers, which the riders ignored until their Commander gave them a nod of approval. Then the soldiers dismounted and knelt to accept the flowers from the tiny gift bearers.

The man in black walked up to the Commander and held out his hand gesturing to the church doorway, "Bring your charges inside, I will receive them in my quarters."

"You still haven't told me your name. I need to be sure you are the man we seek before I will release my charges to your care."

A smirk stretched across the face of the man in black, "My name is Grigori Yefimovich Rasputin and you are escorting Tsaritsa Alexandra and Tsarevich Alexei Nikolaevich from St. Petersburg. I know you have been searching for me since I healed the boy several months ago."

The Commander took a cautious step backward as Rasputin spoke. No one had known or sent word of their journey from St. Petersburg nor had the general public known of the Tsarevich's injury and illness. The Commander studied Rasputin as the man walked back through the darkness of his church's doorway, he hadn't believed what the Tsaritsa had told him about this mystic and prophet; however, now that he had met the man, he was willing to keep an open mind at the very least.

Commander Galitzin strode to the carriage door and bowed his head as he opened it. The Tsaritsa was a large powerful woman, befitting her Germanic background. She moved less with the grace of other royals as with power and self-assurance as she descended the steps of the carriage haughtily, then turned and beckoned the Commander to follow. In her arms she held the Tsarevich, the frail looking child appeared a stark contrast to the usual robustness others toddlers his age were prone to display. He had blue-gray eyes that matched his mother's and even shared his mother's copper tinted hair, fair complexion and, unfortunately, his mother's family's inherited tendency of hemophilia, a condition that rendered the boy's blood incapable of proper coagulation. The disorder is what had left the boy weak and listless, not to mention

8

that the smallest cut or bruise could be life threatening due to blood loss or internal bleeding.

When the infant had initially fallen ill, the Tsaritsa had called on the best physicians to treat the baby but the child continued to worsen. Fortunately, a trusted family member had recommended a *Starets,* called Rasputin, from a tiny town in Siberia. The *Starets* advice seemed too simplistic at first. All he wanted to do was have the current doctors leave the infant's bedside so the boy could rest. Rasputin also agreed to pray for the boy's recovery and, amazingly, the infant did recover. Now, several months since that time, the Tsaritsa had begun to plan her journey to find the spiritual healer, which led her and her escort to his doorstep on this day.

Ascending the steps of the church the Tsaritsa made a cooing sound to calm the toddler, whom had begun to stir slightly in her arms, while the Commander followed close behind and together the two moved into the darkness at the doorway. Initially, the darkness was all encompassing except for the glow of candles in the distance. Then the dark faded away and the majesty of the room they stood in sharply contrasted with the modest appearance church's exterior. Brilliant paintings and murals covered the walls and ceilings while darkly stained glass windows depicted scenes from the bible in majestic splendor. The main congregation area looked much larger from within than the building did from outside and was completely illuminated by candlelight.

Rasputin stood by the pulpit at the far end of the room and waved for his special visitors to follow. He then led them to a stairway where they descended the stone-carved steps into what could have once been catacombs but was now a large open space complete with hearth. Workbenches were placed every wall and books were stacked ten high on each side of each bench. Glass bottles of every size and color were stacked neatly on shelves next to wooden boxes with numeric labels. A small cot was unmade in one corner and clothes were strewn around the makeshift bed with several of the pieces being female undergarments of various shape and size.

Rasputin kicked several articles of clothing under the cot as he circled the room lighting candles along the way. The Tsaritsa and the Commander of her guard walked cautiously behind the *Starets* until the final candle was lit and the sight it revelaed made the Tsaritsa gasp and the Commander draw his Shashka sword. The flame of the final candle was reflected in a mutlitude of mirrors that foucused their illumination on the far workbench where lay a partially dissected corpse of a man who would otherwise have been in his early twenties. The Tsaritsa mumbled a prayer as she clung tightly to the baby while the commander stepped in front of her and raised drew his Shashka to defend her highness and the heir of the Russian throne.

Rasputin noticed their reaction and sighed, "Ah, poor poor Mishka. Several days ago the young fool sought to venture too far from the village at night and was overcome by the elements."

Stunned, the Commander could only say, "You didn't kill him?"

Rasputin whirled to the Commander, "Of course not! I am merely a student attempting to learn what I can so others can benefit from my knowledge."

Rasputin moved to another workbench and waved for the two to come over, "Bring the child and place him on my table."

The Tsaritsa found her composure, resisted the urge to question the *Starets* further about the dead man and began to step forward when the Commander held out his arm to block her way.

"Your highness, I don't..." he began but was quickly interrupted by the Tsaritsa.

"Stand aside Commander," she spoke bruskly as she moved around his outstretched arm, "I have already wagered Alexei's life, your future Tsar, on my belief that this man can help him. There is no point in caution now."

Reluctantly the Commander dropped his hand, but did not sheathe his sword as the Tsaritsa reached the table.

Rasputin unrolled a large reindeer hide and gestured for the boy to be placed on top of it. The Tsaritsa gently laid the child down, who was now awake and staring in wide-eyed fascination at the room and its contents. Rasputin hovered over the boy, placed his hands over the child and prayed softly for a few seconds. Then he placed the boy's hands in each of his own, closed his eyes and seemed to concentrate deeply until a frown creased his brow.

Opening his eyes Rasputin asked, "What is the boy eating?"

The Tsaritsa replied, "Mostly porridge and fruits. He also has his wet-nurses from time to time when he won't take the food provided to him."

Rasputin let go of the boy's hands. Stroking his long beard as it extended from his chin, he began to pace the length of the workbench, nodding to himself as if understanding something that he was not yet willing to reveal.

"Have any of the wet-nurses been...injured?"

"Injured?" the Tsaritsa repeated the question, confused and looked to the Commander possibly for enlightenment. The Commander, who was still brandishing his Shashka, merely shrugged his shoulders in apparent confusion as well, "Injured how?"

Rasputin waved a hand dismissively, "In any way at all? Have any been bitten or bruised by the boy or perhaps taken ill unexpectedly."

"I don't believe so, but I can't really say as I am not present when the nurses go about their duties."

"I see," Rasputin paced a few more steps when he halted abruptly as if he had just realized a thought that had been eluding him. He then moved quickly to the boy's side and stared deeply into the boy's eyes. The boy did not flinch or shy away from the man's gaze in the least. In fact, despite his age and frailty, the boy stared back at the *Starets* with an intensity equal to the one he received from Rasputin. Rasputin's eyes darted as if desperately searching for something, then they froze and all of the blood drained from Rasputin's face as he stepped back from the table wide-eyed and trembling.

The Tsaritsa and the Commander witnessed the exchange and held their breath as Rasputin tried to calm his own. Unable to stand the silence any longer the Tsaritsa spoke out, "What is it? What have you learned?"

Rasputin was still too shaken to respond; however, he did manage to hold up one hand in an attempt to convey that he still needed a moment to recover. When he did speak, his voice was shrill and weak as if he had just undertaken an intense physical exertion.

"You came to me to aid in the maintenance of your son's health and this I will do, but the boy will have to stay with me in order for me to properly accomplish this."

The Tsaritsa was aghast, "That is unacceptable."

Rasputin nodded and chuckled quietly before speaking again, "Then I cannot help him and it would not surprise me if the child was dead within a year."

This was all the Commander could take and he erupted toward Rasputin, "How dare you speak to her highness this way! You will do as the Tsaritsa command..."

The Tsaritsa raised a hand quieting the Commander, "If he were to stay in your care, could you help him?"

A look of surprise flashed over Rasputin's face. Clearly he wasn't expecting the Tsaritsa to accept his terms.

"I believe I can."

"Then you will accompany us back to St. Petersburg where his care will be under your control and yours alone," the words seemed more a regal proclamation as opposed to any kind of request as the Tsaritsa continued, "you shall live under our family roof and share in the privileges as one of the house of Romanov."

Rasputin looked into the Tsaritsa's eyes and nodded sadly, but countered, "I do not recommend this course of action. It would be safer for us all if you would allow the boy to stay here with me until he is of an age to assume his father's throne."

"As I said before this is unacceptable. Alexei is the Tsarevich and is to follow his father as Tsar. He cannot be kept in seclusion." Rasputin looked as though he might protest again and the Tsaritsa held up a hand to silence him, "Accept my generous offer to live alongside the House of Romanov and enjoy the benefits as if a royal yourself."

Rasputin frowned, "And if I reject your offer?"

All emotion drained from the Tsaritsa's face and she clasped her hands regally in front of her, "I do not enjoy to speak of such things, but I think you know what the Tsar's wrath can be on anyone who disobeys the throne."

Again Rasputin nodded sadly and moved to where the again sleeping child lay on the workbench. Gently the tall man lifted the boy up and handed him back to the Tsaritsa.

"I agree to and accept your offer. Please allow me a few days to pack my belongings and gather my family for the journey."

Smiling now for the first time since she arrived, the Tsaritsa asked, "Is there a place in the village where we can stay while you prepare?"

Rasputin chuckled, "None that befits a Romanov. In fact, I believe it will be safer if you, the boy and your escorts were to head back to St. Petersburg as soon as possible."

"I would agree with that," the Commander spoke out abruptly.

"When you arrive back home dispatch three coaches to this village as soon as you can. That should give me ample time to gather myself."

"Agreed," the Tsaritsa said and turned to leave, but halted before climbing the first step. "I am putting a great deal of faith in you Grigori Yefimovich Rasputin, not to mention the future of Russia's monarchy. For all of our sakes I hope you are very sure of yourself."

Rasputin only nodded as the Tsaritsa and the Commander began their climb up the stairs toward the exit of the church. Once the pair was gone Rasputin let out a heavy sigh as he walked over to the workbench where the partially dissected corpse lay. He thought it interesting that neither the Tsaritsa nor the Commander had noticed that the corpse showed absolutely no signs of decomposition, nor was there any smell of death in the room.

He was also relieved that neither of his guests had been inclined to view the small hole in the table, which allowed trace amounts of miscellaneous bodily fluids to seep slowly and drain away from the corpse into a collection bottle beneath the tabletop. Rasputin placed a drain stopper in the hole and then reached under the tabletop and picked up the collection bottle. The quart-sized bottle was made of crystal and was intricately etched and polished as if its importance was far greater than what it was currently being used for. Rasputin examined the cloudy red liquid inside the bottle as he moved to a shelf along a far wall of the chamber. With one hand he opened a wooden box, removed a pinch of a dust-like substance and carefully sprinkled the contents into the bottle. Placing the bottle in front of a candle he slowly began to swirl the contents until the liquid inside turned from cloudy red to clear as pure water.

Rasputin stopped swirling the bottle and regarded it with a sly smile as he said out loud, "All too easy."

Chapter 1
2016: Bangkok, Thailand

"'Well now, s'cuse me thar' pilgrims!" Chris announced to the room, his voice heavily laden with a ridiculous imitation of John Wayne as he brandished his twin Beretta PX4 Storm Special Duty .45 caliber handguns toward the hastily working men at the far end of the hall. Multiple heads shot in his direction with eyes wide in a combination of surprise and panic before their hands dipped to draw their holstered sidearms.

Chris took one more moment to clear his throat and, in that same John Wayne voice, quoted one of the legendary actor's lines, "Fill your hands, you son of a bitches!!!"

Chris' battle cry was the last thing I heard before he unexpectedly opened fire and left a familiar high-pitched ringing in my ears. I could feel the force and air pressure push into the side of my head with each rapidly fired high caliber round that exploded less than two feet from me and I instinctively looked up to see my best friend, and now fellow "vampire" Chris Barnes, rapidly firing the entire 10-round contents of each of his guns, wild west style, down the enclosed hallway we had just entered.

The targets of Chris' attention dove for cover, as the large .45 caliber rounds blew apart whatever they impacted, sending shards of wood, drywall and scraps of paper flying into the air. I tried to shout something to Chris, but in my currently deafened state I really couldn't tell if what I said had been loud enough to register with my gun-wielding, bullet-slinging and "yippie-kay-yay-yaying" buddy.

Chris turned to look at me, his face screwed up in a confused expression while his mouth moved as if he were asking me a question. My look of incomprehension must have been evident because he started gesturing with one of the guns for me to "go." Feeling somewhat stupid that I hadn't instantly realized Chris was eliciting the distraction that I had asked for, I bolted for a side door along the hallway as the last thirty minutes of my life flashed before my eyes.

***

30 minutes earlier.

Chris and I had approached the multi-story strip club, the top floor of which, our source informed us, the CIA had converted into a kind of safe-house. Our source had reliable and in depth knowledge of the floor's layout as he had met with our target, a certain Mr. Pollard, on several occasions at this location, and thus he had been able to provide us with all the details we would need for what we were planning.

As Chris and I entered the club we were practically assaulted by the 'working girls' closing in all around us, like predators converging on some vulnerable prey. The loud techno music blasted our eardrums and the cigarette smoke combined with the cloying humidity in the air making it momentarily hard to breathe. The air also had the lingering scent of multiple perfumes and body sprays that mixed with the smell of sweat and garlic. The press of human bodies didn't help and it was all we could do to politely press our way forward against the tide of smooth skin that was provocatively caressing every inch of our flesh left uncovered by the cotton T-shirts and blue jeans we wore.

Some of the girls actually pulled at our arms in possessive tugs to claim "first dibs" on us, or more importantly, our money. We eased ourselves free of their embraces with simple smiles, feigned mock embarrassment and clumsily performed "wai's", just as any tourist might.

The "wai" is a way of saying "hello" or shaking hands to the Thai people and is performed by extending the fingers and bringing the hands together like a prayer, then drawing your hands up towards your face, so that the middle fingers are just above the mouth, accompanied by a slight bow of the head while lowering the eyes. It is also a way of conveying respect, and as these girls are normally shown very little respect, we made a show with our hands held high on our heads in order to grant them the highest form of respect we could as we turned them down. The girls laughed at our use of the "wai" in a way so inaccessible to their own personal status, but it helped to avoid any injured egos, and they allowed us to pass into the club without incident, or otherwise drawing undue attention.

Once we had reached the bar the music mercifully ebbed, but it was still enough to drown out everything but the closest of conversations, which worked in our favor as we scanned the bar for problems. At first glance it seemed that every patron was beset upon by one or more of the girls, all of whom appeared to be in the midst of one kind of celebration or another. At the bar shot-glasses clinked and alcohol was thrown back, while at the tables every man's lap had at least one provocatively clad woman firmly planted for the night.

Finding him took longer than it should have, given the man's larger than life size, but eventually Chris and I found who we were looking for. He was seated near the back of the bar, sipping a small snifter that held about a finger's worth of cognac, and at his feet lay a small backpack. The tawny color of the alcohol seemed to stand out dramatically against the man's alabaster white hair and skin as he raised the glass to his lips. At first glance the leathers he wore despite the heat of the city would have identified him stereotypically as some kind of giant American biker, but closer inspection would reveal the clothes were made of soft lambskin as opposed to the heavy cowhide leather that the motorcycle clubs favor. His cowboy boots were black but made from the tough, yet supple skin of an ostrich, which indicated that they were likely to be both very expensive and incredibly comfortable. His long leather pants were cut to a custom fit, and the shirtless vest he wore might have been a slight nod to the heat that the rest of his ensemble defied. The vest exposed his lean and muscular arms with skin almost as dramatically pale as his platinum hair, and every flash of colored light from the various neon signs on the walls reflected off of his white skin, making him seem like a hyperactive chameleon.

The employees and patrons of the club didn't exactly make a clear a space around the man, given the packed club's general lack of room at the moment, but everyone near him either consciously or unconsciously kept at arm's length, while he slowly sipped at his drink. A barstool was open on either side of the man, which both Chris and I filled, as we enclosed the man between us.

The man didn't look up from his drink as Chris ordered a round of beers for the three of us. I looked straight ahead into the mirror on the other side of the bar as I quietly said, "I guess you managed to bring them in."

The man smiled and set his drink down on the bar-top, "How astute, as I am sitting here and not in a jail cell. One might think you to be a detective."

I smiled at the jibe as the man's hand fell to his side and dipped into the backpack at his feet. I immediately felt the sensation of something pushing into my side and I lowered one hand to take the package, which I knew contained my Glock 20, plus several spare 15 round magazines. The bartender had dropped off three bottles of Singha beer, and Chris was mid-swallow when his parcel was shoved into his side and, as if written into a vaudeville skit, Chris immediately spit beer into the air in response. Fortunately, the bartender had cleared out of the way to serve other customers and avoided the shower, but he glared at Chris with enough heat to make me think he might want to club Chris to death.

The man and I both covered our eyes, shaking our heads in equal amounts of incredulity before he said, "Sometimes I really wonder if saving you was worth the effort."

Chris feigned offense at the statement, "Oh come on Alpha. We all know how lost you would be without me."

Alpha, leader of the North American "vampire" collective and the man who was as close to me as a father said, "Oh, of course. How did I manage the last 600 years without you?"

Chris only shrugged at the sarcasm, "Walking around the old world like a dumb-ass, most likely."

Alpha turned to look at Chris and the simmering anger on his face was enough to stop time. He was wearing dark sunglasses inside the dark club to hide the twin ebony orbs that his eyes had become. Normally Alpha would have donned full-eye contacts that would simulate normal eyes, but Alpha always said they were extremely uncomfortable and compromising in a fight... and we knew we were in for a fight very soon.

Chris only responded with an over-exaggerated smile that was as much defiance as it was acquiescence.

I broke the tension and asked, "Have you seen her?"

The 'her' I was referring to was my fiancé Lei. She had been abducted by a man we believed to be an active CIA agent named 'Pollard' who, our informant told us, was in the process of shutting down his operation before returning to the U.S.

"No," Alpha said quietly while turning his head back to the bar top, "but Pollard came in just over an hour ago and hasn't come down since."

I nodded, "So we've got him."

Alpha shrugged, "He's still up there, but we are going to have to go up and get him."

Chris grew serious, "That was always the plan."

It was Alpha's turn to nod, "True, but several men have been coming down with boxes and going out the back before

19

returning empty-handed, then repeating the process again and again. I don't think we have much time left."

"How many would you say are up there?"

"I've counted six including Pollard, but there could be more who haven't come down."

Chris swallowed some more beer and screwed up his face, "God this beer sucks. Do they have anything else?"

Alpha and I both looked at Chris with the incredulity that one would use with an impetuous child. Chris looked from me to Alpha and back again several times before he said, "What? I'm thirsty."

"Chris," I sighed, "could you please focus for one minute?"

Chris' face grew as serious as I had ever seen it, "Focus? I'm waiting on you two assholes to stop talking so we can just do this."

I sighed again, "Chris…"

"Steve, stop. Just stop," Chris cut me off, his voice angry, "maybe you forgot that Lei was taken out from under my nose. Or maybe you forgot that this makes her abduction my responsibility. Or maybe, just maybe, you forgot that it doesn't matter if they have six or sixty people upstairs because we know the exact layout, including all the potential entry and exit points, and we will be taking them by surprise. So whenever you guys want to stop gossiping like old women and are ready to act, I am good to go."

He punctuated the end of his tirade by slapping the bar several times getting the bartender's attention. The bartender glared again as Chris waved a hand holding an American twenty-dollar bill.

Chris pointed to the bartender, "Asshole!" he then held up the Singha bottle and angrily said, "Piss!" before slamming the bottle down and pointing to a banner over the bar and read out loud the single word printed there, "Heineken!"

The bartender had started an angry approach, but when he

20

saw the twenty in Chris' hand his fierce expression immediately changed into one that was all smiles and agreeability. He hurried over and opened a large ice chest, digging his arm deeply into the ice and emerging with a green glass bottle. Setting it gingerly in front of Chris, he waited.

Chris nodded and set the twenty on the bar as the bartender used a bottle opener to pop the top. The bartender smiled and "wai'd" several times as he plucked the twenty from the bar top and immediately pocketed the cash. Alpha and I looked disappointedly at our bottles of Singha as Chris took a long pull from the Heineken before setting the now half empty bottle back down on the bar.

"And you guys thought I couldn't speak Thai," Chris said, as picked up the bottle and polished it off on his next pull. He then let out an exaggerated, audible sigh of appreciation for his beverage before asking, "Any of you ladies want to go to the bathroom with me?" Alpha and I looked at each other and set our still full bottles of Singha down on the bar, as we all got up from our barstools. Chris and I headed for the restroom while Alpha disappeared into the crowd. It was eerie the way he could just do that. I mean, the guy was six and a half feet tall, and he vanished into a crowd of people literally a foot shorter than him.

Once in the restroom Chris and I checked that our guns were loaded and ready to fire, then tucked them into our waistbands so the loose fitting shirts we wore would conceal them. We left the restroom and headed for the kitchen, where we knew we'd find a service elevator that would take us to the top floor. There was a fire escape stairwell next to the elevator that would be Alpha's point of entry once the fun began.

A couple of waiters, bouncers or whatever, tried to block our way once we passed through the kitchen doors, each one placing himself in either Chris' or my path. It took a ridiculously small amount of effort to incapacitate them, as Chris and I each

21

knocked one of them out of the way with sharp blows to their heads.

The bustling kitchen froze in silent stupefaction as the entire staff watched the men fall, then refocused on us as we casually moved to the elevator's door. Chris touched the elevator's call button, whistling "Dixie" as we waited for the doors to open, while the kitchen staff remained frozen in place, staring at us. It was like looking at a still life display in a museum as water ran from faucets, flames rose from beneath oversized woks, and steam wafted up from the fresh rice that had just come from the steam pots, but none of the people moved.

The elevator's high-pitched bell went "ding" to signal that the car had arrived, and the doors slid open with a groan of gears that indicated a desperate need for grease. Chris walked into the elevator as if ignorant of the spectacle we had created. I started to follow, then stopped and turned to the restaurant staff while putting one finger to my lips.

"Shhhh," I made the noise with a wicked grin and a promise of violence on my face that hopefully would be enough to keep the kitchen staff from interfering as the elevator doors closed.

We rode the car to the top floor, taking up positions on either side of the doors, just in case someone was waiting for us when we arrived. Again, the doors groaned as they slid open, but the space facing us was empty. I took a quick glance from each side of the elevator, to look for anyone in the hidden spaces to the left and right of the door leading into the receiving area. Seeing no one we then we moved out of the elevator car and onto the floor, covering each other as we went. Instantly, I recognized some of the details I had been told to look for by our informant, which seemed to validate the information regarding the basic layout as accurate.

Following our plan, we turned a corner, entering a hallway with multiple doors along each side of the corridor, that were probably once used as "short-time" entertainment rooms for any of the club's ladies. Our informant told us that these rooms had been turned into offices, safe rooms or jail cells, depending on whom the Agency brought up the stairs. At the end of the hall was what looked to be an open space that might have formerly served as a large congregating area for the girls, but was now filled with four men stacking file storage boxes one on top of another. Quickly realizing that there was no way we would be able to check the rooms for Lei or Pollard without those four men noticing our presence, I had whispered the eight fateful words, "What we really need here is a distraction," and Chris had responded with a simple, "Gotcha," and then the chaos spelled C-H-R-I-S, ensued and my hearing went "bye-bye."

Chapter 2

As Chris went "Wild Bunch" with all the guns blasting down the hallway I rolled to my stomach, crawling the couple of yards to the door of the closest room, I tried the doorknob. It was unlocked, so I hurriedly pushed my way through without doing a proper check first. Quickly I rose to my knees, aiming my Glock in a regulation two-handed grip, moving through the room before I reached to the door on the far side.

I tried the doorknob, but this time the door was locked. A hard kick to the spot just below the doorknob splintered the hardware away from the doorframe and I went in. I quickly checked the corners and blind spots as I entered the room, just as the LAPD had taught me over a decade ago only to find the room empty.

My heart sank at not finding Lei, but I moved on through to another door and realized the ringing in my ears was nearly gone. In the next room, I could discern another volley of gunfire coming from multiple types of weapons. Apparently, the men that Chris had been "distracting" were returning fire. I hoped that the lack of shots coming from Chris meant that he was reloading as opposed to having been wounded, and a pang of worry twisted in my guts for my overzealous friend.

Then a single gunshot from his Beretta boomed, followed closely by Chris shouting,

"Who's your daddy?!"

Boom!

"Who's your daddy?!"

Boom!

"Que es el Padre?!"

Boom!

"Donde esta' la biblioteca?!"

Boom!

…and so forth.

My brain was mentally disgusted with myself as a smile spread across my lips… Chris' behavior could be exasperating but, damn, the guy was such a spectacle I just couldn't help but laugh.

I broke down another door and swept in before immediately having to dive for cover behind a sofa as a shotgun exploded in my direction. The sofa bucked from the impact of the eight pellets of 00 buckshot, but the cushions and frame caught most of it, protecting me from the multiple projectiles. I heard the gunman ratchet another cartridge into the chamber and waited for the accompanying blast when something cut through the air above my head. There was a thud of impact and the gunman's body twisted back with his falling shotgun firing into the floor at his feet. I could just make out the handle of one of Alpha's insane-looking knives extending from the center of the man's chest as the man crumpled to the floor.

I didn't wait for Alpha to come into the room but jumped to my feet and took up position by the door to the hallway until Chris stopped firing. Just as I was about to crack the door open and peek out, I heard Chris shout, "Clear!"

"Clear?" I called back, surprised that Chris could have taken a group of professional agents out with his antics.

"You sound surprised," Chris said, his voice oozing with mock indignation.

I cracked the door open and peeked around the corner to see Chris moving into the larger room, his guns aimed at the door in the far left corner. Alpha appeared to Chris' right and quickly moved toward one side of the door while I left my spot and joined them.

Since I saw no bodies lying on the floor, I asked Chris, "So, what happened?"

Chris never took his eyes off the door, but his voice returned to the John Wayne inflection, "Well, the way I fig'gur it, some folks done need to learn what happens, when Sherrif 'Boom-Boom' Barnes shows up to a gun fight. I reckon' them polecats done be... OW!"

Alpha had smacked Chris on the back of the head, "Quiet, fool!" He then traced a finger over door where one of a multitude of Chris' shots had struck it. I studied the spot Alpha indicated and noticed that the .45 caliber round had not penetrated.

I nodded, "Reinforced steel made to look like a wooden door. Guess we found the safe room?"

Alpha looked at the doorframe and inspected the walls, "More like a barricaded space that they can hold out inside until help arrives, as opposed to a formal safe room."

That news was good and bad. "Good" because a real, professionally-made safe room would be impossible for us to penetrate without the proper tools, and "bad" because there was still the matter of getting to our target, who was locked inside what was obviously a fortified room.

"So," I asked, "how do you want to do this?"

Alpha looked at me and was about to say something when Chris interrupted, "Didn't I hear a shotgun blast a minute ago?"

I pointed to the door I had been crouched behind, "In there."

Chris looked over and nodded, "Okay, be right back."

Chris tucked his twin Berettas inside the waistband of his jeans, and casually walked back down the hall and through the door. Alpha and I exchanged a look of confusion before Chris re-emerged with the shotgun in one hand and Alpha's bloody knife in the other.

Chris held the blood smeared handle of the knife out to Alpha, "You lose this?"

Alpha accepted the blade with a smile, "No, I knew exactly where I put it," and then licked the blade clean of blood.

Chris' face initially screwed up in a disgusted expression,

but then froze as he reconsidered, looking a little deflated, "Wish I had thought of that." He then turned to the door and aimed the shotgun at the doorknob taking a moment to sigh, "Damn, now I'm hungry," before shooting the hardware clean off the door.

Alpha and I both jerked our bodies out of the way to keep from being hit by the buckshot or any shrapnel, as the targeted area on the door cleared of smoke and revealed only deformed steel and a small, quarter-sized hole where the knob had been.

Chris ratcheted another round into the shotgun and stepped back in preparation to kick the door in.

He looked to Alpha and me, "Ready?"

We nodded and Chris launched the bottom of his foot, driven by the entirety of his body weight, directly to the spot he had just blasted with the shotgun. A resounding impact of boot on metal reverberated through the room just before Chris let out a howl of pain and collapsed in front of the still-closed door, while gripping at his knee.

Initially, I worried that Chris might have blown his knee out, but when he stopped groaning and clearly said, "Ow, ow, ow, ow, well that sucked," I guessed that no permanent damage had been done to his leg.

Alpha was smiling broadly, "That was... entertaining, do we have a "plan B"?"

I was shaking my head in a negative way when a shadow fell over the room, just as if someone had put their hand in front of the only light. The three of us turned toward the hallway where the enormous silhouette of a man blocked most of the light coming in from the hall. We all knew the man, but his presence always conveyed a sense of dread whenever he simply appeared like that.

William was nearly seven feet tall and so thick with muscle that it almost seemed he should have trouble moving, but anyone having a muscle-bound impression of him couldn't have been further from the truth. William stepped nimbly through the various detritus strewn about the room, stopping next to where Chris was lying on the floor and leaned down to curl his index finger through one of Chris' belt loops.

"Can you stand?" William asked, his voice a deep and gravelly sound, as he effortlessly lifted Chris from the floor as if he were weightless.

Chris' expression never changed as he dangled from the belt loop in a limp, bent at the waist position. Slowly he flexed and extended the questionable knee before simply nodding his reply. William carried Chris away from the door and gently lowered him until his feet touched the floor.

Alpha rolled his eyes, "Well, I suppose we could try to do this the straight-forward way." He strode up to the door and knocked three times before raising his voice toward the door, "I don't suppose you gentlemen would consider surrendering at this point?"

When no one reply came Alpha knocked again, "Really there's no need for any more violence. We simply wish to gather what we came for and depart."

A voice, muffled behind all of the steel and drywall, could be heard as Pollard called back, "The police have been notified and are sure to be en route. You should be thinking about getting out before they arrive."

As soon as the voice had sounded William shifted to his right, away from the door and traced his broad hand over the wall. He looked at me and gestured with his free hand in such a way that I guessed he wanted me to keep whoever had spoken, talking.

"We aren't leaving without the woman," I offered.

There was a brief silence before a different voice called out, "Woman? What woman?" William shifted to the right another three feet and pointed at a spot on the wall. Alpha seemed to understand and moved to the spot indicated and then William walked back to the door.

"No woman?" I asked as if confirming the information, "Well then, I suppose we should just go then?" I turned away from the door and spoke quietly to Alpha, "You have what you need?"

Alpha had placed his hand on the wall in the same manner that William had, and nodded.

I turned to William, "Count of three?"

"Wait," Chris looked confused but drew his Berettas from behind his belt, ejected the near-empty magazines and replaced them with full ones and then ratcheted both slides to chamber the fresh rounds. He aimed them to one side of William as I simultaneously did exactly the same thing with my Glock, and William turned to me and simply nodded.

I returned the gesture and looked to Alpha, as I held up one finger, "One."

Alpha stepped back from the wall but never took his eyes off the spot that William had indicated.

"Two."

Alpha drew in a deep breath as he readied himself for the third count.

"Three!"

Alpha's fist shot forward driving into and through the wall. There was an explosion of drywall clay and dust, along with the sound of wood splintering as Alpha's fist, forearm and elbow penetrated through the wall, finally stopping at mid-bicep. There were some muffled screams from inside the room when Alpha wrenched his arm back and pulled the body of one of the men through the wall and then flung the limp form to the other side of the room. Alpha immediately sought cover as gunshots exploded and bullets came through the new hole he had created in the wall, just as William's nearly four hundred pounds shot forward into the steel door. Legs the size of tree trunks and a body dense with muscle slammed hard into the reinforced door and the impact shattered the frame and surrounding wall, which exploded inward with a cacophony of sound. The door was ripped from its hinges as William charged forward into the room still carrying it in his hands as he went. Screams of shock and terror came from the men inside who responded with a fusillade of gunshots, but William was using the steel reinforced door as a shield, which must have weighed as much as he, and blocked any bullets fired in his direction. Chris and I followed and shot down the remaining gunmen as they tried and failed to accomodate to what was happening.

I couldn't see him, as William was still holding the door blocking my view, but I heard Pollard screaming as he fired rapidly into the unforgiving steel door that he had so confidently thought would protect him and his people a moment ago. Suddenly the gunshots stopped as William slammed the door into Pollard with enough force to send the man rocketing back and into the far wall of the room where he crumpled to the floor. William tossed the door aside as if were no more than a paper dinner plate, before stepping up to Pollard and throwing the man back into the center of the room toward me. Pollard had barely come to a stop when I lowered my Glock and grabbed a fistful of his shirt. My anger threatened to overwhelm me as I lifted him to his feet while screaming into his face.

"Where is she?!" I screamed through clenched teeth, "Where is Lei?!"

Pollard smiled at me like an adult might at the cute antics of a toddler, "You think you have what it takes to make me talk, boy?"

Something in the way he said "boy" caught my attention and a sick feeling crept into my stomach. I frowned as I read the man's face and realized what Pollard had actually told me. "You're no government agent," I accused, "or at least that's not all you are!" Pollard didn't answer, but his smile grew wider, mocking me.

I took a deep breath and calmed myself... and then I shot Pollard in the knee.

Pollard went down screaming in agony while his lower leg bled and waggled around like a marionette's as the bones had been totally shattered at the knee joint.

I knelt down, "Listen to me Agent Pollard, or whoever you are, you took someone very dear to me, and there is no level I will not stoop to in order to get the information I need from you."

Pollard tried to stifle his groans by gritting his teeth together as he glared murderously at me. In response I moved in closer and whispered, "You should also know that, despite the pain you are in and the atrocities I am prepared to commit upon your person, I am not the one you need to worry about."

Pollard's eyes continued to glare at me, but they had lost a good deal of their fire, as William shifted into place behind me.

I started talking very calmly, "See the giant behind me? Although you might not have been directly responsible for his abduction and torture, you were partners with the people who were."

Pollard blinked rapidly and his head shifted slightly as he took a better look at William before looking back at me. Any trace of threat or defiance had left his face, and I could almost feel his fear as the sight of William overwhelmed the pain he was in.

"You should probably know, if you don't already, that the people you're involved with have his daughter, and as badly as I can make you hurt, it is nothing compared to what that man can do to you."

I could feel Pollard's body shift back as William took a first heavy step toward us, "Are you really an agent of the CIA?" I asked as William took another step, crossing half the distance to us.

Pollard's eyes went wide, as his head swiveled away from William and back to me, "Yes, I am an agent of the United States Government and you can't..."

The moment Pollard tried to stray off the topic I slapped

31

him hard over the wound on his ruined knee. His scream was high pitched and desperate.

"Focus please." Despite the violence of my actions, I kept my voice eerily calm. "Okay, so you are indeed a CIA agent, but am I right at guessing that you are also working with Dimitri Lagos?"

I could sense Pollard's pulse speed up at the mention of Dimitri Lagos, leader of the vampire collective in the territory that used to comprise the former Soviet Union. It had been Dimitri who had provided the information that eventually sent Lei and myself to Bangkok. The bastard had been using us in order to dispose of his former partner and our old enemy, the late Dr. Phineas Whelan.

Some resolve returned to Pollard's voice as he said simply, "Dimitri who?"

William hovered over me, and I had the strangest sense of claustrophobia at being between a solid floor and William. The giant knelt forward and extended his index finger as if pointing at Pollard's knee. Then slowly he extended his arm until the tip of his hot dog sized finger hovered above Pollard's wound.

I looked at the finger and winced at what I thought might follow, before turning to Pollard, "Well, I tried to warn you."

Pollard's eyes looked from the finger to William's face and then back to me as I stepped back. William shifted and pressed one of his ham-sized palms down on Pollard's chest, pinning him to the floor, as he slowly pushed his index finger into the open bullet wound at Pollard's knee. Pollard's body went rigid and his face drained of color as the pain overwhelmed him. He began flailing wildly, but remained pinned to the ground under William's hand, like a still-living insect might after being pinned in a specimen tray.

When William finally removed his finger from deep inside Pollard's knee his hand went into one pocket of his black jeans and removed a small piece of paper. He turned the paper over and then grabbed Pollard by the hair, making him look at it. It took a moment for the tears to clear from Pollard's eyes, but once he could see again he found himself looking at a small photo of a tiny Thai girl.

"This is 'Pha'" I volunteered, "his daughter, and we know that Dimitri has both her and Lei. Where are they?" Pollard only whimpered in response and William casually slapped Pollard hard enough to break his nose. Blood sprayed to the side and Pollard's opposite hand rose in response to the immediate pain and temporary disorientation caused by the blow.

Alpha moved to William's side, and whispered under Pollard's muffled cries, "We need him alive my friend."

A disinterested grunt was all that William said in reply as he looked to me in a silent signal to continue. I tried not to show my concern as I handed Pollard a paper towel from a roll that I saw lying on the floor.

"Where are they?" I asked again as Pollard fought to compose himself. Something seemed to shift in the man as his features tightened and seemed to slowly change into something more feral before our eyes. There was no true physical change to his form, as much as there was a shift in the way he seemed to register the pain he was in. I have to admit the shift was a bit eerie to observe, but not nearly as strange as when Pollard spoke again.

Pollard's voice had changed as dramatically as if an entirely different person was lying on the floor in front of us, "I tell you, then you leave me here," he said with a slight Slavic accent.

I was going to say something, but Alpha cut me off, "Done."

Pollard looked into his own reflection within Alpha's sunglasses, "You speak for all of them?"

Alpha nodded, "I do."

"Um…What just happened?" Chris asked, as baffled as if he had missed a crucial play in a football game that had changed the entire outlook of the game.

All of us stared in stunned silence as Pollard hissed out each breath, but Alpha was either unaffected or completely unimpressed as he knelt in front of Pollard to face him.

"You know who I am?" Alpha asked in a way that managed to convey the entirety of Alpha's insurmountable power behind it.

Pollard stared back and the audible, threatening hiss that his words and breath had held subsided as Alpha faced him. The wounded man kept silent and only nodded his response.

Alpha nodded back, "I have to commend you, and Dimitri, for being able to place yourself so effectively within a United States Government agency. How long have you been in place? Since the Cold War, perhaps? Pollard just stared angrily as Alpha spoke to him, "I'd imagine that has made you a very valuable asset to Dimitri?"

Pollard decided to respond to that, "Yes, and you should know that Dimitri will declare war on you and all your people for what you have done."

Alpha shrugged his shoulders, "He can try."

Pollard let out a slight laugh between teeth still clenched in pain, "We have the numbers, the resources and the influence at our disposal. What do you and your kind have? Your people are either living underground like cowards, or trying to live like humans. Like sheep. Dimitri and my people live like the predators of man that we are. We live above humanity as their superiors. Aside from the couple of dozen Hunters that you have trained, your people are no better than the livestock with whom you choose to coexist."

William started to move, but Alpha held up a hand and the giant froze in place.

Alpha removed his sunglasses and moved his face even closer to Pollard until their noses were only inches apart. Pollard tried to maintain the stare, but the sight of Alpha's black eyes so unnerved him that he began to tremble.

34

"You can think that if you wish, but," Alpha shifted to point toward William, "the next words out of your mouth better tell me where that man's daughter is, and," Alpha's arm twisted back in toward his face with his finger now pointed at himself, as his voice became resounding in its ferocity, "where MY daughter is, or I will take you from this place and slowly feed you, feet first, into a meat grinder."

The shock of what I had just heard made my eyes slowly drift away from Pollard and fall onto Alpha. I had always known that Lei had considered herself Alpha's daughter in much the same way I had always considered Alpha like a father to me. Now it was the emotion in Alpha's voice that made those words convey much more than I had known.

Pollard's eyes went wide and his voice was shaky and uncertain as he said, "N-Nazran."

"What?" I looked to Chris in confusion, "Where?"

Pollard turned to me and in a quick panic said, "It's a small city in Russia near the Mongolian border. Dimitri has taken your people there while he prepares for the Romanov."

Alpha turned to me, confused, "The Romanov?"

I shook my head, "I don't know who he's talking about exactly, but when Dimitri came to Lei and me in our office to set us on this little Bangkok adventure, he said something about 'The Romanov' making a claim for the lands in Siberia that Dimitri currently controls. I can't be sure but I think it goes beyond a simple power play. I think Dimitri is afraid of him."

Pollard chuckled, "Dimitri is beyond such things. He only wants to make sure that since you did not deliver what you were supposed to," he looked at William, "then at least you won't fight against him."

Alpha spoke up, "The city of Nazran may not be New York City, but isn't exactly a pinpoint location. Be more specific?"

I noticed that Pollard started to look sleepy and wasn't

noticing the pain as much as he should be anymore.

Chris noticed it as well, "He's going into shock."

Pollard's words started to slur, but he managed to answer me. "Don't know exactly where, but Dimitri controls the city. It's a safe place for him and our people. Someplace where they can operate in the open."

Pollard's body began to slowly slide over to the side and, perhaps purely by reflex, Alpha reached out to keep him from falling and turned to Chris, "What do we need to do for him?"

Chris was going to answer when his eyes went wide and he opened his mouth to cry out a warning, but before any sound could come out, Pollard's face twisted into a mask of pure hatred and rage as he opened his mouth wide and his head shot forward to strike at Alpha's throat.

Caught unaware Alpha felt the attack coming and tried to shift his weight to keep Pollard at a distance, but his body was not in a position to allow him the proper leverage. Helplessly, I watched as the whole world seemed to slow down while Pollard's white teeth moved closer and closer to the vulnerable spot on Alpha's neck where his carotid artery lay. I could see Alpha trying to move out of striking range, but he couldn't get the leverage needed to avoid the oncoming attack.

Then, even as the rest of the world slowed, something large drove past Alpha's head and crashed into Pollard's oncoming face. In an instant the whole world sped up again to a normal speed, as the bottom of William's heavy boot crunched through Pollard's broken nose and then carried the man's head backward into the floor. There was a sickening crunch as William continued to lean into his strike and Pollard's face collapsed into his own skull cavity under the force. Skin, bone and brain were pulped under the pressure and burst from both of Pollard's ears in a quick and grotesque fountain of gore, as his body went into a spasmodic seizure. Alpha covered his face as the foamy ichor splattered the area, and he quickly rose to keep any additional brain or blood from covering him.

When it was over there was just the nauseating wet, sucking sound as William slowly pulled his foot from the depression it had made in Pollard's head. Everyone was silent for an instant, and in that moment we could hear the sound of sirens in the background. They had probably been on their way since the first gunshot, as Pollard had indicated earlier, but this was the first we heard of their imminent arrival.

Of course, it was Chris who broke the silence first.

"Wow!" He had a strange look of disgust combined with amazement as he noted, "that was without a doubt the gross-est thing I have ever seen... and I'm a Medical Examiner!"

Alpha was less enthusiastic, as he turned to William, "We needed him alive."

William was scraping the bottom of his boot on the carpet to rid it of any residual Pollard detritus and growled hoarsely, "Couldn't risk you."

Alpha sighed at that, and turned away to head toward the stairs. As the rest of us followed, Alpha asked me, "So how do you suggest that we proceed, Detective."

Alpha still called me that whenever he wanted me to use the skills I had developed when I served my ten years as a member of the LAPD.

"I've never heard of Nazran. I think we need to talk to someone who might have spent some time there already."

Alpha's face screwed up in surprise, "You've never heard of it, but you know someone who spent time there?"

I smiled, "It's just a suspicion, but I think we need to talk to our babysitter."

Chapter 3

It may be the sex clubs, the wild and crazy night life, or the beautiful beaches and luxury resorts that come to mind when people think about Bangkok, but most don't know that the country of Thailand does a great deal of exporting. This bustling industry has resulted in several major shipping ports, regulated by the Port Authority of Thailand in conjunction with several private corporations, including Hutchison Ports Thailand and PSA International. The Port Authority itself is located in Bangkok, and on the left side of the Chao Phraya River in Khlong Toei District, is the Port of Bangkok. The port occupies over 900 acres and has a population of support personnel substantial enough to make it a one and a half square mile city in its own right.

Dry docks are common throughout the area for boat storage and repair, so when Alpha, William, Chris and I all walked to a boat storage unit favored by expatriated Westerners, or "Farang" as the Thai people called foreigners, none of the locals gave us a second thought, despite our rather unusual appearances. The interior of the large boat house had all of the basics needed for dry boat storage including "fresh" running water that had a brown haze and fishy stink to it, electricity, and an area sectioned off for the tools and chemicals normally needed for marine-vehicle maintenance.

The four of us walked in and set the duffle bags we carried onto a folding plastic table, before flopping down into the plastic lawn furniture we had procured. The boat house was our temporary base of operations, which we had established weeks earlier after recovering from our assault on Dr. Whelan's compound.

From the back of the unit there was the sound of a door closing and our "babysitter," Major Robert Larson, Navy Seal and SRT Commander, walked over to greet us. Larson took one look at my ragged disposition, grimaced and asked, "It went that badly?"

Chris was pouring himself a cup of coffee from a carafe that had been set on a warming burner for who knew how long, and said, "Actually, it went pretty much exactly as I had thought it would."

There was a slight pause before Larson turned away from Chris and looked at me with sympathy written all over his face, "So, it went that badly."

I chuffed out with a laugh that I was trying to stifle, as William silently shuffled over to the refrigerator. It was a basic unit that stood barely six feet high, but next to William it seemed little more in size than something akin to a minibar. Sifting through miscellaneous juices, bottles of water and beer he found what he was looking for, a plastic pint-sized bag of raw blood.

My people, or at least the vampire collective I grew up in, don't take our blood raw, but instead use a blood derivative that we consume in either pill or liquid form. We also carry around the liquid form of this "serum" in a delivery system called an EpiPen. The EpiPen, developed as a fast-dose delivery system for injecting Epinephrine into the body of someone going into anaphylactic shock, made for a wonderful emergency method of "dosing" our kind whenever the need for blood was starting to take a physical effect upon our physical person.

The reasons my people separated themselves from the raw blood product was as a result of the dangers and difficulties that pure blood represented to my kind. First, there was, of course, the danger we would represent to the outside "normal" human world. After all, every person out there could be degraded down to walking bags of blood, which was how the Russian collective, led by Dimitri Lagos, viewed humanity.

There was also the problem of how my kind reacted when we partook of raw blood. For some, the effect came off as a kind of euphoria, in others it triggered intense erotic impulses and in a very few, the consumption of raw blood caused an uncontrollable,

39

mindless rage. Thus far William had never exhibited any of those particular reactions, but if he were one who became enraged, I don't think that any of us would survive it.

We all glanced over nervously at William when he removed the bag from the refrigerator as Alpha asked, "Are you all right?"

William had been working at the spigot on the bottom of the bag where an IV tube would normally be fastened and looked up. William noticed the concern in our expressions and said, "I'll be fine."

Having been unable to loosen the spigot properly, William simply pinched the thick plastic spout and tore it away as if it were made from a substance that had only a little more resistance than tissue paper. He raised the bag, opened his mouth wide and squeezed, in order to release the blood within, which then oozed out of the bag and into his mouth. The lack of an anti-coagulant in the blood made it extremely viscous, and William had to pinch and refold the bag a few times in order to force some of the congealed solids through the small opening left by the missing spout.

I walked over to Alpha, "That's his second bag in as many days." Alpha didn't respond, and simply continued to watch William as he consumed the blood, "None of us need to dose more than once weekly. Do you really think he is all right?"

Alpha turned his head to me as I had finished asking the question and his face was filled with sorrow. "William is as ancient as I am and he knows his limits as well as any of us, but as you can see," Alpha said while pointing to his completely black obsidian eyes, "our individual progression isn't exactly written in stone."

"So the simple answer would be that you don't know?"

Alpha nodded, "That would be the simple answer."

Chris had walked over to Larson and was in the process of shaking hands, "How's the baby?"

Larson screwed up his face and looked in the general

direction of the rear of the boathouse, "Cranky."

Chris smiled and spoke with a voice dripping with sarcasm, "He's uncomfortable? Gosh, that wounds me so."

"You want to talk to him?"

Chris frowned as he thought before saying, "In a bit. I need a shower and a handful of ibuprofen for my knee first." Chris turned to William, "Hey big guy! Since you're already over there, could you throw me a gel pack from the freezer?"

William had finished the blood bag and was breathing hard. It was a strange sight to see, since he never appeared to have expended enough effort to break a sweat when we assaulted the CIA safe house. Now the big man was panting as if out of breath and he turned to scowl at Chris.

Chris rolled his eyes at the giant, and turned away from him while extending a hand to catch the presumably forthcoming ice pack.

Chris had turned back to Larson, "Did any packages arrive for me?"

Larson had trouble removing his cautious gaze from William, but managed to look at Chris when he replied, "Just a small one. I set it on the table by…"

FWAP!

Larson's words were instantly cut off as an almost frozen gel pack smacked Chris squarely in the cheek. It made a wet sounding slap as it wrapped around the rest of his face. The soft chemical gel in its plastic bag was covered in a small amount of dry frost from the freezer that was helping it to adhere to Chris' face, which was moist with perspiration. The result, although Chris had staggered momentarily from the impact, was Chris standing with his arm held out, and a gel pack stuck to, and wrapped around, his face.

Indignantly Chris lowered his arm slowly, refusing to remove the gel pack from where it stuck, and he turned to face

41

William.

Alpha, Larson and I all froze in silent, but highly amused, disbelief.

Chris made a show of removing the pack from his face, and then began stroking the bag like a puppy in his hands.

"Ah, so refreshing," Chris smiled warmly at William, "thank you, Billy."

William's face was expressionless, in such a way that made him appear far more frightening than any look of anger or rage ever could, but a muffled, choking sound came from him, which sounded almost like he was clearing his throat.

The look, the sound and the danger were all lost on Chris, "Can I call you Billy?"

The giant now went silent, seemed to consider and then shrugged indifferently.

"Okay, then," Chris moved to where Larson had indicated his package had been placed and dropped bodily into a piece of lawn furniture, before placing the gel pack on his knee and inspecting the package, completely ignoring William.

Alpha, Larson and I all turned to watch William, who started making that strange sound again. I turned to Alpha, who was frowning at William as if he were studying the giant, who was also his oldest and dearest friend.

Where Alpha's eyes were completely black orbs, William's eyes had a tendency to turn blood red whenever he felt angry, or when his adrenaline was pumping. Whether this was an effect of his having lived for so long, as was the case for Alpha's condition, or it was a side effect of the tortuous experiments that had been done to him, we didn't completely understand, but when William finally turned away from Chris and looked in our direction his eyes were completely clear of any redness, and Alpha immediately broke into a smile.

"My God," Alpha's accented voice came out rich with

relief, "he's laughing." I looked from Alpha to William and then back again, as Alpha said quietly to me, "Perhaps that fool is worth having around."

Chris' head shot up from the small box he was studying, "Hey!"

Chapter 4
Nazran, Russia.

In all the ways that mattered, Nazran was the city that never was. The city had less than 100,000 residents and had been originally founded as a military fortress in 1817. After the fall of the Soviet Union the town, which was officially became part of the Republic of Ingushetia, it was separated from the Chechen Republic and the city became the Republic of Ingushetia's Capital city in 1991. That temporary title ended because of its poor location and high rate of violence and the town of Magas replaced Nazran as Ingushetia's capital city in 2000. After that, Nazran began the more rapid decline into what it is today.

The first signs of trouble came in 2004, when a raid on Nazran, led by 200 to 300 rebels, reportedly of Chechen and ethnic Ingush descent, attacked the fifteen official government buildings, killing over 67 members of Nazran's security forces, government officials, including their top prosecutors and many United Nations workers. Although the raid only lasted around five hours the witness' reports included stories of raiders being little more than madmen, attacking with a ferocity that seemed far too savage for normal men.

The government reeled from the attacks, and General Tikhomirov, Commander of Russia's Interior Ministry forces, promptly resigned after the incident when the blame appeared to fall directly upon his shoulders. It was never clear who stepped into the vacant command position, but the 'new' government's Federal Security Services that were sent in to maintain order seemed more interested in the total subjugation of the population, as opposed to keeping the peace. Para-military activity included the mass abduction of civilians through illegal arrests, to outright murder/executions that were perpetrated in public, without any hint of concern by law enforcement. Eventually the brazen lawlessness led to a mass protest by the remaining citizens in 2008. The clash between the protestors and the Federal Security Service had the protestors hurling stones, bottles and petrol bombs at the security officers, who responded with tear gas, bullets and batons. The protestors who were arrested were severely beaten and dragged away to waiting vans and most of those arrested were never heard from again. In the aftermath, with the Federal Security Service and Police never revealing how many had actually been taken into custody during the violent clash, Interior Minister Musa Medov told the Associated Press, "Everyone even indirectly involved in organizing or participating, in this protest will be severely punished." More people began to go missing in the night, groups of civilians were escorted into waiting vehicles at gunpoint during the day with some individuals just being randomly grabbed while walking in the city's streets. Throughout all of this no governmental agency was ever identified or held responsible for the acts.

Today Nazran is populated mostly by the predators, prostitutes and derelicts that roam freely and openly on the public streets. There are still several factories and warehouses that sit in boarded abandonment along the outskirts of the downtown area, but simple demolition was too expensive and the buildings were far too dilapidated to be of any actual use in future developmental proposals. As a result, each brick or cinderblock edifice stands, like an enormous tombstone in some gargantuan cemetery, marking this portion of the city to be as dead as its former commercial enterprises.

If there were a focal point to Nazran's physical, mental and emotional decrepitude, then it would likely center on the former police station. Some said the men and women who worked there were the last of those in governmental service to be unblemished by the failing political climate. With most of their officers having been born and raised in Nazran, they had been determined to see the salvation of the city. That final hope was destroyed in 2009 by a "suicide bomber" who drove a van full of high-explosives through the front door of the police station. Twenty-five people were immediately killed, and over 140 were wounded.

Outside of the city's limits, the greenery of the pastures had returned, as if completely ignorant of the decay that was happening in such close proximity. Farming and the raising of livestock was the main vocation in the rural areas outside the city, while the beauty of the hillsides and the ruins of ancient churches had begun to attract a multitude of photographers interested in booking photo tours of the region. Still, the tourists were repeatedly warned to stay with their groups and never enter the city, which was now considered to be one of the most dangerous of all the Russian Republic cities.

Much of the transportation outside the city was still done by horse and cart, but every now and then the headlights of cars, trucks or vans could be seen undulating over the dirt roads. One such vehicle, a white unmarked van, veered off the main road and onto a private drive leading to a farm and a collection of warehouses at the driveway's culmination. The vehicle pulled up to one of the dark warehouse's loading doors and the driver blared the vehicle's horn twice. Within moments the roll-up door began to rise, eventually allowing the van to pull inside. Instantly, the barely audible sound of muffled cries, previously drowned out by the engine's noise, reverberated from inside the cargo section of the van.

The driver could clearly hear the pleas for help from the people begging to be let out of van, but he totally ignored them as he casually exited the vehicle. The driver then moved around to the passenger's door and opened it for an immaculately dressed older man who's appearance was completely out of place in the dark, dank warehouse. Scanning the area the older man moved a few steps away from the van with a swagger about his step and a precision in his demeanor, giving him away as having been in the military at some time and used to giving commands.

Several darkened forms moved in the shadows as they carefully approached the van, but stayed back and well hidden from most of the ambient light.

"Dimitri!" a voice called out to him in greeting from the shadows.

The old man returned the greeting with a wave of his hand, and turning to the driver said, "Bring the woman and the child, but leave the rest in the van." The authority in Dimitri's voice sent the driver, currently standing at attention, to give a quick nod of his head in almost a near salute, to step in front of the van's cargo door and, with a grunt of effort, slide the partially-rusted door open.

Dimitri had only walked a couple steps away from the van when an enormous silhouette appeared in the distance, seeming to flow out of the darkness.

"I see you have been productive," a deep voice spoke from the silhouette.

"Yes, but I am afraid I have some discouraging news as well," Dimitri said with only the merest trace of urgency in his voice.

"Oh?" There was a slight shift in the voice and the silhouette seemed to turn as Dimitri's driver brought the two bound figures to stop and stand just behind him. The silhouette considered the child, her wrists bound with simple twine behind her back and whose eyes seemed to simply have glazed over numbly in shock from the horror of her situation. Without a word the silhouette stepped into the light. Nicholas "The Hunter" Nickolaevich, former Grand Duke of Russia and sometimes referred to as Nicholas the Tall, towered over Dimitri in the same manner he had over his first cousin Tsar Nicholas II, the last Tsar of Russia.

"So this little thing is what will keep your, what did you

call it, 'Ultimate Weapon,' from turning against you?"

Dimitri scowled at the enormous man, but said nothing as Nicholas' attention turned to the other woman. She was filthy, her clothes were in tatters and she was bound in chains that both encircled her waist and entrapped her wrists before looping up and around her neck in such a way that if she tried to move her arms she would end up choking herself. Her mouth was bound by a gag that was stained pink with blood, and much of the rest of her face was covered by a knotted tangle of her long black hair. Despite all of this the woman was absolutely striking. Her body was the stuff that made artists and poets weep, while the mess of her hair and her generally grungy appearance added a kind of wild appeal to her persona that enhanced her appearance, instead of detracting from her looks. The moment she was pushed, stumbling, into the light it seemed as though she commanded all the attention in the warehouse.

Nicholas turned to study her, and his brow furled in concern and confusion, "This one is like us, why is she in chains?"

Dimitri grew angry, "She is not part of our family! She is the American whore I told you about."

Nicholas looked up from the woman, "Ah, I believe you said her name was Lei?" Nicholas stepped close and cupped one large hand over her cheek while using his thumb to wipe away some of the grime that had accumulated on her face.

Lei's eyes burned with murderous intent as she glared up at the large man, who only smiled in response before grabbing a handful of her hair and jerking her head back to expose her neck.

"Wait!" Dimitri called out in warning as Nicholas drew a Shashka sword from where it was fastened at his side.

"We need her as well," Dimitri said while desperately trying to stay calm.

Nicholas smiled and turned back to Lei, looking directly into eyes that had not softened at all from the halted attack,

48

"Who said I was planning on killing her? After all," Nicholas pulled her hair back even further, running his free hand over Lei's breasts "it would be a terrible waste of an enjoyable toy."

Dimitri sighed, "Let her go and get serious, we have a problem."

Nicholas rolled his eyes, but when he saw the look on Dimitri's face his own expression sobered, "What has happened?"

Dimitri looked uneasy, "My informants have notified me that the Romanov has been seen entering the country."

No sound came from Nicholas for a long moment, and then, "Has he found me?"

More shadows flowed to life as other voices began to moan, interrupting him from the darkness surrounding them.

"Release them!" Raspy words from the darkness of the warehouse demanded. "Let them out!"

Dimitri let out an exasperated sigh at the interruption, "Amazing how some people have no patience. You should have better control over them."

"They know their place," Nicholas reassured, but then grew angry, "has he found me?"

"We do not believe so, but he disappeared after passing through customs." Dimitri was genuinely surprised at how upset Nicholas had become, but he maintained a nonchalant attitude, "No matter, arrangements have already been made," Dimitri then inclined his head toward the van, "meanwhile, you and your people are in need."

Dimitri's words seemed to permeate the fog of anger that surrounded Nicholas and his face softened as he nodded his agreement. Without a word Dimitri raised one hand, signaling his driver to step away from the van's cargo door.

Dimitri looked to Nicholas, who seemed uninterested in the van's cargo, "What about you?"

Nicholas gave Dimitri a sideways glance, demonstrating that his anger hadn't completely diminished, "I can wait a little longer."

"Such control," Dimitri smiled as he lifted the van's remote control and pushed a button causing the van to beep once before the sliding cargo door on the passenger side of the vehicle opened to reveal five young adults, all of whom looked like they might have been college students, cowering inside the cargo compartment.

Dimitri turned to his driver, "Secure the two prisoners in the van once the others are out and it is empty." The driver nodded and pulled Lei by her chains to stand next to the girl.

Dimitri turned to the people in the van and yelled, "Go on! Get out of here before I change my mind!"

The promise of booze, partying and general debauchery that many of Dimitri's businesses in Nazran advertised to the surrounding cities always managed to lure more than a fair share of foolish young adults to his doors. Most were given the time of their lives and would return to their homes with wild tales to tell, but there were also a small number that would simply vanish, to never return home or to be heard from again.

This time there were five victims, three women and two men, all in their early twenties and dressed as if they had been out for a night of adventure on the dark side of town. Now their pale faces, which were sweaty and tear-streaked from the stress of a night having gone terribly wrong, cautiously looked out of the open door of the van. No one in the van moved at first, but eventually, one of the males cautiously crawled forward, climbed out and stood extending a hand to help the others get out. Two of the women came next, and after leaving the van, clung tightly to the young man, who again extended his hand inside the van.

Nicholas looked back at Dimitri with a questioning gaze.

"They are for you and yours," Dimitri smiled as he said,

"my driver and I already ate."

Just as the second man regained his footing the shadows once again sprang to life, terrifying the people who hadn't seen the macabre sight until now, and one of the girls bolted for the warehouse's man door. Dimitri and Nicholas watched as a shadow began moving in pursuit until it coalesced into the figure of a man who seemed to materialize out of the darkness. It took mere moments for the man to tackle the girl from behind and roughly drag her to the ground. The girl screamed and tried to keep moving, but the man's weight was on her and she was slowly pushed completely down onto her stomach. The other young people watched in horror as the girl clawed with her fingers into the unyielding concrete floor in a desperate attempt to keep moving toward the exit and freedom. The man on top of her, now exposed in the ambient light of the warehouse, was a horror to behold. His face was covered in weeping lesions, his eyes were bulging, his lips torn and what teeth remained in his mouth were yellowed and in various states of decay. He was clad head to toe in black clothes that were otherwise unremarkable, and despite the state he appeared to be in, he was still physically imposing enough to overpower the girl. He grabbed the girl's left arm and held it behind her back and placed his chest on top of the arm, keeping it pinned while freeing up both his hands. He then grabbed a handful of the girl's hair with his left hand and slowly pulled her head up and to the side while using his right to pin her free hand to the floor.

The girl let out a deep moan that sounded like an animal caught in the clutches of a predator, as the man bent his head down and licked the side of the girl's throat.

Another of the male passengers had seen enough, and probably intended to help the girl as he ran toward the display, but he didn't travel more than a couple of yards before he was hit from two different directions at once, and taken down onto his back.

Immediately his wrists were pinned by two or more different sets of hands, which were also grabbing at his hair and his right ear. The doomed man saw the flash of another ruined face shoot down to his throat, followed by a tremendous pinching sensation on his Adam's apple that grew into a crushing and tearing pain causing far more agony than he had ever before experienced or even imagined. He tried to scream, but it only came out as a loud wet gurgle as a spray of arterial blood burst forth, choking him as it flowed up and into his mouth and nose. The young man didn't really notice the second rending of his flesh at the bicep area, as the suffocating pain at his throat was too intense to ignore. He tried to twist his head away from the pain, but muscles he had always taken for granted failed to respond as more figures ran from the shadows and attached themselves to his body. The young man's cries started to ebb as the pain fell into a dull memory and mercifully, his entire world went black.

The sounds coming from the dying man caused two more of the passengers, apparently a young couple, to abandon the last girl still inside the vehicle as they quickly ran away from their helpless friends, leaving them to their fate. The woman turned back for a final look and saw the man lying on top of the first girl almost gingerly placing his mouth over the neck of his helpless victim in what looked very much like a lover's kiss. That was, until the girl let out a scream and the man drove his mouth even harder into the girl's neck before shaking his head back and forth with incredible ferocity. Blood erupted like a fountain, which seemed to act as a signal for at least a dozen more figures who ran out of the shadows to latch on to her as well.

The pair had almost made it to an emergency exit when the man was hit and lifted off his feet by another dark figure, forcing him to release his grip on her hand. As he landed the impact caused the man's head to strike the cement floor, knocking him into unconsciousness. The woman began screaming at the sight of the

52

figure who had tackled the man and watched as it rose slowly from the ground and regarded her. This time it was a sickly looking woman who faced her but, turning away from her with disinterest, instead began dragging the unconscious man away and into the shadows.

The girl backed away in horror as more shadows came to life all around her and charged past her into the shadows where her lover had been taken. Somehow, despite the panic that threatened to overwhelm her, the girl somehow found the strength to keep moving toward the exit. She reached for the door's handle, turned it until it released and swung it open to the emptiness of the night and supposed freedom beyond. She was about to bolt through when the figure of a woman suddenly appeared in the doorway blocking her path. So close to freedom, the girl tried to barrel her way through the woman in the doorway, but to no avail. The woman easily caught her with one arm and casually dragged her back inside the warehouse before closing the emergency exit door behind her with a free hand.

Nicholas smiled at the scene, his rage momentarily forgotten as he watched his people consume their victims until the last of the human livestock had grown quiet in unconsciousness or death. Then Nicholas turned to look back into the van and the final human inside. Casually he began to walk toward the van with Dimitri at his side.

Nicholas spoke first, "He must be found."

Dimitri let out a deep sigh. "I understand the urgency and have every resource on the hunt."

Nicholas and Dimitri had reached the van where the last passenger, a girl, was cringing in a far corner with her knees pressed into her chest. She had a crazed expression of terror on her face and she was rapidly repeating in Russian, "I want to wake up…I want to wake up…I want to wake up."

Nicholas placed one foot on the sidestep of the van and was

about to enter the cargo area when he stopped and looked back at Dimitri, "When he is found, do not hesitate. Tell you people to be ready and kill him before he can react."

Dimitri frowned, "Of course, but don't you want me to question him first?"

Nicholas shook his head, "We need no information from this man. What we need," Nicholas shot Dimitri a look that brooked no counter, "is him dead."

With that Nicholas hunched his massive frame over and entered the van. The girl began chanting her mantra faster and louder as Nicholas moved into the vehicle's interior, and the van rocked on its suspension with every step the giant took. Nicholas grabbed the sliding door handle and pulled it closed, cutting off all sound just as the girl began to scream.

Chapter 5

Bangkok, Thailand

I suppose I should have gotten more rest and food before choosing to speak with our "guest" but the need for answers after the debacle that our attack on Pollard had become was overwhelming.

"Is our guest in a mood to receive visitors?" I asked Larson.

The man only shrugged his shoulders, "Does it matter?"

"Not even a little," I said angrily and held my hand open to Larson. The major frowned, but placed the keys to the door for the makeshift "holding area" we were using into my hand. "Are you in control?" Larson asked quietly.

I glared at the man, but managed a nod. Larson returned the gesture, but added, "Take the rookie with you, just to be safe."

The "rookie" was the name Larson had given Chris ever since our time together in Thailand. I turned to look at Chris holding the icepack to his knee, "That isn't necessary."

Larson's gaze never wavered, "That man in there is the only lead we have. If something happens to him..."

Larson let the statement hang in the air and I was about to respond with something defensive and indignant. I caught myself before the words came out and I called to Chris, "Chris!"

He didn't look up from his knee, "Yo!"

"Chaperone service!"

Now Chris looked up, "For you or me?"

I sighed and looked back at Larson, "Me."

Chris looked surprised at my response and Alpha turned his attention toward me as well. "Oh," Chris managed, "well, all-righty then." He tossed the icepack on a table and shuffled over to me, "Let's do this."

I could feel all eyes in the room on the back of my head as I moved to the rear door, unlocked the padlock and slid the chains away. Through the door was a large but simple storage area, having one corner completely enclosed, floor to ceiling, with a heavy gauge chain-link fence. The lockable area was a major reason we had chosen this location as our base, but instead of using it to secure valuable equipment or other items of worth, we had locked our "guest" inside.

The man's name was Timberland. Not a first or last name, as far as we knew, but it appeared as though "Timberland" was identification enough for most people. Larson had called in a favor from a friend of his in the FBI, and we had what appeared to be a complete history of the man's activities dating back twenty years. Before that, the guy was a mystery. It was as if he just popped into existence as a guerilla fighter and mercenary at the age of eighteen.

I walked closer to the cage, pulled a folding chair away from where it stood leaning against a wall and opened it. Never taking his eyes off of me, Timberland faced me and knelt into a crouch like a catcher waiting for a pitch, while I sat on the chair.

I felt Chris walking up next to me and I turned to whisper, "Chris, give us some space, would you?"

Chris didn't say anything, he just backed up to stand against the rear wall of the room as I leaned forward in my chair, my face less than a foot from the chain fence that served as a wall of Timberland's cage, and just stared at the man crouching before me. Timberland returned the look, but his expression had a fierceness to it that seemed as primal as any apex predator. I could tell that despite the barrier between us Timberland's body was taut and ready to react, in either attack or retreat, depending on whatever I was planning.

I don't know if I surprised him or not, but he jolted slightly when I simply asked, "What did Whelan do to you?"

Timberland's face lost its ferocity, and a look of genuine concern as if a long held secret had been suddenly and completely exposed.

"He get you hooked on something?" I asked, "Something that you're hurting for now?"

Timberland smiled at my question and shook his head. He stood to his full height and stretched his arms before answering me, "Nothing so basic as drug addiction, I assure you."

"What then?" Timberland seemed reluctant to tell me, so I added, "Listen, I can't help you if you don't tell me what you need."

Timberland's face never lost its smile, "You want to help me? Really?" Timberland made a show of looking at the cage, "Doesn't seem like it."

"In all fairness, you did try to kill us."

"You were a soldier, right?" Timberland asked rhetorically. "Then you know it wasn't a personal thing. I was on one side and you people on the other. Simple as that."

In fact, I was never in the military, but I am and have been what my people call a "Hunter" for almost as long as I have been alive. In the past, Hunters would go out and collect the blood my people needed in order to survive. How they got it? Well, that wasn't always a friendly "social service." Today we have resources that sustain us without our needing to hurt anyone, but I was still trained to be highly proficient in some very ugly and violent skills, just in case I would ever have to use them at some unknown time in the future. Having said that, I have never fought as a soldier. I have never faced and fought in order to kill a foe for no other reason than because someone in an organization with more authority than I possessed told me that I should. Every time I had ever resorted to violence it was because there had been a threat either to my extended family or to me personally while I had been a detective with the LAPD. I have also fought with lethal force in a defensive manner, but I've never harmed a hair on anyone who wasn't a threat. I had never really thought about it before, but a soldier is told to go somewhere and fight, maybe even die, because it was his or her 'duty' and obligation to do so. There's no actual malice toward the human being that a soldier finds in the crosshairs of their rifle, there is only the knowledge that, if the role were reversed, then that person would pull the trigger just as quickly.

Finally I said, "So it wasn't personal? So what? That just means it wouldn't be personal if you killed me or my people once I let you free."

Timberland chuckled and shrugged, "I suppose that's true. So how do we fix this?"

I held up a key to the padlock of Timberland's cage, "We figure out a way for both of us to get what we want."

Timberland froze and his eyes darted from my face to the key and back again.

I said, "I'm thinking it's the only way to make this work."

Timberland moved as close to me as the cage would allow and knelt back down into that crouched position again.

"I take it, as I am not dead or already free, that you didn't find what you were looking for at the strip club?"

I nodded, "We found Pollard, but the girls weren't with him."

Timberland nodded his understanding back, "So that just means Pollard turned them over to Lagos."

I didn't say anything and Timberland read my silence before he said, "But you knew that already, right?"

"Yes," I answered, "so the question becomes, where do we look next?"

Timberland began shifting a little and his face melted into an uncomfortable expression.

"You know where he is, don't you?" My voice grew in volume and a dangerous edge I hadn't intended found its way into my words.

Timberland's eyes met mine and then looked down to the

floor before he replied, "I think I do."

"You think?!"

"Can't be sure," Timberland admitted, "but it's really the only logical location."

"Where?"

Timberland stood and took a couple steps away from his side of the cage, "That information will cost you that key."

I shot up from the chair and grabbed the fence, screaming, "You tell me where or I'll rip you apart and leave you in that cage to die!"

Timberland had jumped back another step as I exploded from the chair and clawed at the fence like I was trying find a weak point to get through. I heard Chris take a couple steps toward me as well and I did my best to calm myself as Timberland smiled smugly at me.

"That isn't going to happen and we both know it." The tone of Timberland's voice made my ire rise again and I immediately tried harder to recompose myself, but not before Larson came running into the room.

Larson was aiming his assault rifle with the red laser sight's beam penetrating through the cage and producing a red dot in the center of Timberland's chest.

Chris had a hand on my shoulder and was talking quietly so only I could hear him, "What's up?"

I struck the cage as I turned away, "He knows where the girls are."

Chris looked at me with concern, but then turned to Timberland and smiled, "He does, does he?"

Something in Chris' expression must have unhinged the man as he immediately objected, "I didn't say that! I said that I believe I know the only logical place where Dimitri Lagos would be."

Larson's eyes were darting back and forth between

Timberland and me, but didn't miss a beat, "And where is that?"

Timberland looked down to the red dot on his chest and swallowed, "The cost of that information is the key to the cage."

Larson looked like he was about to laugh when he said, "Okay, the information for the key."

Timberland pointed a finger at the red laser dot on his chest, "Mind pointing that somewhere else."

"That wasn't part of the deal."

Timberland seemed to regain his nerve, "I think you are missing the spirit of the deal."

"You want to check with your attorney, first?" Chris asked unhelpfully.

"Fine," Timberland sighed and rolled his eyes, "I'll be more specific. That information is the last of what I have to give and, after that, I am going to be useless to you. That means things can only go from bad to worse for me, so I have to…"

As he spoke Timberland's voice suddenly faded to silence and his eyes grew wide as they focused on something behind me. I turned to see Alpha and William ducking through the doorframe to enter the storage area. Alpha was as intimidating and as alien looking an image that anyone could imagine; however, it was William that Timberland's eyes were focused on, as the captured man's body began uncontrollably shaking with fear.

Seeing the apprehension in Timberland, I made a decision. I walked over to the cage and used the key to unlock the padlock and opened the door. Timberland quickly looked at the open door, but didn't move from where he stood in the cage.

"You have a deal," I dropped the key on the floor just inside the cage.

Chris called to me with quiet warning in his voice, "Steve?"

"Go get a laptop with Wi-Fi, Chris."

I could feel Chris' eyes on me, but he backtracked his way out of the room without a word.

Larson kept the red laser dot on Timberland's chest and never turned his head as he asked, "You know if you let him go and the information turns out to be a ruse, then we'll have lost our only asset."

"Yep," I confirmed as I walked into the cage, "but you aren't going to lie to us are you?"

Timberland didn't nod his head rapidly in panic, but it was clear the man was terrified as his words broke when he said, "I-It's all I have left to give you."

Chris came back into the room, sat on the floor and opened the laptop.

I started to say, "Can you turn on that GPS..." when the computer erupted in a piercing cacophony of electronic music that someone had once told me was called "Dub-Step." It was an often repeating, bubbly and obnoxious sound that was guaranteed to make your brain drip out of your left ear if you listened to it for too long without being under the influence of narcotics.

All eyes turned to Chris who quickly closed the laptop in embarrassment, "Um, sorry. I had my earphones on when I last used the..." he pointed to the computer helplessly, "...you know."

Chris ran a finger to the side of the computer and apparently hit a "mute" switch, because the computer remained silent when he opened it again.

"Um, okay... so you were saying something about a "GPS" or whatever?" Chris asked seemingly desperate to change the subject.

I closed my eyes and took a deep calming breath, "I want that thing where we can see locations in real time. Maybe a satellite shot or something like that?"

"Ah, gotcha. One sec."

Chris' fingers flew across the keyboard with only a couple brief pauses for connections to be made before he said, "Okay, tell me where to look."

I turned to Timberland, "You're on."

Sheepishly Timberland said, "Nazran."

Larson's eyes shot wide from behind his rifle and he slowly lowered the weapon to his side.

"Nazran? As in Ingushetia, the Russian Republic? Are you sure?" Larson asked.

Timberland nodded, "Dimitri Lagos basically owns the entire city. I was supposed go there to deliver..." The mercenary paused as he turned to look at William, "Well, you know."

I nodded, "That's pretty much all that Pollard had told us before..." my voice trailed off but, of course, Chris was there to pick up where I left off in his own inscrutable way.

Chris didn't look up from his computer screen but indicated with a thumb in William's direction, "Bigfoot stepped on his head. It went 'squish.' Literally."

Timberland's eyes darted from Chris to William and back again in rapid succession before Larson broke the momentary silence.

"And now we have confirmation." Larson cursed, "Well, shit."

"What?" I asked.

Larson walked over to Chris, "One of the worst Goddamn assignments I ever had was in that corrupt cesspool."

"When was this?" Timberland asked.

Larson stood over Chris as he looked at the computer screen, "September, '93."

Timberland snorted an ironic laugh, "Well, it's a hell of a lot worse now, and I certainly wasn't looking forward to going there."

"Okay, I located a satellite that can visualize the city as a whole or center on a specific street, anything more specific?"

I raised my eyebrows at Timberland who shrugged his shoulders, "I was going to be given a location once I arrived."

"So you want to give me a random city in the middle of Russia and I'm supposed to do… what?"

"Just wait until nightfall," Timberland suggested. "I told you, Lagos owns the city and is running it like some kind of den of depravity for thrill seeking party goers. He'll turn up. Just keep an eye on the screen and focus in on any hot spots of activity."

"Why would an ancient vampire want a...?" Chris had started to ask the question before the obvious answer popped in his head, "oh, never mind."

I looked around the room and saw multiple heads shaking "no" at me. Timberland noticed it too and said, "I know, the information is thin." He glanced down to the key on the floor in front of him, picked it up and held it out to me, "Give this back once you locate him on that thing."

I looked over at Chris who offered, "Might as well, I'm going to lose this satellite picture in," he checked the computer screen, "twenty three minutes anyway. There won't be another in range until half past midnight Nazran time."

I shrugged and looked around the room for anyone to voice an objection. When none came I held out my hand to Timberland and he casually dropped the key into my outstretched hand.

All the hard expressions in the room softened a bit as I backed out of the cage.

Timberland sighed, "Mind if I use the facilities before you lock me up again?"

Chapter 6

Pokrovskoye, Siberia. 1914.

Summer in Pokrovskoye, Siberia was the only time of year where the average daytime temperatures almost reached the freezing point. Currently the temperature was a mere twenty degrees and Alexei had to wear several layers of clothing to protect himself from the cold as he walked across the patches of permafrost that crunched under each footstep despite his attempts to keep his noise to a minimum. His hands were feeling slightly numb at this point and he was considering returning empty handed to the village, but the thought of enduring the scoldings of his teacher Rasputin quickly erased any such inclination he might have had.

He was less than a mile from the village where he and Rasputin would travel once or twice a year so the Starets could either visit with his family or drink excessively with his friends. Alexei felt cooped up the instant they had arrived and his restlessness had gotten the better of him the second he saw the animal tracks along the outskirts of the village. He recognized the track immediately as belonging to a large reindeer, not an unusual track for this area since the villagers raised these animals for transportation, leather goods and food; however, these tracks were of a lone animal with no signs of being part of any herd, domesticated or otherwise.

Although Alexei was only ten years old he had become an exceptional student in the art of tracking and hunting. Rasputin had made sure of that and made sure that the Tsar's game hunters would take Alexei out on several of their hunting expeditions and instruct him in those skills along the way. No one in the royal family understood why Rasputin was putting such emphasis on this particular subject; however, they did see a change in Alexei both physically and emotionally whenever he returned with the hunters.

Given Alexei's otherwise frail countenance under normal circumstances, he would always return looking exceedingly robust after the hunt, which made the Tsar and Tsaritsa even more convinced of Rasputin's genius.

Alexei never told anyone his secret, not even Rasputin, about what he did when he was left alone with the day's kill. As an apprentice to the hunters Alexei was always tasked with the duties of hanging and dressing the kills while the hunters cleaned themselves and their weapons before the evening meal. With a little bit of imagination, not to mention the fact that the hunters were always eager to get to their drinking after the hunt had ended, Alexei was able to concoct a viable story that enabled him to perform the bleeding and skinning of the animals out of sight of the otherwise preoccupied hunters. It was at this time when Alexei could no longer resist the temptation that burned within him the moment the hunting party collected their fallen prey. Now that he was alone to set about his grizzly duties, Alexei would gorge himself on the still warm blood of the freshly killed animals. Sometimes he feasted with such intent that he would have to regurgitate before subsequently resuming his insatiable consumption, until no blood remained. The duty was doubly convenient as everyone at camp mistook his blood-spattered appearance for youthful enthusiasm in the performance of his duties as opposed to the more macabre reality. Alexei never understood why he suddenly had this desperate need when he left the city for the countryside, but he was thankful that he wasn't ever overcome at home; as he feared what he might do if he was ever tempted with no animal resource.

Now Alexei was alone and convinced of his ability to make his first solo kill. Strangely, he wasn't overwhelmed with the need for the blood like he usually was when he left the city, but the thrill of the hunt weakened his resolve to resist. He held the barrel of the rifle directly in front of him as he continued forward, following the tracks until he saw his quarry less than forty yards in the distance. Alexei had watched the hunters load, shoot, and reload the rifles they used so many times that he felt he could do it on his own with ease. When he had stolen the rifle from the blacksmith's shed earlier he was relieved to find it already loaded with its single shot capacity. This meant he didn't have to steal any ammunition, which would have been exceedingly more difficult.

He raised the rifle to look down the sight at the reindeer, taking aim carefully as he had seen the hunters do so many times before. The reindeer was grazing on a small patch of grass that had grown in sporadic mounds wherever the permafrost had thawed and made itself the perfect target. Alexei squeezed the trigger slowly and waited for the rapport of the shot...

"What are you doing Alexei?"

A high-pitched singsong voice spoke so close behind him that Alexei nearly jumped out of his skin. Somehow he managed not to pull the trigger as he whirled around and saw the young woman watching him from less than three feet away. Alexei looked back to his prey and saw the reindeer looking directly at him, before it bounded off in the opposite direction and out of sight.

"Oh that's just wonderful! Look what you did Maria!"

Alexei knew the woman well. Maria Rasputin was the youngest of Grigori Rasputin's children and the only member of Rasputin's family that had regularly visited her father in St. Petersburg. She was several years older than Alexei and already had the appearance of a beautiful young woman as opposed to a teenage girl.

"What did I do?" Maria asked slyly.

"You ruined my shot!" Alexei fumed.

"So? It's not like the great Tsarevich is in desperate need of meat or leathers." She mocked him with a familiarity that few would dare. Alexei may have only been a ten-year-old boy;

however, he was also the Tsarevich and, despite his age, when he gave a command only his father the Tsar, his mother the Tsaritsa and his teacher Rasputin were exempt from following it.

"I needed it," Alexei whined, "you don't understand." Alexei froze; he had almost revealed his secret. Quickly he tried to think of something that would cover what he had just said. "If I go back empty handed I will have no excuse for having left the village or taking the rifle."

"You snuck out, why not just sneak back in?"

Alexei thought for a moment, and then replied, "Sneaking out is easier."

Maria laughed at that and Alexei was surprised how much the sound warmed his heart. As a boy of ten he didn't understand the feelings he had for Maria, but he felt them nonetheless. He found himself unable to keep from smiling whenever she was around. If he was angry or frustrated, and she paid him a visit, all his anger and frustrations would simply melt away. He could only remember laughing out loud at times when Maria had been around. And on those nights when his eyes refused to succumb to sleep all he had to do was think of her and soon he would restfully slumber.

"Well," Maria continued when her laughter had finally ceased, "I suppose if you walked back to the village with me I could sneak you back in."

Trying to maintain his composure Alexei responded casually, "That could work."

The two walked side by side along the frozen bank of the Tura river until they were within one hundred yards of the village.

"Ok, I think I'd better hide you now before someone notices a pair of people walking back into the village."

Despite the cold, Alexei could feel himself start to sweat at the prospect of hiding under her long voluminous coat as she opened the front of the garment for him to hide underneath.

Alexei awkwardly began to move to her when she said, "Perhaps you should hand me the rifle first?"

Alexei giggled in a silly way as he handed her the rifle and wrapped his arms around her waist. He could feel how warm her body was as he pressed himself firmly against her.

"Alexei," Maria whispered.

Swooning, Alexei cooed, "Hmm?"

"You're squeezing me too tight...can't breathe."

Suddenly realizing that he was clinging voraciously to her, Alexei immediately loosened his grip.

"Sorry."

She smiled at him and chuckled quietly. Alexei smiled back at her and they began their awkward walk back to the village.

Once back inside the village Maria whispered, "Where did you   get   the   rifle?"

Alexei's reply was muffled by the long coat, but was still understandable when he said, "Outside of the blacksmith's shop."

Maria guided the two of them slowly to the blacksmith shop when Alexei suddenly stopped in his tracks. Maria, who had no warning that the boy was about to stop walking, nearly fell over. Gently, Alexei pushed himself away from Maria and revealed himself to any who might be watching.

Confused, Maria looked at Alexei and was about to ask what he was doing when Alexei said, "Do you feel that?"

Unlike her father, Maria had only traces of the mystic talents that her father possessed; however, she had heard her father speak of Alexei and his uncanny abilities in mysticism after only minimal training.

"What is it Alexei?"

"Something...something dark and taut, like a loaded spring...just waiting...waiting."

"Where?" Maria scanned the surrounding area but couldn't see anything out of the ordinary.

Alexei didn't reply but he started walking in the direction of the church. Maria didn't return the rifle to the blacksmith's shop. Now she checked it to be sure it was loaded and followed behind Alexei scanning the village as she moved. The Tsar's personal guard bolted to attention the second Alexei came into their view and initially drew their Shashkas in alarm when they saw the woman carrying a rifle behind their charge. When they realized the woman was Maria Rasputin they ran to the Tsarevich in flanking positions with Maria between them for they knew no one was more trusted around the Tsarevich than Maria.

They were nearly in front of the old church that Rasputin had formerly called his home when the doors of the church began to open. Rasputin and a handful of people walked calmly out and began to descend the steps.

Suddenly a woman shrieked and charged the church.

Alexei cried out, "Maria stop her! Shoot her down!"

The guards alongside Alexei immediately pulled him aside as Maria raised the rifle and tracked the woman as she ran straight for her father. She squeezed the trigger but the rifle misfired and sent no intercepting shot at her target.

The woman gripped a long knife and held it at waist level. Rasputin's eyes went wide with surprise at the sight of the oncoming woman. He didn't seem to grasp what was happening as the woman moved up the stairs and plunged the knife deep into his abdomen. Maria screamed as Alexei tried to run to his teacher's side but was restrained by the two huge guards that held him fast. Shock and disbelief seemed to cover Rasputin's face more than any indication of pain as the woman wrenched the blade to the side, disemboweling the man. Eerily, with his intestines hanging limply from his abdomen, Rasputin remained upright and looked directly at the woman as if simply surprised by her presence.

"Khionia...why?" was all Rasputin as able to say before he collapsed backward into the arms of the people who had been following behind him.

The woman was immediately restrained, but she still managed to hold the bloody knife aloft and scream, "My name is Khionia Guseva! And I have killed the antichrist!!!"

The hysterical assassin was dragged away in one direction while Rasputin was carried in another. Somehow the two enormous bodyguards that had been restraining him were suddenly overpowered by their ten-year-old charge and Alexei sprinted to Rasputin's side.

"Father Grigori!" Alexei began to weep and had to shield his eyes from the ghastly vision of the belly wound.

Rasputin's hand shot to Alexei's wrist and Alexei immediately looked at his teacher.

"Your medicine..." Rasputin gasped. "Bring...me...your..."

Alexei knew exactly what his teacher and mentor had requested and he ran faster than he had ever run before to retrieve the intricately etched crystal vial with the strange clear liquid inside.

***

After an intensive surgery and an uncertain two-week isolation period, Rasputin had not only survived the assassination attempt but it also appeared as though he was going to fully recover. He had been returned to St. Petersburg and was housed in the majestic White Palace while being tended to by the Tsar's best physicians. Alexei and Maria barely left Rasputin's side during this time and when Rasputin's eyes finally opened the first thing he saw were the smiling faces of his daughter and his student. Maria carefully wrapped her arms around her father's neck and held him as Rasputin whispered reassurances lovingly into her ear. After a few minutes Rasputin's eyes fell once again upon the ten-year-old boy who stood smiling in the far corner of the room.

Gently Rasputin pulled at his daughter to release her grip from around his neck and said in a thin voice, "Maria, let me speak with Alexei for a moment. Oh, and could you perhaps get me some of whatever the physicians say I can eat?"

Maria looked at her father in a confused fashion momentarily, then nodded and quietly left the room.

"Come closer boy," Rasputin called out to Alexei, who moved to the tall man's bedside and leaned in close so his teacher would not have to exert himself in order to be heard, "tell me, when did you realize that woman was lying in wait for me?"

Nervously, Alexei responded, "I only saw her as she charged you."

Chuckling, then grunting from the pain that the mild laughter caused, Rasputin gently scolded the Tsarevich, "I did not ask you when you 'saw' her. I asked when you realized she was there."

Embarrassed and a little guilt ridden Alexei answered, "I sensed something was wrong almost as soon as Maria and I snuck back into the village."

"And when..." Rasputin's words came to an immediate halt, then he blithely repeated what Alexei had said as if considering the words, "...Maria and I snuck back into the village? You mean...my Maria?"

Alexei couldn't look at his teacher as he told him about his sneaking out of the village, the reindeer, Maria having come after him and his return hiding under Maria's long coat. Rasputin raised one hand to his forehead and he massaged his eyes.

Letting out a deep sigh Rasputin continued, "I see. All right, after you were done disobeying me, your father and your mother by going… anywhere… without your bodyguards, what exactly did you feel when you first sensed the woman?"

"We were headed to the blacksmith shop to return the rifle I had taken when I felt something…out of place within the village."

"AH!" Rasputin seemed excited to hear this, "go on!"

"It was like a black cloud had descended out of the sky and landed on the ground near the church. It is very hard to describe, but I knew that something was out of place and dangerous, just waiting for the right moment. When the woman charged I knew she was the source."

Rasputin stared wide-eyed at the boy. "So strong…so attune. You are truly gifted my boy. Truly gifted indeed."

Alexei didn't really understand that statement, but other questions were nagging at him, "Father Grigori, who was that woman? Why did she attack you?"

Rasputin merely stared off into the distance as if in a daydream. Then he shook himself and waved a hand in the air dismissively, a gesture he was prone to do more often than not, and said, "Khionia? Oh, she was a dalliance of mine who feels scorned by my recent lack of attention. I will have to discover if her actions were motivated by her own will or that of another, once I am fit enough to do so of course."

Confused, Alexei could only reply, "Sir?"

"As a result of my relationship with your mother and father, I have made many political enemies. I don't believe Khionia is someone who would have concocted this assassination on her own and, although she may felt scorned enough to have wished my death, I don't believe she would have carried it out the way she did without someone influencing her to action."

"Do you want me to have Father arrest someone?" Alexei asked, genuinely eager to help.

Again Rasputin chuckled, and paid for it in pain moments later, "No Alexei, well not yet anyway." Rasputin grew quiet

72

before he continued, "Do you understand what you experienced in the village?"

"No sir," Alexei admitted.

"I have been teaching you many, many things Alexei; however, everything I have taught you has always been about one thing...perception. How you perceive the world and interrelate to its mysteries is what it means to be a mystic. This sensitivity that you uniquely possess, it can serve you in many ways; however, I do not know if it is completely natural or if I somehow influenced it by the curative I give you for your hemophilia."

"I don't understand."

"You are special Alexei. What it means to study mysticism and develop the perception as I have taught you for all of these years is vastly different for someone like you as compared to the rest of us. The most powerful mystics develop unique sensitivities to their environment and develop awareness's and abilities that go beyond those of simple logic and circumstance."

Alexei didn't understand and it must have shown on his face as Rasputin chided, "Not to worry my boy, experience will be your teacher after I have gone. I have seen to it."

"What do you mean Father Grigori? You are going to recover from your wound. The physicians all have said as much."

"This time my boy, this time."

Alexei was nonplussed, "and when you recover we shall ferret out those individuals who would do you harm and they shall be arrested."

Rasputin's smile was so radiant that it almost seemed as though the room grew brighter.

"Of course Alexei, of course. Now could you send my daughter back in? I wish to speak with her and then get some rest."

"Yes sir."

Unseen by Alexei as he turned to walk out of the room, Rasputin's face twisted into an insane mask filled with rage and fear. Alexei closed the door behind him and Rasputin spoke out loud as if someone was still in the room.

"Horror awaits us all, my dear ones. All the people of Russia shall feel the terrors and the sadistic tortures that should only be reserved for those in the deepest bowels of hell."

Rasputin could hear the footsteps of his daughter outside his door and his features eased into sorrow, "and judgment day is closing in on some of us faster than others."

Chapter 7

One of the things that had always amazed me about Chris was his apparent ability to forego the normal need for sleep. While the rest of the group returned to their makeshift beds, Chris just typed away on the computer, gathering as much information as he could on Nazran. I think it was guilt that eventually made me give up on trying to get back to sleep, so I tried to sit with Chris as he worked.

I must have nodded off because one moment I was listening to the rhythmic tapping of the laptop keys, and in the next I was being gently lowered to the floor. I tried to shake the sleep out of my head when Chris' voice echoed lightly in my ears.

"You need to lie down before you fall out of the chair. I'll wake you when I find something."

I don't know how long I was out, but when I awoke I could hear muffled voices discussing something close by. My body was extra stiff from having slept on the concrete floor and the multiple pops that my joints made as I stretched were loud enough to alert the others in the room that I was trying to go about getting up.

When my eyes cleared I could see Chris smiling at me, "You should really do some yoga for those creaking joints old man."

I glared at him indignantly, "Have you found something?"

"Yep, but maybe you'd like to get into 'downward dog' position for a bit first?"

I rubbed my eyes as I could hear Chris and Larson, who turned out to be the other person in the room, chuckling at my pain.

"I hate you both," I growled, "now help me up and show me what you learned."

Larson extended a hand and pulled me to my feet as Chris typed away on the laptop. I moved into a position where I could

75

see what was on the screen and recognized the image of a satellite photo zooming in on a cityscape. The sun had set long before and the lights of the city now illuminated the city of Nazran like a pale Christmas tree.

"So what am I looking at?" I asked as Chris stood up to show me what he had done.

"Welcome to beautiful downtown Nazran," Chris said with a flourish of his arms and heavy sarcasm in his voice. "A more beauteous shit-hole you simply could not find on earth."

I looked up from the screen, "That bad?"

Chris blew out a whistle, "I watched three assaults in the last hour. The place seems to be completely lawless, despite the presence of what appears to be a city security force, as well as regular soldiers."

I turned back to the laptop screen as Chris continued, "It's like they have everything they need to maintain some form of order, but no one is interested in doing anything."

"You have any idea what's happening, Major?" I asked Larson.

"Best guess is that the local law enforcement has been given a very specific task in their security duties, probably with explicit instructions to ignore anything and everything else."

"And they can get away with this, why?"

Larson shrugged his shoulders, "When the Soviet Union collapsed, many of their satellite countries, or territories, suddenly needed to fend for themselves without the money, or the means to accumulate the money they needed in order to become self-sufficient. There were immediate petitions to possess these new territories by the people residing with the borders, but that was mostly their pride and greed, without them having any real idea of how to govern. Nazran is just one city inside the territory of the Republic of Ingushetia, but if you try to find out what they do in Nazran, you'll end up just shaking your head in frustration. It is almost as though the one hundred and fifty thousand plus people living there simply don't do anything except officially maintain the town as a town."

Chris turned to Larson, "So they are doing what? Rebuilding or something?"

Larson shook his head, "It's difficult to understand, but Russian territories are classified in certain ways, and supported by the Russian government according to that classification. The territory of Ingushetia is actually quite beautiful, but Nazran is so volatile, with every ethnic background trying to kill off all the others, that it has been deemed the most dangerous city in Russia. It is also a hot bed of governmental corruption signified by the number of people kidnapped or murdered by the government's, so called, officials.

"And I suppose that we suspect the person who has likely been responsible for these government kidnappings, and other associated violence, is actually Dimitri Lagos?"

Larson nodded as Chris called out, "Watch this." He fingered the mouse pad and brought up a smaller screen that sat in a window on top of the satellite's image, "I recorded this earlier."

I watched a line of flashy and expensive cars that seemed completely out of place in the otherwise drab surroundings as they pulled in to park quite neatly along a row of brightly illuminated buildings. On the street a crowd of relatively young and well-dressed people milled around with everyone holding a cigarette in their hand and a 'ready to party' expression on their faces.

"Our guest mentioned that Dimitri 'owned' the city," Chris volunteered. "Well, it looks like the king has come to court with his entourage in tow."

I watched men, dressed in all black with the appearance and demeanor of law enforcement or security personnel, aggressively part the crowd and open the door of the lead vehicle, a beautiful Rolls Royce Ghost Bespoke. Two men dressed in identical designer business suits, which immediately gave them away as Dimitri's bodyguards, exited the vehicle and surveyed the crowd. When they were apparently satisfied the area was secure, the bodyguard closest to the door waved a hand and Dimitri Lagos stepped from the vehicle. I instantly recognized Dimitri from when he had come to recruit Lei and me at my office in Las Vegas, and I knew the small and somewhat frail-looking appearance he sported was a sham that the ancient man liked to project. What I hadn't expected was that he had lost the rumpled business suit he had worn to my office and replaced it with something that I can only describe as "Rock-star" attire, which involuntarily made me think of Mick Jagger... minus the long hair.

I was about to comment on the spectacle when another man's leg emerged from the vehicle. A large head ducked out from under the door's frame, followed by a man's body that just kept coming and coming from within the car's rear seat, until the man was able to stand at his full height, which was more than a foot taller than the bodyguard next to him.

I was about to make the expected comment on the man's size, when something beyond the obvious struck me as odd. The large man was wearing a grey wool overcoat and a traditional "Ushanka" winter hat that made him look more like an old Soviet military man, as opposed to a business man or club goer.

"Who's the big guy?" I asked.

Larson and Chris looked uncomfortably at each other.

I turned from the screen and frowned at their expressions, "What?"

Chris spoke up first, "I ran a facial recognition program on him. We had a hit, but it only registered a 68% reliability."

I raised my eyebrows, "So who does the computer 'think' he is?"

Larson walked to the table where the laptop sat, lifted a small stack of paper and handed it to me.

There was the pixilated image from the satellite feed, along with another black and white photo that took up most of the page. The only type was the name I read at the top of the page and I frowned at the name of "Nicholas Nickolaevich." I took my eyes off the paper for a moment and looked at nothing in particular, "Why does that sound familiar to me?"

"Next page," Chris said as he pointed at the stack in my hands.

I looked back to the stack and flipped the page over and began reading, "Nicholas Nickolaevich, also known as Nicholas the Tall, Nicholas The Hunter and Grand Duke Nickolay Nickolaevich Ro..." my eyes widened as the word caught in my throat, "...Romanov?!"

Larson nodded, "It doesn't really seem possible, but the computer seems to think that we are looking at the grandson of Nicholas the First, of Russia and the first cousin of Nicholas the second, the last Tsar of Russia before the Bolsheviks took power."

My Russian history was next to nothing, but I remembered Dimitri having mentioned 'The Romanov' in my office, along with Pollard's recent confession mentioning such a person as well.

"The man was a public figure. Isn't there a record of..."

Chris cut me off, "If you had kept reading, you would have seen that our man managed to escape Russia before the Bolsheviks could execute him, and lived in Italy where he became the center of an anti-Soviet monarchist resistance group. He remained in exile until his recorded death in the French Riviera in 1929, where he had moved in order to get out the cold winter in Genoa."

"I take it the reports of the man's demise were greatly exaggerated?" Larson quipped, "so, that means he's one of you."

I pointed to a spot in the packet of papers in my hand, "It says here that he was born in 1856."

"Right," Chris agreed, "that would make him over one hundred and sixty years old, which is pretty much the upper limit

79

in age for most of our kind. If he was one of our kind, then he would still look like an old man in the winter of his life, but look at him."

I glanced to the screen as Chris continued, "He's not young, but he's far from the senior citizen that he should resemble."

Larson asked, "Didn't you say Alpha was something like five hundred years old?"

I nodded, "Six actually, in fact, William is around that old as well, but it's pretty rare among our people to be ageless. When it does happen the person seems to resemble a normal human who is around thirty five years old."

"So how do you, account for Dimitri?"

Chris responded, "He has a point Steve. Dimitri is supposed to be one of those 'ageless' what-ever you might call him, and he looks older than dirt."

I shrugged, "There's no written record that can explain what happens to us if we keep on living like that, but Alpha has said it is different for everyone. Just look at Alpha as compared to William. Alpha's eyes have become black orbs, while William still looks pretty much normal."

Chris laughed, "Normal being a very relative term."

I heard Larson cough to hide his own laugh as I continued, "Fair enough. I simply mean that as far as we know, the condition might manifest in a different way for anyone afflicted."

"So it is still possible that this "Nicholas" is one of your 'Ancients'?"

"Quite likely, actually," I confirmed as I studied the photo of Nicholas Nickolaevich Romanov, "I don't know, but I think we are going to need to be very careful. Dimitri wanted William as a weapon against someone he called, "the Romanov" and given the similarity of their sizes I am thinking this might have been his target."

"They seem pretty chummy to be enemies," Chris

observed, "unless Dimitri is using him to get what he wants and then plans on eliminating him."

I let that thought roll around in my head, but I couldn't shake the feeling that there was something we were missing.

"Why does Dimitri need such a man?" I asked to the room in general.

Larson turned to Chris, "Did you say something about this guy Nicholas being an 'anti-Soviet monarchist'?"

Chris looked back at his screen and nodded.

Larson shrugged, "Sounds like your answer right there. Dimitri recruited an ally who is a military expert, at least he was back in his day, and is likely highly motivated by the prospect of reclaiming at least part of what used to belong to his family before he was forced to abandon it."

Maybe it was the old Detective instincts I developed back in my days with the LAPD, but I shook my head, "We're still missing something." I turned to Chris, "Are there any other living descendents of the Romanov's?

Chris nodded his understanding, "Give me a sec," the screen started loading a new page and I could see Chris' eyes vibrating as he read the words. "Says here that the Tsar and his entire family were killed by firing squad in some kind of storm cellar where they were being held by the Bolsheviks." Chris continued reading and his face grew ashen, "Christ, his children were little more than babies at the time, but none of them were reported to have been spared."

"What was this Romanov's relation to the Tsar?" Larson asked.

I re-read the paper for Larson, "First cousin, once removed."

He nodded, "I'm no genealogist, but it sounds like anyone with a more direct link than this guy," Larson pointed at the tall man on the screen, "was either executed or hunted down and killed."

I sighed, "Ok, let's focus." I changed the subject, "In the end it doesn't matter who this 'Romanov' is, because I really don't give a shit about Dimitri's plans. He has Lei. He has Pha. We need to go and get them, period." I gave that uncompromising statement a moment to sink in before asking, "Have you figured out how we're going to get into the country yet?"

Chris smiled and hit another set of buttons on the keypad. The screen went blank and then faded into a YouTube video called "The Mystic Land of Ingushetia." Immediately the video began playing modern music with what might have been lyrics native to the region, as panoramic shots of beautiful mountains and landscapes with ancient looking ruins in the background rolled artistically across the screen.

"Lovely, but what am I looking at here, Chris?" I asked.

Chris pointed to the video where people were standing to one side photographing the ruins. "It would appear as though photographic tours of the countryside surrounding Nazran have become popular amongst photography enthusiasts."

"So you'll need to go in as photographers," Larson said matter-of-factly.

Chris nodded, "I can put enough credentials together to make the three of us appear to be a professional photography crew on assignment to photograph the historical ruins throughout Ingushetia. With Nazran being more or less centrally located it would make sense that we set up a base of operations for our work in the city."

I looked questioningly at Larson, "You're not coming?"

Larson lowered his eyes as Chris looked over. Chris had apparently missed the fact that Larson had said, "You will, need to go in as photographers" and not "We will need to go in as photographers," thereby effectively taking himself out of the equation.

"Can't," Larson said simply, as Chris and I waited for an explanation. Eventually he got the hint and expanded, "I'm still active military status despite my ongoing hiatus of the moment. If any Russian official were to learn that a member of the United States Special Forces has crossed the border into Russian territory without the permission of the Russian government, or the knowledge of the United States government, then I and anyone with me would be as good as dead."

I looked at Chris, who shrugged his shoulders and said, "Hard to argue with that."

I nodded and asked, "What will you do?"

Larson jerked a finger at the room where Timberland was still locked in his cage, "You said you were going to cut him loose?"

"I will, unless I suddenly change my mind and believe he's a threat, then I'll just shoot him."

Larson frowned, "You don't currently think he's a threat? Why not?"

I held up my hands in a helpless gesture, "I'm only guessing, but the bottom-line is that he's a mercenary and mercenaries aren't loyal, or at least their loyalties are for sale. His employer abandoned him to die back in Thailand, and probably a far greater betrayal in Timberland's mind, is the fact that he has been left unpaid. My guess is he'll go back to wherever he came from, and wait until he has a chance to avenge himself on his former employer."

Larson thought about it and said, "Maybe, but I think I'll follow him and see if he turns over any rocks that might help."

"Not a bad idea." Chris volunteered.

Larson nodded, "Just make sure you keep a satellite phone with you so I can contact you as needed."

"Can you prep us for the trek to Nazran?" I asked.

Larson grimaced at the thought, "Fair warning, it is going

83

to suck. But sure, I can even give you the name of someone who can get you geared up, once you're in Nazran."

I shook my head to clear it of disbelief, "You're on friendly terms with arms dealers in the middle of nowhere?"

Larson smiled, "Well, I did tell you that I had been there before, and I have an ongoing relationship of sorts with a particular individual there."

"I don't suppose your 'friend' can help us sneak across the border instead?"

Larson laughed, "You aren't familiar with the terrain around that area are you?"

I shook my head soberly, "Not even a little, but from your expression I take it that was an ill-advised suggestion?"

Larson nodded, "The geography of the region is one of the reasons that Nazran was originally founded as a military base. Anyone foolish enough to attempt an invasion would be physically spent scaling the mountains, not to mention that any supply trains would never be able to get to the troops.

"Okay," I said, "scratch the idea of sneaking in. Do you think we could falsify our way through customs?"

"Why would we have to?" Chris asked.

I was about to scold Chris when Larson cut me off, "He's right. The place is so backward in its networking abilities, that they probably wouldn't be able to run a check on you even if they wanted to. Add into the mix a well-placed bribe to expedite the process, and they'll probably carry your bags, as they hustle you on through."

I thought about that and let it roll around in my head a moment before asking, "Is there any chance that the bribe would do us more harm than good?"

Larson shrugged, "There's always a chance you could end up arrested and thrown into whatever is passing as a jail in Nazran these days, but the corruption runs so deep that bribes are pretty much expected. It might even be construed as rude not to offer a bribe." Larson grinned wickedly, "Hell, you could be stopped simply because you have American passports, because the camera equipment is worth more than the bribe you are giving, or simply because the person checking you through is in a bad mood. There's always a risk."

I frowned at Larson, "Try not to enjoy this so much."

Larson laughed, "Definitely relishing the 'better you than me' moment here."

"That only leaves us with two big problems," Chris said as he held up two fingers, Larson and I remained silent as we waited for Chris to explain.

"Tweedle-Dee and Tweedle-Dum in the other room," Chris pointed to the room where William and Alpha were resting, "are never going to pass for professional photographers."

He was right, even if we could convince the local authorities that William and Alpha were a legitimate part of a photography crew, their larger than life presence and unsettling appearance would certainly attract too much attention.

"So what do we do about them?" Larson asked, "I don't know them all that well, but I don't think they will like the idea of being left behind."

"Alpha has his ways, "I said cryptically, "just tell him the destination and I'd bet that he and William will beat us there."

Chapter 8

When Larson had said the ride to Ingushetia was going to suck, it had been an understatement of such magnitude that I might actually give him a nomination for the "Biggest Understatement in the History of Mankind" Award. The flight to Istanbul just sucked in general, but the drive from the airport, over the waterways and across the border into Georgia while bouncing in the back of a truck, sucked a lot more. The boat ride up the Terek river from Georgia to southern Ingushetia was a frozen and turbulent catastrophe, which also sucked, while the final Cessna flight over the mountains and its subsequent landing in a pasture just outside Nazran was the pinnacle of all suck-i-tude. And finally, I kid you not, there was an actual fully harnessed horse and cart, accessorized with wooden wagon wheels, for our final ride into Nazran. Meanwhile we were showing falsified passports, and handing out bribes like candy on Halloween, just for the honor of traveling in such decrepit splendor. It was almost as if Larson had arranged for us to suffer just as he had two decades ago, and he didn't want to deny us the experience of nearly three days-worth of aggravation, discomfort and possibly death, in transit. Chris and I made a pact to kick Larson in the ass, once for each leg of the trip, for his efforts in preparing our journey, yet personally opting out of this little adventure, regardless of the legitimacy for his reasons.

When we finally arrived in Nazran we both felt beaten and bedraggled, as we climbed off of the cart and ambled from the marketplace into what appeared to be a decent hotel, decent in this case referring to the fact that there wasn't any graffiti on the building, or squatters sitting outside the establishment. Once we stepped inside the hotel every eye in the joint scrutinized us as if we had just been added to the menu.

The front desk clerk was nice enough and seemingly extra helpful once she saw the color of our money. Chris and I got separate rooms, although the second room would serve more as a decoy and extra storage space in case anyone came looking for us, forcing a split of their forces between the two rooms. For our part, we had no intentions of separating ourselves at night, and would sleep in shifts, as if we were on watch in hostile territory, which was probably an accurate description of our situation.

Once we unpacked and separated our gear, including the handguns from the camera equipment, Chris asked, "So do you want to sleep first, or get started now?"

Instantly my mind flew to Lei, and the desperation I felt at wanting to locate her, but we had been traveling hard, and I knew we wouldn't be helping her if we weren't at our best.

"Sleep, shower, eat and then make a plan." I said with a sigh of resignation.

"Okay," Chris nodded, "do you think you can stay awake long enough for me to take a shower?"

I only nodded my reply and Chris rose to walk into the bathroom. I think I managed to keep my eyes open until I heard the water from the shower stop, because after that I only remember Chris shaking me awake three hours later.

I rubbed the sleep from my eyes and asked, "Everything okay?"

Chris turned back to his laptop and starting punching keys, "So far so good."

I spelled Chris and let him catch a couple hours of sleep as I showered, checked the guns, and strapped my Glock into the shoulder holster I preferred. The gun wasn't overly large, and could easily be concealed under my jacket. The shoulder holster was cumbersome and I wouldn't win any quick draw competitions, but my priority was concealment and, as long as I wore the jacket, no one would know I was armed.

I sat quietly as Chris slept and my mind drifted to Lei. I smiled and shook my head as I thought how, even though we both looked to be in our early thirties, we both were approaching eighty years of chronological age. We had known each other for nearly our whole lives and had been in love most of that time as well, but we had only become engaged a little while ago. Looking back I couldn't imagine why we, or more specifically, why I had waited so long to ask. Sure, we lived dangerous lives, as our people's "Hunters," but that hadn't been the reason that kept us from tying the knot. Maybe it was because the marriage ceremony had always seemed something for regular people? If I were to be honest about it, then I'd have to admit that the whole thing had always seemed like a silly religious or legal binding that supported the coupling of two people into a marriage within our modern society. As Lei and I, by design, weren't part of that society, it had always seemed sort of unnecessary to me. We were together, so what more was required for the likes of us?

Then I had left her, and the rest of my people, over a misunderstanding that still stabs at my core when I think about how arrogant I had been. I still remember the look on Lei's face when I finally asked her to marry me. I remember her shocked look, as my question had caught her off guard. The way she trembled as I fumbled over the words that came out of my mouth. The nervousness that I had no reason to feel as I asked the question, as well as my combined relief and exultation when she accepted.

I was wrong. Marriage was a very big deal, regardless of our being part of society or not. Then, just as soon as we had gotten used to the idea, she was taken from me. I shook my head to clear the anger and sadness from the front of my thoughts, and felt a cramp in my right hand. I looked down to see my fist clamped tightly in a ball with small trickles of blood peeking through the creases. I had been clenching my fist so hard that my fingernails had driven into the flesh of my palm. I wiped the tiny amount of blood away on the black jeans I was wearing and turned to look at

Chris' laptop. He had the satellite image up of the main street where we had previously located Dimitri and his entourage.

I watched the screen in a kind of trance-like state, as miscellaneous people walked by and various cars drove past. I only looked up one time, and that was only when I heard footsteps in the hall just outside our room. This wasn't the kind of place that had room service, turn down service, or any other service for that matter, but that didn't mean there weren't other people staying in the hotel. I removed my Glock from its holster and aimed it at the door as the footsteps grew louder, but whoever was out there simply continued past the door and the footsteps gently faded away, until I heard a key unlock a door further down the hall. I could hear the door close, but I didn't put the gun away until a couple of minutes had past.

When I finished holstering the weapon I turned to find Chris sitting up and alert as if ready for whatever might happen next.

"Everything all right?" he asked.

"Guess so. You up for good?"

Chris rubbed some sleep from his eyes, "Yeah, did you order any room service?"

I laughed, "You would trust this place with room service, assuming they had any in the first place?"

Chris looked bewildered for a moment then, even though I saw the comprehension fill his eyes, he asked, "So, no room service?"

I reached into one of our bags and pulled out one of the protein bars that we had been living on for the past couple of days.

Chris let out a moan as he looked at the bar, "I never thought I'd develop a distaste for chocolate."

At those words my head shot up and my eyebrows raised as I stared at Chris. He had unwrapped the bar and was in the process of taking a huge bite when he noticed my expression and froze, mouth agape and bar halfway inserted into his maw.

His eyes rolled from me, down to the bar and back before he slowly lowered it from his mouth and asked, "What?"

"Are you sure you're hungry for food? Lack of interest could mean you're in need."

The "need" I was referring to was the concentrated serum that my people use to stave off the effects of the Porphyria.

Chris looked at the bar, concerned, "I can usually go a week before I feel the slightest need for a shot."

"I know," I said sympathetically, "but the travel was tough. Your body may have burned through it early."

Chris looked up, "You seem okay."

"I'm older than you." It wasn't a great answer, but it was true. Chris was relatively new to being one of us, while I was born with the condition. As a rule, the whole "turning a normal human into a vampire thing" is a bit of a false legend. In fact the only time I have ever seen it done in my lifetime was in Chris' case, but that was because he received a near total transfusion of Alpha's blood after he had been gut shot and was almost dead anyway. Alpha has blood type "O" which makes him a universal donor and the combination of his blood, plus my kind's natural resistance to any viral infections or bacterial pathogens had saved Chris from both the lethal blood loss, and the septicemia that a bullet wound to the gut usually causes. The trade-off for saving his life, was that Chris couldn't go back to being "normal" again, as Alpha's blood changed him on his cellular level.

Chris looked down at the bar and quickly took a bite that reduced it by a half. Chewing quickly, he forced the bolus down, and took the other half with the same vigor until it too was in his gullet.

I frowned, but Chris said, "If I'm still not right in fifteen minutes, then I'll take the shot."

Concern faded from my features and I smiled back, "Fair

enough, but if you have any doubts wake me up, right?"

"Okay mom," Chris mumbled while reaching for a bottle of spring water, "Get some rest already."

I nodded and switched places from the desk chair to the bed as Chris pulled a towel out of the bathroom and doused it with the water from the bottle. I remember him wiping his face off and moving to the desk chair, but that was the last thing I can remember before Chris was again shaking me awake.

"Steve! Wake up! He's here," Chris was pointing excitedly at the laptop screen. "Dimitri is here!"

Chapter 9

When Chris was saying "here," what he meant was the satellite imagery being played on the laptop showed that Dimitri had arrived in front of the buildings that he owned and ran as nightclubs. Just like the similar images we had been watching via satellite, before we had started out. The scene played out pretty much as it had before, with three Rolls Royce vehicles in varying colors arriving on the scene and the celebrity-like people emerging from the vehicles, followed by the bodyguards parting the lookey-loos, and clearing a path for Dimitri and his entourage to access his establishments.

I first scanned the crowd and then the car windows for any sign of Lei, not that I was really expecting for her to be in tow as Dimitri made his kingly rounds, but I had to look in any case.

"To the roof!" Chris exclaimed as he grabbed an expensive pair of Swarovski binoculars from one of the camera bags and made for the door.

It was all I could do to keep up with Chris as he lunged for the door, but I managed to grab my own set of binoculars before heading to the stairway that would take us to the roof. Chris reached the roof access door before me, only to find it locked. I'm not sure if that violated any of the building's safety codes, or if there even were any safety codes in Nazran that could be violated, but the thought was quickly put aside as Chris began pounding his shoulder against the locked door and latch.

I watched him bang against the seemingly immovable door a couple more times before asking, "You done?"

He stopped and rubbed his shoulder while peering at me with a look that was a mix of indignation and embarrassment.

Before Chris could make one of his patented quips I asked, "Did you even check to see if there was an alarm?"

Chris had his index finger raised at me as if about to scold me like a disconcerted parent, which froze mid-wag as he looked from me to the door frame. He scanned the door for a couple of seconds, then said with a satisfied and mockingly official tone, "There doesn't appear to be any wiring or electronics attached to it that would indicate it an alarm."

I nodded my head and shrugged my shoulders, "Okay, just wanted to be sure," and then I kicked the heavy metal door just beneath where the latch of the door was fitted into the frame. There was a sound like a gunshot, as the metal reinforced door bent and tore and the latch ripped through the wooden frame, and the door flew open to the outside.

Chris had ducked instinctively from the sound, then looked at the opening and shook his head. He muttered, "Goddamn show off, that's what you are..." There was more mumbling, but he had moved through the opening I had created, and I couldn't hear him clearly after that.

Chris may have become one of us since Alpha's blood had transformed him, but he hadn't had the benefit of a lifetime of living in the abandoned Las Vegas silver mines where rock climbing was considered a mode of transportation. That life had made me very, very strong.

We worked our way through some of the machinery that had been installed on the roof and stood near the edge. In the distance we could only see a collection of lights from the cars and street lamps, along with the general movements of the crowd of people in the ambient wash of those lights. The binoculars were powerful with a rating of 12 x 90 and their magnification pulled us in close, so that we could see almost as well as if we were standing on top of a building right above the crowd. I could see that Dimitri had already made his way into the building and his bodyguards had taken up positions outside the door of the nightclub and began restricting entry at this point.

"Same routine every night," Chris said as if confirming a

question that I had asked.

"You're sure?" I said.

Chris lowered the binoculars, "Yup. At about seven o'clock the dinner rush starts to slow down, and by eight thirty the waiters have started coming out of the back, moving into the alley over..." Chris paused as he raised the binoculars back up to his eyes, "...there, where they begin to stack the folding dinner tables. See?"

I raised my own binoculars and scanned to the left where Chris had indicated. The alley was dark, but it still had enough illumination for me to see the wall of stacked folding tables. Further down the alley I could see a pair of homeless men who were just ambling over to one of the nightclub's dumpsters, where they would probably search the trash hoping to find their evening meal.

Chris continued, "By nine o'clock the last of the diners are finished, and the remaining tables are stacked. Then the club closes for thirty minutes, and the bouncers get the people who showed up early to form a line on the street outside. The club reopens at ten o'clock and pretty much everyone who is in line gets allowed into the club, but anyone who shows up after that initial opening has to wait, except for certain "VIP's" who also arrive in fancy cars, to be escorted into the club by the bouncers. Dimitri's arrival is the only variant, as he can show up anywhere between eleven o'clock and midnight"

I lowered the binoculars and asked, "So how does this help us get Lei back?"

I looked at Chris who was still scanning the area with the binoculars. He shrugged, "Always a good idea to know their routine, right?"

I hadn't registered the cold, but when I blew out a frustrated sigh my breath made a plume of chilly mist. It turned into a wispy, disintegrating cloud in the air in front of me. I knew that Chris was right, but I had really been hoping against all common sense that

I'd catch a glimpse of Lei, or even for that matter, Pha. Just something that would tell me that they were still alive and unharmed.

"Uh-oh!" Chris' voice was jovial as he spoke so I didn't react strongly to the outburst.

"What's up?" I asked.

"Working girls at ten o'clock."

I smiled, sighing at Chris' ridiculously naive and effortless ability to be distracted by the opposite sex, especially when it came to the more provocative women of the world. The guy was a world-class sex hound, and now he was one of us, meaning that he was completely immune to the dangers of STD's, which was like giving him a special license to fully indulge in what would otherwise be highly risky behaviors. Keeping track of him in Bangkok had been especially trying, and some of the positions we had found him in, passed out drunk and ensconced among of any number of paid partners, were bordering the ludicrous.

"Don't suppose you could keep your mind on..."

"Whoa! No pants!" Chris cried out as his finger rapidly spun the focus dial on the binoculars, "That one isn't wearing any pants in public!"

"Chris, what..." the inane statement caught me off guard and I raised my own binoculars up to witness the spectacle for myself, "Where?"

"They're one alley over from the back of Dimitri's nightclub."

I looked but all I could see were a trio of club goers, who I guessed were taking a shortcut from wherever they had parked for the night.

"Um, Chris...Those are guys, and they all are clearly wearing pants."

"What? How could you...?"

I could hear Chris shuffle his feet before he said, "No, no, you scanned too far. You're looking two alleys away."

I was about to adjust my view when a shadow appeared behind the jovial men I had spotted and started to slinking towards them. Realizing what was about to happen I wanted to call out, but remembering that we were nearly a block away and several stories above street level there was no way anyone could hear me, even if I had a megaphone, which I didn't.

"Just keep walking guys. Keep walking," I muttered to myself, as I watched the shadow close the distance between itself and the trio.

I heard Chris' concerned voice ask, "What's up?" but I couldn't tear my attention away in order to answer. The trio had only taken a couple steps before they would walk out of the alley and into the lighted street. They were nearly to safety when, of course, one of the men began searching in his pockets for something.

"No, no, no. Don't do it," I said aloud, as the man pulled a pack of cigarettes out of one pocket and fumbled to remove what I guessed would be a lighter from another. He stopped as he pulled the lighter from his pocket and began falling a couple steps behind his friends, who turned to look back at him. I saw the shadow dart behind some garbage cans or some other stacked up alley trash when the two men turned to look back toward the alley, but a couple quick flips of the smoker's wrist sent his friends on ahead, and he continued to fumble with his lighter. No sooner had his pair of friends turned away from their colleague than the shadow burst from its hiding place grabbing the smoker from behind. One dirty hand clamped tightly across the man's mouth while the opposite arm encircled his throat, simultaneously lifting and dragging the smoker back into the darker shadows of the alley.

The attack had been so quick and well executed that the smoker's pair of friends never heard nor suspected a thing, as they walked away chatting, none the wiser.

I heard Chris take in a quick breath and knew he was watching the same thing I was with all of his previous interest in the women of the night momentarily forgotten. The shadow dragged the smoker to the far side of the alley where it opened onto a perpendicular street. Light spilled into the space near where the attacker dropped the smoker's now unconscious body and the thief turned out to be nothing more than an ordinary man, who began to rifle through the smoker's pockets.

"Everywhere I go, there's always an asshole," Chris sighed as he watched the mugging take place.

I refocused the binoculars and could just make out the rising and falling of the smoker's chest, "The guy's still alive. It's just a robbery."

"Think so?" Chris asked, "I'm not so sure."

I lowered my binoculars, "Why not?"

"Because there's a cop watching the whole thing from across the street and clearly able to see into the opening of that alley."

"What?!" I quickly raised my binoculars and traced a path from the alley up to the street where it opened, and indeed there was a uniformed man watching the entire crime and doing nothing to stop it. I didn't recognize the uniform, but with his "nightstick" and sidearm he did seem a lot like he might be the local constabulary.

I looked back into the alley and saw the mugger finish stashing things in his pockets and then turn towards the street. The criminal froze momentarily when he saw the "cop", but it seemed to register on him that the officer wasn't going to do anything, so he slowly turned to walk away from the scene.

The cop watched the mugger go, and turned back to the body that lay unconscious just inside the alley. He seemed to consider what to do for a few seconds before the smoker's friends reappeared on the far side, obviously having realized their friend hadn't followed them. Apparently they had come back to locate their missing buddy and were moving hurriedly up the alleyway calling the man's name.

I looked back at the cop, thinking he might make a show of concern now that there would be witnesses to his presence, but he instead pulled a radio from his pocket and spoke into it briefly before reattaching it to his belt. The smoker's friends had just reached the halfway point, when four men appeared on the street and closed off each opening to the alley.

"Wha..? Where the hell did they come from?" Chris asked, as he watched the escalating situation.

One of the newcomers was a big man and he sported a splint over the wrist of his right arm. I didn't know the man personally, but I did recognize him and his injury. The guy's name was Mikhail and he had accompanied Dimitri Lagos in an unexpected visit to my office in Las Vegas a couple of months ago. When he had pointed his shotgun in my face Lei had rewarded him by shattering his wrist and arm. Crushing fractures like the one Lei had given him took months to heal, and his infirmity had apparently resulted in his demotion from personal bodyguard to... what I didn't know.

"Those are Dimitri's people," I said deadpan.

Chris recognized what was happening and said, "I suppose it's a dumb question, but should we do something? Call the police or..." He seemed to remember the concern shown by the cop on the street and sighed, "Right, never-mind."

"We couldn't get there in time anyway," I commented, "but maybe we'll learn something?"

I could feel Chris' eyes on me as I continued to watch through the binoculars, "You once told me that the Russians still hunt for live blood, right?"

I didn't want to answer, but not answering or even lying outright to Chris wasn't an option I even considered, "Yes, they

98

do."

"Damn, then it's four against two," Chris commented. "That just doesn't seem fair."

I grunted, "It isn't supposed to be. And it's five against two if you count the..." I had moved the glasses to look and see what the cop was doing, only to see him lying flat on the ground. Whether he was unconscious or dead, I didn't know, but whatever the case he had been taken out quickly and efficiently.

"What the hell?" I said out loud.

The smoker's friends had suddenly realized the danger they were in and began backing away from the closer pair of men walking toward them, while casting nervous glances behind them at the more distant pair.

"Now who the hell is this guy?" Chris said as I focused on the downed cop. I shifted my binoculars and found the subject of Chris' confusion to be a homeless man, maybe one of the one's I had seen about to go dumpster diving for his dinner earlier, and who limped weakly into the alley behind the pair of Dimitri's people and appeared to be studying the situation.

"Might want to get out of there old man," Chris said as we both focused our binoculars on the tattered clothes of the hobo's back.

We watched as the homeless man shifted his gaze to the different men in the alley, and then without any warning he sprinted forward with a powerful stride and no indication of any sign of infirmity.

Chris and I both nearly jumped out of our skin as we saw the man moving with a speed and grace that belied the man's appearance to such a degree that it seemed unnatural. In less than a second he had reached the first pair of Dimitri's men, who had no idea that the newcomer had even arrived, and he slammed into them with enough force to literally knock them off their feet.

Chris and I could see the body language of the four other

men in the alley, prey and predators alike, jolt to attention as all eyes turned to take in the latest arrival and the scuffle he had begun at the far end of the alley. The newcomer wasn't huge, but he wasn't small either. Maybe six feet tall, with a shock of shoulder length black hair and a full, but close-cut beard. He was wearing oversized tattered jeans and a filthy sweatshirt that, if cleaned, wouldn't be out of the ordinary for any other man of his apparent age to be wearing. The only thing out of place was a strange looking messenger bag that seemed to be made out of some kind of animal hide that he carried slung over his shoulder.

I shifted the binoculars to see the big one, Mikhail, take a step back as if he recognized the man before pulling a long curved blade from his belt with his uninjured hand. The man next to Mikhail looked confused but followed the big man's lead by pulling his own knife.

The former homeless man looked at the party-goers who had become potential victims, and gestured by pointing finger at their unconscious friend, and then waving for them to get him and go. Hesitantly they moved to their friend's side, but froze as the man alongside Mikhail started to move toward them. The homeless man moved as well, as if to attack, and Mikhail's partner backed off. The club goers picked up their friend and ran back past the homeless man, who continued to face Mikhail and his partner.

Mikhail decided he wanted to talk, but despite seeing his mouth moving I couldn't make out what he was saying. The homeless man never responded, but casually slipped one hand inside of the messenger bag. Mikhail saw the move and his face turned white with what seemed to be fear, as his adversary's hand came out of the bag clenching something small within his fist.

Seeing that the man hadn't removed anything so obvious as a gun or knife, Mikhail's partner became emboldened and strode forward with a smile on his face. Mikhail reached out to the man, but seemed reluctant to move forward in order to catch him. I thought I could just make out Mikhail's voice on the wind calling out to his partner to stop, but instead the man foolishly rushed forward in a low crouch and thrust the blade in his hand upward diagonally toward the homeless man's upper torso and neck.

I watched and couldn't help thinking it was a competent strike that was sure to have a lethal result if it connected, but the homeless man effortlessly backed out of his attacker's reach and raised his clenched fist to his lips. In one motion he opened his fist and blew the contents of his hand into a green cloud of powder or ash that blossomed from his palm and enveloped the attacker's head. The man was completely taken by surprise as the vapor invaded his mouth, nostrils and eyes and made him falter in his tracks. Immediately he began coughing and desperately rubbing at his eyes as his initial discomfort quickly escalated into a confused and painful panic. Blood began seeping from his nose and streaming down his face from his eyes like blood-colored tears as the man began clutching at his throat, flailing around helplessly, until he finally just fell to his knees, clawing at his face and hacking out black globs of vile looking fluids.

I could hear Chris' breathing growing rapid, as we watched the scene through our binoculars, with their added magnification making it seem as though they were only a few yards away. With our full attention on the victim of... whatever that green cloud had been... we didn't notice that Mikhail had attacked the man as well. When I looked up I saw the homeless man dodging backwards from left to right to avoid the slashing attacks of his knife. Mikhail had apparently wanted to press his advance before the man could pull anything else out of that pack of his and, considering what it had done to his friend, it was probably as good a plan as any. The itinerant newcomer wasn't trying to counter the attacks in any way, rather he was just getting out of the way without retreating completely.

"What's he doing?" Chris asked, as we continued watching.

"He's not trying to fight back?"

I nodded, "It's almost as though he were trying to..." my words caught in my throat when I understood what was happening. "He's drawing him in."

"Drawing him in close? For what?" Chris asked, "Is he gonna hit him with his purse?"

"I..." my voice caught again, as the vagrant dodged to one side when Mikhail thrust his blade forward and left himself slightly off balance and overextended as the blade passed harmlessly by his opponent. I could just make out the homeless man reaching for something at the small of his back before there was a flash of motion and, in the next moment, Mikhail hit the ground with his knife arm severed just above the elbow while the homeless man stood over him with an enormous Bowie knife held out to one side. The sheer length and mass of the blade was more than should have been concealable, and I would have sworn that he had been unarmed.

Before Mikhail had a chance to realize what had happened, the homeless man lunged and delicately swept the Bowie knife across Mikhail's throat in a killing stroke, which was much more like the slash of someone accustomed to a sword, as opposed to a fighting knife. I could see Mikhail trying to raise his head, before his pink vampire blood erupted from his throat and the dramatic drop in blood pressure from his pair of grievous wounds immediately rendered him unconscious.

The homeless man knelt in front of Mikhail as the man died, then wiped his Bowie knife on Mikhail's shirt before standing and returning the knife to its sheath beneath the shirt on his back.

I looked over to Chris, who had lowered his binoculars as well and saw the frown on his face. Chris turned to me and asked, "What the hell did we just see?"

I shook my head, "I'm not sure, but it looked like Mikhail, the big guy, recognized that homeless guy."

Chris' face was nearly wild as he said, "You knew one of them?"

I nodded, "Lei gave him that arm injury a couple months back. He had come calling with Dimitri in Las Vegas."

Chris seemed to calm and remembered what I called the newcomer on the street, "Homeless guy? Really?"

I shrugged, "I know, but what else do I call him?"

Chris' face relaxed a bit but the concern was still apparent in his features, "Maybe... really scary, S.O.B.?"

I smiled an ironic half smile, "Too many words," and raised the binoculars back up to my eyes. Suddenly my breath caught in my throat as a cold tremor rose up my spine and threatened to make my knees give out with fear, as I looked through the binoculars.

Chris must have noticed my reaction as his instantly demanded, "What?!"

Through the lenses I could see the homeless man staring directly up at me, the magnification of the binoculars, making it appear as if he were only a stone's throw away. The intensity of that glare made it seem as if he was not only aware of our presence, but also looking directly into my eyes. I tried to lower the binoculars, but I was completely frozen under the man's angry stare.

Chapter 10

I couldn't move. Hell, I couldn't even breathe, as I was held by the crystalline gaze of the man's eyes. I knew Chris was calling out to me but his voice was garbled, as if I were listening to him while submerged in water. I started to feel dizzy and was desperately trying to will my lungs into taking in a breath of air, but any conscious control I previously had over my body was overwhelmed by the need to not break eye contact with the man on the street far below me. Finally, just as I started to lose the sense of my legs beneath me, I saw the his frown change into something more like confusion, and he broke eye contact with me. Instantly I was able to suck in a breath of air, dropped the binoculars from my face and fell to my knees. Chris was at my side instantly, catching me before I could topple over, while I just panted for more air.

"What is it? What's wrong?" Chris was demanding, but I still hadn't recovered enough air to be able to answer him. I held up a hand instead, trying to relay the information that I was going to be okay, and to just give me a second. I guessed that Chris got the message, because he stopped talking and went into doctor mode, checking my pulse and looking me over for any signs of injury.

When I finally felt as though I could stand I said, "Okay help me up," and Chris lifted me to my feet but didn't release my arm as I walked to the rooftop door.

Seeing I was back in control of whatever had weakened me, Chris asked again, "What happened to you out there?"

I shook my head, "I'm not sure," I said honestly, "I was looking through the lenses, but when I locked eyes with the guy who had attacked Dimitri's people..." I tried to search for the right words without being overly melodramatic, but failed miserably, "Well, it was like I was caught in the guy's gaze, like when a snake mesmerizes its prey before it strikes."

Chris frowned, "You think he could see you? Knew we

were up here?"

"Seemed that way to me."

Chris thought about it for second, "Even if that were possible, we'd be tiny smudges on top of a building over a block away. There's no way he could see with enough detail to stare directly into your eyes."

I sighed, "I know, but I'm telling you his eyes weren't scanning around haphazardly looking at a shapes in the distance. He was on me. No question about it and..." My voice trailed off as a chill spread through me, and I thought about the expression in those eyes as they held me immobile.

I looked up to see Chris frowning at me with concern, then he shook himself as if clearing the thoughts from his head, "Okay, so let's focus more on what we do now?" When I raised a confused eyebrow at him he continued, "Assuming for one second the guy didn't give you anything more than a really bad case of the 'stink eye', what do we do about it?"

"Do?"

Chris shrugged, "If he realizes we are up here, then shouldn't we be preparing for some unwelcome company?"

I thought about that for a moment and then shook my head, "I don't think so."

"Why not?"

"I remember the look on the man's face as he broke off eye contact. It wasn't aggressive as much as if he was confused. Almost as if he had "read" my intentions and realized we weren't a threat."

"Could have been a feint. Maybe he's just a good poker player and wanted to give you that impression?"

I took a deep breath, and relished it as I became more aware of the icy cold air that both calmed and refreshed me, "I think we're okay, but it wouldn't be a bad idea to leave the roof and then get back on task."

We headed back down the stairs and walked into our room. Chris immediately began enlarging the grid of satellite feeds on the screen of his computer. "You looking for our homeless friend?" I asked.

Chris ignored the question, "Dimitri's cars are all still parked on the street in front of his favorite club, so what's the plan from here?"

I moved behind Chris so I could look at the computer's screen, and pointed to one of the small video feeds that sat in a checkerboard pattern on the screen, "Is that the front of the club?"

Chris nodded as he used the touchpad to move the cursor to the point I had indicated, and clicked, which enlarged the shot. The party seemed to push its way into the street, and the huge number of people that had been waiting for entrance to the club were now dancing around like revelers at Mardi Gras. Several of the patrons held bottles of champagne, vodka or beer over their heads, as they danced around like well-dressed fools with ridiculous clown smiles on their faces.

"Looks like someone bought a round of something for everyone waiting in line."

I scanned the perimeter of the crowd and cursed.

"What?" Chris asked.

"Look." I pointed at the edges of the screen, "More people are walking over and, from the way they are dressed, they're locals, not party-goers."

"So?"

"He's deliberately drawing a larger crowd around the club."

Chris enlarged the video screens that connected to the one in front of the club. Indeed, everyone and anyone who happened to be on the street began ambling over to the scene in front of the nightclub. Instantly the new arrivals were engulfed by the gyrating crowd as more bottles of booze appeared out of nowhere, to be passed around to anyone with empty hands.

"I don't get it," Chris admitted, "What's the point?"

"Best guess is that the bodies of Dimitri's men in the alley were found, and he's building a wall between himself and whoever might be attacking him."

Chris looked up from the computer screen, "A wall?"

I nodded, "It would be kind of hard to storm through the front door at this point, don't you think?"

Chris looked back to the screen as he said, "There's a back door."

"Which is likely being fortified by Dimitri's people. My guess is that Dimitri's men are going to search the area behind the club, and then scoot him out of there in some rather inconspicuous kind of vehicle."

Chris inclined his head to me without looking up from the computer as he reduced all of the video images on the screen before enlarging the image of the back of the club. Men and women, all clad in black attire, were winding through the alleyways behind the club when an overhead roll-up door began to rise. Slowly an unmarked white cargo van pulled out into the alley, and casually rolled away from the club.

As I watched I raised a hand and said sarcastically, "Goodnight Mr. Lagos."

Chris chuckled, "Okay, so there was a reason you made 'Detective' rank so quickly when you were with the LAPD. However, if you are done showing off, it doesn't change the question of what do we do now?"

I rubbed at my eyes, which still seemed to be aching from the stare off with that homeless guy. I walked to the bed and opened a bottle of water that had been set on what passed for a nightstand.

Chris watched me as I walked to the bathroom and poured some of the water onto a towel and wiped my face with the damp cloth.

"You sure you're okay?" Chris asked as I draped the damp towel over the hanging rack for it to dry.

"Yeah, I'm okay," I hesitantly admitted, "but I feel vulnerable and completely unprepared to move against Dimitri or his people at the moment."

Chris waited for me to finish the thought, and I asked him, "Do you still have the name of Larson's contact? The one who made the arrangements for smuggling us into the country?"

Chris pulled out his cell phone, and after punching the screen a couple of times, nodded and held the phone toward me, as if I could read it from across the room.

"Yep, got it." Chris said with a smile once he saw me roll my eyes at the phone.

"I think we need to see him, and maybe get some better gear and any recon info available on the club, or more importantly on whatever the story might be regarding the relationship between Dimitri and the local authorities."

I could see the wheels turning in Chris' head, "That cop on the street during the mugging?"

I nodded, "If they aren't here to 'protect and serve', then what is their purpose? And are they a threat we have to worry about, in addition to Dimitri's people?"

"That seems to be clear enough already." Chris volunteered sarcastically.

"True, but I'd really like to get the story from a local. It might reveal something that we hadn't considered."

Chris nodded, "Makes sense." There was something else Chris wanted to say but he seemed hesitant to ask.

"What?" I asked.

Chris could see how shaken up I still was, but to his credit he asked, "Should we ask about our 'homeless hero' too?"

"Why?! What are we going to ask him? Have there been any lethal, homeless hypnotists plaguing the streets of Nazran lately?!" I hadn't expected to respond so sharply or defensively, and was immediately sorry for the outburst.

For Chris' part, he couldn't have reacted less if I had whispered the whole thing. It was almost as if he had been expecting the outburst. Then, after the briefest of silences, and without otherwise missing a beat he calmly said, "We should probably phrase it differently than that, but basically yes."

Again I knew Chris was right, but I hated the fact that the question, not to mention my outburst, had brought the image of the homeless man to the front of my thoughts. My head was starting to throb and I felt like I really needed more sleep, so I just nodded my agreement, moved to one of the twin beds and dropped limply on the hard mattress.

I was pretty much asleep as soon as my head came to rest on the pillow when I managed to hear Chris say in a flustered voice, "Oh no, please let me take first watch. I insist."

Chapter 11

December 16, 1916. Moika Palace, Russia.

Grigori Rasputin sat at a table in a guest room of Prince Felix Yusupov's Moika Palace after the Prince had summoned him several days ago. Now he focused intensely on what he was writing, completely ignoring the fine pastries and wine that had been laid out for him.

Everyone around him had noticed the change in Rasputin over the last few weeks. He had become jittery, was startled by the most benign events and was extremely impatient. He had not slept much for days on end; also, he had been drunk for the last two weeks, except for the last two days when he partook of no sustenance whatsoever.

Quickly, he finished the letter he was writing and sealed it in an envelope before her took out a fresh piece of paper and stared blankly at the page for a few moments before he began writing once more. With the first stroke of the pen Rasputin's body seemed to deflate. Muscles, which that had been cord tight, relaxed and his shoulders slumped forward as if a great weight was finally being lifted off his back.

Tsarevich Alexei Nikolaevich,

My boy, I fear I must leave you now, which is probably for the best, as I have nothing left to teach you. You have excelled at all of your lessons and have made them a part of who you are. As you go forward into the future, your experiences, your life, will be your new teacher, as you will learn more and more with each passing moment.

But I cannot leave without at least warning you of the dangers that are coming. The terror that will run rampant over Russia will be the end of all you have known, but you must survive it. You will be tested most harshly, brutally and sadistically before the end and I greatly fear for you. My only advice would be to

110

watch over yourself when the trials come, for if you futilely squander your abilities on others you will fail both them, yourself and, ultimately, all of Russia.

Use what you have learned my dear Tsarevich and someday, when you have reached the full extent of your potential, may you also forgive me for what I have done to you. Forgive what a zealous man saw in your eyes on that first day and made a decision that he had no right to make. Know that my intentions were...

A gentle knock came from the closed chamber door. Quickly, Rasputin folded the unfinished letter, placed it in an envelope and rose from his chair. Cautiously, he opened the door and saw a servant, bundled in burlap rags, standing outside his doorstep.

Curiously Rasputin eyed the small man, and then his eyes went wide.

"Alexei?!?"

The bundle of rags didn't speak but nodded and Rasputin hurried the boy inside.

"Alexei! My God, what are you doing here?! I thought you were with your father in Mogilev?"

Alexei began to unwind the various scraps of burlap from around his head and shoulders.

"I was with my family in Mogilev, but I had another experience that made it necessary to come here. What I sensed felt very similar to that day when the woman attacked you over two years ago in Pokrovskoye. Only this time it was much, much larger and far more terrible."

Rasputin guided Alexei to the table and the two sat as Alexei continued.

"After, I was overwhelmed by your image in my mind and I knew I had to come."

Rasputin held out his hand to clasp the boy's shoulder but winced when he saw how badly his hand was shaking. Alexei noticed it as well and the fear he felt for his mentor increased tenfold.

"Why are you shaking Father Grigori?"

"Be calm my boy, be calm. It is only my having gone without food or drink for too long," Rasputin lied. "As you can see all is well here as I am safe within a Romanov household." Rasputin poured himself a glass of wine and picked up one of the many cakes that sat on a silver tray next to the wine bottle and took several bites of the pastry.

Alexei sniffed the air, and then looked at the cake. "It smells as though the cook burned the almonds in your cake."

Rasputin froze, his hand trembling again far worse then before. He held the cake out in front of him and eyed it suspiciously. Alexei immediately saw the look of concern of his teacher's face and, although he had no idea why, he braced himself for whatever was to follow.

Alexei was not prepared for what he saw.

Rasputin threw his head back and laughed. And laughed. And laughed. He laughed so hard that he began pounding his fist on the table as tears began to fall from his eyes. It took almost three minutes for the elder man to gather himself; however, when he did he quickly finished the cake and grabbed another. Alexei began to giggle at the sight of his teacher stuffing cakes to capacity into his mouth then drank wine directly from the bottle to wash them down. Rasputin ate heartily until only one cake remained.

When Rasputin spoke it sounded as if he was still about to break into another raucous round of guffaws.

"Now...ha heh heh... now my boy, you need to go back...heh ha...to your father."

Alexei couldn't help but smile at the spectacle that was his teacher, despite the fact that he felt as though he desperately

112

needed to stay. Alexei still felt that Rasputin was in grave danger and he had to be here to help protect him.

Before Alexei could protest, Rasputin held up the two letters. He sealed the second envelope and held them up for Alexei to see.

"Since you are here you can do me a great service. This letter is for your father, please see to it that he gets it immediately." Rasputin placed the unfinished letter, which was actually written to Alexei, into Alexei's hand.

Alexei looked at the letter, then back to his teacher. Alexei knew that Rasputin was just trying to get him to leave and he wanted with all of his heart to protest.

"That letter is of vital importance and your father must get it as fast as possible. Understood?"

Alexei lowered his eyes, "Yes Father Grigori."

Rasputin nodded in satisfaction, "Good. I have one other task for you." Alexei looked up earnestly as Rasputin raised the second letter into the air, "This..." Rasputin hesitated, "this will need to be placed in my secretary's hand before the sun rises. She is in St. Petersburg at...oh, you know where she is, don't you?"

"Of course."

"Good...Good. Can you do it? Can you get to her in time?"

Alexei looked at the sky. The sun had just retreated behind the horizon and the last wisps of orange and red were quickly fading from the sunset.

Alexei turned back to his teacher, "If I leave now I can be there in time."

Excellent! Then..." Rasputin's words caught as he turned to his door.

Something was very, very wrong.

Alexei had "felt" it too and he knelt down on the floor. Placing the fingertips of his right hand on the floor, Alexei could feel a series of arhythmic vibrations getting stronger and stronger

113

with each passing moment. Recognition of the vibrations came quickly as Alexei realized that men were climbing the stairs in a large group while making an effort to muffle the sound of their footfalls as they ascended.

Rasputin apparently didn't need to feel the floor to come to the same conclusions as Alexei had, "Quickly Alexei! Under the bed!"

Alexei did not hesitate as he dove forward, slid past the bed linens and came to a halt under the mattress. He spun himself around and raised the bed skirt just enough that he would have a clear view of the room without being detected.

A loud knock sounded on the door as Rasputin sat back in his chair, picked up his wine glass and called out for the person or persons to enter.

The door opened and Prince Felix Yusupov sauntered into the room followed by several others. All of who looked confused and nervous as the Prince spoke.

"Good evening Father Grigori. Please forgive the intrusion, but my associates and I were heading to the dining room and wondered if you might join us?"

Rasputin smiled wickedly at the Prince. "Ah, the Prince is too kind, but I am feeling quite satisfied at the moment. After all you were so considerate to have these wonderful cakes sent to me upon my arrival and I fear that I have overindulged in them."

The Prince and all of his "associates" looked at the remaining cake as Rasputin lifted it and said, "They are quite delicious."

The Prince stammered as he agreed. "Yes I...I am...particularly fond of them."

Rasputin's eyebrows lifted in what appeared to Alexei to be mock surprise.

"Really? Well let me be considerate in return and present you with the last of the cakes." Rasputin held out the pastry to the

Prince...and saw the briefest flicker of apprehension flash across the Prince's eyes.

"Oh! No, no, no. I never partake of sweets before I have my supper. Although I thank you for your consideration."

Rasputin's smile faded and he grew very serious. "As I thank you, my Prince."

The room fell into an uncomfortable silence as Alexei watched his Uncle and his teacher lock eyes.

Finally, the Prince broke the spell. "Yes well, we are off to the dining hall then. Let any of the servants know if you are in need of anything."

"Again I thank you my Prince." Rasputin rose to his feet and inclined his head as the Prince and his associates left the room.

Closing the door behind them, Rasputin turned to the bed and beckoned Alexei to come out.

Alexei slid out easily and quickly moved to his teacher. Rasputin grabbed the boy and shoved the second letter into the boy's hand, "Alexei you must go now!"

The look Alexei saw in his teacher's eyes chilled him to the core and he didn't resist as Rasputin began to hand Alexei the burlap fabric he had arrived in.

"Hurry, assume your disguise and go!"

Alexei dressed and was about to leave when Rasputin grabbed him by the shoulders. "My boy, I want you to know that I could not be more proud of you." Alexei looked at his teacher confused and concerned. He would have said something but Rasputin knelt forward and kissed him on both cheeks then spun him around and pushed him away from the room. "Now go!"

Alexei couldn't think straight as he ran from the room and began to descend the stone steps toward the east entrance of the palace.

Rasputin watched him go and whispered. "Go with God my student, my friend, my son. Go quickly before you are washed away by the blood that is about to flood this palace."

***

The Prince paced the floor as Grand Duke Nicholas Nickolaevich watched nervously. The two men were the culprits, along with the four noblemen who sat against the wall, who had lured Rasputin to the Moika palace and had poisoned the refreshments that the man had apparently consumed. Now they were reassessing their next move after witnessing Rasputin still whole and hearty despite having eaten the cakes and drunk the wine.

"How is he not dead?" the Prince spoke anxiously to no one in particular. "He seems as though the poison had no effect on him at all, how can that be?!?"

Nicholas turned to one of the nobles in the room. "Vasily, are you sure you that you used enough poison?"

Vasily Maklakov had been holding his head in his hands when he looked up to the Grand Duke and nodded vigorously. "I put enough cyanide in his food to kill several men. I was not subtle and my only fear was that he would realize the poison was there before he consumed enough of the sweets."

Nicholas rose from his chair. "The sweets?!? You didn't poison the wine? I told you to poison both!"

Quickly the nobleman protested. "There was no way of knowing what vintage he would request from the wine cellar, so the cakes, being the only food available to him upon his arrival, seemed to be the better choice."

Prince Felix walked to the Grand Duke and placed a hand on his arm. "I watched Vasily poison the food and he is telling the truth about the massive dose he placed in the dough. It should have been more than enough to do him in."

Nicholas quieted his demeanor and turned away from the trembling nobleman. "What are we to do? Our opportunity to remove his body undetected during the changing of the staff is dwindling. If we don't act now we will miss our chance."

Everyone in the room looked expectantly at the others but no one seemed willing to speak up. Then, finally, after almost a minute of uncomfortable silence the Prince removed his revolver from his belt and said, "I'll finish him."

One of the noblemen was quick to speak out. "But the shot will be heard throughout the palace!"

The Prince looked solemnly at each of the noblemen. "If anyone in my employ is still around to hear, then this is my home and my staff. They will follow my orders and cover any doubt cast upon us. It has to be me who does this deed.

Every head, except for the Grand Duke, began to slowly nod in agreement as Nicholas held out his hand, "Let me see your weapon."

The Prince frowned as he handed the pistol over to his relative. The Grand Duke unloaded the weapon, held it up to the light and inspected the barrel and wheel, then reloaded the weapon and handed it back to the Prince. "You have taken excellent care of the revolver. It should fire true for you."

The Grand Duke embraced the Prince, who appeared bolstered by the act, and all the men in the room stood and nodded at their cohort. Then without another word the Prince removed his jacket and covered the hand holding the pistol and left the room.

He made no attempt to conceal the sound of his boots as he quickly ascended the stone steps until he reached Rasputin's room. Taking a deep breath to calm his nerves, the Prince laid one hand on the latch, pulled it free and burst into the room. Throwing his jacket off the revolver, he pointed at his target ahead of him with his finger resting on the trigger.

Rasputin stood with his back to the door looking out the window over the countryside and the night sky. He made no attempt to turn and face the man who had just burst in and instead stood calmly with his arms at his sides as he spoke.

"I don't suppose you want that last cake now my Prince?" Rasputin's fingertips glided effortlessly over each other and, if the Prince could see the man's face, he would have seen that Rasputin's eyes were closed in concentration.

The Prince didn't hesitate a moment more and he fired the weapon, point blank and at heart level, into Rasputin's back. The force of the round torqued Rasputin's torso as it collided and penetrated his body, accompanied by a spray of blood that covered the window frame as the bullet exited the man's chest. Rasputin silently stumbled forward then tried to brace himself by grasping the window drapes without avail as he fell and pulled the fabric down on himself as his body gave out.

The Prince watched Rasputin fall then waited in order to determine whether the wound was sufficient to be fatal. When Rasputin had remained motionless for almost three minutes the Prince walked over and checked the body to see if the man was breathing.

He wasn't.

The Prince hurried from the room and ran to join the rest of his group, "It is done," he said as he entered the room and met the expectant looks of all inside. "How do we proceed?"

Nicholas spoke quickly, "Now we must divide ourselves. Take two men to the stables and prepare a wagon, I will take the rest and get some bed linens from the laundry to wrap the body. Remember gentlemen, we should avoid all witnesses from this moment on. Ready your weapons as any who gaze upon us need be dealt with most severely."

The men all hurried from the room; however, the Prince was less than halfway to the stable when he remembered he had left his jacket in the room. Terrified with the thought that someone could possibly find the jacket before his group had returned to clean up the scene worried him. Ordering the noblemen to the stable to make the proper preparations the Prince ran back to the palace, raced up the stairs, and entered the room where he had done the deed. Initially, he averted his eyes from the spot where Rasputin had fallen and reached to pick up his jacket from the floor.

His hand froze inches from the garment and his eyes shot wide as the breath caught in his chest. Slowly the Prince inclined his head to the spot on the floor that he had seen in his peripheral vision. The spot where Rasputin's body had landed was now an empty space identified only by a small pool of blood.

The Prince shot to a standing position and began to search the room but found no sign of Rasputin. Then he realized what must have happened...The window! Somehow Rasputin had survived the shot and had climbed out the window to escape. The Prince ran to the window, but as he tried to open it he found it securely locked.

Confused he backed away from the window when, behind him, he heard the the sound of the door slamming shut, which caused his heart feel as though it would lurch from his chest. The Prince spun to see Rasputin making a show of securing the latch on the door, his eyes wild with rage and pain as he turned and pointed a bloody finger at him.

The Prince opened his mouth to scream for help but Rasputin crossed the room and had both of his large hands around the Prince's throat before a sound could be uttered.

The Prince collapsed to the floor under the weight of the attack and Rasputin came down on top of him giving his hands even more leverage to choke the breath from the Prince's body.

The Prince flailed and kicked, his fingers desperately looking for purchase on the hands that held him fast. Rasputin was smiling in a vicious grimace and bloody spittle shot from between his clenched teeth while the Prince's face began turning a pasty blue as his body began to convulse.

Through gritted teeth Rasputin rasped, "Kill me? Only a fool of an assassin such as you wouldn't know that cyanide degrades to its harmless components when heated. Poisoning baked goods with cyanide does little more than flavor the food."

The Prince's face began to darken to purple as his resistance waned.

"Now die with the knowledge that it was your own ineptitude that ended you!" Rasputin squeezed even harder. "DIE!"

The Prince's tongue protruded purplish and swollen from his mouth as his body stopped moving and finally came to rest. Rasputin continued his efforts for a few moments more until he finally released the Prince's throat and made his way to the door. His cramped hands fumbled at he latch as he unlocked it and began to hobble for the exit when, after rounding a blind corner, he collided with Grand Duke Nicholas. The two men fell backward; however, the Grand Duke regained his footing quickly while Rasputin's bullet wound greatly hindered his recovery. When at last he did stand Rasputin turned to face each of the four noblemen as well as the Grand Duke aiming their revolvers at him. Rasputin spun to run back the way he had come, but he never had a chance to take a step as each of the men fired their weapons. Blood burst from three new locations on the his back as he was thrown forward, crashing bodily on the stone steps a moment later.

Cautiously the Grand Duke approached the body followed by the rest of his conspirators. At first there was no movement as the group circled, then Rasputin suddenly lurched and tried to get up. The Grand Duke began to club the wounded Rasputin's head with the butt of his revolver. Soon the sickening sound of bone splintering could be heard as the pistol grip came down again and again on Rasputin's skull while the rest of the noblemen began to pummel him as well until Rasputin again was motionless on the stone floor.

"Quickly now, wrap the body in the linens and let's get him out of the palace," Nicholas said between gulps of air.

Rasputin's body flopped limply as it was rolled in a sheet and then carried down to the stables. From there it was placed on a cart and taken to a bridge that crossed over a partially frozen river. The Grand Duke watched as the men removed the body from the cart and heaved it over the side of the bridge. The ice was thin this time of year and the corpse exploded through the surface ice and splashed into the freezing water beneath. The Grand Duke and the noblemen stood at the bridge railing as they watched the body disappear under the ice and drift away downstream.

Unbeknownst to them a small figure, wrapped in head to toe in burlap, had followed them from the palace and was watching them from a distance away.

Chapter 12

It only took a couple of moments for Lei to aclimate to the darkness when she awakened. Feeling the small, warm body of a girl lying next to her on the mattress brought her mind back to the reality of her present situation, and kept her from bolting upright and thrashing at her restraints.

She wasn't blind in the dark as her eyes had adjusted while she had slept, and she could soon easily make out her surroundings. She and Pha were lying on a king size mattress in the center of the room inside a converted office space that had been otherwise cleared of all furnishings. Both of them were wearing the grey cotton sweatpants and sweatshirts they had been given by their captors to replace the clothes they had been wearing when they had been abducted. The soft material was an anathema to Lei, as it was shapeless and hid the more provocative features of her body, which she always used so effectively as a weapon. Still, bound as she was, the sweats offered her protection and warmth, falling loosely over her form, not to mention the fact that they were comfortable and clean. Plastic bottles of water and a large plastic washbasin were also provided, but if either had to use the bathroom they had needed to call for assistance. There always seemed to be an armed guard available to unlatch the chain from the eyebolt that had been drilled and secured into the center of the concrete floor, while the other end of the chain was connected to the heavy leather collar encircling Lei's neck. Lei knew she could escape the collar easily, but she hadn't tried because her captors had threatened to harm the young girl if they detected any signs of her having tampered with the restraint. As it was, she had no idea what was waiting for her outside the office space, and until she knew that she could safely get the child away Lei couldn't risk the girl by attempting an escape. Instead she chose to bide her time and wait for an opportunity to present itself.

Besides, Lei considered that despite being collared captives they hadn't been treated badly. They had been fed better food than what would otherwise have been expected, given their circumstances. They had instant access to a toilet facility, as well as a shower and the basic toiletries for personal hygiene. Perhaps most surprising to Lei was the fact that no one had attempted to molest either of them since their arrival.

The quiet of the moment was interrupted by the sound of a loud crash followed by a thud that came from outside the door of the office. Lei checked Pha, who continued to sleep undisturbed by the noise, as the sound of the door lock turned and clicked into the open position. Lei dropped her head back down onto the mattress next to the girl, while keeping her eyes barely open to see the silhouette of a figure enter. The figure moved fluidly within the shadows of the already darkened room and shifted into position over the child as she lay motionless on the mattress, entwined in Lei's arms. Then Lei felt the girl's body slowly begin to slide out from her embrace. Fear instantly overtook Lei and she bolted upright and she lashed out with one hand.

The figure yelped at the sudden motion and moved back from Lei's outstretched hand so quickly that the fabric of the girl's sweatshirt tore where the figure had grabbed it. The subsequent jolt instantly awoke the girl, who found herself staring right into the disfigured, pock ridden face of one of Dimitri's people and she screamed in a shrill, little girl's cry of terror.

This wasn't one of the well-organized and fit guards that they had seen before. This vampire was a young man, maybe mid-twenties with his face covered in lesions and his eyes sunken in a way that made him look far older and very sick. Perhaps it was having been discovered, or maybe it was the girl's cries that made him go wild in that moment, but he bolted forward with both hands outstretched, seeking to grab the child. Lei knew that the restraint around her throat would prevent her from getting in between the

123

man and the child before he had a hold of her so she pivoted on one hip and thrust her foot into the man's abdomen. The kick should have sent the man reeling, but instead the vampire's body folded around the impact of the kick and he kept coming. Lei thought she could feel something snap and give within the body of the young man, but he still kept pressing forward and it was all she could do to keep him away.

There were more sounds behind her, but Lei couldn't risk taking her eyes off of the wild man who was all but impaled on her foot. Deciding to take a chance, Lei bent her leg and leaned back and away in order to avoid being grabbed by the vampire's outstretched hands as his ragged fingernails clawed at her face. The shift gave her the leverage she needed to kick her attacker again and it landed with another crunching thud that sent the man off of her. The vampire didn't fall but staggered drunkenly as it tried to regain its balance and never saw either the giant figure it collided into, nor the man's large hand which shot out encircling his neck as massive fingers immediately synched down on the vampire's throat like a vise.

Lei watched as this new and far larger masculine silhouette came fully into view, still holding the young man aloft by the back of the neck. He was bigger than Alpha, and might have given William a run for his money in the overall size department, but unlike William, who was more a creature of instinct, this giant had eyes that seemed to analyze and plan while he surveyed the entirety of the scene.

Nicholas Nickolaevich's eyes were hard as he peered at Lei, while still holding the flailing vampire aloft, but once his eyes came to rest on the Pha's torn sweatshirt his head jolted back to the vampire he held in his grasp.

"Idiot!" Nicholas screamed, as the young man desperately began reaching, clawing, and trying to get away from the giant hand on the back of his neck,

"You have been repeatedly warned that these two were not for eating!"

Lei watched as more diseased and emaciated looking vampires ambled and jerked into the room, making no attempt to attack the giant nor to help the young vampire, or make any move toward the mattress where she and Pha lay. Gurgling sounds began, coming from the trapped subject in Nicholas' grasp, growing in intensity and becoming more desperate with each passing second. Nicholas' face began to contort with the physical effort of crushing the man's neck as the face of the vampire began to discolor to purple. Squeezing even harder the giant of a man kept at it until the vampire's arms and legs ceased flailing and fell limply to its side. Then, with disgust, Nicholas flung the limp form across the room, where the body smacked hard into a wall, sending a tremor through the entire makeshift office.

Nicholas was breathing with only a little extra effort as he called out to everyone in the room, "Let this be a final warning to all of you. Control yourselves and follow my orders, or die. I offer no additional warnings or chances. Understood?"

Slowly each head in the room nodded with what could best be described as clouded comprehension, and as they did Nicholas' angry countenance softened, "Good," he pointed to the body, "get him out of here and dispose of his body with the others."

Lei felt a chill at those words. Who were the others? Had Steve, Chris and Alpha tried to rescue her and been caught or killed? She pushed those thoughts from her head, they would be no help for her at this point, and she focused all of her attention on the big man who was apparently in charge of the multitude of vampires within the office space. Most of the vampires that had been drawn to the conflict began to slink out of the office, while two came forward and cautiously moved to the dead vampire, lifting him quietly up and carrying him out of the office, never speaking a word.

Once the body had been removed Nicholas took a deep breath, which he let out with an exasperated sigh and spoke to Lei and Pha in a voice heavily laden with a Russian accent,

"I am sorry for that. I pride myself on having better command of my soldiers."

"Soldiers?" Lei hadn't intended to speak but the surprise at hearing the word had shocked the word from her.

Nicholas looked at her questioningly, "Yes, soldiers. They have been tasked to follow my orders, and I expect nothing less than total adherence to the task. I do not brook either disobedience nor insubordination within their ranks."

Lei shook her head, "These soldiers of yours are all in various throes of the Porphyria madness. You've starved them to the point that they are little more than zombies, barely having the ability to think, and you're surprised that they disobey you?"

"I have done no such thing." Nicholas spoke with patronizing patience, as if he were talking to an ignorant child, "They can think clearly enough, and have been fed adequately to maintain their sanity." Nicholas inclined his head at the door where the body had been carried, "That fool simply wished to give in to his baser desires, and that disregard for proper protocol is a weakness I can't allow to spread."

Silence filled the room for a moment as Lei and Nicholas held eye contact with each other, before Nicholas asked, "Are either of you hurt?"

Lei could feel her own anger rising at the manner in which Nicholas was talking to her, "We're your prisoners, so you'll have to excuse me if I am not convinced that you're looking out for our wellbeing."

The big man shrugged his shoulders, "In general, that is true. You and the child mean nothing to me, and if it were not for your value in remaining untouched and alive, I would throw you both to the horde and let them rip your bodies to pieces without a

126

second thought."

The cold, matter of fact manner in which Nicholas spoke chilled Lei. She had killed several times before, but there had always been either rage or reason behind her actions. Never had she heard anyone speak of violent murder with such dispassion and apathy.

Nicholas knelt in front of Lei and she could feel Pha's grip on her get tighter as the big man moved closer. "Make no mistake girl, I am not your friend, but I do have an interest in your wellbeing, so you have nothing to fear from me as long as you can manage to keep from doing anything foolish."

Lei could see the slight pulsation in the veins of Nicholas' neck and felt her fingers tingle at the prospect of raking her sharpened nails across the soft flesh, opening his vessels and feeling the warm burst of life explode from the giant's body. She might have taken the chance too, had it not been for the small girl wound around her and hugging her body tightly, thereby hindering her movement.

Nicholas seemed to read her thoughts and he smiled in a humorless, wicked grin, "You have spirit, but you are weakened by your worry for the child." Nicholas reached out and ran a finger through Pha's straight black hair. The girl moaned and clung even more desperately to Lei at the touch of his fingers. Lei slapped Nicholas' hand away, which only made the giant laugh at her as he stood.

"You see? I know your weakness, and it will hold you in obedience better than any chain I could fasten to you." Nicholas turned to leave, but stopped at the door, "Are you or the child in need of anything?" The sincerity that came from Nicholas was a complete turnaround from the creepy and threatening manner with which he had just been speaking. "Your stay with us need not be unpleasant. We have every accommodation the two of you might require, and it is yours for the asking."

Lei looked up at Nicholas from where she knelt on the mattress, "Are you trying to convince me we are actually guests?"

Nicholas shook his head, "No. You are prisoners, but ones that are to be treated with respect and courtesy." The big man paused a moment as if reflecting on some long repressed memory, "There is no greater dishonor that one can place upon himself than to abuse the power of incarceration."

Lei just stared at the man blankly in confusion, as Nicholas looked back at her and said, "I have some history in this regard. You can trust me in that."

Lei frowned, but decided to ask, "Is there any chance you could move us somewhere that has access to a bathroom, so we don't have to be calling for an escort all the time?"

Nicholas frowned as if the thought had never occurred to him, "There is a storage shed inside the main warehouse. It is smaller than this room but it is adjacent to the toilet facilities. Would that suffice?"

"Is it clean?," She asked.

"I will see that it is cleaned and made comfortable for you. Anything else? Food?"

Lei could feel the pang of hunger in her belly, but knew it wasn't for food, "I need my serum."

Nicholas inclined his head in confusion, "Serum?"

Lei looked at the man's blank face as her own thoughts faltered at his confusion, "You know, the blood substitute we all use to stave off the hunger?"

Shock filled Nicholas' eyes, but he quickly calmed and offered, "I'll see what I can do," before he stormed out of the office.

Once he was gone Lei could feel the girl loosen her grip and lay back down on the mattress. Lei reached for a bottle of water and offered it to Pha who drank several sips. The girl said some words in Thai, but quickly switched to broken English when

Lei's face went blank at the Thai.

"What we do?" the little girl asked in her high-pitched voice.

Lei looked at the girl with the most reassuring expression she could manage, "We bide our time. They don't appear to be trying to poison or sedate us, so we eat everything they bring us. Drink whatever they bring as well and do our best to keep our strength up and wait for that moment when they let their guard down."

"You think wait?" The girl asked, "wait for what?"

Lei smiled, "For an opportunity." Lei's smile faded, "Listen to me. I need you to be brave and do what I tell you to do, when I tell you to do it, okay? We may only have one chance, and if you hesitate or are too afraid to act, then we may never get out of here."

The girl looked at Lei blankly for a moment and Lei worried that the child's English wasn't proficient enough to grasp everything she had said. Then Pha nodded and put on a brave, indignant face and balled up her fists, "Father taught me be smart. I can do as you say."

Lei was so startled by the change in the girl's demeanor that she wondered if the girl had been putting on an act the whole time she had been clinging and cowering while Nicholas was in the room.

Lei studied the girl as she stood with her chest out and her back straight, in a defiant and strong stance. Lei wondered if, as a child, she herself had owned the same kind of resolve and fighting spirit. Maybe she had, but if so her handlers had been methodical in torturing it out of her. It had taken her liberation from slavery by Alpha, along with years of training and learning to trust again, to bring her back from the brink. Sadness crept into Lei as she stared in joyous wonder at the child's strength, and despite everything that had happened in this young girl's life, the innocence was still holding fast and burning within her. Experience had taught Lei

129

that, despite a strong will, a child is still only a child, and there are adults cruel enough to relish in the power they can wield over someone so much weaker.

"I can fight too!" Pha suddenly said without prompting, "But I be better if I had my knife. Big doo-doo head took it when I not ready."

"Big doo-doo head?" Lei asked while desperately stifling a laugh that had shocked her out of her melancholy, "Do you mean the man who was just in here?"

Pha shook her head, "No, not really big man. Small, old man, but very big doo-doo head."

Lei could only guess that Pha was talking about Dimitri, in which case the girl was right. "I think I know who you mean, and yes, he is a very, very big doo-doo head."

Chapter 13

I awoke before the sun was up and let Chris catch a few hours of sleep before we would to head out to see Larson's contact. I showered, which wasn't really an appropriate action for someone "on watch," but the aches and pains in my body would restrict me and demanded my intervention. Still, it was a quick shower in any case, and I toweled off and dressed in rapid succession. The shower helped, but the pain was still gnawing at me and I tried to distract myself by sitting at Chris' computer and doing some random internet searching. I had always found YouTube to be a great choice for exactly that kind of activity, where I usually looked up comedy routines or music videos, but this time I just searched Yahoo for the latest news. The Yahoo news channels were reporting on the latest disaster or celebrity indescretion, peppered with shadowbox advertisements for some "extreme baby cuteness" video that had gone viral. I absently clicked on one of those videos about a giant dog that loves his new human baby, and watched as this enormous mastiff tried to curl itself around a three month old without crushing its tiny form.

As I watched I felt my heart drop, and it wasn't the adorable nature of the scene that deflated me, but rather because Lei really loves this kind of scripted-reality video. . When we were killing time in our office back in Las Vegas she would repeatedly call out to me until I came over and watched the latest video she had found. It was a near-daily ritual, that could get a trifle annoying at times, mostly because she seemed to always want me to come watch a video clip when I was involved in something that commanded my full attention. Still, Lei was a force of nature, and deep down I knew I wasn't going to be off the hook until I dropped everything and went over to her desk to share in the "Oh, how cute" experience of some kitten, puppy or other newborn creature's video.

I could almost sense her next to me as I watched, and chuckled as the big dog started to whine when the baby moved away, and the dog had to put in another round of careful circling followed by a great flopping onto the floor, as only large dogs can do, with the infant once again perfectly encircled by the dogs girth.

I scratched at an itch on my cheek and my fingertips came back slightly damp. I frowned and stared at my fingertips thinking I had cut myself, but the wetness was clear. Pressure on my shoulder startled me, but not enough to make me jolt, and the reassuring weight of Chris' hand made me realize I had been crying.

"We'll find her," Chris said, speaking in reassuring tones that were completely without doubt and would brook no debate. I wiped at my eyes, more to compose myself than as a result of any self-consciousness. Chris and I were brothers and I had no secrets from him.

I could only nod my response, which prompted a reassuring squeeze and manly shoulder pat, before Chris broke contact and moved into the restroom. I turned to see that not only had the sun come up, but it now appeared high enough in the sky to have burned off some of the grayness of the misty sunrise. I shook myself and stretched, while I waited for Chris to emerge from the bathroom. Every fiber of my being was either sore or tight with muscle tension, and I knew I needed to get moving. I was going to say as much, when Chris waked out of the bathroom fully dressed and back to his old self.

"So," he said with more enthusiasm than was warranted, "let's go see if this backward town of former Communist heathens has a Starbucks yet."

***

It turned out that Nazran was, in fact, one of the last

132

remaining places on earth without the Starbucks franchise. We found coffee though, at what passed for a tiny farmers market mostly featuring potatoes or other root vegetables, but we were not provided milk or sugar. I tend to cream and sugar my coffee to the point where it is more like melted coffee ice cream, as opposed to a hot and bitter beverage. Lei took hers black, and after seeing me fuss over my brew with the cream and sugar, would generally make a snide remark about how big a pussy I was. I'd follow with something snippy, along the lines of what it indicated about a person's true nature, who enjoyed such bitter flavors, and the verbal dance would go on until we were both laughing and ignoring the coffee that had started the whole debate.

Chris pulled out his cell phone and entered several passwords, before opening the "notes" section on his phone. Reading the directions and realizing we were only a few blocks away from where we needed to go we decided to walk, as opposed to attempting to hail one of the infrequent cabs that drove past. The morning was still a bit overcast, shedding a pale grey light and depressing the already ugly city to an even greater dimension. The city was a wide-open space, more reminiscent of the way in which cities in the Western half of the United States had been planned, as opposed to skyscrapers abutting each other in New York's Manhattan. Most of the windows of the buildings had been blown out, likely by earlier artillery fire, and the few that looked intact were dilapidated in a multitude of other ways. All of the buildings seemed to be made of a filthy grey concrete and without any adornment, evocative of the "No-Frills" mentality that many government offices seem to engender. We could see the rubble of a number of buildings, which had either been bombed, blown up, set on fire or riddled with bullets. The area's capacity for damage suddenly made me realize that the space between the buildings made sense in a purely survivalist manner.

There were few people on the streets, and those who were

133

hanging around seemed as though they had probably slept there. They hovered in their spots in a way I associated with the homeless back in the states, although without the shopping carts loaded with "found treasures" nor the backpacks of belongings they frequently defended. These folk were dirty, haggard and in as much a decrepit state as was their surroundings, but they were cognizant enough to turn and eye Chris and me, as we walked by.

"Isn't this interesting?" I whispered.

Chris frowned, "What?"

I inclined my head towards a trio of people who just sat and watched us walking along the street, "They look like street people, but no one has held out their hand or asked for money."

Chris turned away from me and back to the trio I had indicated as we were passing them, and he recognized the look in their eyes. "They're afraid of us perhaps?" he asked. I nodded as he continued, "and it's also my guess that they don't quite know what to make of us."

I thought about that, and given Dimitri and his people's reputation for living like the vampires of old by feeding off of the fresh blood of others, it sort of made some sense. These people probably knew that we weren't part of Dimitri's group but, despite that, we were walking the streets of one of the most dangerous cities in the world unarmed and seemingly unafraid, which meant we were either completely stupid, insane or so dangerous that even the risks of Nazran were of no consequence to us.

"We might want to consider finding a route with fewer spectators," Chris spoke in a voice not much higher than a whisper.

I nodded my head in agreement, "These people look like they have been effectively cowed, but we are attracting a lot of attention, and even though they may not attack us directly, one of these enterprising souls might try to sell our presence to someone on the lookout for strangers."

Chris rolled his eyes, "Seems kind of late for preventing

that."

I smiled, "True, but I'm a big believer in not making a bad situation worse." I pointed at Chris' phone, "Can you use that thing to get us off the main road?"

Chris nodded and studied the map on the screen of his phone, "We're almost there. We can walk between a couple of the buildings and make a shortcut of it."

"We aren't taking the quickest route?"

"No, I had thought we were doing a casual recon of the city as we walked to the Green Fairy."

I tried to let the words roll over me, but failed miserably, "I'm sorry, the what?"

Chris laughed, "I'm embellishing. The joint we're heading to is a liquor store specializing in Absinthe and the various associated accessories."

Chris had always been interested in myths and legends, even before he actually became one, so it was no surprise to me that he was aware of the legend of the "Green Fairy" that was associated with Absinthe. Absinthe is a high-volume alcohol drink or "spirit" having a proof rating from at least 100 to a usual maximum of 140 and contains the psychotropic chemical Thujone, which naturally resides in the drink due to the inclusion of wormwood within its recipe. Absinthe has been labeled the inspiration, and possible detriment, for a number of bohemian artists, musicians and writers throughout history. This close association with the creative process resulted in the legend of "The Green Fairy" or "The Green Lady" who would appear when the spirit is properly concocted and consumed. Ultimately, due to the presence of Thujone, the drink was thought to be a dangerously addictive and psychoactive drug that altered one's perceptions, thoughts or emotions to the point that people could become insane. Recent studies had proved that the quantity of Thujone was so low in the "spirit" that it had little, if any, effect on the body. As it turns

135

out, the dangers of Absinthe were the simple and mundane dangers of regular alcoholism, and the ban on the liquor was lifted in the 1990's.

There were no signs or numbers on the door of the grey shop we approached, which made me wonder how Chris knew where the shop was.

"GPS," Chris volunteered before I could ask, "pinpoints exactly where we are and where we need to be."

I walked to the door and pulled, only to find it locked. Chris nodded as he pointed to the cell phone screen, "Larson's notes say that the shop would likely be closed, but the owner is always there."

I frowned, "So we just knock or something?"

Chris shrugged, "Guess so." Chris knocked on the door and, after a few seconds without anyone answering Chris knocked again, but this time added in a sing-song voice, "little pigs, little pigs let me in."

I rolled my eyes, "Now that's just creepy."

Chris pointed at his nose to indicate himself and said, "Vampire."

I pointed at his nose and said, "Idiot."

Chris smiled, "You're no fun, you know that?"

I ignored him and said, "Knock again or something."

Chris smiled and turned to knock on the glass when a voice demanded something in what I guessed was Russian. I scanned the door and the space around it. The voice had the electronic and tinny sound from coming through a cheap speaker, but I couldn't see any sign of an intercom or speaker box.

"Speakee English?" Chris responded in half chuckle that was offensive enough to make me sure we wouldn't get a response, even if the person speaking did have some command of English.

To my surprise a heavily accented voice immediately came back, "Who are you and what do you want?!"

Chris was still in "Chris" mode and called out loudly in a false baritone, "Little pig, little pig, let me... OOF!"

I punched Chris hard in the shoulder to cut him off. Despite the sting of the blow I just had given him, Chris looked as though he might break out in a huge laugh and I was about to start chastising him when the voice came back, "Robert?"

The angry words in my throat froze and I looked back at the door in dumbfounded disbelief. Major Larson's first name was Robert and the whole "Little Pig" thing had been a password he evidently used with his the contact in the Absinthe shop.

Finally I found my voice, "We're Robert's friends. I believe he told you we were coming?"

"Ah! Da, da. He told me of you. Wait a moment."

Chris was smiling at me with a smugness that made me want to hit him again.

"Say it," Chris chastised me.

I growled, "No."

Chris' smile grew wider as he taunted, "You know a "real" man admits when he made a mistake."

I turned my face away from him lest his smile become infectious, which absolutely would not be appropriate at this time, "Not my fault if you don't tell me everything," I complained.

Chris would not let it drop, "C'mon, say it. You know you should."

I let out a breath and threw my hands in the air, "All right! I'm sorry I hit you in the shoulder," but I quickly followed with, "but you were so...

Chris cut me off, his smile growing ridiculously wide, "No, no. An apology with an excuse attached isn't an apology." He was enjoying making me uncomfortable way too much.

I let out a defeated sigh, "Okay, you win. I'm sorry for hitting you in the shoulder."

Chris' smile turned to satisfaction as the door to the shop

opened and a small round man beckoned us inside, "Come, come. Quickly."

"After you," Chris gestured regally with one hand and, as I turned to head inside, he socked hard me in the shoulder.

I yelped, and the man holding the door for us looked as though he was going to bolt inside and lock the door behind him, but Chris walked inside before he could act on his impulse.

I bit my lip both in the pain of the shot he gave me as well as stifling the laugh that threatened to overwhelm me. Chris was many things, but best of all was the way he could cheer your spirits and push a smile out of you when you needed it most. I had been feeling such worry for Lei that it was threatening to overwhelm me. Now, with a mock look defeat on my face and a hand over my punched shoulder, I shuffled meekly into the shop and let the man close the door behind me.

Chapter 14

The impoverished appearance of the sparse and somewhat rundown exterior of the building was stripped away the instant we stepped inside. The shop was of a basic rectangular box shape, with display shelving on the long sidewalls and a bar countertop at the far end. Exotic hardwoods covered the floor and spanned seamlessly up the walls and into the cabinetry, as if impossibly cut from a single log. Along one of the sidewalls were bottles too numerous to count of various Absinthe brands, which were arranged neatly to become as much a part of decor as the woodworks. The opposite wall displayed an enormous collection of intricately designed silver Absinthe "fountains" and slotted sugar spoons. Absinthe fountains are used to dilute the alcoholic spirit with water, which is usually dripped over a sugar cube that is resting on a slotted spoon spanning the opening of a specially designed crystal drinking glass. Most of the pieces utilized by connoisseurs were of basic design, little more than funnels, but with the added ability to regulate the water flow. The Absinthe fountains in this shop went way beyond the principles of mere functionality as each was a wonder of hand-crafted art that could have served as a museum quality steam-punk masterpiece. Such was the artistry that each piece looked as though with a turn of the spigot, the fountain would not only dilute the beverage, but would likely animate itself and fly away with strains of some classical music chiming in its wake.

Chris and I both hesitated while taking in the dreamlike majesty of the shop. Not very professional on either of our parts, but the surreal way the interior appearance contradicted its exterior, and with Nazran as whole, was just too much to be ignored.

The man who had opened the door for us smiled at our awe as he casually locked the shop door. Any traces of anxiety on his face at our presence or behavior melted away as he, too stopped to join us in appreciation of what he had presumably created. Chris walked over to the wall where the Absinthe fountains rested on the oversized display shelves that stabilized their bulk, while still keeping them accessible to whomever might be looking at them.

Stepping in front of a fountain with a particularly gothic design, Chris' eyes twinkled like child's, who has just entered a major toy or candy store for the first time, and turned to the shop owner, who answered with a nod at the wordless "Can I touch it" question on Chris' face. Chris ran his fingertips over the detailed workmanship that was so fine it looked as though it had been created under a microscope, as he traced the path the water would take from the fountain's reservoir until it reached one of its many terminal spigots.

"Is this functional?"

The owner smiled wickedly and responded in that heavy Slavic accent, "Oh da, very much so."

"It doesn't seem possible," Chris wondered, "it seems as though the water has to defy gravity to get to its destination."

The owner nodded happily, "Indeed, that is exactly how it was supposed to appear, but it is simple case of the water pressure from the reservoir overwhelming the weight of the actual water in the piping so it rises as though lifted by the fairy herself."

I chuckled, "Poetic."

The owner turned to me and shrugged his shoulders, "It's Absinthe, would you expect any less? The mystical legend of the spirit is half the fun."

The owner walked past us and rounded the bar at the far end of the room, "Now as much as I am flattered by your admiration of the art in my store, you are here to do business, Da?"

"Business?" I said in confusion, "Major-"

Chris stopped what I was going to say by resting a warning hand on my shoulder. I turned to him in confusion, "What?" but he was looking at his cell phone screen and ignored my question.

After a few seconds Chris raised one eyebrow at the cell phone screen and mumbled a quiet, "Hmm, who knew?" before pocketing his cell phone and turning back to the owner.

"We are looking for a very special bottle of Absinthe. Our friend told us that you would be the one to talk to about acquiring it."

The shop owner shrugged, "Robert is prone to flattery, but I can try. What are you looking for?"

I stood dumbfounded, "He didn't tell you why we were coming?"

The smile on the owner's face faded and a worried expression crept into his features, "No, only that you might be arriving in this week. He said you were connoisseurs and that I might have exactly what you needed."

Chris looked at me, "Do you want me to hit you in the shoulder again?"

"What?" I said in surprise.

Chris didn't answer, instead he placed his index finger to his lips and silently "shushed" me.

I raised the palms of my hands in a "what's going on?" motion, but Chris had turned back to the owner and said, "We are hoping to find a bottle or bottles from a producer called J.L.T."

The owner's eyes widened, "You... you know of J.L.T.?"

I couldn't help myself, "That surprises you?"

The owner made a move with his head and neck that wordlessly conveyed incredulity and said, "J.L.T. is extremely rare and the producer is not recorded in any documentation or literature. We only know of the work from the bottles found in forgotten cellars that date pre-ban, and usually are from the mid seventeenth century. Such a bottle of Absinthe is not for drinking. It is for a collector... or a museum."

"And," I asked, "You have one?"

"Perhaps," the owner's eyes grew very serious, "was there a particular year you were hoping for?"

Without missing a beat Chris said, "1876."

The owner nodded and removed a bottle of water from beneath the counter along with three crystal glasses, three slotted spoons and a small bowl of sugar cubes. "Come over, I have what you need." Chris and I exchanged looks of confusion as we stepped up to the bar. The owner placed three small silver chalices, each resting on four winding legs, next to the glasses on the bar and turned from the bar to look at the wall of bottled Absinthe, before approaching and carefully selecting one of the bottles from the wall. He walked back around us, and with a practiced precision opened the bottle of spirits to set it on the bar for us to inspect.

"Oh!" Chris exclaimed as if understanding and picked up the bottle to smell the contents.

"That doesn't look like the bottle we asked for," I said, stating the obvious.

"No, no it isn't. You are right. This is a very young bottle of Absinthe, but it is a fine example of the spirit. You will join me in a sampling?"

"Smells like licorice," Chris said as he set the bottle back on the counter, "I thought all Russians drank vodka?"

The owners face screwed up as if Chris had just placed something fecal under his nose, "Vodka?! Peah!!" The owner had turned and mimicked spitting something foul from his mouth, "Tasteless potato water without any soul. There is no art to Vodka, only purity."

The owner lifted the bottle and poured enough of the contents to fill each of the glasses in front of us about a third of the way up from the bottom. Then as he placed one of the small silver chalices on top of each glass he said, "See how the Absinthe is white and pale as it sits in the glasses now?" We nodded as he placed a sugar cube on each of the three slotted spoons and slid

142

one of the spoons under the legs of each chalice to rest above each of the three glasses.

"Those things are Absinthe fountains? They seem so... basic, compared to the wild things you have on your wall."

The owner nodded, "Yes, these are for individual tastings of only the finest bottles. My creations on the walls are for more..." he searched for the right word, "...commercial use. Mostly I sell them to the various Absinthe bars that are cropping up since the ban on the spirit was lifted in 1990's. They add the right ambiance to the room, as well as perpetuate the myth and majesty of Absinthe, but they are meant more for commercial use in diluting portions on a large scale. For us, we will concentrate on the singular glass as our sole focus"

Twisting the cap off of the water bottle, the owner filled each of the individual serving fountains, opening a spigot in each base. I watched as the fountain released the water, drop by drop in rapid succession onto the sugar cubes, which then dripped their way into the glass.

With a flourish of waving hands the owner gestured to our glasses, "Now watch for the green lady to appear."

I wanted to roll my eyes at the David Copperfield-esque showmanship the owner was throwing at us. Of course Chris, former LAPD medical examiner and forever science nerd, was completely enraptured. His enthusiasm was addictive, so I turned back to my drink and watched as the sugar water dripped. At first nothing happened, however, as more of the sugar water dripped the contents of the Absinthe in the glass began to change. Before I knew it, I too, was watching with fascination as the translucent white liquor changed color until, when the last drop fell, the Absinthe was now a deep rich translucent green.

"The lady has arrived," the owner declared and lifted his chalice off the top of his glass. Chris and I followed suit, and together the three of us raised our glasses to one another. "To friends and business, the best comrades make." The owner supplied the toast and placed the glass to his lips.

Sensing the chance to ingratiate myself where I might have fallen short earlier I said in Russian, *"Za fstrye'-tchoo."*

Both the owner and Chris looked at me as if I had just lifted a glowing hunk of Uranium out of my pocket. The owner smiled and translated, more in surprise than need, "Yes, 'to our meeting,' excellent sentiment." He gently clinked glasses with me and together we shared a drink. It tasted very sweet, more so than the sugar that had dripped into my glass should have made it taste, and the flavors of licorice and floral herbs resulted in a flavor unique to any alcohol I had ever tried. There was little, or possibly none of the burn usually associated with alcohol, despite the surprisingly high percentage it contained.

I lowered my glass to see the shop owner looking expectantly at Chris, with Chris looking back and forth nervously between the owner and me. He hadn't sampled his drink yet and looked a little unhappy. My nerves suddenly perked up and I was worried that I had again missed something.

Chris shuffled his feet, now looking more self-conscious than worried, "I... I only know one toast..."

"What's up?" I said.

Perhaps it was his life revolving around alcohol and those who drank it, but the owner immediately had a smile spread across his face, "Oh, I can tell, this shall be a good one! Please continue!"

I looked from the bartender to Chris, "What...will be a good one?"

Chris shrugged, his inner turmoil vanishing with the words the owner had spoken and with a deadly serious demeanor on his face.

"Here's to the girls we love the best,
we love them most when they're undressed..."

"Oh crap..." I muttered as I put one hand over my eyes as if massaging a headache. The owner was near giddy with anticipation, his eyes twinkling with merriment as he listened to Chris' bawdy toast.

"We love them sitting, standing, lying;
if they had wings we'd love them flying.
And when they're dead, buried and forgotten;
we'll dig them up and fuck them rot-"

"Chris!" I cut him off on the last word, "Jesus man!"

But the owner got it and began to laugh. He laughed so hard that he had to put his drink down on the bar-top in order to support himself with his hands. Chris was laughing too, but if it was at his own toast or the owner's reaction I couldn't say. It was infectious and I found myself chuckling as well when the owner grabbed at his chest, feigning a heart attack as he continued to laugh uncontrollably for another few seconds. Eventually we managed to regain some form of composure as the owner retrieved his glass and raised it to Chris, "That was wonderfully horrible. Thank you for that."

They clinked glasses and drank. I drank the remnants from my glass as well and, as we set the glasses down the owner removed another set of keys from his pocket and turned to what appeared to be a storeroom door. He beckoned for us to follow him and, as Chris and I walked around the bar, I heard the owner chuckle some more and repeat the last line of Chris' toast under his breath before he opened the door to the storeroom and we all walked through. We found ourselves in a storage area with many crates, each filled with bottles of Absinthe and stacked haphazardly throughout the room.

"This business was far more lucrative when Absinthe was illegal throughout the world. I could sell it on the black market for several times its actual value, but then they lifted the ban and I thought I'd have to drink all of these myself. Thanks be to God and the internet for saving my business. Here help me with this."

The owner pointed at a particularly large crate and together we all found a handhold and slid the several hundred pound box of booze to one side, revealing another small door.

The owner used yet another key to open it and said, "Watch your heads," as he hunched over and went through. Chris and I did as we were told and walked into a completely dark room. A familiar scent filled my nose, but before I could give a name to it the lights came on and we found ourselves in a huge space, lined floor to ceiling with military grade weapons. The scent had been gun oil and cleaning solvent and for the second time in less than half an hour my eyes went wide in shock at what they were seeing. Automatic rifles, assorted handguns and shoulder mounted Stinger missiles were mounted on the walls, while grenades and other anti-personnel devices were in bins or stacked in neat piles on the floor. Folding tables were filled with collections of surveillance equipment on one side of the space while multiple pieces of body armor hung on clothing racks on the opposite side. The middle of the room was cleared from end to end, except for one small display case sitting in the center of the room and, once my eyes had gotten over the shock of the arsenal, both Chris and I found ourselves drawn to the display. The display was an old wooden stand topped by a glass box that rose seamlessly from the wood. Inside was a single bottle of 1876 J.R.T Absinthe, still covered in the cellar dust from which it had been discovered.

The owner noticed us looking at the bottle. "That is the Absinthe you requested, but the two of you are really here for the other items in this room, da?"

I managed to tear my eyes away from the bottle and nodded to the owner, "Yes."

Chris was mesmerized, "Is it real? I mean, drinkable?"

The owner tilted his head inquisitively, then smiled, "Older bottles have been found, although not of this brand, and the spirit inside had only improved with time, as opposed to turning into vinegar or such as would wine."

Chris frowned, "So it's not possible you have little more than salad dressing in there?"

The owner made a flourish of his hands like a magician taking a bow. "Only when the seal is broken and the liquid inside sampled will we know for sure." He let those words hang in the air before adding, "But the chance of the Absinthe being... not only viable, but exquisite, is a very safe bet."

The owner moved to the center of the room and stood next to the antique bottle of Absinthe, "Now gentlemen, I believe formal introductions are in order."

"Fair enough," I said, "my name is Steve Jacobs and this is my partner Chris Barnes."

"Partner?" the owner's face screwed up in surprise.

I frowned at his expression, but Chris laughed, "Not that kind of 'partner' you Commie bastard."

The owner shrugged, but there was a humor in his eyes when he said, "When it comes to dealing with you subversive American pigs, one must be prepared for all sort of things. In any case, my name is Igor Tonichev, and as a friend of Major Larson I expect you will find all you require here. If not, I can locate most things within a day or two, just let me know what it is you need."

So I said, "Chris, give him the list, please."

Chris removed a piece of paper from his pocket and handed it to Igor, who pulled a pair of reading glasses from an inner pocket to begin perusing the items we had listed.

"So," Igor asked as he studied the list, "how have you enjoyed your time in our beautiful Nazran?"

I was going to say something benign about the city when Chris chimed in, "To say this place is a festering armpit would be a compliment to the town and an insult to the festering armpits of the world." Then he added, "But you have a lovely shop."

Igor laughed, "Thank you, and yes, Nazran is shit. I'd leave if business were not so good here."

Shaking my head at how much better Chris related to people than I ever could, I asked, "Can you come up with the equipment we are requesting."

Igor walked over to a crate and sat down on the planks, "Most of the items are indeed within this room." He pulled a pen from his pocket and circled two items on the list, "These two will take me a day or so to acquire. You can wait or you will have to do without."

Igor pulled out another folding table that had been leaning against a wall. It was heavy and of the old wood and metal variety, so I was surprised to see how easily the little round man was able to move the piece of furniture. Once the table was set up he lifted a duffle bag from the floor, set it on the table and zipped it open. He removed several boxes of ammunition of varying sizes first, and then removed what looked like a briefcase. Setting the briefcase on the table, Igor popped the latches and lifted the lid to reveal a disassembled Dragonov (SVD) Sniper rifle.

Chris instantly recognized the weapon, "Oh, that's mine! I call dibs!""

Seeking a long-range support rifle, the Soviet Union had held a contest among its elite gunsmiths to fill the void in their arsenal. In 1963 Yevgeny Dragunov's design was victorious, and the rifle design went into service within the Soviet Military. Very little has changed from then until now within the production of the rifle. The wooden stocks had been replaced with black polypropylene, and the original 7N1 ammunition, with its lead core and a steel jacket, was replaced by the 7N14 with a steel core within the steel jacket.

Chris scanned the boxes of ammunition, "I don't see any sniper rounds?"

Igor sighed, "Yes, acquiring that ammunition might have raised eyebrows around here, but the rifle shoots the standard

7.62x54mmR just as well."

I frowned, "Acquiring the guns doesn't raise alarms, but looking for the bullets would?"

"I already had the guns," Igor informed me, "but when they changed from 7N1 rounds to 7N14 I lost my stockpile of ammunition." Igor closed and latched the case before sliding it aside. Next he pulled out two of the smallest automatic rifles I had ever seen.

"The Tsniitochmash 9mm SR.3M assault rifles. The rifle is effective to two hundred meters with iron sights, or four hundred meters with an optical sight, and is only sixteen inches long without the folding stock or silencers."

I could see the folding stock attached to the side of what otherwise looked like a two-handed handgun and asked, "Were you able to get silencers for them?"

Igor smiled and set the rifles down on the table before lifting four cylinders that were almost the same length as the rifles, "The suppression system should last you between six hundred to one thousand rounds before degrading. A lot of shots to be sure, but I have an extra silencer for each weapon should the need arise."

I blinked at the matter of fact professionalism Igor was showing as he described the killing machines he was presenting to us. He went into ballistics, armor penetration capabilities and a bunch of other informative characteristics for the rifles. The technical information passed completely over my head, but Chris was in a rapture and was hanging on every word. Igor removed everything else from the duffle bag, including body armor, surveillance equipment, Government issued GPS tracking devices, along with a first aid kit and flashlights.

When he had finished, Igor asked, "Now, have you found a need for anything else since you arrived? Anything not on the list?"

"Just some answers, if you have them." I said.

Igor seemed to consider the idea for a minute before saying, "All of my customers' information I keep confidential. It is an important part of the way I do business, not to mention my own safety."

I held up my hands, "We aren't looking for any specific information about any of your clients."

Igor raised an eyebrow, "No?"

"No," I said, "what we are interested in is information about what is happening in Nazran."

Chris jumped right in, "We saw some things last night that don't make a great deal of sense."

Igor turned to Chris, "Like what?"

"Like the way a police officer just watched as a mugging happened right in front of him and he did nothing to help. Then after the mugger had run off, instead of checking on the victim he called some men on the phone who looked as though they were going to collect the body."

Igor looked at me suspiciously, "And then what happened? What else did you see?"

I considered telling him about the homeless man who attacked Dimitri's men, but decided against it, as the story might seem a little unbelievable to someone who hadn't witnessed it.

"Nothing else after that." I said calmly, hoping my poker face was functioning properly.

I felt Chris come to attention when I said those words. Having witnessed the entire spectacle as well, he knew there was much, much more, but he read my intentions and went along with me without giving anything away.

Igor had been looking at my face the whole time, so I don't think he noticed Chris' initial reaction. "Come," Igor said in a friendly manner, "let's go back into the shop where we can talk over a drink and I'll send Sasha to get us some food." He gestured at the duffle bag with a wave of one hand, "You can leave your gear here and collect it when we are finished talking."

I wondered if Igor had grown suspicious and wanted to distance us from the room and bag of weapons that we might turn against him, but he seemed calm and eager to please.

I hadn't seen anyone else in the store, but once we were back in the main shop there was a young man, probably in his mid-twenties, behind the bar.

"Sasha," Igor said jovially to the young man, who smiled warmly back at Igor before the pair began speaking in rapid Russian. Sasha looked only a little put out by whatever Igor had said to him, but he smiled at us as he came around the bar and headed for the door. "Sasha will bring back the food and join us in a little bit. Now, please sit and ask me whatever you'd like, as long as it doesn't break my rules of confidentiality."

The way Sasha and Igor interacted made a thought pass through me that was interrupted when Chris asked, "How old is your son?

Igor stopped and turned to him, "My son?"

Chris pointed after Sasha, "Your boy, how old is he?"

I covered my eyes with my hand and made an audible groan. Chris looked stupidly from me to Igor clearly bewildered at what he might have done.

Igor just laughed before saying, "Igor is not my son."

"Oh, I thought..." Chris started, but Igor cut him off.

"No, he is my 'partner.'" Igor used his fingers to indicate parentheses as he said "partner," and then continued to laugh at what must have been the look on Chris' face.

Under the sound of Igor's laughter I whispered to Chris, "How does that foot taste in your mouth, Mr. Tactful?"

Chapter 15
Yekaterinburg, Russia. July 17, 1918

Following the Russian Revolution of 1917 the Tsar and his family were all taken into captivity and initially held in the city of Tobolsk, but constantly transferred several times over the next few months until they ended up at the Ipatiev House in the city of Yekaterinburg in May of 1918. Alexei, unable to gain access to either raw blood or the medicine that Rasputin had previously provided him, had grown so weak at this point that he could no longer support his own weight and was confined to a wheelchair. Throughout their ordeal the family preservered through this trying time; however, something changed in Alexei after the arrival in Yekaterinburg. Nightmares plagued him and some nights he could only be quieted by his sister, Anastasia, who whispered to him in the darkness and soothed him back to sleep.

"Anastasia!!!" Tsaritsa Alessandra called to her youngest daughter who was fast asleep in her room, "Anastasia, get to your brother. He's calling out again and I want him quieted before he wakes the entire household."

Groggily, the seventeen year old got out of bed and eased into a robe. When she went into Alexei's room she found him rocking back and forth, sweating profusely and rambling. She gasped at how pale her brother had become and resisted the urge to run from the room.

Gently Anastasia knelt next to the bed and placed a hand on her brother's cheek, then recoiled in horror at the touch of his skin. He flesh was so cold that it almost seemed that all of the warmth had been unnaturally drawn from his body.

"Alexei," She whispered. "Alexei, wake up. You're dreaming…and you're scaring me."

Suddenly Alexei's hand shot out and grabbed his sister by the arm.

"Get away!" he croaked in a voice too weak to be more than a whisper. "You must get away now!"

Despite the ferocity with which Alexei spoke, Anastasia remained calm as she began to stroke his matted hair, "Be calm, you were just dreaming again."

Alexei pushed her hand away and tried to sit up, but Anastasia placed a hand on his chest and kept him from rising.

"No. Not a dream this time. The black clouds descend. The terror has arrived for us!" Alexei was desperate as he spoke, then his body shuddered and he passed out from the strain.

Anastasia was about to run for help when her father, Tsar Nicholas II entered the room.

"Anastasia, go get dressed quickly. They are moving us again."

***

Yakov Yurovsky had always been a simple man from a simple working class family. That was until he joined the Bolsheviks, rose quickly through the ranks and now he was a commander in the Bolshevik secret police. The "secret" to Yakov's rise through the ranks in the newly formed Soviet Union was spurred by his overzealousness to commit acts of severe brutality while maintaining an aire of dispassionate professionalism that chilled his superiors. Now he fulfilled his duties with intense pride at having been granted the honor as the man responsible for guarding the deposed Tsar of Russia along with the royal family.

Yakov reclined in his creaky wooden chair and poured himself a celebratory shot of vodka. He was nervous, but the feeling was not as a result of anxiety, rather it was the significance of what he was to do and the honor that had been bestowed upon him that caused his current trepidation.

153

A knock at his door startled him and he quickly downed his drink before rising from the chair. Taking only the briefest moment to straighten his uniform, he called out for the person's outside the door to enter.

Yakov's aide, Vladimir, entered the office followed by seven additional men who were dressed in civilian garb and overcoats.

"Are these the men I asked for?" Yakov asked as he inclined his head at the men.

Vladimir responded immediately. "Yes sir, they are all from the 1st Kamishlov Rifle Regimen, comprised solely of soldiers of Hungarian descent. The men are all completely loyal to the party and none speak a word of Russian, only German, as requested."

Yakov looked each man over and made his own mental assessment. Having lived in Germany for years before returning to Russia to join the Bolsheviks he would be able to communicate with these men while keeping his orders private from the general staff of the house. True the Tsaritsa was originally from Germany and Yakov knew his orders would not be private to her, but he wasn't overly concerned.

"Excellent Vladimir, now get the rest of the squad together and inform the prisoners that we will be moving them to another location."

Vladimir snapped a salute and was about to leave the room when Yakov asked, "You know where to hold them once they have packed and prepared themselves?"

Vladimir looked back at his superior and nodded slightly, and then exited the office without a word.

Yakov watched his man leave and knew he had only a few minutes before his squad had the entire house ready to go. Turning to the seven men who remained in the small office he asked in accented German, "Who speaks for you men?"

None of the men spoke; however, a large man near the back stepped in front of the others. His face was sunken and scarred with one eye that appeared discolored as it stared off in an unseen direction.

"Have your orders been explained to you?" Yakov asked.

"They have comrade," the rifleman answered.

"And?"

"We live to serve the state."

Yakov nodded. "Excellent, now follow me."

Yakov led the seven riflemen from his office and down the stairs into the cellar. Soon the royal staff, the Tsaritsa and her four daughters joined them, all of whom stood against a far wall away from their jailers. Each was dressed in simple clothes that would do little to shield them from the cold, if not for the multiple layers they wore, and made them look to be little more than the peasants they previously ruled over.

To the former Tsaritsa, Yakov asked, "Where is your husband and son?"

"The Tsar..." Tsaritsa Alexandra proudly began.

"FORMER Tsar and enemy of the people." Yakov interrupted.

The Tsaritsa looked at her jailer with a vacant expression for a moment then continued, "...is helping our son get dressed and will be here shortly."

Yakov frowned at her, but did not reply. Instead he turned his back on the woman and her brood and waited, rather impatiently, until the rest of the family arrived.

Eventually, Nicholas II descended the steps carrying his fourteen-year-old son in his arms. Immediately, upon seeing the state her son was in, the Tsaritsa asked for a chair to be provided for Alexei and, as if on cue, Vladimir appeared on the steps with a dining room chair. Vladimir placed the chair on the far side of the room, then returned to the stairs and ascended. Gently the boy's

155

father placed Alexei, who was now awake and apparently coherent, in the chair and stepped to his wife's side.

"This is not the first time you have suddenly moved us, but it is the first time that the need has come at such an hour. Why would it be so important for us to leave at this time of night?"

Yakov looked at the man, studied every aspect of him, and was appalled by the arrogance the man seemed to project. This pompous fool who had fallen from such lofty heights to arrive in his care didn't seem to understand what was happening.

"It is no longer your place to be informed of anything comrade; however, I have orders that need to be fulfilled and, unfortunately, they were specific enough as to prevent me from doing things in my usual manner." Yakov paced the room as he spoke and was oblivious to Alexei who, despite his exceedingly weakened state, sat very straight in his chair and held his arms loosely at his sides.

Yakov smiled, "You see comrade, together we shall make history this day."

The former Tsar grew impatient, "What are you talking about?"

Yakov seemed to ignore the man, "I never allowed myself to dream that my name would ever find its place in history. Individual achievement is not something one should openly strive for when one also happens to be a member of the communist party, you understand."

The Tsar frowned at the man and something in his demeanor seemed to grow wary as Yakov stopped pacing and spoke in German to the riflemen who had accompanied him, "Prepare yourselves."

The riflemen stepped forward in single file line that was parallel to the family then turned one quarter to the right in order for each of the men to face the prisoners as they raised their rifles.

Suddenly each member of the former royal family and their staff realized what was happening and wailed in the face of the terror that was their fate.

Tsar Nicholas II quickly stepped in front of his wife and daughters. "You cannot do this! You don't have the authority!"

Yakov withdrew a single piece of paper from his breast pocket. "Actually comrade, the order for your execution came earlier this evening."

Fear drained the blood from Nicholas' face as his head dropped. Then he raised his head to his executioner and said, "My execution? Mine?"

Yakov couldn't believe what he was hearing. Did this man have such arrogance that he could be indignant of what was about to befall him?

Nicholas continued, "Does that mean...my children...?"

"Ah," Yakov said as he realized where the former Tsar's thoughts had led him. "I am supposed to carry out the sentence upon your entire family."

Panic began to ensue among the girls who cried and held each other fiercely, while the Tsaritsa stood proud with her eyes cast to someplace far away.

"But I will do you one last service Nicholas and spare them your fate."

Tsar Nicholas II, former ruler of all Russia, dropped to his knees and bowed his head toward Yakov Yurovsky.

"I...thank you."

Yakov smiled, removed his revolver and shot Nicholas in the stomach. Nicholas' body shuddered and his hands flew to the area where the bullet entered his abdomen. The girls all screamed and the Tsaritsa dropped to her knees, tears falling from her eyes.

Yakov bent forward and whispered into Nicholas' ear, "I don't think you understood me comrade. I said I would spare them YOUR fate. Them, I shall kill quickly."

Nicholas raised a bloody hand in an attempt to grab at the throat of the cruel man before him, but the damage was too severe for him to succeed.

Yakov stood upright and walked behind the row of riflemen and took one last, long and satisfying look at the horrified family of royals all as they desperately clung to each other cowering and weeping on the bare stone floor. All except the sick boy, Alexei, whose eyes had suddenly, frighteningly, gone very hard.

Yakov's tried to give the order to shoot but his voice caught in his throat as the look Alexei gave him chilled him. There was a moment where Yakov couldn't even draw a breath as a violent shiver rolled through his entire body.

Then, the moment passed and the chill faded. Suddenly Yakov could feel himself regain control and, although his voice came out in more of a high pitched squeak than its usual barratone, he shouted"*Schitzen!*"

All seven rifles fired and the rounds found their intended targets as the Tsaritsa, her daughter Tatiana and the five staff members all were wrenched backward by the force of the projectiles impacting their bodies. Mercifully, the riflemen were skilled and almost every shot was instantly fatal. A wet, guttural sounding scream burst from Nicholas upon seeing blood erupt from his wife and daughter as they fell motionless to the dirt floor. Desperately he attempted to crawl toward his family, but the riflemen calmly loaded another round into their rifles and slammed the bolts closed readying the weapons to fire again.

"*Schitzen!*" Yakov ordered again and the riflemen fired, the sounds of the shots muffling the anguished moan coming from Nicholas as his remaining three daughters were rocked back into the wall behind them before coming to rest on the floor that was becoming a pool of Romanov blood. In that volley of shots one round had penetrated Alexei's chest, but passed through the boy as if he were made of little more than air. Blood trickled from the wound, yet he remained seated his eyes glaring mercilessly at Yakov.

Yakov frowned as fear and confusion filled him and then saw some slight movement coming from the group of bodies on the ground.

Calling to the riflemen, Yakov said in German, "Bayonets."

Nicholas dragged his failing form to Yakov's feet, "Please!" he rasped, "Show mercy!"

Yakov looked down at the dying man, "I am showing mercy. The bayonets will end them quickly." Yakov waved his hand, ordering his men to proceed.

A final burst of rage filled Nicholas and his bloody hand flew to Yakov's pant leg and grasped the fabric, trying to take his executioner down to the ground.

Yakov never swayed, rolled his eyes and lowered his revolver between Nicholas' eyes and proclaimed "For the State!" before pulling the trigger.

The first rifleman had crossed the room and savagely plunged his bayonet into Alexei's side. The boy's body recoiled from the force of the blow and fell from the chair. The other riflemen began to pierce each wounded victim regardless of the fatality of the initial gunshot until they found the source of the movement. It was Anastasia; she had survived but was now helpless against the multiple stabs from the riflemen's bayonets. Perhaps some mercy had been granted to her as she had lost consciousness in the instant before the first stabbing blow could be delivered and she seemed not to notice the blades as they pierced her body over and over.

Alexei was not so fortunate as he continued to struggle weakly and hold his glare on Yakov.

Then something happened…The riflemen stopped their attack practically in mid motion and looked at each other, fear filling their eyes.

Turning to Yakov the rifleman in charge said, "This is unnatural! The boy will not die!"

Yakov was still staring at the remains of Nicholas' head when he asked, "Then why are you stopping?"

The riflemen looked at Yakov then to each other and all of them stepped away from the victims, "We were brought here to be a firing squad; however, it is customary for our Commander to apply the Coup De Grace."

The ground had become so saturated with blood that it now flowed down the unleveled floor heading toward the far corner of the room. Yakov sighed and snatched a bayonet from one of the riflemen. He walked over to Alexei and pointed the blade at Alexei's heart when he again noticed the young man's eyes. Yakov hesitated and the stare between Yakov and Alexei seem to go on in eerie silence for nearly a minute before Alexei looking far more dead than alive, began to rise. Yakov began to shake at the sight as he watched the boy, his face so white from blood loss that it had turned a grayish color, begin to walk toward him.

Dropping the rifle, Yakov reached for his revolver that he had holstered after shooting the boy's father, and fired point blank into the Alexei's chest. The boy recoiled from the impact, staggered back a few paces, then righted himself and again took a step toward Yakov. Yakov tried to fire again, but the gun misfired and only made a gentle "click." Desperately Yakov's fingers worked at the single action mechanism of the revolver as Alexei took step after step in his direction. Alexei had nearly closed half the distance between them when the revolver fired and again tore into the boy's chest.

The riflemen were so stunned by the spectacle that they all simply stared dumbfounded and afraid, making no attempt to assist their commander as Yakov gathered his courage and fired one last time. Alexei's body stiffened and his eyes rolled upward before his body finally collapsed to the floor.

Nervously, Yakov walked forward, gun at the ready, as his shaking hand gingerly checked the boy for a pulse and then blew out a breath he had been holding when he couldn't find a heartbeat.

"Listen to me," Yakov said between gulps of air, "I want no one to speak of this. No one will believe it and it will look like a sign of weakness and failure if word of this gets out. Do you all understand?"

The riflemen all nodded.

"Good. Everyone out, now!" Yakov ordered and the riflemen quickly complied. Yakov stared at the body of the boy for another moment before he collapsed to his knees just as Vladimir came running down the steps. Quickly Vladimir lifted Yakov to his feet and assisted his superior up and out of the cellar while hollering for medical assistance.

Alexei's body lay face down with his abdomen draped over his sister while his head lay to one side on the floor as the accumulated blood of his family continued to flow and pooled all around him. Then, the open wounds in his body began to fill with the blood of his family…

…and Alexei gasped.

Chapter 16

"I guess we can start with the police officer," I said to Igor, who sat behind his bar on an elevated barstool while Chris poured the coffee Sasha had prepared while we were conducting our business in the back rooms.

Igor considered the question and then shook his head, "It is better to start at the beginning." he said, rubbing his face as Chris set a cup of coffee down in front of the man. Igor thanked him, took the sugar bowl, and dumped nearly a quarter of the contents into his large mug. I must have had a stunned look on my face regarding the coffee to sugar ratio because Igor suddenly became self-conscious about it.

"Sasha is an excellent cook, but he likes his coffee much stronger than I can take it."

Neither Chris nor I said anything as we held our cups without sipping. Igor looked between us as if waiting for one of us to try the brew, in order to see if he was right, but after a few seconds he set his cup down and placed his hands on the bar's countertop to begin his story. "When the Soviet Union fell, all of its acquired territories reverted back to being responsible for themselves, at least to some degree. Most were already in a dire state of poverty, and it was only the influx of Soviet financing that kept the commerce flowing and the people employed. In the case of Nazran, that had meant the government jobs, sponsored by the Soviet Empire in the various oil fields were going to go away."

"Why would the new government want to shut down an oil field? Chris asked. "I would think that would be something to hang on to indefinitely.

"Unless the oil field wasn't producing?" I volunteered.

Igor shook his head, "No, the fields were fine, but the location of the fields were too far from the refineries to make production worthwhile especially in this new capitalistic society. Technically, Russia had no claim over the territory anymore, and they felt there were better ways to get more oil as it was needed. In fact the oil drilled from the ground in Nazran was used primarily to support factories, troops and other military installations here, as opposed to supporting areas outside of Ingushetia. Oil was shipped out and the refined gasoline, along with other supplies, were shipped back in return, per the old communist method. Now, the cost of shipping the oil in and out became prohibitive so the government simply abandoned the operation."

"I'm surprised no one jumped at the opportunity," Chris noted.

Igor shrugged, "Some did, but the clash between the rebel Chechens and Ingush, against the new government in 2004, made everyone think twice about setting up a base of operations here. The rebels had killed some high-ranking officials, leaving what I believe you Americans call a 'power vacuum' in their wake."

"So who took control?

"At first, no one knew," Igor offered, "but when people started disappearing everyone thought the government had reverted back to the old Soviet system, and the KGB were the ones given the task of controlling the city."

"Disappearing?" I said, feigning ignorance.

"There was a constant military presence supporting a small group of what we thought were civilians. These men came and looked over our town, along with its oil fields, and then were never seen again. Soon after that people started disappearing. Sometimes the ruins of a body would turn up, but for the most part the people who vanished were gone without a trace, very similar to the way the KGB used to take people away for "re-education" back in the days of the U.S.S.R."

I listened as Igor spoke and watched as the man's eyes began to glisten, while he seemed to be recounting his first hand

163

memories of the experience. "Eventually the strain and fear grew to the point that in 2008 there were an number of violent protests against the government, but despite the belief that the government would restrain itself with the world watching, the protestors were met with a military response."

Igor paused to wipe at his eyes, "I'm sorry. I lost my share of friends during that time."

Both Chris and I nodded in silent understanding and let Igor compose himself. Once he had control again he continued, "It wasn't anything overt, but people began to grasp that it wasn't the government that was the cause of our fear. This time it was worse, because no one knew who to watch out for. Someone, or some group, was controlling the police, the utilities, the import of goods and labor, and no one had any idea who it was. More protests erupted against the government, but nothing changed and eventually people either just left the city or lost their will to resist. Now they just continue on, living day by day until they are either called upon to be a part of whatever is coming or until they too become one of the vanished."

I screwed up my face, "Whatever is coming? What does that mean?"

Igor shook his head again, "Mostly rumors. Some say that this new group is gearing up to reopen the oil field. Others say they are prospectors in search of coal and will need workers once they find it. Things like that."

"What do you think?" Chris asked.

The expression on Igor's face dropped and became very sad. "I think this town is a graveyard, and the people in it already dead on the inside. The only hope for them, and likely the only thing they have that keeps them going day after day, is the illusion that something is coming to breathe new life into them. They see that parasite Dimitri Lagos and his army of thugs throwing money around in the nightclubs, they see the way the wealthy young

164

people come from all over Russia to feed their erotic pleasures, and they have turned to selling those wealthy children drugs, providing them with prostitution or other vices, just for the ability of continuing their lives while they wait.

The mention of Dimitri Lagos made me stiffen and the involuntary response wasn't lost on Igor.

"Ah," he exclaimed, "I see you know of Mr. Lagos?"

"You could say that," I said as cryptically as I could.

Igor looked nervous, "And you are a friend of his?" I think I managed to keep my poker face intact, but Chris chortled a laugh and said, "Not exactly."

Igor looked suspiciously from Chris and then to me as silence filled the shop.

"What can you tell us about Dimitri Lagos?" I asked, unsure if I had changed the subject or added to Igor's paranoia.

Igor lifted his cup and swallowed a large mouthful of coffee. I drank from my cup as well without thinking and nearly gagged on the bitterness of the brew. From behind me I heard a hacking sound followed by a string of choked curses as Chris sputtered after having taken a drink of his own coffee. I turned to see him flailing around looking for a place to spit the remaining liquid in his mouth and then, finding no appropriate place to emit the offensive brew, he covered his mouth and made a move for the door. Igor raised a finger as if to say something to Chris, but Chris had arrived at the door only to find it locked.

Chris turned and slowly walked over to the bar, his cheeks distended from still holding coffee within them, and he pulled out his barstool and carefully sat down in it.

The look on Igor's face had turned from the stern and suspicious countenance he had held a mere moment ago and was now one of poorly concealed hilarity. Igor reached out, and while averting his eyes from Chris, slowly pushed the sugar across the countertop, he let it come to rest in front of Chris.

With a great effort and look of defeated disgust, Chris' cheeks deflated as he sickeningly swallowed the coffee he had been holding at bay. When finished swallowing he immediately grabbed the sugar and upturned it into his open mouth, letting the crystals stream in for about three full seconds, before righting it and returning the bowl to the bar. Chris chewed and swished the sweet contents around in his mouth for a moment and then swallowed again.

Without missing a beat and completely disavowing the scene he had just caused, Chris said, "Please continue."

Igor smiled warmly and extended a hand to Chris in a sarcastic gesture of congratulations. Chris accepted the gesture, shook Igor's hand and then took another shot from the sugar bottle.

"Dimitri Lagos," Igor continued, "is the first sign of new money that has come to Nazran since the Soviets. His nightclubs employ many people, but as I said, even more survive off the selling of drugs or prostitution to their patrons. He basically owns the police, who are in place more to clean up after the messes that surround the clubs' operations, than they are to enforce any laws. What you saw was probably exactly what I am talking about."

I thought about the ramifications of what I just heard. It sounded like we were going to be going up against not only Dimitri and his brood, but the police force of Nazran as well.

"How well fortified are the police here?"

Igor cocked an eyebrow at me, "What do you mean?"

"I mean are they well-funded? Well trained and armed? Where is their headquarters?"

Igor snorted, "They are as bad as the criminals they are supposed to apprehend. In 2009 a suicide bomber drove into the police headquarters and killed most of the legitimate force. Those who replaced them were, rumor has it, personally chosen by Dimitri Lagos. Still, they are not well funded and anything they have comes from Dimitri as opposed to the government.

"So they are going to be loyal to Dimitri as opposed to any body of authority." I sighed and with heavy sarcasm said, "Perfect, just perfect."

Igor studied me for a silent moment and then asked, "May I ask you a question?"

His words brought me out a daydream, "Of course."

"The police officer you saw ignoring the crime? When was this?"

I frowned, but saw no reason to lie or not answer, "Last night, why?"

Igor's frown never diminished, but he nodded and said, "Last night. Was there anything else you might have seen?"

I hesitated as the conversation came full circle, not sure whether I should mention the homeless vigilante that had shaken me up so much with his impossible stare.

Chris volunteered, "I saw a couple of working girls." He leaned in and whispered conspiratorially to Igor, "Sans pantolones."

Igor looked confused at Chris, as his French and Spanish mashup apparently being beyond comprehension, but he responded to the statement in any case, "Yes, the girls are abundant these days, but I meant something more..." Igor seemed to be searching for the right words, "...out of place."

"Like what?" I asked as best I could without giving anything away.

Igor searched my face for a moment, then closed his eyes and shook his head, "Never mind, it isn't important." He stood up from his barstool with his manner suddenly changing to one that was all business, "I am afraid that is all the information I have for you, so unless there is something else?"

I was surprised by the sudden bum's rush but I really didn't have any other specific questions that needed answering, so I stood as well and started to make my way around the bar to get our duffle bag of supplies. Igor watched me warily, but made no attempt to stop me other than stepping in front of me to politely lead us out. I collected our things and thanked Igor once more, just as the sound of the front door unlocking came from the other side of the shop. We all turned to see Sasha walking carefully through the entrance with the food he had gone to get us. There was something wrong with the expression in his eyes, and I could tell he was desperately trying to cover it up as he made his way over to the bar. Carefully he set the bags of food down and whispered something in Russian to Igor. I don't know why he bothered, it was pretty obvious that neither Chris nor I spoke the language. He could have shouted it to the mountaintops and we still wouldn't have a clue.

Igor picked up the bags of food and said, "I am sorry my friends, but something has just happened that requires my attention. Feel free to take this food with you, along with my apologies for being an improper host."

"If there is anything else we might need?"

Igor quickly handed me a business card with only a telephone number typed across the surface, "You have but to call me."

Igor placed the bags of food into Chris' empty hands, and before we could object he had escorted us to the front door of the shop, which Sasha had left open. Chris said his thanks and was ready to walk through the door, but first I grabbed Igor by the loose fabric of his shirt, and in the same motion proceeded to force him through the opening first. The small round man stumbled a couple of steps onto the pavement outside, but other than the offended expression on his face, nothing else happened. No shots rang out and no ambush occurred. So I waited a moment more, before I stepped outside as well, carefully scanning the area.

Chris followed me, and as I turned back to Igor I could tell that the man was furious. I couldn't tell if it was because of the way

168

I had manhandled him, or the fact that I thought he might have betrayed us in some way. As I waited, expecting a torrent of curses to be rained down upon me, his irate expression melted into one more of resigned understanding as he said, "Again, my apologies. You have only to call me if you need anything else. *Dos vidaniyah.*"

With that he stepped back inside his shop, closing the door behind us and locking it. We heard the sound of the door's tumblers latching, and with nothing left to do but stare at the door, Chris asked, "What the hell was that all about?"

I stared for another second, before becoming somewhat self-conscious from just standing there out in the open and replied, "I wasn't sure and I thought he, or maybe Sasha, had betrayed us somehow but," my voice trailed off.

"So? Back to the hotel?" Chris asked.

"You want to walk through this town carrying a bag of guns, explosives and electronics on your back?" I asked.

Chris shook his head and made a gesture with the food in his hands, "My hands are full, thank you."

As if on cue, a car engine turned over and I looked to see that a long four-door vehicle which had been parked by the curb was pulling into the road. As it drifted slowly in our direction I tensed, but the car silently coasted to a stop a few feet away from us and the driver-side window lowered.

The driver called out to us, "Mr. Tonichev said you would be needing a ride." The trunk popped open as he spoke, but the driver made no attempt to climb out of his seat. "Put your things in the back, and I will take you wherever you need to go."

Chris asked me, "We doing this?"

"Any better ideas?" I responded.

"No, not really," Chris chuckled as he opened the rear passenger door and moved inside, while I put the duffle bag in the trunk and then joined him.

169

"So," the driver asked, "where are we going?"

I gave the driver the name of our hotel and turned to Chris, "What's in the bag Chris? I'm starving."

Chapter 17

"You know, it would be ridiculously simple to blow your head completely off your neck right now," Chris' voice resonated through the Bluetooth receiver in my ear.

"Thanks for that tidbit of comforting info," I replied, "now is there any chance you could keep your mind on the job at hand?"

It had been nearly six hours since we had made it back to our hotel, inventoried our new equipment and came up with a tentative plan for the evening. Now Chris was on the roof of our hotel and looking through the telescopic sight of his new Dragunov sniper rifle covering my movement, while I worked my way down the street toward Dimitri's nightclub.

"Ah, I'm just verbally admiring how well the scope on this rifle zooms in on you," he said, and the thought that the gun was aimed at the back of my head sent a chill down my spine. "It also makes everything seem brighter than it really is, some top-notch optics at work here," Chris said with admiration.

"It's only as good as the guy pulling the trigger," I teased.

There was a short silence before Chris asked, "So, you're worried?"

"Very," I confirmed, still joking.

Chris sighed audibly, "Yeah, you probably should be. I mean, it's not like I have ever shot this thing before. Or had a chance to sight it in."

I stopped walking as what Chris was saying registered in my head. I hadn't been worried because I knew that Chris was extremely competent with a long-range rifle. It was something he had excelled at before he... well, before Alpha saved his life by bringing him into our world. "And I don't know what the wind patterns might be as they pass through the buildings and alleys," Chris continued.

I inclined my head without directly looking at the roof of

our hotel. It was far less than a thousand yards, but just as definitely over five hundred. Chris had told me that he had made longer shots with less accurate rifles and his confidence had reassured me. Now he was shooting holes in his own abilities and doubt was beginning to take refuge in my mind.

"Um...Chris?"

"And I have a hangnail on my index finger that stings like the dickens," Chris hadn't stopped talking.

"Okay, cut it out. I'm sorry."

Chris laughed, but grew serious once he calmed down, "Look, I'm confident that I can pretty much my hit target with the first shot, but this is still an untested weapon in my hands. It may take me a shot or two before I start getting pin-point accurate with this thing."

"Meaning?"

"Meaning that you are going to need to remember to watch out for your own ass, at least until I get a couple of shots off and have a modicum of feeling for this thing. I can be your eyes in the sky, but as I was trying to tell you before you left all in a rush to get down there, you are going to be on your own in the very beginning."

I'd be lying if I said I hadn't, on at least some level, already known this. Hearing Chris speak it out loud did raise my anxiety level a bit more than I needed, but the reminder put me slightly on edge, and it was probably a good thing.

The basics of tonight's plan was to get inside Dimitri's circle at the club. Dimitri would have a literal horde of his people with him, and I'm not sure what I intended to do other than look for an opportunity. What opportunity? I didn't know. I'd just have to be ready to react as soon as I saw it.

I was armed with a minimum of weapons, most of which were supposed to elude detection from the metal detector. My handgun was a Glock, and even though it was made mostly from a

172

polymer, as opposed to metal, the ammunition would set off any detectors. As a result, and to my regret, I had to hide the gun just inside the opening of an alleyway adjacent to the row of nightclubs and hoped none of the city's homeless would accidentally discover it. All I had on me, after hiding my gun, was one of ColdSteel's Nightshade knives that are made of a fiberglass-reinforced plastic, and I had it neatly sheathed in my lower back with a set of 'brass knuckles' that were also made from a space-age plastic, as opposed to actual brass. The pseudo-blade at my back was a Karambit style knife like the one Chris preferred. The wickedly curved and pointed blade is a particularly gruesome weapon, as it is designed for maximum efficiency in opening throats and disemboweling its intended targets. Normally the non metal version of the knife was used for advanced training as opposed to actual combat, because the blade on the knife, while very pointed, is not steel and has no edge for cutting. Still, the extra hard nature of the space age plastic made it a very effective stabbing and ripping tool that would have to do. Think of it like a large cat's claw that could still open you up when used with enough force.

The "knuckles" were made of Lexan and I was able to stow them in my pants without causing any unusual bulges or an impairment to my natural gait. Don't ask me exactly where I had them stored, but let's just say it's a place that a male bouncer usually is reluctant to grab when doing a cursory frisk... and at least Lexan didn't get cold like metal would.

The evening's early birds had already made it inside, and now a sizable line was forming on the sidewalk as the crowd began stretching onto the street, just as they had done every other night. I shifted around the outskirts of the line and the crowd, and tried to mentally place all of Dimitri's security people, who were standing out in their all-black commando gear. I also tried to pay attention to the way the crowd moved, just in case there were any people who also seemed out of place. I had a feeling that there were some

173

of Dimitri's people, dressed as the club goers, mixed in with the crowd as an extra measure of security.

Once the music had begun to play the party attitude from inside the club almost immediately spilled outside to the revelers in the street, just as Chris and I had seen from the previous night's recon. The entire crowd began to bounce up and down in time with the bass line of the music, as it boomed through the outdoor speakers, while people raised bottles of champagne or some other liquor over their heads and attempted to bounce and drink simultaneously.

I pushed my way into the crowd as young men in designer suits flapped their arms while young women in provocative evening wear waggled and bounced along with the guys. I had made it to about the middle of the scrum pile when I heard something in my ear that I knew was Chris trying to talk to me. Unfortunately, the noise of the people and the music made for a surrounding volume so loud that I couldn't make out what he was saying. I turned toward the street to look for the headlights of Dimitri's caravan, but saw only darkness before I felt someone's hand dip into my back pocket.

My initial reaction was that of a pickpocket alert, but when I felt an assertive squeeze followed by a second hand sliding its way into my other pocket I realized it wasn't my wallet that was in danger. I turned to find myself looking down into a pair of the largest eyes I had ever seen on any person. I kid you not, the woman was like a Disney cartoon, but for some reason it had a nice effect on her face, giving her an extra, extra cute appearance. The cuteness of her face was completely in contrast to the way she was dressed, which was so sheer and revealing that I couldn't help but wonder if she were cold.

She tilted her head and looked up at me with those too cute to be real eyes and smiled, "Hi."

She was so short and petite that I had to look twice to make sure I was looking at a grown woman as opposed to a child. Eventually it was only the size of her bosom, and the way she was flaunting it, that made me guess she was old enough to be groping me in such a manner. I admit it wasn't the best form of age identification, but I suddenly wasn't thinking with my head as much as another part of me.

"Hi," I responded stupidly, and had no idea if I could even be heard over the cacophony that enveloped us.

She stood on her tip toes and barely made it to my shoulder as she half-yelled something in Russian, but ended in what sounded like the name, "Maya."

I looked around and noticed that there wasn't anyone paying particular attention to us, so I said in English, "Hello Maya, I'm Steve."

Her eyes widened even more, which I hadn't thought possible, and in nearly perfect English with only a trace of accent said, "You're American?"

Again I heard the sound of Chris talking to me through the earpiece, but couldn't make out what he was saying as I nodded to Maya my confirmation that I was indeed an American.

Maya said something else to me but it was a garbled jumble of words lost in the sound of the crowd and I just smiled and shrugged my shoulders at her to convey my lack of understanding.

It was then I saw the illumination of the headlights from the first of Dimitri's vehicles as it came around a corner and headed toward the club.

"I said," Maya was doing that standing on her toes and screaming into my ear thing again, "are you here alone?"

I didn't look at her as I nodded my head absently. At that moment I wasn't really listening to her anymore, and if she'd asked me if I rode here on a cow I would have responded the same way. Realizing my mistake I quickly turned back to her and was going to excuse myself when she surprised me.

"My friends and I are going to get inside when Mr. Lagos arrives. You want to party with us?"

I blinked at her and then looked around at the younger, better dressed and apparently wealthier men bouncing around us like rhythmic rabbits. She wanted me to join her over all of them? I like to think of myself as a decent looking guy, but... well, you know that statement about something too good to be true? She did say the word "party", which was a relatively common term for a working girl to call her services, but the look on her face didn't have the predatory personality that call girls typically have when soliciting their "John's."

I opened my mouth to say something, then thought better of it and just nodded my head excitedly at the idea. My reaction was, for the most part, feigned. After all, I was here looking for Lei and any seduction act this little girl thought she could pull on me was pure amateur hour, compared to what Lei could do. Still, it didn't take much acting to give her the impression that I was interested. Maya returned my sentiment with equal enthusiasm and began to lead me through the crowd to where, I presumed, her friends were waiting.

Maya seemed to know where she was going as she led me out into the middle of the crowd. It was incredibly difficult to see through the throng of party goers, but when I was able to distinguish my position I could see that we were about to exit the main crush of the crowd and move into a space on the street that would leave me exposed as Dimitri exited his car. Not a good thing as Dimitri knew my face. I turned to the street and saw all three of Dimitri's vehicles had parked along the curb and the door to Dimitri's Rolls Royce open.

I began looking around for a place to shield me from view, but found nothing but the wall of the nightclub behind me, and a perfect line-of-sight to the parked vehicles in front. Maya was looking at me, her expression having lost some of its bubble factor and been replaced by a wariness. She must have noticed my change in demeanor, and I had expected her to break away from me. Instead she moved in closer and ran her fingers down the front of my shirt and whispered a breathy, "What's wrong?"

I could see Dimitri's head as he ducked to clear the doorframe of the vehicle, and heard a crackle in my ear as Chris was invariably trying to warn me to get to cover. I made the only decision I could, and tried to remember everything Lei had ever taught me about what she called the 'thrall', and focused all my attention on Maya. Inside I felt stupid, as I really didn't know what I was doing, but I bent down and encircled one arm around Maya's waist in a quick and powerful, yet tender embrace. I stood back up to my full height, lifting Maya off her feet with her body pressing tightly into mine in a very intimate manner. She let out a little yelp which could be surprise, pleasure or fright, as my free hand gently caressed and cupped one side of her face, forcing her attention to remain completely on me while I was looking deeply into her eyes and holding her gaze.

Her eyes were wide with what I thought was a mixture of excitement, joy, fear and then I felt the connection that Lei had described to me countless times before. I could feel the conflict in her as Maya's body reacted in a need to pull me closer, while her head fought to push me away. Lei had told me about this internal struggle, and how she overwhelmed her "victims" resistance when they would go through the same internal fight. There is a primitive part of the brain and the body will always want what is being offered. It didn't matter if you were young or old, beautiful or ugly, fat or thin, or any combination of the attractants that serve to possess and impose one's attraction toward another. All that matters, to a certain part of our person, is that we know what we want instinctively and it's within our nature to take advantage when such is offered.

That isn't to say women have different "buttons" to push in

177

these matters, but if you tap into the right part of any brain, then there would be no resistance. Men only needed a proper attitude to be displayed in order to go completely monkey-brained. I hadn't believed it and had asked Lei, if that were true, then why go through the whole production and overt display of her over-the-top sex Goddess body and face? She had smiled, and replied that it made everything that much easier and that sometimes the hard part is getting noticed in the first place. But Lei had told me that for women it was different, because the animal brain in women still reverts back to a time when finding a mate was about looking for the biggest, baddest and most powerful man in the cave, so that she could get a proper hunter, provider and protector for her and her offspring. I honestly didn't know how to tap into my inner caveman, but Maya hadn't started screaming for help yet, so I took it as a positive sign. I stepped forward and gently pinned her back, feet still aloft, to the wall of the club. This left the back of my head to the cars, which is what I wanted, and I leaned in closer to her with the threat of a kiss. Initially she had placed one hand on my chest, resisting my advance as her eyes narrowed and turned into a frown, but when I brought my lips within millimeters of hers, feeling the warmth of her rapid, excited breaths flow over my face, I could feel her resistance and her strength ebb, as her hand's pressure slackened so it merely rested on my chest while I gently ran my lips over hers. It was more a caress of the lips than a kiss, but I could feel the first pass send a shiver through her body. I slid the second caress at a slower pace over her lips and I felt her free arm move around my neck in response. On the third pass her legs slid up mine, before wrapping around my hips, trying to pull me more tightly against her body. She squeezed her legs and pulled with her arms to try to press our lips together, but I held her fast, and only made the lightest contact with my lips on hers, which pulled a slight breathy moan out of her.

In the background I was aware that the crowd had begun

cheering, presumably as Dimitri had fully exited the vehicle, but I found it harder and harder to concentrate on what was going on around me as the seduction I was putting on Maya progressed. Finally, with her body straining and quivering for me to relent, I pressed forward and kissed her passionately. She let out a deep moan into my mouth before returning the kiss with an even greater intensity. The hand she had placed on my chest slid under one of my arms and intertwined with the arm already around my neck while my hands slid over the sheer fabric of her party dress, massaging whatever exposed skin they could find. I could feel her giving in to the seduction as her breath pushed into my lungs. The soft, wet warmth of her mouth and the action of her tongue became insistent as our kiss grew even more passionate. I noticed that there was a strange buzzing around one of my ears, but it was too minor to be any kind of distraction, and Maya's hips began rising up and down my body, which instinctively reacted to the pleasure I was experiencing.

The buzzing at my ear was growing more insistent, and it took all my effort to remove one hand from the amazingly smooth, soft skin it had found on the curve of Maya's upper leg to swat at whatever it was. Maya never broke the kiss but managed to find my loose hand and guided it back, this time beneath the strap of the thong she was wearing to find the full flesh of one buttock. My hand nearly encased her entire cheek and I felt the smooth texture of her perfect skin as my fingers squeezed possessively and assisted her body in its up and down rhythms as her hips slid over the length of me.

That background noise, which had been little more than a hum before, was growing louder, although no more distinguishable, but a part of my mind was telling me something was wrong. I didn't want to break contact with Maya, but a part of me needed to know what was happening. I gently extended my neck in order to break the kiss, but as Maya sensed what I was going to do she grabbed the hair on the back of my head and pulled herself along with my retreat. Her legs cinched tighter around my hips and she arched her back to allow me to feel her breasts and hard nipples as they gently slid over my chest, no longer just quietly pressing firmly against me, but now actively tantilizing me.

I swooned at her response and felt my legs begin to wobble as Maya shifted her small frame, and I found myself moving along with her and completely oblivious of the crowd that was around us, when something struck a part of the wall just to the left of our heads. The impact must have been immense, as tiny pieces of brick and dust covered the left side of my face and stung my cheek. Distracted, I turned toward the impact and saw a softball sized indentation in the brick wall about three feet away from where our heads had been. I frowned, confused because it looked like a bullethole, but there hadn't been the sound of gunfire. I turned my head a little more to see that the crowd hadn't noticed the cause of the indentation nor the spectacle that Maya and I were putting on. I could hear Dimitri's voice addressing the crowd as my ability to hear returned to normal, when Maya shifted her mouth to my ear that was free of the Bluetooth device.

Why had I been wearing a Bluetooth? I shook my head and tried to clear my thoughts. I knew where I was. I knew what was happening around me. But I couldn't remember what I was supposed to do. I felt the warmth of Lei's body against mine as she lowered her feet from around me, and set them back on the ground while she worked her mouth away from my ear and down to my neck. I chuckled as Lei gently bit a particularly ticklish spot that she had found when...

Wait... Lei...?

I was here to get Lei back...

But if I was here for Lei, then who was kissing my neck? My head jolted back and my hands pushed Lei away from me and held her at arms distance. No not Lei. Maya. She had said her name was Maya.

Maya looked at me more startled and confused than upset, and opened her mouth to say something when the voice in my ear exploded.

"Wake up you asshole!" Chris was literally screaming at me through the Bluetooth. The crowd was parting, some were running away from something that was happening on the street. The music was still blaring but no one was dancing any more as all eyes were trained on something, no not something, someone in the street. I looked back to the girl and saw that Maya had lost all interest in me and was also fixated on whatever was happening. I leaned over and placed one hand on the wall to steady myself. Why was I so disorientated? I hadn't ever felt like this since the first time Lei and I had...

Realization hit me like a ton of bricks and my mind jolted back to one hundred percent clarity.

"Oh, son of a bitch!!!" I exclaimed as I pulled the polypropylene Karambit from its sheath at my back. At the sound of my voice Maya spun back to me and her eyes momentarily went wide with surprise, before they narrowed and a loud hiss came from her throat as her face contorted into a mask of rage.

Bad move. If she had cried for help she would have had plenty of people turn to assist. Instead her decision to stand up to me went unnoticed as my fist crashed into her jaw. Little as she was, her body flew back a greater distance than I had expected, before falling in a heap to the pavement unconscious.

I looked to the crowd and a few of the partygoers had turned to see Maya hit the pavement, but they were already in full retreat mode from something else that had them way too scared for their own safety and no one felt the need to assist some random girl.

Chris' voice in my ear sounded desperate, "Everything's blown! Go for your gun now! I'll cover you!"

It was then, that one unmistakable voice rose above the hum of the crowd and the music, which was still coming from the exterior speakers. The voice spoke with such authority and clarity that it could not be ignored.

"*YBENTE ERO!*" Dimitri Lagos screamed, "KILL HIM!"

Chapter 18

5 minutes earlier

"What the hell?!" Chris had said out loud when he watched Steve get friendly with one of the locals. He shifted the rifle and saw that the door to Dimitri's car had been opened and the old man was climbing out. Understanding that Steve was using the girl for cover, Chris chuckled into the headset, "Oh, very James Bond of you, but Lei is going to kick your ass when I tell her about this."

Chris kept the crosshairs on Steve for a moment longer but, as the entanglement Steve was in grew in erotic intensity, he uncomfortably returned to scanning the crowd for any sign of Lei or Pha.

"Okay, you officially have made me ill," Chris mumbled into the microphone, "don't get too into your role."

Chris swiveled the rifle toward Dimitri's Rolls Royce and saw the old vampire standing on the vehicle's step and facing the crowd. The music and general sounds coming from the crowd were too loud for Chris to make out what Dimitri was saying, so he just watched and centered the crosshairs of the riflescope on Dimitri's temple. Chris felt his finger tighten on the trigger and had to will himself to relax it up and away, lest he accidental discharge the weapon. Chris thought about how easy it would be to put an end to Dimitri. Just a simple exhale and squeeze and the man's head would literally burst like a ripe watermelon as the large caliber, high velocity round exploded in and through his head. If it weren't for their need to retrieve Lei and Pha he'd be able to put an end to this right now.

Chris indulged his idle thoughts of killing the leader of the Russian vampire collective for another moment before he saw Dimitri's head jolt to one side and look toward the street. Chris could see several other faces do the same as the crowd's attention turned away from Dimitri and toward something that must have been happening on the other side of the cars and crowd. Chris gently turned the rifle to see people jolting quickly away from where they were standing and moving quickly toward the curb in front of the club.

Then Chris saw bodies lying in disarray and unmoving in the middle of the street, but whether they were unconscious or dead he couldn't tell. There was no blood or signs of violence, but the sheer number of them gave the scene such a frightening sense that Chris could feel it to his core. Chris continued to pan the rifle as more and more bodies accumulated on the pavement, but now Chris could tell that these bodies were clad all in black suits, shirts and pants identifying them as Dimitri's security people. Chris scanned each of the bodies until his crosshairs finally fell on a pair of boots belonging to the one person still standing in the center of the fallen bodies.

The figure was a man, maybe just over six feet tall, wearing black boots, jeans and a long "hoodie" style of over-shirt that resembled something more akin to what a monk would wear as opposed to a sweatshirt that an athlete or modern youth might wear. The hood was up over his head and had enough fabric to drape loosely over the man's face and encase his features in shadow. Chris studied the man, who without any weapons in his hands, seemed rather non-threatening and unimpressive. However, a distinguishing feature that stood out from the rest of the man's appearance was the messenger bag the man had slung over one shoulder, and it had the appearance of having been made from some exotic leather or hide.

All eyes shifted between Dimitri and the figure, who remained motionless under Dimitri's gaze.

Chris quickly shifted the rifle back over to Steve, who looked almost as though he were literally having sex with the girl he had pinned to the wall and was apparently completely oblivious to what was happening a few yards away.

"Jesus man!" Chris screamed into the microphone, "something's happening out there! Snap out of it already."

Chris was moving the rifle back to Dimitri when one of his security people stepped forward and pointed his finger at the figure in what Chris could only guess was a kind of "Who are you?!" gesture.

Chris moved the rifle onto the hooded figure, who responded by very slowly and deliberately raising an arm to pull back the hood from his head. Although he didn't know him, Chris recognized the man's face before the hood had cleared his head. It was the homeless man that had taken on Dimitri's goons from the other night, but he was now clean, shaved and looked far, far younger than he had while he was in his homeless attire.

Chris looked back to Steve, and was surprised to see him still locked with the young woman, but now there seemed to be something wrong with his legs. They were buckling, like he was losing the strength to stand while his body was swaying and in danger of falling over, as if lost in vertigo. Chris frowned at the scene, and despite appearances to the contrary, it suddenly seemed as though his best friend was in danger.

It took a limp-limbed drop of one of Steve's arms to his side while to girl held on tightly for realization to dawn on Chris, and he flipped the rifle's safety off. Quickly he tried to calculate the slight breeze as it passed over his cheek and set the crosshairs on a spot of the brick wall four feet to the left of Steve's head. Chris prayed the sights were true, at least to the point that they would not send the shot wide right and he gently squeezed the trigger. The silencer swallowed most of the report from the shot and Chris watched as brick exploded less than three feet from Steve's head. Tiny pieces of the brick burst out in all directions, some of which hit the pair in the face and as a single unit they ducked, jerking away from the multiple impacts from the brick shards.

"Wake up dude!" Chris shouted into the microphone, "kick that bitch in the nuts and get moving! She's putting Lei's vampire boner-whammy on you!"

Chris watched as Steve shook his head and gently pushed the girl back.

"C'mon!' Chris was yelling into the night air, "Wake up you asshole!"

Initially the girl looked surprised, but then she had her attention caught by the commotion on the street. Chris, having seen the bullet's strike inches away from his aiming point dialed in the correction on the rifle's telescopic sight by turning the micro adjustable wheels of the scope so his next shot would fly true.

Chris called out to the night and into the Bluetooth microphone, "Everything's blown! Go for your gun now! I'll cover you!" and he trained the crosshairs back on Dimitri who was gaping wide-eyed at the figure in the street. Chris watched as Dimitri's face contorted with rage and, although Chris didn't hear the next words that came out of Dimitri's mouth, he could both understand and feel the power in them.

"KILL HIM!!!"

Men dressed in the black clothes of Dimitri's security team immediately jumped into motion. Chris saw the homeless man dip one hand into that old and odd-looking messenger bag at his side, before flicking his hand out again. At the crest of the maneuver the man opened his hand and a plume of powder or ash was sent billowing into a cloud in front of him. Initially Chris thought it was to blind the attackers, but watched in shocked surprise, as the first vampire to come in contact with the cloud began screaming and clutching madly at his face, with his exposed flesh instantly erupting into blisters.

The homeless man shifted his position, and Chris could see a glint of reflected light near the man's side as he pulled out an enormous knife, rushed forward and began carving his way

186

through Dimitri's men.

At the first sign of blood the crowd panicked and people began to run in every direction, but despite the ferocity and speed the "homeless guy" was using to cut down his opponents, Chris could clearly tell that he was avoiding the general crowd and was deliberately focused on Dimitri's people.

Chris shifted the scope and saw the girl that Steve had been getting busy with was lying unconscious on the ground a few feet away from him. Unfortunately, Steve still looked to be in a daze. Shifting the scope slightly back to the crowd, Chris could see some of Dimitri's men who had held back from the initial charge looking at the girl, and then turning to Steve.

"Uh oh," Chris whispered to himself before calling into the microphone, "Steve, time to move!"

Steve didn't move. He just kept looking around as if trying to figure out where he was and why. Chris saw three security men start moving in on Steve, violently pushing the panicked party goers from the crowd out of the way, as they came for him.

Chris yelled into the microphone, "Go man, go!"

That command seemed to click as Steve hesitated only a microsecond to tap his earphone before breaking into a sprint toward the alley where he had stashed his sidearm. The three security men followed hot on his heels and Chris could see Steve pull the polypropylene "knife" from where he had sheathed it at his lower back as Steve's words came over the earpiece in a weak-sounding tone.

"How many are following me?"

Chris aimed the scope to see the security men sprint after Steve.

"Three," Chris paused, "one sec..."

Waiting for the trio to move into an opening in the crowd, Chris held his breath and led the sight ahead of the security man in the rear of the sprinting trio. If he could take that guy out with a

187

silenced shot then the other two might not realize they just lost a man, which would give Steve an advantage on the street. Chris squeezed down on the trigger and the rifle fired the suppressed shot with only a mild clapping sound. Once Chris had recovered from the recoil, he could see that only two of the security men continued to run after Steve.

"Make that two," Chris said with a smile in his words.

Steve called back with no sign that he was winded from his run so far, "Nice shooting Annie Oakley."

"I always pictured myself more a Buffalo Bill. And you're welcome."

"Okay Buffalo Bill, can you take the other two?"

"Hold on," Chris didn't like the angle he had to work with, as Steve made his way into the alley. Still he held his breath, led his target and squeezed the trigger. The high caliber round flew straight and true, but impacted the ground behind the remaining pair and one of the men heard the noise, turning to see what had happened. He didn't necessarily see the crater the bullet had created, but did see the unmoving body of his friend lying twisted on the concrete with a portion of his head missing. The man nearly skidded to a halt before ducking into a doorway to take cover. Chris knew he had no shot at the man as long as he remained behind the cover of the solid brick doorway, but he put two more shots into the brick as the man tried to call out to the remaining pursuer.

"Got one pinned down," Chris reported, "but I can't keep him there and take out the last guy, too.

Steve understood, "Okay, I got it. Do you know if these guys are armed?"

"They aren't running with guns in their hands, but that doesn't mean they're unarmed," Chris answered.

"Okay," Steve seemed back in full control of his faculties, "let me know if you lose the one you have pinned down."

"Check," was all Chris said and he turned his attention back to the brick doorway.

Chapter 19

Chris was better with his new rifle than I had thought he'd be, but I could hear the footsteps of the remaining member of the security force still chasing me and closing the distance between us rapidly.

The alley was only about thirty yards away at this point, but I knew I couldn't risk going for the gun once I made the turn. I felt the handle of the Karambit in my hand and slowed my run. At the last moment I spun, whipping the point of the blade at my adversary's throat. He was good, using his forearm to block the stab and his forward momentum to slam his shoulder into me hard enough to send us both sprawling.

I felt a pain in my hip as I hit the pavement, but managed to roll away and get some distance between us before springing to my feet. As I stood I saw the man reach for something at his back, and fearing that it would be a handgun he was reaching for, I immediately charged forward. The polypropylene blade wouldn't cut deeply through his jacket, but the point was sharp and extremely strong for stabbing, so I raised the weapon like a fencing sword thrust it at the man's face. His arms instantly both came away from whatever he had been reaching for and grabbed my arm. I felt a jerk, and then had the sensation of my body being aloft, before I realized the man had flipped me up and away from him. I rolled with the impact as I hit the pavement and jumped to my feet, but held off on another charging attack as I saw the man drew a real, steel-bladed knife from the sheath at his back.

I should have been more disconcerted at the sight of the knife, but all I felt was relief that it wasn't a gun. The man made one quick look past me to check where his comrades might be and seemed to shrug off the fact that they were nowhere to be seen before he began calmly stalking toward me. I waited, watching as he flipped his knife into an underhanded grip so the back of the blade was against his forearm. He said something in Russian that sounded like a taunt to a seriously inferior opponent, but I had no idea nor care of what it might have been.

I opened my mouth as if to reply, then thrust the point of my weapon at his face. He leaned back and out of the way while slapping my arm aside with his free hand. I barely had time to retreat, before I watched the man's body spin closer to me followed by his blade as it slashed across my abdomen from right to left cutting deeply. I reacted just in time to avoid the edged weapon as it came back around, this time threatening to cut even deeper from left to right in a upward diagonal slice meant to totally disembowel me.

I managed to dodge out of the way as my opponent used the momentum from the second cut to reach for and grab the fabric of my shirt with his free hand before thrusting the point of the blade toward my heart in a killing stroke. Realizing what he was intending I raised my arm and blocked the stab with my free hand, holding it immobile with what, to him, must have seemed an unnervingly effortlessness move.

I might not be a vampire like the legendary creatures of horror fantasy, but I am strong. The man's eyes went wide with surprise, thinking that his first cuts had eviscerated me. His eyes darted down seeing only the shredded fabric of my shirt and revealing the razor thin slices through the outer lining of the Kevlar body armor that I had was wearing.

I could feel him try to pull his knife hand free but, with my strength restraining him, it was little more effort for me than what it might have been like to hold onto a small child. I responded by squeezing down more tightly on his wrist, and I knew the squeeze had to hurt. Squeezing bones together like that hurts, a lot. The man was tough and only gritted his teeth before letting go of my shoulder with his left hand and darting at me with his thumb as a move to gouge up at my eyes.

191

I'll admit it was a good plan, and I had thought he'd either try for my eyes or my throat as he attempted to break my hold on him, so I was already bringing my knife into play as his hand reached for me. The point of the polypropylene blade pierced straight through his attacking wrist with little resistance and left his whole extremity in pain as it became momentarily impaled on my weapon. I quickly wrenched downward and pulled the blade free before thrusting it back up and into the man's throat, shattering his Adam's Apple and piercing his windpipe. The man dropped his knife as instinct forced him, too late, to be defensive and try to protect his throat, but I was holding his other wrist tightly and used my leverage to spin the man's body toward the alley opening. I pulled the knife free and felt the hot explosion of the man's blood splatter my face, before kicking his chest hard enough to send him flying into the darkened, shadowy spaces of the alley's interior.

Darkness enveloped him and I couldn't see where he landed, but I did hear the crash as his body fell among the various detritus strewn about the interior of the alley. I listened for any sounds of the man trying to rise, but I was met with only silence coming from the alley, as the sounds coming from the commotion still happening in front of the nightclub drowned out the end of the fight.

Chapter 20

"What's happening, Chris?" I called out.

Chris winded voice came back, "Ah, you're okay. I thought he gutted you."

"Body by Kevlar," I said confidently. "Are you on the move?"

"Yeah," Chris' replied, "on my way to you."

"What about the guy you had pinned down?"

"He stuck his head out when you started fighting his buddy."

"You took him out?"

"No, but the shrapnel from the bricks I exploded near his face made him think twice about staying there. I think he went for reinforcements, so I thought I had better change positions."

I nodded to myself because it was the right thing to do, just in case they figured out where his shooting position had been located. Chris continued, "I grabbed as much of our gear as I could and ditched the rifle as soon as I got outside. Hopefully we'll be able to collect it later."

That worried me, "Is it somewhere secure?"

"Secure enough as long as the sun's down, but in the light of day it will be far less so. Are you clear?"

"Clear for the moment, but I have to move as well." I walked into the alley and squinted, looking into the shadows until I found the man I had killed lying in a heap near an overturned garbage can. His blood, too pinkish to be human, was pooling into a puddle as it dripped from his cooling body.

"Did you get your gun?" Chris asked.

I turned away from the body and moved to the spot where I had covered the pistol, which was still firmly lodged in its Kydex holster and lying under a box I had topped with several random pieces of garbage. I pulled the Glock from its holster and quickly checked it over before re-holstering it and fastening the holster back onto my belt. "I'm moving to the far end of the alley and will try to get a look at what's happening."

"Gotcha," Chris said, and he was no longer breathing as hard as before. "I'm at my new location and armed with a red-dot scope on an MP7. I'm within range to cover you, but without a silencer it's going to be loud. Let me know when you're going to stick your head out and I'll make sure the coast is clear."

I quickly and quietly shuffled toward the far end of the alley as I whispered, "What happened out there?"

I heard Chris chuckle before asking, "Do you want to know what happened before or after that girl put Lei's 'boner whammy' on you?"

I knew what Chris meant. The girl had been one of Dimitri's people and she, like my wife Lei, was a seductress, accomplished at exploiting lust by inducing a kind of hypnosis. Lei was a master at the process but, after the first time, she could never make it work on me again. Alpha liked to say it was because we "fell in love, at first sight, with one another..." so either Lei's heart wasn't in it to enthrall me, or that I had just as much effect on her as she did on me. I had always arrogantly thought that I was simply immune to the process. I used to watch how quickly Lei could capture either a man or woman with her skills, so the idea she couldn't do it to me had given me the false sense of confidence that had almost been my undoing.

"I guess I should thank you for shooting at my head earlier?"

Chris chuckled again, "First, yes you should. And second, I put the bullet three feet away from you, so don't start whining about that."

As I reached the far side of the alley and slowly peered around the corner I could see the remnants of Dimitri's people picking up the bodies of their dead. Some had severed or mangled

194

limbs, while others were simply sporting hideous gashes which had eventually killed them, but with less efficiency. There were no club-goers still on the street, but several were lying, either unconscious or dead, near the entrance to the club.

I ducked back around, "Chris, what the hell happened here." The seriousness in my voice was sufficient to bring a halt to the expected ball-busting I was sure to receive about being put under another woman's Thrall.

"Our friend from the other night showed up and set Dimitri off."

"Which friend?"

"The homeless guy who offed Dimitri's goons, including your buddy Mikhail."

"What?"

"Yeah man, total weirdness too. Used some kind of voodoo on Dimitri's people and then started carving them up with a knife so wicked looking it should be in Alpha's collection."

I shook my head as the words hit me. Who the hell was this guy?

Chris kept talking, "I saw Dimitri mouth some words, but couldn't make out what they were. Did you catch any of it while you were playing grab ass with the bad guys?"

I let out a sigh... there was the end of my reprieve. "So considerate of you to be so sensitive to my compromised condition that you would allow me some space, yet it only lasted a whole sixty seconds."

"Serves you right Mr. Grabby-hands."

I ignored Chris' immaturity, "Am I clear to move?"

"That's your new name, you know. Mr. Grabby-hands."

I really tried to ignore Chris' immaturity, "Chris?"

To my relief Chris got back to business, "Well, 'clear' is a relative term. Dimitri is still there yelling orders, and a couple of his guards are pinning down our newest friend somewhere across the street. The idiots finally figured out not to run at him, and instead are shooting at him from a distance."

"Any sign of Lei?"

"No."

I thought for a moment and then asked, "So everyone's attention is on the man across the street."

"Yep, they..." Chris went silent before complaining, "Wait! Uh, wait... Wait-a-damn-minute. What are you thinking? It may be chaos, but everyone has their hair up and guns out. One glance in your direction and your Swiss-cheese."

"How much you want to bet he had his car reinforced?"

"Dimitri? Bullet-proof?" Chris said incredulously, then asked, "So what?"

"All I have to do is get him in the car and drive off."

"Ooooooooooh, is that all?" Chris' sarcasm was so thick it was positively cloying.

"You don't like my plan?"

"That's not a plan."

I laughed, "Besides, I have you to watch my back."

Chris didn't answer.

"How many are still out there?" I asked him.

Chris counted, "Eight, plus Dimitri."

I sighed, "All right, cover me!"

I slid around the corner of the alley and began shifting from cover to cover, as I closed the distance between Dimitri and myself. Shots were being fired regularly from various handguns, as Dimitri's people kept 'Mr. Homeless' pinned down and I hoped the noise would prevent anyone from hearing me. I made it to within thirty feet of Dimitri, who was standing behind his car shouting orders, positioned with the rear passenger door open so that, presumably, he could jump inside if things continued to worsen. His security force had regrouped itself and they were advancing on their supposed victim, as I quietly watched, waiting for my

196

opportunity. I decided to wait until the shooting started again, and then, under the covering sounds of the gunshots, I would spring forward and tackle Dimitri, driving him headfirst into the backseat of his own car so that I could disappear with him quickly before anyone realized what had happened. Hopefully my surprise attack would leave him vulnerable just long enough for me to knock him out and get the door closed behind me. After that I wouldn't have to worry about the security forces getting to me as I would be inside the locked and armored vehicle. I could just crawl into the front seat and drive off. Of course, that presumed the keys were in the ignition, otherwise I was going to have to try to hotwire a Rolls Royce. It wouldn't be my first hotwire, but frankly I didn't even know if it was possible to hotwire a Rolls Royce. If it all went to hell there was Chris, my backup, who would be picking off the remaining security people as they tried for a potential rescue and I made good my retreat, in theory anyway.

As each of the remaining security team inched their way toward their target and away from me, with their guns at the ready. I was balanced on the balls of my feet and ready to spring at the first shot, like a sprinter waiting for the starting gun. Then a sound to the side broke my focus, as the doors to the club opened.

I heard the terror in Chris' voice whisper into my ear, "Oh my God," as more men poured out of the club, all of them carrying AK-47 assault rifles. The last man to exit had to duck his head in order to fit under the door's frame, and he was glaring menacingly across the street at the source of the conflict.

I was completely out in the open with no cover, nowhere to run and so I did the worst thing possible and just froze in place. Nicholas pointed his finger and opened his mouth to give his men orders when he suddenly froze, too. Slowly his eyes moved to the side, and his head followed them, ending up looking in my direction. Our eyes met and for a few microseconds neither of us moved as we just took in the sight of each other. Suddenly rage contorted Nicholas' face and his eyes went wild with fury as he began to twist his body towards me. I came out of my stupor and moved faster as I raised my Glock, firing repeatedly at Nicholas, and the nightclub's doorway in general, while bolting across the street. Surprisingly the giant was able to alter his movements with such quickness that he managed to duck, and was back inside the club for cover. Some of his men weren't so lucky.

The security people must have taken my shots as a signal to open fire on our homeless friend, but it was Dimitri who realized something was wrong, turned to see me shooting back at the entrance to his club, and without any hesitation jumped into his vehicle and shut the door behind him, while my plan officially went to hell. I turned my attention to the security people who had been working their way toward our homeless buddy. As they realized that there was someone shooting at their backs, they scattered, diving for whatever cover they could find, and I ran past them toward the spot where Mr. Homeless had taken cover. Swinging my Glock from one side to the side, I managed to shoot down two of the retreating security people, before the my ammo clip was empty. As I released the empty clip I saw Mr. Homeless watching me as I made my way toward him. Turned out he was hiding behind a parked car, and realizing what I was about to do, he ducked to the side, as I made with a 'Dukes of Hazard' slide over the hood of the sedan, dropping into place next to him behind the car.

No sooner had I landed than I felt something roughly press across the front of my throat, and I realized the man had placed the edge of an enormous hunting knife at my throat. I froze as I felt the razor-sharp edge of the blade grip at the flesh over my throat and instinctively I knew that with the slightest flick of the wrist that blade could kill me.

I raised my empty Glock up, "Do we really have time for this?"

I had gambled that he, having seen me shooting down Dimitri's people, would realize that we were on the same side. After a moment, he glowered at me and lowered the blade. I nodded and finished popping a new clip into the Glock.

"So?" the man asked in a heavy Slavic accent, "I suppose you have plan?"

Chris' voice echoed in my ear, "Who was that?"

I answered, "Our homeless friend asked if I had a plan."

"Oh, well I'm guessing the answer is 'yes,' but I'm also equally sure that it's a terrible one."

I raised my eyebrows at the man and opened the front passenger door of the sedan. Climbing into the front seat I dropped under the steering wheel and ripped the wires from their housings. "Going to need a few uninterrupted moments please," I said into the earpiece loud enough for both the man next to me and Chris to hear as I began the hotwiring process. The car was an old Lincoln Continental that had been refurbished recently. I felt a pang of sadness for the owner, who would eventually find the vehicle riddled with bullets. I hoped there wouldn't also be two bodies bleeding out next to, or inside of, the car as well, as I finished stripping the wires with my teeth.

"Pass me your gun," the man said and held his hand out expectedly, as I turned away from my work to look at him in stunned surprise.

He arched one eyebrow and used my own words against me, "Do we really have time for this?"

I clenched my teeth and passed him my Glock. The man studied it for a half a second, rose and fired three shots before ducking back down. Return fire hit the sedan in a volley, some penetrating through the door over the top of me, as I worked on getting the car started. A felt a hot shock in my fingertips as the electrical connection was made, and the sedan coughed to life. The man smiled at me, then rose to fire again and I stuck my head up in

199

time to see Nicholas and the remaining men raise their AK-47's. My eyes widened in panic knowing there was no way to avoid the hail of bullets that would penetrate the car like tissue paper.

A single shot rang out from a distance and I could hear the man who it hit scream in agony, as someone else yelled, "*Chan'nep!*"

The homeless man ducked behind the vehicle, "Is the sniper yours?"

"Yep, get in!"

The man flung himself though the door and into the backseat, as I straightened in the driver's seat, put the car into drive, and slammed the gas pedal to the floor with the rear wheels doing a slight chirp before catching the road, and suddenly we were racing forward. I heard the sound of automatic fire and the rear windows exploded before it suddenly stopped. I guessed Chris had fired again and shot the gunman.

I rounded one corner then accelerated down one street before turning again at the next. Once I had gained some distance I checked the rear view mirror to see that we weren't being pursued, or at least not yet, and I yelled into Chris' earpiece, "Stay put, I'm going to circle around and get you!"

Chris answered, "Don't bother, they're still not sure where I am and I think I can clear out of here without being detected. Where do you want to meet up?"

I considered that for a moment and realized I was going to have to trust that Chris could handle himself.

"All right, we can meet at the..." I heard the door of the car open before I could finish talking, and my head swung around to see the homeless man jump from the car, roll to the sidewalk and run down an alley. I was about to hit the brakes when a pair of headlights suddenly appeared from around the corner behind me and accelerated toward the car.

I cursed, "Chris, I have a tail. I'm going to need to lose him first."

I only received static on the other end as Chris didn't answer.

I prayed that Chris could still hear me as I said, "We'll meet up at the Absinthe store."

It was the only, relatively friendly place I could think of, as I floored the gas pedal and felt the car blast forward.

A loud rattle sounded from the engine of the Lincoln as I pressed it for more speed. I suppose it was unreasonable of me to believe that the engine could have gone completely unscathed from the gunfire, but I had hoped it had enough left in it to get me away from whoever was pursuing me. I had barely finished the thought when a loud "PANG!" sounded, and the car lost all power as if someone had flicked an "off" switch.

I looked back, saw the headlights coming up fast and reached for my Glock, only to remember that I had given it to Mr. Homeless mere moments ago. With no other options I got out of the car and ran in the hope to find another shadowy alley to hide in before the car overtook me. The driver of the other vehicle had apparently spotted me as I heard the engine revving faster and louder as the oncoming car closed the distance between us.

Suddenly, gunshots from a familiar sounding weapon reverberated in the dark and the oncoming car swayed awkwardly to one side and then quickly tried to correct itself. If Dimitri Lagos had armored his personal vehicle, then he had apparently neglected doing the same for his subordinate's vehicles. I couldn't see what damage had been done by the shots, but heard tires skid and felt the concussion of the impact as the car careened off of a building, before rolling to a stop less than ten feet from me. I had stopped running when I heard the initial skid of the tires and I now turned to peer at the damage. Through the cracked windshield I could see that the driver was either unconscious or dead, as he lay in a bloody heap stretched over the steering wheel. Passenger doors creaked open and three men fumbled their way out of the wrecked vehicle as they tried to collect their wits and their bearings by quickly surveying the area. Realizing they were all still carrying weapons I backed away from them and was about to take off, when more gunfire erupted. Each of the three men twisted convulsively before falling to the ground and I saw my homeless friend walking casually toward the downed men as he pulled the clip from my Glock and checked to see how many rounds he had left before pushing it back in place. Walking nonchalantly past the bodies, the man strode up to me and held the weapon out to me, butt-first.

"A fine weapon," he said approvingly, "you have two rounds still in the clip."

I carefully accepted my gun and holstered it, saying "Thank you."

The man nodded to me, and I asked him, "So, who are you exactly?"

The man smiled, "That is a long story, and I think we had better get off this street before more men come looking for us."

It was my turn to nod, "Can you at least let me know your name?"

The man gave me a sideways look, but said, "Alexei."

"Alexei?" I asked, "That's it? Just, Alexei?"

The man's smiled widened even more, "For now, it is enough."

I rolled my eyes, "Fine then, Alexei. My name's Steve."

Alexei nodded at me, "Very well Steve, you have safe place for us to go?"

I nodded. I wasn't sure how the liquor store owner was going to react with my bringing a stranger to his shop, but what other choice did I have?

"Safe enough anyway. C'mon, it's a bit of a hike from here."

It took almost thirty minutes to get to the street where the liquor store was located, although it might have taken less time if I hadn't gotten us lost twice along the way. When the store was in sight Alexei, who had been following me pleasantly the entire time, even when I had clearly gotten us lost, suddenly stopped in his tracks and looked at the store. Realizing he wasn't on my heels anymore I stopped as well and looked back.

"What's wrong?"

"You are going there?" He pointed to the Absinthe store that was my destination.

I looked to the store and then back at Alexei, "Yes, why?"

Alexei's eyes widened jovially and a slight smile spread across his lips. He mumbled something under his breath and shook his head, in an ironic kind of way, before saying, "I should have asked where we were going."

Concerned I asked, "Is there a problem?"

Alexei chuckled, "Not at all, but I could have gotten us here faster."

I watched Alexei start to happily jog toward the store, and so I followed him, not understanding if his sudden jubilation was a result of knowing the owners or just having a preference for Absinthe. Alexei walked to the door, but stood to one side and gestured for me to ring the bell while wearing a foxlike, 'Cat-that-ate-the-Canary' grin on his face.

I frowned at him, but pressed one finger down on the ringer. After a moment of silence I heard Igor's voice over the speaker explode out at me in a language I couldn't understand, but felt sure that I and my entire lineage was being well cursed out.

Alexei covered his mouth with one hand in the apparent attempt to stifle a laugh as the verbal onslaught continued.

"Um, Igor?" I said as the man was forced to pause in order to take a breath, "mind if we come in?"

The response I received was louder and more enthusiastic cursing, this time the tirade was peppered with English swear words so I was able to catch a few insults involving my mother.

At the next pause Alexei called out, "Igor! Ycnokon'te cebr, moero apyra." (Calm yourself, my friend).

The sound of Igor's shouting suddenly stopped, and we stood in silence outside the shop. When Igor responded his voice was authoritative, but had a certain cautiousness about it as he asked, "Who is with you American?"

I opened my mouth to speak, but Alexei beat me to it, "Bbi ctonb bbinvtbi choba, yto bbi he npv hatete mov ronoc?" (Are you so drunk again that you don't recognize my voice?).

Silence.

This pause was much longer than before, but what ended it was the sound of locks turning and the door being cracked open as Igor peered out at me with one eye. The eye frowned deeply at me until Alexei shifted positions and came into view. The eye went wide and the door was flung open to reveal Igor standing, slack armed and gaping at Alexei. The semi-automatic shotgun he had been holding slipped from his hand, and he awkwardly took a step forward.

"You?" Igor said hesitantly as tears welled into his eyes. Alexei raised his hands and the two men stepped into an embrace that was evidently long overdue.

I watched them, wondering how the one contact I had in this entire country, much less this region of the world, could possibly have a common connection to this stranger, with whom we shared a common enemy.

Chapter 21

The two men let go of each other and stepped back smiling just as Chris came bolting around a corner, still a block away and at a full run. He had apparently ditched his weapons in favor of speed, and as soon as he saw us he began screaming and waving his arms in what I interpreted to be a "get inside" motion, but he was too far away for us to be able to hear what he was saying.

Sensing the obvious danger I lifted my Glock, with its two remaining rounds, as Alexei picked up Igor's shotgun from where the man had dropped it.

"Get inside Igor," Alexei commanded to the shop owner.

"Not a chance in hell," the small man responded then called out, "Sasha!"

Sasha appeared from behind the door, brandishing two very new Glock Model 20, Gen 4 15-shot 10mm semi-automatic handguns, and handed one to Igor, along with a few extra magazines.

Chris made it to the halfway point between us and the corner he had just rounded as Alexei and I began walking toward him. Seeing our intention Chris waved his hands even more vigorously and started screaming, "Get inside! Get inside!"

It was then that at least a dozen men came running around the same corner as Chris. All of them were apparently from Dimitri's security force, and were wearing various pistols and revolvers in their shoulder holsters, although they hadn't drawn their weapons. Perhaps their intent had been to take Chris alive? But there was no doubt that, as soon as they saw us armed and already putting up a defensive front, they would stop and draw on us.

Chris kept running, and to his credit, managed to maintain his distance without slowing. I stepped in front of the others, "Get ready," I said and behind me heard the distinct clatter of slides being ratcheted and cartridges being chambered as our the weapons were made ready and brought into firing position.

I was aiming down the sights of my Glock, past Chris but directly at the security man running closest to him when someone else came around the corner behind all the security men.

The sheer size of the man running after the initial gang chasing Chris made my eyes widen with shock. I turned to look behind me and saw that the others had registered him as well. Shock and fear covered their all of faces, all except Alexei whose eyes grew more intense at the figure in the distance.

I called out, "Get inside!" and turned to push the others through the doorway. Sasha didn't hesitate, but Igor and Alexei were mesmerized by the sight of the giant. I shoved Igor through the door and grabbed Alexei by the shoulder and began dragging him inside when another figure landed, and I mean landed as if he had dropped out of the sky, between Chris and the men chasing him. This figure was wearing familiar black leather, had skin as white as Italian marble and a long mane of pure white hair that fell to the middle of his back.

Alpha stood and faced the oncoming men who quickly pulled up short in their run as their hands flew to their weapons. Not a single man was able to get his gun out in time, before the giant figure running from behind crashed into them like a freight train. The sounds of bones breaking could be heard over the distance as William barreled through the highest concentration of the security force. Alpha surged forward as well, his strange knives drawn and glinting in what light the streets provided as blood, diluted pinkish vampire blood, erupted from the members of the security force and began to coat the street.

Chris had reached me by that time and was about to scream at me when he saw the look on my face and paused to turn and look for himself. At least four of the security team lay dead or bleeding out on the ground, while Alpha and William engaged the others.

"Oh!" Chris chortled, "when did they get here?" Chris didn't wait for an answer and instead drew his knife and turned to run back into the melee.

Confusion at seeing Chris pull his knife momentarily paralyzed me, until the realization that firing into the fracas would be too risky, with William and Alpha dodging in and out between multiple opponents. Chris had made the right call on selecting his knife, so I holstered my Glock and pulled fiberglass Karambit out of its sheath. As I stood I saw Alexei holding that giant Bowie knife in his hand as he looked at me and smiled.

I sighed, "Always the hard way," as Alexei and I both ran into the fray. As I charged in, my eyes locked on one of the men who had seen me coming. He had managed to draw his own knife and was ready to meet me head on. I crouched low in my run and then had to duck even lower, as a body of a different security man came flying at my head. At first I thought it was an attack, but the way the man's arms were flailing I realized that William had just tossed him aside like a rag doll. I rolled under the man as he sailed over me and came up with my dagger in my hand like a fencer's foil. I thrust the tip of the dagger forward toward the man's belly, but he retreated out of range in time for me to miss, then shifted his weight and lunged forward with a slashing motion aimed at my throat. I anticipated the strike, slid further forward and raised my left forearm to block his slash and hoped I had closed enough of the distance to block the man's wrist, as opposed to the edge of his blade. I felt that hard smack of bone on bone as the man's wrist hit my forearm, stopping his strike cold. Wisely he didn't try to overwhelm me or force the point to my throat, but instead tried to pull the blade back quickly in order to slice my forearm along the way. I knocked his knife away and then spun my body around and kicked out with my right leg, knocking both of his legs out from under him.

207

The security man fell flat on his back with his legs in the air as I continued the spin bringing the dagger straight down and into his chest over his heart. The sturdy design and pointed tip of the dagger forced its way between the ribs and slid directly into the man's heart. His whole body shuddered and he grabbed at my wrist, but I had already begun pulling my blade from his chest and I fell back before he could catch me in his wildly flailing death throes.

The man was dead before I could get to my feet and as I stood looking for another target, I noticed William holding one man aloft by the throat and squeezing the life out of him, while Alpha spun first to his left, slicing through one man's throat, and then reversed his spin to disembowel another. Chris was taunting two others who were trying to draw their side-arms, but kept having to abandon them in order to fend off the quick sweeping strikes of Chris' Karambit.

I started to make my way toward Chris when one of the men stepped back far enough to give himself a chance to draw his sidearm. I threw my Karambit at his head and it landed hard on the flat side of the handle, not penetrating, but the mass of the knife was enough to make a loud "crack" sound as it hit. The man grabbed at the side of his face and then turned to me. Unarmed, I ran toward him as he reached for his gun.

As I have said before, I'm very strong and fast, so when I leapt at the man his eyes widened with surprise as I sailed the twenty foot distance between us, driving the web between my thumb and index finger into his Adam's apple, shattering his hyoid bone and sending the bone fragments into his windpipe. The man initially staggered backward grasping at his throat, but then fell to the ground, writhing in pain while suffocating on his own blood.

I looked up to see Alexei engaging three of the men while moving at a speed that rivaled Alpha's. The man twisted, parried, lunged, ducked and countered with such fluidity that one could only think of a master swordsman, as opposed to someone who was just proficient with a knife. The more I watched him move the more I realized that this was exactly the case. I remembered reading how Jim Bowie had been an expert with the saber and he had designed his famous knife to be a practical fighting tool that was reminiscent of his prior weapon of choice. Before I could register what he had done Alexei had cut down his third attacker and used the momentum from that final strike in order to position himself within range of the two men Chris was facing. With two quick and powerful strokes Alexei took them out, too and faced a startled and awestruck Chris.

Of course, Chris being Chris, he broke the silence with an uneasy, "Um... yay team?" He held the palm of his free hand up, "Up top?"

Alexei turned and looked for any further threat, but by that time all of Dimitri's security forces were lying either dead or unconscious on the street. He looked back at Chris and then at his still raised hand, awaiting the "high-five."

"Um," Chris said nervously, "don't leave me hanging, bro."

Alexei looked back at me, his eyes a question.

I answered, "Alexei, meet Chris, my sniper."

"AH!" Alexei's face went from suspicion to elation as he stepped in, ignoring the raised hand and gave Chris an exuberant man-hug. Chris 'oof-ed' at the force of the hug and was smiling as Alexei stepped back. Not yet finished with Chris, Alexei grabbed Chris by the wrist and raised his free hand again. He then slapped the palm of Chris' hand, completing the "high-five" and saying with his deep accent, "I not leave you hanging...bro."

Alpha still held his knives at the ready, but his body language eased as he realized the fight was over, while William knelt over one of the security men and checked his neck for a pulse.

I walked over to Alpha as he sheathed his knives, "How'd

you find us?"

Alpha smirked, "There was a gun fight on the street in front of Dimitri's main businesses. It wasn't that difficult to figure out where you were, or that you might need a hand. Once we arrived, we saw Chris fleeing the scene with Dimitri's men in pursuit and followed."

"Why didn't you tell me you had arrived?" I asked not bothering to hide the frustration in my voice, "We could have formulated a much better plan with the four of us working together."

"William and I had our own leads to follow before we made contact with you," Alpha said with that annoyingly inscrutable tone he could pull off so well.

I knew better than to try to get him to talk about something he didn't want to talk about, so I just asked, "Any progress locating Lei?" I looked over at William and inclined my head at the man, "Or Pha?"

Alpha let out a breath of air in frustration, "No, despite our best efforts we are no closer to finding the girls."

Alexei and Chris walked over to us and I introduced everyone. "Alpha meet Alexei, Alexei this is Alpha."

Alexei smiled at me, "Only 'Alpha?'" but he then extended his hand to Alpha.

I rolled my eyes at the jibe and Alpha raise one white eyebrow in confusion over our inside joke, but accepted Alexei's hand warmly.

"So you are the Romanov that Dimitri is so worried about?"

At Alpha's words I saw Chris frown and look away as if a memory had been triggered but was having trouble coming to the surface.

A sound like a large animal snarling sounded behind us and all four of us spun to William who had risen to his immense full height and faced us with murderous intent. Actually, "us" wasn't exactly correct. William's entire focus was on Alexei.

Alexei instinctively lifted his knife, but went white with fear, "Boishe Moi!" Alexei whispered in apprehension, "His eyes! What is happening to his eyes?!"

William's eyes had gone blood red with no evidence of iris or pupil left within the orb. The condition was a holdover from the experiments Dr. Phineas Whelan had perpetrated on him back in the jungles of Bangkok that were intended to heighten William's already incredible physical abilities, as well as mold his mind with a kind of brainwashing technique in order to keep him under control. The experiments were funded by Dimitri Lagos, with the intent of turning William into a biological weapon in order to kill...

"Oh shit," I hissed as realization struck me, "Alexei we need to get you out of here now!"

Alpha turned to me, "What? Why?"

"You just identified Alexei as 'the Romanov,' the man who William was programmed to kill."

Chapter 22

Alpha sheathed his blades and stepped toward his oldest and dearest friend, his hands palm up in gentle supplication, but William's blood red eyes never wavered from Alexei. An image from earlier in the night flashed through my mind and I whispered, "Alexei, can you do that "smoke-thing" to William, like you did to those people back on the street in front of the nightclub?"

I could tell Alexei didn't want to make a sound, lest it trigger an attack from William, but he still answered, "Yes, but as it is, the ash will kill him."

I gritted my teeth and slowly turned my head away from William to look at Alexei, "Do you have anything else that will help?"

I could see Alexei's eyes dart around as he desperately thought, then they stopped and widened slightly, "I may have something, but if he attacks me before I am ready..."

As if on cue, William charged. Alpha braced himself and met William head on, but was batted to the side as if he weighed nothing. Alexei retreated as I ran toward William and dove at his legs. It was like being hit by two tree trunks in the ribs, but I had timed it right and William toppled face first to the pavement. I braced myself for him to land on me, but the giant was far more dexterous than I had expected, and he rolled over a shoulder, coming instantly back to his feet and using the momentum of the roll to propel himself at Alexei.

Alexei had dipped one hand into that messenger bag he wore at his side, but had to abandon whatever he had been reaching for as William charged him. With a quickness that my eyes could barely follow, Alexei had his knife in his hand and thrust it at William's throat. I was about to scream out, "Stop!" but William raised a forearm between his throat and the blade causing the knife to pass straight through his forearm and lodge itself between the two bones therein. If there was any pain, William gave no indication of it as he ripped his arm to the side, taking the blade with it and disarming Alexei in the process.

Wide-eyed with shock at the maneuver, Alexei tried to retreat, but William hadn't so much as hesitated as his arm was impaled, and he grabbed Alexei by the throat with his uninjured arm. Alexei was instantly and effortlessly lifted into the air, his legs kicking wildly as his hands desperately dug at the fingers that encircled his throat.

I staggered to my feet and was about to shoulder block William again, when Chris jumped on the giant's back.

With a ridiculous Hollywood-style karate cry of "Hi-yah!" Chris clapped his hands over both of William's ears. There was a sinister 'pop' at the impact, and William released Alexei from his grip and staggered as his equilibrium was sundered. I immediately grabbed William by his uninjured arm near the shoulder and wedged my body into the giant's side to lever him up and over, then slamming him bodily into the pavement. Alpha was at my side in an instant and held the arm with Alexei's blade still protruding from it. Blood began to trickle from William's ears indicating a rupture of the eardrums, which at any other time I would have taken as a bad sign. In this case, I doubted that we could have managed to keep William down if Chris had not so thoroughly shattered the man's equilibrium.

I looked up to see if Alexei was in any state to help and, to my surprise, he was already kneeling in front of William's face and covering his mouth and nose with one hand. A powdery mist plumed with every one of William's next few exhalations until I could feel the big man's body start to relax.

It likely took only a few seconds for William to go limp and then fall into unconsciousness, but it felt as if an eternity would pass before I felt it was safe enough to let go and back away from his limp form.

"He's going to be all right?" Alpha asked as he released William's arm to inspect the damage the protruding knife had done.

Alexei shook his head, "I have never used that much of the sedative before," he pressed two fingers into William's throat and considered what he felt, "his heart rate is as it should be, so I think he will be all right."

Alpha grew angry, "You think?"

Alexei looked up and directly at Alpha, his eyes meeting Alpha's fury head on and unwavering, "I'm sorry for your friend, but who is he to me other than another person wanting to see me dead?"

I spoke quietly in protest, "That's not really fair..."

Alexei turned to me as his face relaxed and looked sympathetic, "So you say, but that doesn't change the situation. I won't let your friend kill me because his circumstance is unfair."

Igor came running from the door of his shop, shotgun in hand, "Is everyone all right?"

Chris didn't answer Igor, speaking to the group as a whole instead, "We should probably keep Alex and "little Willie" separated for the time being. I don't want to have to deal with Willie waking up and going postal again."

I turned to Igor, "Think you can get your driver to come back and take Alexei somewhere safe?"

Igor looked as though he might protest, but a glance at Alexei stopped whatever protest he was going to make. "Of course."

I nodded, "Chris, you should go with him."

I was expecting a smart-ass remark and was surprised when Chris didn't offer one. Instead he simply regarded William's limp form and asked Alexei, "I should stay with William and make sure he recovers as best I can." He turned to Alexei, "What did you use to knock him out?"

Alexei looked to Chris before answering Chris' question

with a question, "You understand chemistry?"

"I'm a Doctor."

Alexei nodded, "The powder is a combination of ash, botanicals and spider venom, but when all is said and done, the result is the same as Chloral Hydrate and the body perceives it exactly the same way."

Chris looked shocked, "You have a natural compound that mimics Chloral Hydrate?"

Alexei didn't answer and instead moved his head close to William's chest to, apparently, listen to his breathing. "Is that a problem?" I asked.

Chris looked concerned, "No one really understands how Chloral Hydrate works to sedate people before surgery. If this is some kind of 'witches brew' I won't know how to reverse the effects, not that I have the reversal agents in any case."

Alexei reached into his bag and produced what looked like a plastic zip-bag filled with leaves.

"If his heart slows too much or his breathing loses rhythm, then place six leaves in his mouth. It would be better if he chewed them, but whether he holds them in his mouth or chews them, he shouldn't swallow the leaves, only the juice."

Chris took the bag, looked at the leaves and mused, "Coca leaves, interesting."

Alexei's eyes widened slightly with surprise and the man inclined his head in a respectful nod at Chris, "You know these leaves?"

Chris looked slightly flushed, "I experimented... in college... just looking to see what they'd do, you know?"

Everyone was silent while I frowned at Chris.

"What?" Chris asked before stating, "It's not like I was cooking up anything illegal... in the chemistry labs... after hours... for, you know... tuition..."

I rolled my eyes, my interest in Chris' alleged illicit past notwithstanding, "Alpha, can you take William somewhere safe?"

Alpha looked at me, "I take it your hotel is no longer an option?"

I shook my head, "Can't risk it. It's a death trap if Dimitri's people catch you there."

Alpha thought for a moment, "I think we can go back to the farm we stayed at before we entered the city. The family there was prepared to help us further if the need arose.

"Okay," I said, "take William there and wait for word from me."

Alpha looked at me, "You are not going with us, Detective?"

"So what's the plan?" Chris asked.

I sighed and shook my head, "I'm going to give one attempt at diplomacy."

"Wow!" Chris laughed, "now you want to talk to Dimitri? If that isn't the height of stupidity I don't know what is."

My response came out far more harsh than intended, "It seems clear to me that we are just bumbling around in this city and getting nowhere close to Lei and Pha."

Alexei regarded me with narrowed eyes, "Dimitri is holding people of yours?"

Alpha answered for me, "He has two of ours," he then pointed at William, "one is a child, his daughter."

A mixture of pain, anger, indignation and horror all spread across Alexei's face simultaneously, "Perhaps I should accompany you on this 'diplomatic' journey?"

I quickly shook my head, "I can't risk any harm coming to Dimitri until we have located the girls."

"I am not here for Dimitri or interested in his ridiculous grab for my family's former claim to the land he seeks. I am only here for the Wolf-killer."

"The Grand Duke? How do you...?" Chris' face was

216

contorted with thought as he peered at Alexei.

"Yes, the Wolf-killer," Alexei confirmed, "Grand Duke Nicholas Nickolaevich.

Chris' eyes went wide, "Nicko... Aha! You're Alexei Nickolaevich, aren't you?"

Recognition struck me at the mention of Alexei's full name, "Dimitri called you the Romanov?" I asked, "You're the son of Tsar Nicholas the second? Last Tsar of Russia?"

Alexei sighed and rolled one hand as if it would help the words come out faster, "And the true ruler of Russia, at least from a certain point of view." Alexei looked abashed, "I haven't been recognized in over eighty years, and now in only a couple hours, you identify me." Alexei sighed, "I must be getting old."

I shook my head, "I remember reading about you in world history class, when we were studying Rasputin. You were the Tsar's hemophiliac son who Rasputin managed to cure when no other doctor in Russia could, am I right?'

Alexei laughed, "Father Grigori didn't cure me, so much as recognize that what I suffered from wasn't hemophilia, even though my Mother's family had the hereditary trait that ran toward that condition."

"Rasputin knew you were like us?" Chris asked before melodramatically adding, "A vampire?"

Alexei nodded, "Rasputin held a great deal of knowledge that assisted in giving him the reputation as the 'Mad Monk.' One such bit of information was the knowledge of the existence of Dimitri's people, and the reality of what they truly were. When my mother initially brought me, as an infant, to Rasputin, the monk had seen the truth of my condition and became my physician and mentor years before what has been recorded in the history books.

"You knew Rasputin?" Chris said, awestruck. "Wow, that must have been something."

Alexei shrugged, "To the world he was either an angel or a

devil. A holy man and *Starets*, what you might call a "mystic" in English, or a madman with Machiavellian intentions for the ruling of Russia by influencing my father's decisions." Alexei's eyes drifted as if seeing a vision the rest of us were not privy to, "But to me he was simply a teacher and friend."

"This is all well and good, but can we take the conversation inside?" Igor asked and was clearly getting nervous.

I tended to agree with the man, "Okay, Alpha you take William and Chris back to the farmhouse. I'll contact you as soon as I can. Alexei..."

Alexei cut me off by raising one hand, "My friend, we may share a common enemy, but that does not make me your subordinate." His words were matter of fact and held no malice, but they also conveyed an air of certainty that brooked no compromise as he said, "I go where my own conscience takes me."

I frowned at Alexei, "You don't think it would be better if we worked together instead of potentially getting in each other's way?"

Alexei considered for a moment and then said, "I think I have ways of doing things that do not work well with others. Having said that, I feel we will find ourselves working in tandem regardless of our going separate ways for the time being."

I looked at Alpha, who seemed to be considering Alexei's words before turning to William and lifting his prone form off of the concrete with a heave.

I shrugged, "All right Alexei. I don't like this, but I can't force you to work alongside the rest of us." I turned to the rest of the group, "Are there any questions, or a need for clarity, from anyone before we split up?"

Silence reigned as everyone looked from one to another.

I turned back to Alexei and held out my hand, "Good hunting."

Alexei accepted my hand in his, "To you as well."

We were about to turn away from one another when Chris chimed up, "Oh! Wait! I have a question."

Alexei and I turned back to Chris.

"Do you know if that enormous penis on display in the Moscow sex museum 'Totchka G' is really Rasputin's?"

Chapter 23

Lei nudged the sleeping child lying next to her. "Wake up Pha, it's time we got out of here." Pha rubbed the sleep from her eyes and peered back at Lei, fear evident on her face. "Don't worry," Lei whispered, "we'll sneak out of here before any of those freaks ever know we're gone."

Lei had been formulating an escape plan ever since Nicholas had moved them into their new holding cell. His only mistake was in not blindfolding her before taking her out of the old location. En route, Lei had studied every aspect of the space within the warehouse that she could. It had taken her nearly two days to process the details of what she had seen, and now she was at a point where the beginnings of a plan had begun to take root. Assuming no drastic changes had been made since that time, Lei was convinced they had a chance to make it out of the building. Once outside, well, that was where the plan fell apart. Still, Lei believed that once they were outside she could hide herself and Pha from Dimitri's relatively mindless drones.

The problem was Nicholas.

The man seemed extremely capable and he would likely be the determining factor in the success or failure of her plan. She had thought of killing him, which was a possibility if she were fighting him one on one, but with a girl in tow and an unknown number of Dimitri's people in the warehouse, a physical confrontation wasn't a good idea. Instead, she had noticed that the warehouse had a very different energy, or attitude, about it when Nicholas was on location, as opposed to when he was absent, so it seemed that her best bet was to try to sense when Nicholas was away, before she made her move.

The high-energy bustling of people working outside her cell had diminished to such a degree that it even sounded lethargic, and that was her indication that Nicholas had left the building, so she set her plan into motion.

"Okay," Lei spoke softly to Pha, "once we're outside stay close to me, but if we get separated, then you run and keep running until your legs won't carry you anymore. You understand?"

Lei had expected Pha to cringe and cling to her, but life on the streets of Bangkok had, while not so much preparing her for this particular moment, taught her how to survive. A steely resolve morphed onto the formerly teary face, and the determination in her countenance was intense beyond anything a girl of nine years should ever be able to project. It took Lei momentarily aback, but then a smile creased her face as she recognized her own spirit within the child.

"That's my girl. Okay, do as I told you."

Pha nodded and began calling out in Thai to whoever might have been placed on guard, "Excuse me, we need more water please."

No sound came from the other side of the door as Lei and Pha waited. The seconds ticked by like minutes, and Lei was about to have Pha call out again when the sound of the locking mechanism unlatching resonated from the door. The door to the locked office space where they were being kept prisoners opened a crack, and a single frightening eye peered in.

At the first sound of the door unlocking Lei had let her body fall slack against the floor and she forced a tremble to shimmy through her whole body, as Pha cradled her head in her small lap.

Pha stroked her forehead as she looked up toward the door, "Please, we need some water or more food or something." Pha looked down at Lei with concern marking her every feature... just as Lei had instructed her to do. "Please, I don't know what's wrong with her."

Lei was mimicking the initial stages of what any of her kind began to go through when they hadn't taken in enough blood,

221

or in Lei's case the substitute that she and all of Alpha's community used in lieu of actual blood.

Instead of the usual armed guard, one of Nicholas' deprived people stared into the room and opened the door wider to consider the scene on the floor of the office space. Supposedly tasked with the wellbeing of the captives, the "guard" should have reacted by going for help or backup, but Nicholas kept those in the warehouse in a deprived state, barely nourished with enough blood to keep them from becoming little more than animals. Lei supposed that it was done intentionally to make the people of the warehouse more akin to guard dogs. A dangerous and ravenous collection of creatures that would ensure anyone imprisoned would either remain so, or be destroyed in the case of an escape attempt.

The "creature" was male, perhaps young although it was hard to tell as his skin had become pock-marked with the tell-tale blisters of moderate deprivation. He started to turn away and close the door, but froze in mid motion and seemed to scan the exterior of the warehouse as if searching for something.

That's right, Lei thought, *you remember what Nicholas did to the last person who threatened us.* Lei let out a slight moan and went even limper in Pha's hands. Pha, as instructed, let out a little cry of what was supposed to be panic and began whispering urgently to her as she cradled Lei's head.

The man at the door looked back into the room without making a sound.

Lei squinted through one eye to see the door open wider as she thought, "That's right, come in. You still have enough control to take some blood without killing us. They keep you so hungry that it is hard to think straight. Just a little blood from each of us and you will get your mind clear. Just a little from each, how could that hurt?"

When the man moved it happened with surprising speed. He shut the door and had a hand over Pha's mouth before Lei had even realized he had moved, Pha let out a small squeak in surprise and alarm, but then grabbed onto the man's wrist with both hands. Thinking Lei was unconscious, the man had ignored her. Lei bolted upright grabbing the man's head in her hands, before twisting sharply. There was no audible crack, but the man went limp and fell to the floor in a daze and Lei was immediately on top of him, entwining his arms and legs in her own. The dazed man tried to shake his head to recover from the trauma that, like a knockout punch in a boxing ring, had negatively stimulated the nerve clusters in his neck. Lei released one of the man's wrists and thrust a sharpened thumbnail deep into the hollow of his throat. The man's eyes went wide with shock and horror at the mortal wound and his body convulsed under Lei as she pulled her thumb free. The man tried to punch her off with his free hand, but Lei re-established her grip on that wrist and once again pinned the man to the floor before latching down on with her mouth over the neck wound. Lei didn't drink the blood, it wouldn't fortify her in any case, but she forced any and all blood that pumped from the wound back down in to the man's windpipe both suffocating and silencing him as he thrashed beneath her.

Lei rode his bucking form, as the man sputtered and gurgled pink blood from his mouth, while his body tried to clear his lungs of his own body fluids, which were drowning him. Yet the more the wound bled, the more his lungs filled with his own blood.

Finally, the man's body relaxed as he passed out from lack of oxygen and Lei slowly removed herself from the unconscious form. Raspy, horrible sounds were coming from the dying man as Lei looked to Pha. The girl's expression was a mixture of surprise and uncertainty as she stared at Lei.

"I'm sorry you had to see that," Lei said as she wiped at her mouth, "are you all right?"

Pha looked down at the man who let out a rattling sigh as

his life faded away, then she looked up to Lei and asked in heavily accented English, "He would kill me, wouldn't he?"

Lei nodded her head and Pha turned back to consider the corpse on the floor, as something shifted in her demeanor and her former resolve returned to her small face. Pha stood and made a show of brushing off the sweat clothes she wore for dust that wasn't there.

"I'd like to go now," Pha said, in a manner that was so matter-of-fact it sounded less like a request and more like a command.

Lei smiled and knelt, hugging the girl, which was returned by Pha, along with light reassuring pats on Lei's back. "Okay honey, time to go," Lei said as she moved to the door with Pha following to stand behind her..

She cracked the door open and peered out, seeing a few of Dimitri's people shambling around, moving or unpacking boxes, with the majority of the commotion happening near another of the office spaces. In fact, most of the attention was focused in that particular area, which gave Lei and Pha the opportunity they needed.

"Let's go, stay close."

Lei held Pha's hand as the two of them stayed in the shadows along the wall, while they worked their way around to a stack of shipping containers for additional cover. Lei led Pha to a hiding spot behind the containers as she checked to see if anyone had noticed them. No one looked in their direction, nor seemed the wiser as to what they were doing. The next part of Lei's plan was a little trickier. She had noticed a fork lift near one of the roll-up doors, but had never heard the engine ignite for the entire time she and Pha had been held here. The previous room that she and Pha had been stashed in held a box on the wall with several hanging sets of keys. Those keys had been retrieved, used and replaced by Dimitri's people many times while she and Pha had been locked in the room, yet one single set had never been touched. The keys looked similar to car keys, but were shorter and thicker than one would expect from the keys to an automobile. Lei guessed that these were to the forklift, so her idea was to sneak back into their previous jail cell, retrieve the keys, get to the forklift and drive right through the roll-up door and out of the warehouse. Obviously, they were going to draw a significant amount of attention the moment they started the forklift engine, but Lei hoped that there would be enough confusion to buy them the precious seconds they would need to get outside and lose any pursuers that might follow.

Pha tapped Lei on the shoulder in a warning as one of Dimitri's people, a small woman lazily wandered past in front of the crates. Lei could see the mottled flesh on her face and the glaze in her eyes that was indicative of the woman's need for blood. Lei could only imagine the amount of pain the woman was in, and her hatred for Dimitri twisted in her core, wondering how he could leave his own people in such a state.

Once the woman had walked far enough away, Lei squeezed Pha's hand and the two made it to the next hiding place Lei had chosen, stopping right beside the machine. The forklift was smaller than Lei had remembered, but the controls seemed as though they were more "layman–friendly" than most heavy machinery. A simple gear shift of "drive, neutral and reverse" was evident, along with the steering wheel. Foot pedals, which were likely to be the accelerator and brake, sat reassuringly where they would be expected. There were some other levers that probably controlled the lift, but Lei wasn't really interested in that. She didn't see a choke switch, which was also a good thing as some equipment needed to be started with the choke in a specific position, and she had no idea how this particular machine was supposed to be started other than with the turn of a key. Every moment she had to spend trying to figure out how to make the forklift run would be time for Dimitri's people to catch up with her,

225

so the more she could mentally note about its operation, the better.

Satisfied that she knew as much as she was going to concerning the forklift, Lei turned back to the open area of the warehouse. Pha was still at her side and doing surprisingly well, considering her young age, and that the nature of what they were doing demanded that she be quiet.

Lei said, "Okay, I want you to get into the forklift and lie on the floor. I'm going to get the keys and come right back."

Panic flashed momentarily in the girl's eyes, but it didn't last, as she wordlessly climbed up and into the operator's cabin, staying low and being as quiet as possible, before coming to a rest on the metallic floor.

Lei cautiously closed the door of the lift, making as little sound as possible and then sprinted for the far wall. Her footfalls were soft, silent, and drowned out by the ambient noise of the work being accomplished inside the warehouse, as she finally came to rest in the shadows next to the office where they had previously been held.

She tried the door. It was unlocked and the knob turned easily in her hand. She didn't open the door fully right away, as much as just cracking it open, in order to listen for the sound of anyone inside. She couldn't see or hear anything, and there was no way of knowing for sure if there was anyone inside until she actually went in and cleared the room. With a quick breath Lei bolted upright, the fingers of her dominant hand with their reinforced nails hooked in a claw shape, ready to rip at any enemy who stood in her way, and she swung the door wide open.

The room was empty and relief washed over Lei as she quickly bounded to the wall where the various sets of keys were hung. She removed the set she had guessed were the forklift keys and was about to leave when she noticed something through the window on the wall opposite from where she had just entered. She had known the window was there, but while she and Pha were

226

captive in this room the lights had always been out and the adjoining space that the window overlooked had been dark as well. Now the entire space was aglow in the white/blue shine of multiple fluorescent lamps, revealing the entire contents of the adjoining space.

It was filled with makeshift military cots, hundreds of them, spread out in perfect and precise rows. The sheer immensity of the adjoining warehouse was so vast it must be some kind of an airplane hangar, yet it was filled with cots instead of aircraft, and on every cot was a motionless, supine body. People of varying ages, sizes and ethnicities, all in an apparently induced sleep, each with a single intravenous line extending from the back of their hand. Lei froze, as the nightmare of Pharmanetics and the lab where Dr. Whelan had harvested the blood from her abducted people came back to her with such clarity it was like being slapped in the face. But the more she stared at the scene, the more she realized this was something different. Before, the purpose of the lab was to siphon off the blood of her people for the creation of medicine that was to net the corporation billions, if not trillions of dollars in anti-bacterial and anti-viral medications. Here, there was no indication that the people in the cots were being drained of their blood and Lei recognized that the back-of-the-hand location where the I.V. needle had been inserted was meant to deliver whatever the I.V. bag held into the sleeping people, as opposed to taking anything from them.

Lei tried to make sense of the whole scene, when the sight of a young Asian woman lying still in a cot reminded her of the younger, smaller Pha lying on the floor of a forklift, awaiting for her return. Lei pulled her eyes away from the scene at the same moment that the door of the office space opened, and she dropped to the floor in a crouch, as whoever entered the office space turned to switch on the lights.

The man was one of Dimitri's armed, black clad security

people, looked to be in his middle ages and reeked of cigarettes. Casually, he moved from the door to the desk as Lei scurried silently across the floor and into position. She rose to her full height and placed one hand over the man's mouth while encircling her opposite arm around the man's throat. The shock of the attack buckled the man's legs and he fell immediately to the floor, before his brain caught up to what was happening. He struggled against Lei, but by that time she had shifted her leverage on the man and had his body trapped against hers as she applied the "sleeper" hold. It only took a couple of seconds before the cutting off of the blood supply to the brain rendered the man unconscious, and Lei quickly rolled him off of her and returned to the door. Killing the man might be noisy, as some people just don't go quietly into death, so she had let go of the man to allow his blood supply to restore itself. Eventually this would rejuvenate the man, but he would be dazed and confused for a minute or two before he fully regained his faculties, which was all she was going to need to make good her escape.

Lei peered through the door, checking to see if anyone was looking in her direction, and seeing none, bolted straight for the forklift.

Chapter 24

Lei almost made it before a shrill, screeching sound erupted from the far side of the warehouse. Lei looked back as she ran, seeing every head turn toward her to raise their own ghastly sounding cry of alarm, before breaking into a sprint right for her. Lei reached the forklift and opened the door to find the operator's cabin empty. Pha had been lying on the floor of the forklift when she had left her, but now there was no sign of the girl. Panic shot through Lei, but as she moved to the driver's seat she realized that the zombie-like people in the warehouse had only raised an alarm when she had left the office and not because they had seen the child wandering around. Lei tried the first of the three keys on the ring and it fit snugly into the keyhole ignition. She turned the key and there was a slight cough in the engine before it turned over, rumbling into life.

Quickly she shifted from neutral into drive and slammed the gas pedal to the floor, just as the first of Dimitri's emaciated people reached her. The forklift lurched forward, slamming into the bodies of two zombie-like creatures sending them flying wetly away from the blades of the forklift. Lei was thrust back and forth as well, from the initial momentum of the lift's movement, before she got herself and the lift under control.

She turned the steering wheel and aimed the forklift at the rolling doors as more of Dimitri's people jumped onto the back of the machine. Hands reached for her through the lift mechanisms and Lei had to lean forward over the steering wheel to keep them from being grabbed by her hair or clothes, as the roll up door loomed closer and closer.

With an explosion of screeching, straining metal the forklift punched straight through the aluminum door scraping all but one of Dimitri's zombies off the speeding machine. The remaining zombie had his shifted position and held on, until the roll up door's housing mechanism failed, sending the door crashing to the ground like an anchor and ripping away from where it had been installed. The shearing force of the thin metal cleaved straight through the remaining zombie, practically cutting the man in half as blood erupted from his massive wound to saturate the exposed rear engine of the lift.

Sparks flew up from the engine and a foul smelling smoke, the by-product of the sizzling, burning zombie's blood on the engine, wafted into Lei's nostrils while the forklift's motor coughed and finally stalled. Lei desperately turned the key in the ignition and tried pressing down on the gas pedal, but the engine refused to turn over. A quick look over her shoulder and she realized she had no more time to do anything but run.

Clamoring out of the forklift just as the first of Dimitri's people reached for her, Lei spun, grabbed the arm that was extended toward her and snapped the bones at the elbow joint. The poor wretch was far too emaciated and, despite his height, likely weighed the only as much as Lei did. She reversed her momentum, flipping the man onto his back and delivered a kick like a footballer's punt to the side of the man's face.

More arms encircled her from behind and lifted her up and off of the ground, but Lei thrust her head back, hoping to slam the back of her skull into the nose of her attacker. Pain shot through the point of impact on her head as she felt her attacker's nasal bones and cartilage crunch like a potato chip and a high-pitched cry of pain erupted while the grip around her body went slack. Lei spun, found her target and thrust a clawed hand into the her attacker's throat. She could feel her reinforced fingernails sink deeply into soft flesh as she tightened her grip, before they struck something more solid, like cartilage or bone. With a violent, wrenching twist and pull movement Lei tore the flesh away from the body of her attacker opening his carotid arteries and twin fountains of pink blood sprayed everywhere.

More of Dimitri's people came for her. Dozens were emerging from the warehouse and Lei recognized the impossibility of standing her ground. She turned to run but was hit hard from the side, the shock of the impact knocked the wind from her body as she tumbled to the ground. The arms released her and Lei rolled away before righting herself in a crouched position. Lei's eyes focused on her latest assailant was surprised to see that she faced a woman. Long luxurious brown hair flowed over a sensually curved, yet striated and powerful physique clad in the balck combat gear of the security team. The beautiful face that mockingly smiled back at her was in no way emaciated, nor had she any of the signs of the decrepitude that the other figures in the warehouse sported.

"Well hello there," the security woman spoke in a chiding voice, "I'm Andi."

Lei's eyes shot to the side to see more of the emaciated people arrive, but then shuffle to a stop as they looked nervously at Andi. Were they afraid of her the same way they were afraid of Nicholas?

Lei met the woman's mocking glare and smiled pleasantly, "Hello Andi, I'm Lei."

"You're pretty good," Andi began to circle to the left and Lei matched her by circling the opposite way to the right, "please don't tell me you are going to disappoint me and surrender?"

"Well, since you'd be so disappointed, no," Lei inclined her head toward the others who were watching them, "they aren't going to help you?"

Andi chuckled, "Oh no, you're my prey now."

"Prey?" Lei burst out with a laugh, which wiped the smile off of Andi's face, replaced by anger as Lei noted, "someone has been watching too many movies."

The woman moved, no, writhed to the side like a serpent while Lei crouched and matched her movements step for step.

"You should think about the child," Andi said confidently, but Lei was sure it was a bluff. If they had Pha they would have dangled the girl in front of her like a worm on a hook in order to get her to surrender.

"Nice try, but I'm guessing she is so far away by now that you'll never be able to find her." And now, Lei thought, time for a little distraction trick of her own, "I wonder what Nicholas will say when he learned she escaped from right under your nose?"

Without warning Andi lunged forward so quickly that Lei stumbled as she backed away from the oncoming assault, barely avoiding the knife that appeared from nowhere in the woman's hand. Lei rolled and came to her feet just as the woman thrust the tip of the blade toward her face in a fencer's lunge. It was a powerful attack, but left the woman unbalanced on her forward leg, and Lei took advantage by sliding under the attack and slashed her nails at the woman's torso. Lei's nails struck, but succeeded in tearing only fabric as the woman spun with the strike and slashed a counterstrike down the length of Lei's arm. Lei had seen the attack coming but was too slow to act before the blade parted the flesh over the back of her forearm from the elbow to her wrist.

Pain shot through Lei's arm, but the slash was shallow, despite the copious blood that initially flowed from the elongated wound, and no arteries or nerves had been severed. Lei kicked at the woman, forcing her to retreat a few paces enabling Lei to momentarily distance herself from her assailant.

The woman smiled at Lei and licked the blood from the blade before looking down and seeing the horizontal tears in her outfit. The smile was replaced by confusionas she looked to Lei's hands.

"That was interesting," the woman stated indifferently.

Lei smiled back at her having noticed that the woman was slightly unnerved, and asked,"Sorry this turned out not to be as unfair a fight as you had thought?" Lei couldn't restrain the smile that creased one side of her face as she grasped the wound in her arm with her uninjured hand.

The woman steeled herself and charged in again as Lei whipped her hand away from her wound in response to the attack, sending a stream of her own blood toward the woman's face. Droplets covered the woman's visage and she winced from the mild impacts as instinct caused her to turn away to protect her eyes. Lei ran forward and thrust her shoulder into the woman's abdomen bending the woman's body over on impact and sending her blade flying from her grasp. The pair tumbled to the ground with Lei controlling her roll so she would find herself straddled on top of the woman. Before her opponent could recover, Lei started raining punches down with her good hand against the woman's face. Blood flew from the woman's nose on the first blow and the second sent her eyes rolling up into her head. The third punch split the woman's lip and her body went limp and, as Lei opened her striking hand to drive her fingernails deep into the woman's throat, she was tackled from the side and knocked off the woman.

Dimitri's people, seeing one of their people about to lose the battle, came to life and entered the fight. Lei was hit again and again, as body after body fell on top of her, pinning her to the ground and holding her arms and legs in place. Foul smelling breath and body odor made every inhalation cloying as Lei desperately struggled to no avail.

Only her head was free of the crush of bodies that lay on top of her and, as Lei turned her head away from the blow she knew was coming, her eyes widened in shock to see Pha running away from the warehouse and into the night. Lei watched as the small child disappeared into the blackness unnoticed by Dimitri's people, all of whom had focused their attention on the struggle that had just concluded.

"Go girl, go!" Lei thought to herself as she quickly turned her head back, so as not to give away what she had seen, and lightning flashed before her eyes as the expected kick connected with her temple.

Chapter 25
Moscow, Russia. June, 1938

The office building was poorly lit and very cold as uniformed men and women went about their daily rituals of cleaning off their desks and preparing for the end of the workday. Soon that time would come and each would hurry to wait in line for various supplies such as bread, milk or other such necessities.

One office was larger than the rest and stayed illuminated well after the end of a normal business day. The Chief of Soviet State Treasury was known to work late in his crusade for uncovering corruption at any cost. He was deep in thought when his secretary bruskly opened the door to his office and broke his concentration.

"Will there be anything else before I leave Comrade Yurovsky?"

Yakov Yurovsky did not look up from his documents as he spoke. "No my dear, I have everything well in hand."

The secretary nodded and began to close the door when Yurovsky added.

"And Tanya...If you ever come into this office again without knocking I will shoot you in the face."

In reality it had been a long time since Yakov Yurovsky had killed anyone, he was more of an administrator these days, but his reputation as a "Hero of the People" for the execution of Tsar Nicholas and his family still gave those around the man a sense of wariness that he could make good on his threats.

At first Tanya smiled awkwardly thinking the man had made a poor joke. Then Yurovsky looked up from his papers and when their eyes met she knew that the man had not just made a joke or even an idle threat. There was a terrifying lethality to his stare and Tanya had to look away.

"I'm sorry sir."

"Goodnight Tanya." Yurovsky looked back down to the papers he had been studying earlier.

Tanya waited, afraid to move, and her hands unconsciously let go of the doorknob allowing it to swing fully open before gently striking the door stop against the wall. She only paused another second or two before she finally managed, "Goodnight Comrade Secretary." Tanya had to reach for the doorknob as she made an effort to slowly, quietly shut the door behind her.

Unbeknownst and unseen by Tanya or Yurovsky was the space behind the door that was revealed as it was shut. In that space, was Alexei.

Alexei studied Yurovsky as the man sat behind his desk reading over his papers. The stocky man looked the same as he had over twenty years ago, if one ignored the gray that covered his temples and flecked through the rest of his hair. Alexei stepped forward, his fingertips gliding over one another, as he closed the distance between himself and Yurovsky. When Alexei was standing directly on the opposite side of Yurovsky's desk he stopped rubbing his fingertips together and waited. All at once Yurovsky seemed to realize he was not alone in the room and, when the man nonchalantly glanced upward, the shock of Alexei being so close, so right on top of him, made him scream in startled fright.

"Boishe Moi!!! How did you get in here?!?"

"Relax Comrade, "Alexei chuckled, pleased with the start he had given the man, "I wouldn't want you to have a heart attack… at least not yet."

Alexei turned his back on the man and began to walk to the door as Yurovsky frowned in confusion as he watched the young man step to the door and lock it.

When Alexei turned back around he saw that Yurovsky had not lost his composure and realized the man must be hiding a weapon somewhere on his person.

236

Yurovsky shot the same look at Alexei as he had at his secretary, "I would very much like to know who you are and what you are doing here before I have you arrested," Yurovsky said in a confident manner.

Alexei smiled back as he asked, "Who I am? You mean you don't recognize me?"

Yurovsky frowned and waved a hand nonchalantly as he shook his head, "No, I am afraid not. Should I recognize you?"

"You should always remember the faces of those you have killed," the smile faded from Alexei's face.

Yurovsky laughed, "Who I killed? Ha! I am quite sure that anyone I killed would not later show up on my doorstep." Yurovsky laughed again; however, this time something flickered in his eyes as he quieted and searched Alexei's face.

Alexei watched Yurovsky's face as the man began to remember, "I, for one, have never forgotten your face," Alexei snarled.

Yurovsky's eyes darted from side to side as the images raced in front of his mind, replaying the entire scene from the cellar of the Ipatiev House. When the memories ended Yurovsky seemed to wake from a daydream and his hand immediately shot to a desk drawer and the sidearm holstered inside.

"It...it isn't possible!" Yurovsky stammered as he struggled to remove the weapon from its holster.

Alexei watched, before asking, "Did you want some help with that?" Yurovsky froze at the words and he looked up at Alexei, his eyes now filled with fear as Alexei continued, "the guns didn't do the job last time. What makes you think they will work now?"

As soon as Alexei had finished speaking Yurovsky went back to removing the gun from the holster and Alexei quickly stepped foward. The gun came free but Alexei had Yurovsky's wrist before the older man could aim the weapon. Yurovsky punched at Alexei, but Alexei swatted the blows away with his free hand before slapping Yurovsky across the face so hard that the man's knees buckled and he fell back into the seat of his chair.

Alexei maintained his grip on Yurovsky's wrist, but the old Bolshevik managed to squeeze off a shot. The barrel of the gun was aimed harmlessly at the ceiling, but Alexei quickly took the weapon out of Yurovsky's grip before he could fire it again.

Alexei tossed the gun aside and hovered over Yurovsky as he sat in his chair, "No!" The old Bolsevik screamed, "Stay away! I killed you!"

Alexei swatted the man again with a blow that rocked his whole body and threatened to send the man out of the chair. Alexei caught the man before he could fall and righted Yurovsky's body so was sitting upright in the chair. Outside voices were being raised as the few remaining people in the building reacted to the gunshot. Commands to open the door came from what must have been the soldiers tasked with security of the building and, upon hearing them, Yurovsky seemed to regain some of his composure.

"They heard the shots and will break down that door to get to you soon enough. It will be easier on you if you surrender now," Yurovsky said meekly while attempting to put a small bit of steel back in his voice.

Alexei was still smiling as he looked from Yurovsky's face to the office door and back again.

"I suppose it would," Alexei said as he looked to the door, "but they will not save you."

Yurovsky saw the look in Alexei's eyes and his face blanched white. Somewhere deep inside the man he managed to speak and the few words came out him in a broken, desperate plea, "Don't... please... I beg of you..."

Alexei placed one hand on Yurovsky's throat and slowly pushed his knife into Yurovsky's stomach. Yurovsky's eyes went wide with pain and shock as the cold steel went deeper into his body until the point passed out his back. His body began to shudder as the pain intensified, but Alexei pushed more steel forward until the blade puncture the back of the chair, pinning Yurovsky where he sat.

When he realized Yurovsky was fully impaled Alexei triumphantly stood to his full height and watched as Yurovsky raised his hands in an attempt to pry the knife from his abdomen.

Yurovsky looked up pleadingly from the knife in his belly, "I was...I was a...soldier... following orders..."

Alexei nodded, "I know. I have grown to understand the politics behind my father's execution and what it represented. Perhaps, as heir to the throne, I could understand mine as well." Alexei leaned forward and grabbed the handle of his knife as he peered, unblinking, into Yurovsky's eyes, "but you could have sent my mother and my sisters into exile. Instead, their execution was nothing more than a Bolshevik act of sadism that I cannot forgive."

Yurovsky seemed to know what was coming as Alexei tightened his hand on the knife's handle, and the Bolsevik eeked out, "No!... orders... all of you... betrayed..."

Something inside Alexei made him pause as that singular word flowed into his ears. Frowning slightly, Alexei asked, "What do you mean?"

The door to the office burst open and six soldiers filled room and screamed for Alexei to surrender as they took in the ghastly scene.

Alexei didn't move as Yurovsky's eyes darted from Alexei to the men funneling through the doorway. Yurovsky coughed a laugh as, in his deteriorating mind, he thought himself saved.

His confidence restored, Yurovsky managed a snarl, "I win."

Alexei's eyes never left Yurovsky and he returned the smile, "You lose."

Alexei ripped the blade up and out of Yurovsky causing an explosion of gore that sprayed the room.

The soldiers froze at the sight as Yurovsky's blood covered them and Alexei turned to face them, blood dripping from the elongated dagger he held, "My name is Alexei Nikolaevich and today I have justice for my parents, my sisters, my friends and myself. May God have mercy upon all of you black hearted, murdering Bolshevik scum, for in the end, I will not!"

For a moment none of the soldiers could move. Most were understandably in shock from the graphic display that they had just witnessed. Eventually all eyes turned away from the ruin that was Yurovsky and focused on Alexei, but none of the half dozen armed soldiers made any move to restrain Alexei.

Alexei smiled, "I would advise anyone who wants to live to leave now."

Two of the soldiers raised their rifles but, before they could properly aim, Alexei was moving. The rifles weren't meant for such close quarters and the soldiers fired without regard for their surroundings as Alexei dove behind Yurovsky and his heavy oak desk. Bullets ripped through Yurovsky's corpse and splintered the wood as Alexei reached into one of his pockets and withdrew a handful of what looked like ash.

Now the riflemen held their fire so the other soldiers could push their way into the room, handguns drawn, in an attempt to capture Alexei, but Alexei drew in a deep breath, held it and was on the move again. He threw the powder into the air toward soldiers and then dove behind a filing cabinet as more shots from the handguns exploded in his direction. Instinctively the soldiers ducked as if Alexei had thrown something solid at them, but they quickly realized that no object was hurtling toward and they again lifted their guns toward the filing cabinet… but hesitated.

Confused expressions spread across the faces of the soldiers as the first one audibly tried to clear his throat, then another began to cough and hack, until all of them desperately grabbed at their throats. Within moments their faces turned as gray as the ash Alexei had thrown and they dropped to the floor while they asphyxiated on the substance.

Five bodies hit the floor, leaving only one still standing and struggling to breathe. Apparently he had inhaled less of the ash than the others, but Alexei didn't give him the chance to recover. Bolting up from his position behind the filing cabinet, Alexei barreled into him, lifted the soldier off the ground and slammed the man against the office wall where Alexei held him aloft and pinned. The rifle was knocked out of the soldier's hands and Alexei wrenched the man's head to one side exposing his neck. Without thinking Alexei plunged his head forward and drove his teeth into the side of the man's neck, bit down hard and ripped the flesh away. Blood erupted in rhythmic pulsations as the man screamed. Spitting the chunk of meat in his teeth to one side, Alexei clamped his mouth over the wound and quickly began swallowing as much of the blood gushing out as he could.

Alexei held the pinned soldier fast despite the man thrashing wildly in panic and pain. Soon the soldier's thrashings began to fade and his body grew limp, as what was once a gush of blood became merely a trickle. Alexei swallowed a final mouthful and eased his grip on the now dead man allowing him to drop to the floor.

Slowly, reality began to return to Alexei who now stood wide-eyed at what he had done. He had never killed a man for blood before as he had always received the blood he needed through the animals he had hunted, from butcher shops or, as a child form the medicine he had received from Rasputin.

Killing a man the way he just had left him nauseous; in fact, the next thing Alexei knew he found himself retching, but his convulsions came in the form of dry heaves as opposed to the purging of a stomach full of blood. When it was over Alexei managed to compose himself to enough of a degree that he knew he had to get away. More people would have heard the shots and others would come to investigate.

Alexei ran.

He had planned his escape but, as the revulsion wore off, he was shocked at how strong he felt. He was running faster than he ever had before and when he came to a wall that he had expected to climb, he scaled it with far less effort than he ever believed was possible. It was not a superhuman effort, but it was as if his body was performing at the very maximum of its ability. He wanted to test himself, but the sounds of soldiers arriving in the distance cleared his mind.

All of that could wait. Now his only goal would be to get away and he used every bit of newfound speed and strength available to him to get home again. Back home to the United States of America.

Chapter 26

There was no secret concerning the owner of the new five-story office building that held Nightingale Industries. The building, a gleaming beacon of shining new glass and steel, was standing alone in its splendor beside the ruins of Nazran's other structures. I stood across the street from the building staring up at its majesty and I couldn't help but feel how out of place the building looked amongst the dilapidation of the rest of the city.

How, or better yet why, Dimitri would construct a building in such stark opposition to the rest of the city was puzzling. Certainly the city required the new growth to make any sort of comeback, but he was making a target of himself with such a lavish display of fortune. Then again, Dimitri was anything but subtle. Perhaps the ostentatious display was, in its own way, a challenge, a defiance or a dare, for anyone to try to threaten what he had built, or by extension, himself.

I scanned the area, realizing that despite my having found what I felt was a satisfactory hiding space, I was the only person in the vicinity who was not going into, or coming from, the Nightingale building. The only cars that passed on the street in front of the building were the ones that would ultimately turn into the building's parking entryway. No pedestrians walked past the building. People who weren't leaving, were entering the building through its front doors.

I had been watching the building for most of the afternoon, just to get a sense of what security might be in place. My plan was to get inside the building and confront Dimitri in a similar way to which he had met with me less than a year ago in Las Vegas. My plan was simple in principle, if not in application. I was going to sneak in, bypassing security, and wait for Dimitri in whatever he used for his office space.

Simple right?

Chris, before he had left with Alpha and William, had done quite a bit of the proverbial "heavy lifting" with the computer when it came to finding out about the floor plan and the basic security of the building. In a way that seemed to me like modern magic he had hacked into the building's security system and hijacked the feed from the security cameras spread throughout its interior. From the comfort of our chairs we had been able to see every hallway within the building, although we were still blind to whatever was inside each of those office spaces. The front lobby consisted of only a desk with a single security officer stationed behind it. The desk was situated in front of a set of elevator doors, to which the security guard controlled access by punching in a code that called the elevator back to the lobby from the other floors.

This was a pretty significant problem, as the guard's hackles would be raised the instant someone walked into the building whom he didn't recognize. I could probably incapacitate the man before he set off any alarms, but then I'd lose the ability to access the elevator, and despite the blatant safety violation, neither Chris nor I could see any sign of a stairway.

The cameras inside the parking garage revealed a better option. If I could get through the initial security gate, then the elevator could be called from within with a normal push-button call switch. There was a security presence of three guards within the garage, two stationed near the elevator at what looked like a valet parking kiosk, while a third pedaled a bicycle around the two stories of parking spaces. I don't know if it was the presence of the additional personnel, or if it was the fact that every car had already passed through some degree of security measures, that gave the men stationed within the garage their more relaxed demeanor, as compared to the one displayed by the guy in the lobby, but they definitely seemed bored by comparison.

"So," Chris had said, "it looks as though once you get past

these guys you can get to whichever floor you'd like."

I nodded, "Unless there are cameras in the elevator car."

Chris shook his head, "Normally I'd agree, but I can't find anything in the system for the elevators or the office spaces. My guess is that it was either an oversight, or for some reason Dimitri and his people didn't want the security people to be able to see what was happening in the elevators and offices."

I had frowned, "That make any sense to you?"

Chris had thought a moment, "No, not really."

Chris and I studied the video feeds for another moment before Chris asked, "So how do you plan on getting past the gate?"

I smiled wolfishly at Chris, "I'm going to take a lesson from our regal friend Alexei's playbook."

Chris frowned at me, not understanding.

"Don't worry," I told him, "I have no intention of actually getting past the security guards, because in the end, I don't think I'll need to."

When I told Chris the plan his face had blanched, "You know how bad they're going to beat your ass?"

I sighed, "I'm hoping that there will be a certain level of professionalism in the security personnel."

"You mean the guys who stand around all day, bored off their asses and waiting for the chance to earn their pay by showing how willing they are to break heads for their employer? Those very professional guys?"

I sighed again, and with my sarcasm honed to a fine edge I said, "Thank you for sending me in with the proper attitude Chris."

I had spent the morning scouting the innumerable homeless people living on the streets of Nazran until I had found one that was roughly my size. The man looked terrified as I approached, but when I offered him one hundred U.S. dollars to trade clothes with me his apprehension turned to excitement. Fifteen minutes later the man walked proudly away in a new pair of jeans, cotton

245

T-shirt and leather jacket with one hundred dollars in the pocket. I, on the other hand, was wearing his filthy overalls and flannel shirt. The stink wafting from the fabrics nearly turned my stomach and made my skin crawl as I slipped them on. I was fairly sure I'd need to be de-loused and get a tetanus shot once this little adventure was over, but his clothes would more than serve in order to convincingly sell the illusion.

It was around four in the afternoon when I decided to make my move. I lumbered out from where I was hiding, shuffled drunkenly to the other side of the street and into the driveway of Nightengale Industries until I was standing behind the next car that waited at the entrance to the underground garage security gate.

The driver saw me coming and rolled up his window, probably thinking I was going to ask for a handout. I didn't say anything as the glass slid upward, I couldn't speak the local lingo in any case, but I still held my hand out and tried to look as desperate and sorrowful as I could.

The look he returned was one part repulsion and another part predatory exhilaration, which gave me an impression that he might jump out of the car and try to make a meal out of me before the security gate to the underground garage had a chance to open. To my relief the gate began rattle as it started to slide into its fully open position, which also served to snap the driver out of his daydream. I could see the driver through the tinted glass as he took a deep breath, apparently to settle himeslef, then release the brake as his car began to roll forward.

At this point I made an effort to shamble after the car and, when the gate started moving back to the closed position, I feigned a trip and "fell" down the decline of the entry driveway, which rolled me past the gate before my body came to a halt

The driver must have noticed my tumble as the car screeched to a halt a few yards inside the gate. The driver immediately climbed from the car and slammed the doorbehind him while cursing at me in something that sounded like Russian. In response I only moaned and held one arm up to the driver as if to ask for a hand up, but I also tensed my torso in preparedness for what I knew was going to happen. The driver swatted my hand out of the way and launched a kick to my ribs that would have shattered bone had I not been anticipating the blow. The driver must have realized his kick did less damage than he intended as he quickly threw in several more kicks that were less powerful, but came in rapid succession. I maneuvered my body so the force of the blows were insufficient to do any real damage beyond being painful and raising bruises. The trick was to keep rolling and moving so he never managed to kick the same spot twice. I blocked a few kicks with my arms as well, and I could feel the man begin to tire as each kick landed with less and less force.

Voices called out from the distance and echoed through the garage. Initially the driver ignored them, but as his breath began coming in heavy gulps of air from the effort of kicking me, I knew it wouldn't be long before he would need to rest and he would answer.

The voices called out again in Russian and the driver responded with a tone in his voice that resonated with annoyance and frustration. He made a gesture to the far part of the garage that looked as if he were telling whoever else was out there that he didn't need any help. I heard some laughter echo as the other voices acknowledged the driver and seemed to fade away, probably as the people who had come to assist were walking back to their posts.

Hands suddenly grabbed at my shirt and jacket and hauled me back to my feet. I raised my hands as if to cower and protect my face while I snuck a glance into the garage and saw the pair of security men walking away just before they disappeared into the shadows of the garage.

The driver began dragging me toward the car, opened the

rear door and tossed me inside. He slammed the door, and then went back to his own seat and started the engine. I let out small whimpers that I thought would be consistent to the type of damage the driver had hoped to inflict, as I felt the car roll forward. The sounds of a cellular phone dialing could be heard over the hum of the car engine and then the driver spoke hurriedly between labored breaths, as the car once again slowed to a stop. When the driver climbed out I had expected he would pull me out as well, but instead he just shut the door and left me in the backseat. I turned my head and could see the driver speaking with the two other guards that were stationed next to the elevators as well as the third, who was wearing what looked to be a bicycle helmet. Apparently the commotion had brought the bicycle guard to the scene as well. I smiled as the plan was going even better than I had expected.

It took about five minutes before the elevator doors opened and two men wheeled what looked like a hospital gurney out of the elevator and walked over to the car. The driver pointed to the back seat and one of the men stuck his face up to the window to peer through at me. I turned my head away and began rocking back and forth as if in significantly more pain than I actually was, but the presence of the gurney had sent a shiver into my spine. I hadn't expected more than a beating that would bring all the guards together to share in the momentary respite from the daily tedium. Now a new prospect had been added that I hadn't accounted for, because if they strapped me down to the gurney I would be trapped, and that lack of freedom was going to significantly alter my plans.

The driver opened my door and launched me out of the back seat by pulling hard on my feet. I felt my upper body go airborne and then my back and shoulders violently struck the concrete. I had only barely realized what was happening in time to tuck my head and prevent the back of my skull from smacking the ground hard enough to render me unconscious. After that I felt several pairs of hands grab my arms and legs until, at last, I was lifted off the ground and dropped unceremoniously onto the gurney. I lolled my head back and forth as a belt strap was tied around my waist, but this restraint was more to prevent me from falling off than it was to truly incapacitate me. To my relief they did not secure my hands or ankles, and the gurney started rolling toward the elevator.

When the doors opened the two men dressed in light blue surgical scrubs stayed with the gurney, as did the driver, and I listened until the ambient noise of the garage was muffled by the elevator doors closing. I felt the elevator begin to move before I began to make a choking sound deep in my throat. The men glanced down at me in an uninterested fashion before their eyes returned to the floor numbers above the elevator door. I made the sound again, this time louder and swayed my head from side to side as if in slight distress. Still the men ignored me and watched as the numbers ascended until the elevator doors opened onto the third floor.

I waited until the cart had cleared the elevator doors and then opened my eyes as I continued to sway my head back and forth in order to survey the surroundings. The third floor opened into a large expanse, looking very similar to a hospital Emergency Room, but without any walls or separation of treatment rooms. There were cots lined along one wall and medical equipment on wheels, as well as several desks and office type chairs spread all throughout the large open expanse. I.V. racks were in abundance and several of the hanging bags were flattened as if drained of their contents, but were also stained with the remnants of dark red liquid that could only come from blood.

Uh oh.

Chapter 27

I felt the butterflies of adrenaline flutter inside my stomach as the orderlies wheeled me into position next to one of the cots. I could see the ALYX blood donation machine on a small table next to the cot and an errant thought ran through my head. The ALYX machine is used to perform what is called a double red blood cell donation when people volunteer to give blood. Essentially the whole blood is drawn, spun in a centrifuge separating the red cells from the plasma before the plasma is pumped back into the donor's body to prevent dehydration. The process is repeated a second time and the end result is the donor has safely been able to give twice the amount of red blood cells than he or she would have been able to donate if they had donated whole blood. Most of the donation centers in the United States have switched to this machine because the red blood cells are the portion of the donated blood most needed in transfusions, and as a result the centers can get twice the amount of red blood cells from the same number of donors.

In the case of my kind, vampires suffering from our particular type of Porphyria need to supplement our bodies with the "heme" part of hemoglobin, which is present in the red blood cells. My own North American collective has been utilizing the ALYX machines to speed the production of our serum from well intentioned donors so they can donate more of what we need while keeping them safe from dehydration. The machines were expensive and, given the fact that the Russian Collective still took most of their blood from unwilling vitims, I didn't think the ALYX machines were here to maintain the wellbeing of any donors. Then again, if the ALYX machines safety measures were ignored, then a donor, or victim, could technically be fatally exsanguinated in a far more efficient way than by simply opening an artery or major venous canal. The only question was, why would they bother?

My mind snapped back to reality as my gurney came to a

stop and one of the orderlies clicked the wheel brake to keep it still. I was pretty sure I could take out the two orderlies hovering over me, but the driver was still near the elevator and there was no way I could take him out before he could raise an alarm. Worse, although I hadn't noticed anyone else moving around in the vicinity, that didn't mean the driver and two orderlies were truly the only people on the floor. I felt one of the orderlies start to unbuckle the strap around my waist as I saw the other one put on a pair of rubber gloves, which told me I had to move soon. If they managed to draw any of my blood and noticed the pinkish hue that my people have as a result of our condition, then my cover was blown, and my opportunity at diplomacy would be over before it had begun.

As soon as the strap came off my waist I started coughing and making a choking sound. The orderly who undid the strap stepped back as I hacked and gagged in his direction.

His partner looked at him, "What happened?"

"No idea. All I did was undo the strap."

The sound of English nearly shocked me out of my performance and I had to curl up into the fetal position in order to hide the surprise that I was sure was showing on my face. I also began gasping for air in between coughs and gags as if I had something caught in my windpipe.

The guy who undid my straps just stared at me as I convulsed on the gurney, "You think he swallowed his tongue or something?"

"How should I know?" the second orderly replied.

"So, check him." said number one.

"Why me?" responded number two.

"You already have the gloves on," the first orderly teased, "not that you need to worry about infection in any case."

The second orderly grumbled as I felt his hands forcefully grab my hair, turning my face toward his and saying, "I'm not

251

worried about infection, but the street people here are beyond disgusting."

I made a particularly noxious gagging sound just as the guy tried to pry my mouth open and he stepped back in fear of an imminent projectile vomit.

"What is going on?" I heard the driver call out in heavily accented English.

"Not sure," one of the orderlies replied, "this guy's maybe choking on his tongue or something."

I could hear the driver's footsteps approaching, curiosity making him investigate. When he spoke again, it sounded like he was standing right next to the gurney. I heard the unmistakable sound of an automatic handgun's slide ratcheting to load a bullet out of the magazine and into the pistol's chamber so that it was now loaded into a firing position.

"Want me shut him up?" he asked in broken English.

Before I could react one of the orderlies shouted, "No!"

Relief washed through me as I heard the driver chuckle, "You are afraid of gun?"

The orderly sounded winded as he spoke, "No, of course not, but I am the one who is going to have to clean up your mess afterward... Or were you planning on doing that?"

The driver continued to chuckle, but I heard the click of the gun's safety, as he put it back into its holster. It was at that moment that I grabbed onto the rails on one side of the gurney and thrust a heel kick into the driver's abdomen hard enough that I actually thought I could feel the kick hit the man's spine. The driver's body bent neatly in half before being catapulted through the air and landing a couple of yards back. The orderly closest to me let out a yelping sound before trying to jump on top of me, but I had used the momentum of the kick to push myself into a backward roll off the end of the gurney and into the other orderly who, upon seeing me strike the driver, had tried to turn to run. I grabbed the back of

252

his head with both hands and violently pulled up and backward, the momentum causing his body to lift off the ground with his feet swinging out in front of him. I shifted and altered his momentum to slam his head and body straight down to the floor. The back of his head hit first with a loud crack, and his body fell limply in a heap next to me.

The last orderly was facing me, his hands up and in a fighting position, and the look on his face was one of uncertainty, as if he were torn as to whether he should stand his ground or make a break for it. The driver started gagging in response to the kick I had given him and both the orderly and my eyes flicked to him and back again. I don't know how badly I had broken him up inside, but the pale blood coming from his mouth and nose was a pretty good indication that he was out of the fight. The orderly took a slow step toward the driver, and for a moment I had the impression that he was going to check on the guy to see if he was okay. Sudden realization sparked in my brain as the orderly quickly dove toward the driver, or more specifically, for the sidearm the driver had dropped when I flattened him.

"Oh shit!" I exclaimed leaping into motion, without even realizing I had spoken, as the orderly slid to a stop, scooped up the sidearm from where it had been lying on the floor and was twisting his body toward me as I finally slammed into him. Both of my hands grabbed the orderly's wrist holding the gun and pushed the barrel away from my body, but he took the opportunity to use his free hand to punch me squarely in the face causing my grip to loosen enough for him to gain some leverage and begin to inch the barrel slowly toward my head. We rolled, fighting over control of the weapon until I somehow ended up lying flat on my back with my hands over my head still holding onto the guy's wrists. The orderly was kneeling and using his weight and gravity to his advantage to force the barrel back toward my face... and he was winning the contest.

I only had one chance, but I knew that if I miscalculated by only a fraction of an inch that I was as good as dead. I gave a sharp pull on the guy's wrists in what seemed like an attempt to draw the weapon in closer and pull the orderly off balance. On pure reflex he responded by shifting his weight and pulling back against my effort at which point I relaxed my arms let go of my grip. The guy hadn't been expecting it, and the force he had thought to use to counter my move was now a severe overcompensation. The guy began to tumble backward, but not before righting the gun and pointing it directly at me. I knew I wasn't going to be fast enough, but I heard no gunshot as the orderly's finger squeezed the trigger. Unfortunately for him he had forgotten that the driver had engaged the safety after threatening to shoot me earlier, and nothing boomed out of the weapon.

I kicked both of my legs up and over my head curling my body into a backward roll before bending my legs and bringing my knees down hard on the man's stomach. He let out a loud, "Oof!" and I shot my legs out straight again kicking him with all the force I had in both of my legs, directly in the face. The orderly's nose crunched and blood sprayed as his head whiplashed violently backward and forward, and then he collapsed like a rag doll to the floor. For my part I didn't slow down until I had removed the gun from his limp hand, checked him to make sure he was truly out of commission and, once satisfied that he was unconscious, I checked on the other orderly who was also unconscious. Then I walked over to the where the driver was now lying in a curled up fetal position. I put the gun against the man's temple, but he didn't stir, and then I checked for a pulse at his neck. I didn't find one.

Crap, so much for diplomacy.

Chapter 28

It didn't take me long to drag the driver's body into a corner and put each orderly onto a cot before tying them down and then gagging them for good measure while praying that no one else was going to work on this level after hours. I really didn't need for them to be found before I had finished what I had come to do. I had tried to time my break-in after what would normally be construed as regular business hours so there were fewer people around, but then again, we were talking about vampires who thought they were living like the legends of old, so who knew what kind of office hours they kept?

Deciding that my best chance was to move as quickly as possible, it fortunately only took me a minute or so to find my way to the top floor and the space designated as Dimitri Lagos' office. I had speculated to Chris my doubts that such an old and, for lack of a better term, stereotypical vampire would have a use for such a space, but Chris had assured me that Dimitri not only had the office space, but he had hacked surveillance video that showed the old vamp had a routine of being in the office daily, just like his nightclub routine later in the evening.

I put one hand on the large wooden door and pushed it open. What greeted me was something akin to a reception area, with sofas against the one wall and a small desk against the opposite wall, while straight ahead was a large pair of ornate doors. Apparently I had made my way into the reception area, where a normally present secretary would have notified Dimitri that his visitors had arrived, assuming he didn't already know via the security cameras at the entrance to the building.

I cautiously walked across the room, but froze when I heard Dimitri's voice coming from the doors in front of me, "Tell Nicholas to send as many people after the girl as he can spare!" Dimitri's voice was incredibly agitated and I felt my heart ramp up at the mention of the "girl." Had Lei and Pha managed to escape? No, I thought, he had said "girl" singular, as if only one of them needed to be found.

Dimitri's pause told me he was on the phone as opposed to speaking to someone in his office, "Is the other one secure?"

Another pause before he replied, "No, we still need her. Don't kill her, but make sure she is... damaged to the point that she won't be able to make any further escape attempts."

Rage shot through me like an electric current and any caution or subtlety I had been employing vanished in an instant as I kicked the doors open and aimed the driver's automatic at Dimitri's head and said with a low growl, "You might want to rethink that order."

Dimitri had turned away from the door as soon as he had registered the sound of the wood splintering under the force of my efforts and he had rebounded from the sound by coming back up with a snarl on his face, until he registered who he was facing... as well as the gun I was holding. Mild surprise washed over his face for a second, and then it was gone, replaced by a frown as he calmly spoke into the phone.

"Wait fifteen minutes, if you don't hear from me after that, kill her," and then he quickly hung up the phone before I could do or make him say anything else.

My eyes flicked down to the phone in shock, before I let out a sigh and said, "You can certainly think on your feet. That was well played, hanging up like that so if I shot you down you wouldn't be able to call back to save her life."

Dimitri's conversational voice was as low and raspy as I remembered from our meeting in Las Vegas as he stated, "I haven't lived as long as I have because I'm an imbecile."

"Of course not," I agreed, "but what's to stop me from shooting you in the legs until you pick up the phone and give the order."

Dimitri smiled, "Do you think it would be that simple?"

I considered his smile. It was unnerving to say the least, as I was the guy holding the gun and the archaic asshole across the room was the one smiling. So why didn't I feel as confident as I apparently should have? Because Dimitri was old, very old, and the fact that he had managed to live so long was a not only a sign of his being an Ancient but was also a testament to his more than extraordinarily abilty to survive.

I flicked the gun barrel at the phone, "So let's say that instead you make that call, and I lose the gun. Would that work for you?"

Dimitri frowned, "To what end?"

Now it was my turn to smile, "So we can talk detente."

Dimitri's frown deepened, but I could also see from his expression that there was a curiosity or at least an interest on his part. I remained silent as Dimitri looked me over for nearly a minute before his expression softened, "I never wished to start a war with you or yours."

Steve frowned, "You do realize yours actions speak otherwise?"

Dimitri shrugged his shoulders, "Had you done your job and delivered the one you call 'William' to me we wouldn't be here now, would we?"

I coughed out a laugh, "I think you knew that as soon as I realized your 'property' was, in fact, William my intentions would change. That's why you had your man take Lei in the first place."

Dimitri shrugged his shoulders as a confident smile spread across his wrinkled face, "Hedging my bets as you Americans say."

I really wanted to shoot that smug look right off his evil face, but I said instead, "Are you going to make that call or not?"

Silence filled the room again as Dimitri let some time tick off of the clock for another minute before he raised his hands, and then reached for the phone. He dialed a number and then pressed a speaker phone button on the receiver. The phone rang only once before a voice said, "Da?"

"I believe everything is under control here," Dimitri said smugly, and in English for my benefit and then held out his hand toward me for the weapon.

I lowered the gun and stepped toward the ancient vampire, before releasing the magazine and ratcheting the slide to remove the lone bullet from the chamber and then gently placed the gun in Dimitri's hand, without breaking eye contact. If that old son of a bitch even looked as though he was going to betray me with his next words I was prepared to take him down, hard! Or at least I was committed to making the attempt in any case.

Dimitri seemed to realize my intentions, and his smile widened even more before he asked, "Is the woman still alive and unharmed?"

The voice answered in what I thought might have been Russian and I felt my stomach lurch when Dimitri's face slightly lost its smile, and he turned slightly to peer at the receiver, before he recovered and said simply, "I see. Well, see that no..." Dimitri looked away from the phone receiver, and directly into my eyes, "no further harm befalls her. And tend to her wounds immediately."

My fists clenched in anger, but what could I do other than stand there literally trembling in impotent fury, as Dimitri calmly disconnected the line. He could see my rage and the smile returned to his face, as he tensed in preparation for violence.

He was silent a moment longer, before saying, "Perhaps this was something that would have been served better by simply calling me?

I hadn't even realized I was holding my breath, until I made a conscious effort to let the air out. My hands were shaking so badly in their need to demolish the man standing in front of me

258

that I didn't trust myself to move, so I just forced myself to take in a deep breath, trying to relax my clenched jaw, along with the rest of my too tightly wound body.

Eventually I felt my fingers unclench and my jaw loosen enough to reply, "I thought it better to speak with you in person." Dimitri seemed to regain a certain measure of his own composure at my words, and the realization of this fact shook me out of all the rage that had been burning through me. Dimitri, leader and Lord of the Russian vampire collective and quite possibly the oldest of all our kind had, just now and for at least the briefest of moments, been afraid of me.

With a strangely renewed confidence Dimitri said, "A very presumptive move on your part to have come here uninvited."

"I am not interested in presumption Dimitri, only in diffusing the situation that has escalated between us."

"Indeed? And how do you propose we do that?" He asked.

"Russia and the outlying regions belong to your clan and, as far as I am concerned, as long as your actions don't threaten the rest of us, I have little right nor the responsibility to act against you."

Dimitri frowned in confusion and then, using my own words against me, "You do realize your actions speak otherwise?"

The rage returned and I growled, "The only reason we are here is because you have our people."

Dimitri's anger seemed to grow as well, "Truly? And how do you explain your alignment with the Romanov?"

I initially had a mental hesitation before realizing he meant Alexei, "We were in the same place, at the same time, with the same people wanting to shoot us. That's it."

Dimitri let out a scornful laugh, "You expect me to believe that?"

I took a step back, hoping to ease the tension that was building between us with distance, "The situation created the necessity last night, that's all."

Dimitri studied my face and looked as though he was going to throw another accusation at me, but the words never made it out of his mouth.

Taking advantage of his momentary speechlessness I asked, "What is it with that guy anyway? I mean, I get that he has some voodoo that is a little bit beyond my understanding, but he's only one man."

Dimitri nearly shouted his answer at me, "He's not just one man! He is *Starets* and Grigori's finest student!"

"Grigori?" I asked, "you mean Rasputin?"

"Of course!" Dimitri looked at me with eyes on the verge of madness and he slammed his fists down on his desk shattering the heavy wood where his fist had hit.

I stepped back again at the sight. Dimitri was small, frail looking to the point that it seemed as though a strong wind might blow him off his feet. Clearly that impression was about as far from reality as it could possibly be, and I suddenly felt very relieved that it had not come to blows between us.

Dimitri looked down at the ruin of his desktop and then at his hands before visibly calming, "You don't realize what such a man is capable of."

I shook my head at the ironic whiplash that those words brought with them.

"Are you actually trying to tell me that Alexei represents a greater threat to the world than you?"

Dimitri studied me and then said, "Not Alexei, at least not exactly." Dimitri looked away from me and sighed, "You are very young and have little knowledge of what Rasputin was beyond what the history books have described. You weren't here when the man began to study and meddle with forces that no man," Dimitri suddenly looked back into my eyes, "even one as old as myself, should ever trifle with."

I thought I had read that Rasputin had dabbled in the occult, but I hadn't known if that were real or just more conjecture, enhanced by Hollywood. Now it would seem there was some truth behind those stories. Or, at least Dimitri believed there was.

Dimitri seemed to read my thoughts and his eyes lit up in recognition, "So you do understand, at least a little."

"You're talking about some kind of occult knowledge that Rasputin passed along to Alexei, then?

"Not just some arbitrary wisdom found in old periodicals, but the origins of our kind."

I froze, the breath stuck in my lungs and my eyes darted from side to side as my brain processed what Dimitri had just said. Even though I repeated those last four words out loud, I was saying them more to myself than to Dimitri, "Origins of our kind?"

Dimitri's voice turned hard and mocking, "Do you truly think that we are some kind of genetic mistake? That some abnormality as random as a birth defect in our genetic code could turn us into the most superior creatures on the planet?"

It wasn't something I "thought." It wasn't medical theory, or even an educated hypothesis on the part of scientists who were tasked with filling in blanks when the facts ran out. Our condition was fact. Hard cold science, with no room for guess work, no room for error. The cause of our vampirism and its related effects on our bodies was as certain as the fact that we need oxygen to breathe, or that our ears are for hearing and our nose for smelling.

I just stared at Dimitri dumbfounded and silent as he continued, "Look at me, I was an Ancient before your Alpha was ever born. I have seen the rise and fall of empires, and gained knowledge that could fill every library in the world twice over." Dimitri held out his wrists to me, "Our blood holds the secret to immortality, can you think that this a mistake?"

I just shook my head, not in any kind of disagreement with the statement as much as I was trying to shake the proverbial

261

wheels in my brain so they would begin turning again. "So," I asked in an attempt to stall for time while my brain tried to catch up with what Dimitri was saying, "what are we then?"

Dimitri smile and raised his hands up and out to the side, "We! We are gods manifested on earth! We are divine entities walking in this world that belongs to us and us alone! This world, and all of its bounties are ours to harvest in order to enhance our lives. We are the inheritors of the world."

"And the humans?" It felt strange, differentiating myself from the rest of humanity as I had always believed that both my people and I were a part of the greater whole of humanity, as opposed to being something quite different.

The excitement left Dimitri's face and he just shrugged at the question, "They have their place, and I will give them credit for the creative advancements they have made in the last century, but in the end they have been placed here on earth for much the same reason as horses, chickens or cattle are here. They are resources for our use and have the sustenance we need to survive."

The indifference Dimitri clearly felt toward human beings was disconcerting, as it was clear that Dimitri felt the human race was little more than clever livestock.

I shook off my unease and tried to change the subject, "And what does this have to do with Alexei's potential knowledge of our origins?"

Dimitri sighed, "Given the length of my life, I have seen things that go beyond understanding. Things that science cannot now, nor ever will be able to explain." Dimitri paused, as if reflecting on a particular experience from his memory before he began again, "There is power in that knowledge, but in all my years it was never something I could understand."

I waited as Dimitri laughed, "Perhaps I was always too afraid, so when I heard of a man, a human, who could guide me and instruct me in gaining and understanding that power, naturally

I sought the man out. It didn't hurt that he was Russian."

"Rasputin?" I said aloud, as the answer came to me, "you knew him?"

"Of course," Dimitri confirmed, "we traded knowledge. He tried to teach me about the occult, and I taught him about our kind, but where I struggled to understand what Rasputin was teaching me, he absorbed everything I showed him without effort. Eventually I realized what that demon of a man was doing."

My eyebrows raised, "What was he doing?"

Dimitri pressed his lips together in a silent snarl before saying, "He was deliberately misleading me, putting conflicting information together in such a way that I would think myself too simple to be able to understand what he was trying to teach me. He..." Dimitri made a visible attempt to calm himself before continuing, "the arrogance of that man. To think he could take advantage of our arrangement, and then use what I had taught him in order to endear himself to the Tsaritsa by 'saving' her child. The child that I could have 'saved' just as easily, had I not been detained on a trip in counsel with Tsar Nicholas."

I didn't know why but Chris' face flashed in my head as a memory, or aberrant thought, fought its way to the surface of my mind. Chris had been human until he had been mortally wounded by a gunshot to the abdomen and would have died if Alpha had not given Chris a direct transfer of his own blood. It only took me a moment to connect the dots and my eyes went wide with shock as I turned to Dimitri, "You... the child? Alexei?"

Dimitri stood with his chin thrust slightly forward, "The boy was the final piece of the puzzle that would have given me control of the entirety of the Russian Empire." Dimitri shrugged, "The power behind the throne perhaps, but then that is always the way it is, isn't it? Kings, dignitaries, and in today's world Dictators, Despots and even Presidents are little more than figureheads for the real rulers of the land."

"But the Tsaritsa panicked and sought out Rasputin, instead of waiting for you?" I said.

Dimitri growled, "I told the bitch to leave the child alone and let his physicians attend him in my absence, but we never liked each other and she used my absence to spirit the child off to Grigori. By the time we had returned to the White Castle the child's body had recovered from the transfusion I had given him before I left, and even though the secret of the boy's true condition and how he came to contract it was never revealed, Rasputin had poisoned the Tsaritsa against me to such a degree that she forced the Tsar to cast me out."

I heard the words coming from my mouth before I realized I was saying them, "You admit your intentions to use the child as a pawn for a power grab and you have the unmitigated gall to be indignant that the child's mother might find you a threat and have you removed?"

Dimitri whirled on me, his eyes filled with rage, "Power grab?! Have you not been listening to me?" Dimitri began screaming at me, "We are gods! A god does not have to justify why he does what he does, he only has to be obeyed!"

It was at that moment that my plan completely devolved. I had been planning to bargain the girls' freedom by reciprocating with whatever Dimitri demanded in return, at least to a degree. Now I could see that there would be no negotiating with this creature, this monster, who needed to be put down once and for all.

I tensed my body in anticipation of violence, as I said simply, "You're insane."

Instead of exploding with an even greater rage, Dimitri seemed to calm and the smile returned to his face, "Insane?" He regarded me with a patronizing expression, "I am about to set into motion a plan that will net me all of Siberia. Either my connections within the government will grant me control of the territory or the late Dr. Whelan's biological bombs will render the area

264

uninhabitable to anyone but our kind."

Dimitri stopped his tirade for a moment as he appeared to internally consider something, then he slumped his shoulders and spoke in a confessional tone, "Personally, I tire of waiting for the current adminstration's permission."

I mocked, "And gods don't have to justify themselves."

He missed my sarcasm and nodded his head in agreement, "The time has come for more drastic steps. There will be opposition, of course, even the threat of nuclear retaliation but, in the end, the truth is that Russia desperately needs the resources coming out of Siberia and would never risk destroying it in simple revenge. They cannot reclaim it, so they will have no choice but to make me an ally, as opposed to an enemy."

I shook my head, "Completely insane."

Dimitri shrugged his shoulders and walked to one side of his desk and sat on the edge, "History will tell, but today it was far more insane for you to come here."

Dimitri crossed his arms in front of himself and smiled, then with a bolt of speed he reached to where he had placed my gun on his desk.

I had removed the ammunition so the move surprised me, but I instinctively charged forward at the sight of the gun anyway. Dimitri whipped his hand toward me and the hard steel of the weapon slammed against my face. Stars burst like fireworks in front of my eyes and I stumbled back. Dimitri moved with me as I retreated and one of his hands shot into my pocket where I had put the ammunition clip. My mind was slow to register what Dimitri was doing, but when I felt his fingers in my pocket and about to curl into a fist around the magazine, clarity quickly returned. I grabbed his wrist, trapping his hand in my pocket, but Dimitri wrenched his arm back with such power that it lifted me off the ground and tore the fabric of the pocket sufficiently for him to remove his balled fist along with the clip. I fell to the ground hard

265

and heard Dimitri laugh as he slid the clip into the gun, ratcheting the slide to get a cartridge into firing position and aimed the gun at my head.

I never heard the door open, nor any footsteps or sound of any kind that would indicate that someone else had come into the room, so when Dimitri suddenly looked up, eyes wide with shock and pointed the gun away from me, my head couldn't process what was happening.

The sound of steel ringing on steel chimed in the air and the gun flew across the room. Dimitri pivoted and retreated behind his desk as someone leapt over me in pursuit.

I had noticed the umbrella stand set on the floor next to Dimitri's desk when I had come in and had even taken note of the different umbrellas that had been sitting inside. Given Nazran's often rainy weather, an umbrella stand was not a surprising sight to see in any office space and I had paid it little mind. I watched from the floor as Dimitri's hand dipped into the forest of umbrellas as he ran past the canister, but when it came up again it held an ornamental walking stick. Dimitri twisted the ornamental handle and quickly pulled a long slender sword out of the walking stick. Shifting his weight to the balls of his feet Dimitri raised the sword defensively over his head. I watched in shock as Alexei slashed his hunting knife down at Dimitri who managed to parry the strike with the part of the walking stick that had been the sword's sheath. Alexei barely flinched as he swatted the wooden sheath aside and continued the chase, with Dimitri leaping over his desk and thrusting the point of the sword at me. I rolled to the side, kicking Dimitri's legs out from under him, sending him sprawling to the ground. Alexei immediately came over the desk and would have pinned Dimitri to the ground like an insect specimen in a display with that massive blade of his had I not caught his wrists.

"No!" I yelled, "he still has Lei!"

Alexei looked like he was going to argue, but any words he

was going to say were abandoned as both of us had to jump back from the point of Dimitri's sword as the Ancient slashed it at our legs. Dimitri's face was enraged by Alexei's appearance and he directed his attack in Alexei's direction. Alexei retreated but Dimitri expertly pressed his attack, continuing to drive Alexei back by using the longer length of his sword to thrust with deadly strikes, yet remaining outside of Alexei's reach with the hunting knife.

I tried to move in, but without a weapon of my own I wasn't going to do much good. I scanned the floor searching for anything I could use when I saw the glint of steel, under a leather chair in the far corner of the room. I ran for the gun, but Dimitri saw me move, and after a thrusting strike at Alexei's chest, reversed his steps and charged to intercept me. Dimitri had the angle and managed to cut me off with a slash of the sword before I could get to the gun. He might have tried to retrieve it himself if Alexei hadn't also been pursuing him. He stood in front of the gun and held his ground, as I watched his sword become a literal blur of rapid strikes while Alexei's hunting knife appeared to barely move. I couldn't believe that Alexei hadn't been stabbed a half a dozen times until I realized that each slight movement of Alexei's blade was parrying the longer thrusts of Dimitri's sword. The rapier like blade that Dimitri was using was a stabbing weapon and only the point was truly deadly. By altering the direction of each thrust to a small degree the point was passing Alexei's body harmlessly with what seemed like minimal exertion as compared to the full body thrusting that Dimitri was employing.

I watched as Dimitri tried to twist the blade mid-strike in order to redirect the point from what appeared initially to be a heart strike, yet ended as thrust to the throat. Immediately I realized that Alexei wouldn't be able to get his knife up in time to parry, but this time Alexei didn't even try. Instead he juked to the side like a boxer and attempted to move inside the range of the sword. Dimitri was ready for the move and slashed the edge of the sword down, the sharpened edge slicing a shallow line across Alexei's back as he tried to duck forward into striking distance. Alexei arched in pain but still managed to launch his own strike, albeit towards a non-lethal part of Dimitri's left thigh, and his hunting knife sliced through the fabric of Dimitri's slacks as well as the flesh beneath.

Both wounds were painful but shallow and far from incapacitating. The fight had an elegant style and conveyed a sense of mastery on the part of both men, making it almost like watching the perfectly coordinated and choreographed dance. I, therefore, felt like a complete heathen when, as Dimitri parried Alexi's latest move, I took the opportunity to lift the heavy leather chair and swing it baseball bat style into Dimitri's side. My inner caveman rejoiced even further as the sensation of the bone jarring impact traveled up the length of the chair before it broke over Dimitri's body, which collapsed at the point of impact and crumbled to the ground from the sheer force of my swing.

I picked up the gun from the floor when the high-pitched "ping" of the elevator sounded from outside the office. An interruption by security forces right now was going to be a serious problem for us, but no sense wishing it were otherwise as they were on the way.

Alexei moved first and slapped my shoulder and then pointed to the large window overlooking the city. I understood in an instant and picked up a larger piece of the chair that had broken near my feet, I think it was part of the seat and arms, as I threw it at the glass, which completely shattered in thousands of tiny pieces. Alexei didn't wait for me and ran for the opening as if to dive through, despite the fact that we were nearly five stories in the air. I looked back to see Dimitri rising to one knee, as he recovered from blow I had given him with the chair and then the office began to fill with several black clad figures as they bolted from the elevator car, all of whom were carrying automatic rifles equipped with silencers. There was no fighting those odds, so despite my lack of understanding and under the threat of imminent doom, I ran for the window and leapt through just as Alexei had, only to find myself plummeting down toward the empty concrete street five stories below.

Chapter 29

I had only dropped about ten feet and was about to scream in terror when something grabbed me by the waist. I felt my body bend uncomfortably as my fall became a swing back toward the face of the building and I crashed through a window on the fourth floor. I could feel my clothes and skin being torn by the glass and I barely had time to shield my eyes before my body hit the floor just inside the room.

I was afraid to move for fear the glass that I was covered in would cut my skin even worse than it already was, but I still managed to look up in time to see Alexei's swinging legs come into view, as he kicked himself back for momentum and then artfully levered himself in through the smashed opening.

Alexei looked down at me, "Get up quickly, they will be coming down after us."

Forgetting the danger the glass shards represented I rapidly stood up as Alexei had requested and leaned over to look outside. There were no apparent hand or footholds that could have possibly supported our combined weight and the impossibility of what Alexei had just done bamboozled me to such a degree that I almost missed seeing the head of one of Dimitri's guards peering out of the shattered window above. The guard immediate pointed his weapon down at me, but I managed to pull my head back in before he could fire a shot.

The fourth floor was set up like any normal office space, complete with hallways and several individual adjoining spaces. Alexei was checking the window view of each office space for something and I ran to join him just as the elevator again made its pinging sound.

"Here!" Alexei called out beckoning me to follow and I made it to the office door just as the elevator door opened and again the men inside fired off a cacophony of shots in our direction.

I closed the door behind me, for all the good it would do, turned to Alexei and said, "What's the plan?"

We could hear Dimitri screaming at his men in Russian as Alexei opened the window and looked down.

"There!" He pointed to an enormous dumpster, the kind that was normally used on construction sites during demolition. It appeared to be the same size as the cargo space on a trailer truck with the lid open and displaying that the inside was filled with what looked like garbage bags, as opposed to demolished wood, concrete and drywall.

I pulled my head back in, my eyes wide with shock, "That only works in the movies!"

Alexei smiled before involuntarily ducking his head, as the door to the office began to pop and splinter as the bullets burst through it.

"No choice! Try to land as flat a possible!" Alexei had said as he grabbed my arm, twisted his body and flipped me out the window. I don't remember screaming as much as gasping for air while I fell and felt the wind rush by me. There was a loud snap, crackle and pop that filled my ears as I hit the detritus in the dumpster, exhaling sharply as the wind was knocked from my lungs. Despite the violence of the impact and my inability to breathe, I didn't feel that much pain, which made me wonder momentarily if I was paralysed before the sound of something else crashing into the dumpster next to me brought me back to my senses. This time the crash was accompanied by a resounding "clang" of something solid striking metal and I had recovered enough from my landing to realize that it was Alexei's limp form lying next to me. I reached out and shook him but got no response and guessed that the metal clanging sound had been Alexei hitting part of the metal container as he landed. A chill went through me as I realized that if he had hit his head on the side as he dropped

271

inside he was as good as dead, so I quickly felt his neck and immediately found a strong pulse. I guessed that he had instead struck his head against the thin inner walls of the dumpster at some point during his landing, but now I had to drag his ass out as well as my own.

I kicked my legs over and hung suspended at the waist on one side of the dumpster as I pulled Alexei up and out by the shoulders. I had just managed to leverage his torso over the side when the sound of bullets hitting the trash strewn around us gave me a reason to hurry. Without another option I just heaved Alexei out and we both flopped to the ground at a point behind the container, where I hoped we would both be out of the line of sight from the gunmen in the window.

There were a multitude of "pangs" from the silenced rounds hitting, and often penetrating through the dumpster, but none of the bullets seemed to be able to find their way through both sides. I couldn't make a run for it without the risk of being shot in the back, not to mention the fact that I'd be leaving Alexei behind, so I needed to come up with a plan and fast.

I looked at the base of the dumpster and saw that it was on wheels, but it still likely weighed over a thousand pounds and there was little chance that I could get the thing moving.

Damn, I was sure that most of Dimitri's people were on their way down while a single guard or maybe two kept us covered to prevent our escape, but what could I do? Alexei started moaning as he regained consciousness and I put a hand on his shoulder to prevent him from trying to get up and exposing himself as a target to the gunmen above us.

Desperately I looked around and was trying to come up with something that could save us, but with the chaos happening all around me I was coming up blank. Then, from above, there was a cry of pain and surprise followed by silence until something hit the side of the dumpster hard enough to jolt the entire container. I kept my back pressed against the wall of the dumpster but rolled my eyes skyward to see an arm hanging limply over my head, and still tethered to the automatic rifle that it had been holding. The bullets stopped hitting the dumpster and I took the opportunity to improve my position and saw one of Dimitri's guards was folded neatly in half over one side of the dumpster. The guard had a hole in his forehead that had blown out the back of his skull. How the hell had that happened, I thought, but didn't waste time wondering as I immediately grabbed onto the rifle that was still slung around the guard's body. Unfortunately for me, the fall had entangled the shoulder strap around his head and I'd have to pull him out of the dumpster to get it off of him, which would likely expose me to any remaining gunmen. The bullets hadn't started raining down again, but that didn't mean I was in the clear. I decided to go for it and stood to lift the guard off the side of the dumpster when about six more guards ran around the far corner of the building and spotted me. I immediately ducked down and was about to pull Alexei around to the far side of the dumpster for cover when a sound of something cutting through the air came from over my head and the guard in the front of the pack suddenly contorted, flying back and falling to the ground.

The guards all pulled up short and began retreating, as I turned my head in time to see a muzzle flash come from the building I had been hiding in earlier in the day. I heard another guard cry out in pain, as I took the opportunity to grab the rifle, scoop up Alexei in a fireman's carry, and then run as fast as I could across the street to the building where the shots were coming from.

Bullets zinged off the pavement to my right so I darted left before I saw several flashes come from the sniper that had been covering me, and the hail of bullets following me ceased. I jumped over the curb and bounced Alexei roughly on my shoulders, which apparently jolted him to full consciousness, as he began kicking wildly to get off of my shoulders. I obliged with relief, and pulling

Alexei in the direction I thought we should run when, from around the corner, the limousine belonging to Igor's friend fishtailed, righted itself and then, with its engine growling as the driver gunned it into action, the large car shot in our direction.

I was already moving for the car when Alexei grabbed at my shoulder and pulled me down. I looked at him as he directed my attention across the street. There was a combination of Dimitri's black clad guards running out of the alley we had come from, and a multitude of security personnel bursting through the front door of the building. No shots rang out from above us, which meant our beneficiary sniper was gone, or perhaps just changing positions.

"They're going to turn the car into confetti as soon as it stops," I snarled.

Alexei gave my shoulder a squeeze, "Just be ready to go when it get's here."

I frowned at him, "What? Where are you going to be?" I didn't get answer before Alexei stood and ran.

The guards instantly began firing at him, making the concrete of the building explode in a cloud of dust that trailed Alexei as he bolted. I have no clue how he wasn't riddled with bullets, but the guards kept firing their rifles as the bullet strikes trailed his path. Then all four of the black clad guards bolted after him. The guard in their rear flashed hand signals to the arriving security personnel and pointed toward the spot where I had taken cover, apparently telling them to stay on me. There were several of them, and they seemed to register the orders they had been given as they started toward me. They had barely taken a step when they realized that the limousine roaring down the road was going to pass between us. Their eyes darted from the car to me and back again, but it wasn't until the car screeched to a halt that they looked for cover or dropped to their knees and prepared to fire their weapons at us.

At that moment Chris popped half his body out of the limousine's sunroof with an automatic shotgun in his hands.

"Spartans!" Chris hollered in his best imitation of actor Gerard Butler's King Leonidas, "What is your profession?!" The guards' eyes went wide with shock as their minds registered the weapon in Chris' hands just before Chris opened fire with the shotgun. The recoil of the weapon resulted in double ought buckshot spraying wildly in their direction without any real regard for accuracy. Still, the guards scattered, diving to the ground before attempting to crawl to safety, and I took the opportunity to run for the car.

I had barely cleared the door as I jumped in before Alpha slammed his foot down onto the accelerator and the car lurched forward. Chris was whiplashed with such force that he dropped one of his shotguns before he could get down from the sunroof and settle back into his seat.

"What the hell are you guys doing here?" I asked in both fury and relief.

"It was decided that your decision to attempt diplomacy was stupid," Alpha said with about as condescending a tone as I had ever heard come from him.

"We voted," Chris volunteered, "and it was unanimous. You're officially an idiot."

I stared at Chris blankly, before the relief of being out of the fray finally sank in, "I suppose you guys were right."

"Gosh! You think?" Chris stated with mock incredulity. "In fact, I wanted to have a vote in favor of changing your name to "Stevie Stupid-pants" but I couldn't get anyone to second my motion."

Alpha groaned before asking, "Where is Alexei?"

My wide grin faltered, "He took off leading three or four of the guards away."

"Did he say where we should meet him?" Alpha asked.

I shook my head, "No, I had actually hoped you guys had talked about it before hand and it was a part of a plan."

"Uh oh," Chris whispered, "so what do we do?"

On instinct I said, "Last I saw of him, he had run to the next street and turned right with the guards in pursuit. Let's see if we can find him."

The vehicle shot forward until we reached the corner when Alpha spun the wheel and hit the brakes, fishtailing the heavy vehicle into a turn that maintained a good portion of its speed. The street was empty, but we scanned the buildings and any spaces between them for a sign of Alexei.

When we approached another intersection Alpha called out, "Which way?"

I tried to think and give a most likely or logical answer. Alexei was leading the guards away and turning right would be the beginning of a square or grid pattern that could lead the men back in our direction, so he wouldn't choose a right turn. A left turn would have interrupted his pursuers line of sight, albeit momentarily, where running straight ahead would give him no advantages.

"Go left!" I answered and Alpha repeated the sliding turn to the left that he had done earlier. We had only traveled about fifty yards when Alpha suddenly hit the brakes and the car skidded to a halt, flinging both Chris and myself forward against the front seats and dashboard, respectively.

Alpha's eyes were locked onto something to the left of the vehicle, and I turned in that direction to see what had caught his attention. The building Alpha was staring at was only a shell of its former self, and appeared to be mostly rubble strewn around a warped and rusted, but still standing, frame. Blackened marks indicated artillery fire had blotched the face of the concrete rubble and twisted the building's metal structural support, which was partially melted down into the natural shadows of the ruin, giving the entire crumbling structure an organic feel, as opposed to something that once had been engineered.

I was about to ask Alpha what he had seen when he quickly got out of the vehicle and jogged over to a towering concrete block with rebar sticking out of it in several places. Chris popped his body out of the sunroof and brought his sniper rifle up to cover Alpha as he quickly but cautiously peered around the block before disappearing behind it.

I heard Chris hiss, "No! Don't..." followed by a huge sigh, "...go out of my line of sight."

I wanted to call out to Alpha, but he called out to us first, "How many were following him?"

I thought for a second before answering, counting off the guards in my head, "Four!" I called back,

Alpha came walking back around the far side of the concrete block dragging one of the black clad guards behind him by the ankle, as if the man weighed no more than a child. He nonchalantly lifted the man's limp form with one outstretched arm to make sure Chris and I could see what he had found. In true Alpha form, he had no regard for the incredible feat of strength he was displaying. He then dropped the man, discarding him like the inanimate object he apparently was and walked back to the vehicle.

Once he climbed back inside he said, "All four of the guards are over there. Two look to have what appear to be knife wounds while the other two look as though they simply dropped where they stood with no signs of injury."

"Like the guy you just held up?"

"Yes, the very dead guy I just held up."

I looked away from Alpha and back toward the ruins, "Any sign of Alexei?"

Alpha shook his head, "No. No blood, or anything else that might help us track him, he's just gone."

Chris dropped back into the car, "So what now?"

"Nothing we can do at this point," I said with a sigh, "let's go collect William and discuss our next move.

I had a sick feeling as Alpha put the transmission into drive and took us out of the area. I didn't like leaving anyone behind, especially not someone who had just saved me from my own shortsightedness. I had truly expected Dimitri to want to get us out of the way badly enough for the ancient, evil, Russian bastard to make a deal with us. I had also been arrogant enough to think that if things went sideways I could take the old man out on my own. I cursed myself for a fool.

With the exception of Alpha, and William of course, I had always been the fastest, strongest and most capable of my kind. I was Alpha's lead Hunter, but I needed to remember that this didn't mean I was Alpha, or even in his league. The Ancients, like Alpha and Dimitri, were playing on a level that only time and experience can muster, and Dimitri was older than Alpha. I had gone toe to toe with Alpha in the past and got my ass handed to me, but had not been overly surprised by the beating I took, because Alpha looked the part. Alpha was tall, muscular and moved with a grace of motion that practically shouted what a danger he was. On the other hand, Dimitri used his frail appearance to make his enemies, like me, underestimate him by thinking him to be the old man he appeared to be. And he had a sword. Even if he hadn't taken my gun from me, he had still accessed a blade in an instant. Maybe I could have survived a hand to hand skirmish or at least found a way to run away, but once Dimitri had armed himself it would have been over. In fact, after having tangled with both Alpha and Dimitri, I wasn't sure Alpha could have handled him either. Alpha was definitely the stronger of the two, but if Dimitri was armed, then he would likely have chopped Alpha to pieces.

The image of Alexei having fought Dimitri to a standstill, with that machete he called a hunting knife, suddenly became far more impressive to me, and even though he had apparently

278

escaped from his pursuers, I could only hope that he had survived the encounter intact.

We were definitely going to need him in the coming fight, if we could find him.

Chapter 30

Pha's lungs screamed for air and her legs were burning with exertion as she ran. She hadn't eaten since she had started running more than a day ago and only stopped once to drink. When she made that stop she drank as much as she could force into her stomach from a fast moving stream before going back to running again. She remembered what her new father had told her back in Bangkok, about fear and how to channel it into strength. Back in her birth city she had been afraid of people, mostly her mother and later the Madame of the brothel where her mother had worked. But she had never known such fear as she felt now, because here in the wilderness there were no labyrinths of hidden streets or alleyways with dark shadows that could hide her from anyone who would want to hurt her. There were no people here, and as much as she knew that people were to be feared, she was running through a wild landscape, where her imagination placed every dark predator and demon she had ever read or heard about, hiding and ready to pounce from behind each tree she encountered.

In time she had reached the edge of the forest just as the sun was beginning to set and she stopped to peer out of the trees. A small farmhouse was in the distance with an area surrounded by a wooden fence. Ambling around inside the fence were unusual looking animals that she had never seen before. They somewhat resembled large goats, but covered with a thick and curly fur that didn't sway in the wind. They had gentle faces, but a few had large curled horns that were enough of a warning for her to avoid trying to sneak past them. If they were aggressive she was certain the large horned animals could run her down in a second.

Smoke billowed from the chimney of the simple stone and mortar house, and the scent of cooking food immediately sent her stomach churning with hunger. She needed to eat and replenish some of the energy she had expended if she were going to keep running. Eventually hunger overwhelmed her fear and she slowly walked from the edge of the woods to approach the gate in the fence. Several of the goat creatures were grazing on grass by the gate and lifted their heads as she approached. She froze, and the animals quickly lost interest in her and went back to their meal.

She continued walking and began plucking small yellow flowers that were growing wild in the field surrounding the farm. She had remembered that the goats in her grandmother's village had liked to eat the flowers on the jungle floor more than grass, when they could find them, and she hoped the same would be true for these creatures.

The animals didn't lift their heads again until she was standing next to them with only the gate standing between her and the animals. Her close proximity had made some of the beasts amble back and away from the gate, while others started braying an alarm for the rest of the little herd. One of the larger horned animals approached warily and stomped its small hooves on the ground as she stared at them from her side of the gate. Slowly she stuck her hand through the openings of the gate, offering a couple of the flowers to the agitated creature with the horns. Initially it stepped back from the her outstretched arm, but then seemed to notice the flowers and quickly stepped up to accept them. The animal immediately switched from making angry sounds to satisfied grunts as it began munching on the flowers, which spurred the other animals in the herd to saunter over and begin bleating at her, not in alarm, but instead for their own portions.

The girl chuckled at the creatures. They even sounded a little bit like the goats she had taken care of in her the village. Although their calls were louder and deeper than the animals back home, the familiarity was comforting. She was handing out the last of the flowers when a loud barking came from the house and a large dog ran at full speed toward her location. A man walked out of the house as well, holding a rifle in his hands. Every part of her

281

being screamed at her to turn and run back to the forest, but she knew she'd never be able to outrun either the dog or a bullet, so she dropped the remaining flowers she had been feeding the animals onto the ground and stood her very still. The dog came up fast, snarling, growling and flashing it's large teeth at her, but at the last minute it pulled up short to just begin barking wildly, as the animals that had been eating her flowers quickly dispersed.

The man was running as well and shouting something in a language she didn't understand, but she never took her eyes off the dog's eyes. The dog was hopping around in a half circle trying to get a reaction out of her, but the girl made no move to run and the creature's predatory instincts were confused.

The man who approached was sounding angrier and angrier, and his deep voice began to crack in frustration as Pha realized that the man was yelling at the dog, not at her. He grabbed the dog by its collar and repeated an order until the dog reluctantly sat and became quiet. The man regarded her with a stern look on his face. He said something abrupt to her and flicked the arm that held the rifle at her in a "go away" motion. The girl felt some relief that he was not going to hurt her, but leaving was not an option anymore. She needed help and, if this man meant her no harm, then she had to find a way to get him to help her.

The man repeated himself, but seeing no reaction from the girl his face screwed up in a look of confusion as he knelt down on one knee to look at her in more of an eye-to-eye level. His voice softened as well, and when he spoke again his tone was filled more with concern than anger. She still didn't know how to react, and remained standing still, until the man put the rifle down and held out his hand to her. She didn't mean to flinch, but years of wariness around strangers made her react instinctively.

The man, upon seeing her reaction, pulled his hand back quickly and held it up with his palm facing her. She began to lose her nervousness as the man spoke softly and tried to communicate with her. The man scolded the dog sharply once more, and then turned his head and shouted something she didn't understand back toward the house. A woman's voice answered and the two spoke a few words to each other before the woman walked from the house holding the hand of a small child.

When the woman and child arrived the Pha's eyes went wide at the sight of a little girl holding on to the woman's hand, and the immense number of colored ribbons tied within her braided hair. Seeing her staring at the ribbons the little girl reached into a pocket of the dress she was wearing and held out a tiny handful of colored ribbons to her. Pha looked from the girl's hand to the man and woman, and they were all were smiling warmly at her.

Finally the man broke the silence and waved at Pha to get her attention. She watched as he pointed to the child, who was likely his daughter, and said, "Mishka," before pointing back to her, his bushy eyebrows raised as if asking a question.

Understanding leaked in and she pointed to herself as, in a voice that cracked her words, she said, "Pha."

Chapter 31

After searching the streets for Alexei without any luck, Alpha, Chris and I had driven out of town to meet up with William, Igor and Sasha at their rented farmhouse. The owner initially seemed overjoyed with the extra income Alpha provided him in return for his hospitality. But after resting his eyes on William, he had decided that it was a good time to take his sheep out to pasture. His wife, on the other hand, made herself out to be the doting hostess, and almost magically she had a variety of breads and cheeses set out for us when we walked through the door. She immediately took on a matronly role with us, as if she had known us our entire lives, and she seemed to otherwise revel in the fact that she had guests. I was sure the food, and likely the overtly sunny disposition of the woman, was more rooted in the fact that we had paid nearly three times the couple's asking price for using their dilapidated barn as a personal shelter for our small troop, and also for a storage space for our gear for at least the next few nights.

Chris and I tucked into the food and Alpha went out to look for William, who we all unnervingly noticed was quite absent from the bed in which he was supposed to be recovering from the wounds he sustained when we prevented him from killing Alexei.

"So, what exactly do we do next." Chris asked between mouthfuls of bread and cheese.

I shrugged my shoulders, "You didn't much care for my last idea."

Chris nodded, "Well, the fact that it went south leaves me with the pleasant ability to say 'I told you so.' On the other hand, it's not as though any of us had any better ideas."

I shook my head and sighed, "To tell you the truth, I think I was acting out of desperation, as opposed to any kind of inspiration."

Chris kept eating, but his eyes were locked onto me, wordlessly expressing his desire for me to continue.

"I'm pretty much tapped out here. I know you are all looking to me for a plan, and expecting my experience as a Detective to just 'Sherlock' something out of thin air." I put some of my food back onto the plate in front of me, as my appetite suddenly diminished, "I am literally a stranger in a strange land here. I don't even know where to begin to start sleuthing around, and even if I did, I can't speak the language to conduct a proper interrogation because I don't know how to form the words in order to ask the questions that might begin to give us a lead."

Chris listened to every word I said without making his usual commentary and then seemed to consider his next words before speaking them, "Frustrating, isn't it?"

I frowned, "What?"

Seeing my negative reaction to the question, Chris held his hands up, "I'm just saying it's a frustrating feeling to have the skills to accomplish what you need to do, but circumstances prevent you from using them."

My frown deepened, but not in anger. Chris was circling around a point he wanted to make and, despite his usual frivolity, he had moments when he could be quite inspired, even profound.

"I don't think I can remember ever feeling helpless before," I confessed.

Chris nodded, "Back when I was working as a Medical Examiner there were times when I knew, I mean I just knew, that I was looking at a homicide, but nothing would come back from the lab to indicate making such a report. Blood work was clear, no signs of intentional trauma, no allergic or other chemical reactions that could be associated with foul play, still I knew something was wrong, and I had to figure out how I was going to get the answers."

"What did you do?"

Chris smiled a wolf's grin at me, "I asked the corpse."

"You mean you studied the body and let it reveal its secrets as you continued your examination?"

Chris looked at me like I was crazy, "No, I started a conversation with the corpse, and once we had fully broken the ice and developed a friendly report, I flat out asked the corpse what had killed him or her."

I waited for the sarcastic zinger to follow, but it never came. Chris just sat there looking at me expectantly until I responded, "You spoke to the corpses?"

"Sure, we talked about all kinds of things. From the weather to whatever game might have been on the radio the night before. Just idle chat, of course, kind of like anytime you are trying to get to know someone new."

"And the bodies spoke back to you?"

Chris admitted, "In a way. Listen, when you spend hours upon hours in the morgue, eventually the dead will either become something akin to a puzzle, or maybe similar to a machine comprised of like parts. The danger is that your humanity gets sucked away when you start looking down on a formerly living human being like this. The magic and mystery goes away, which leads to a very pragmatic way at looking at life as a whole. Eventually everything becomes so empirical that we lose something in ourselves that we desperately need."

"Which is what?"

"We lose our imagination. Our creativity. Our ability to theorize outside of what is most obviously right in front of us, and it's my experience that tells me this is where and how the answers reveal themselves."

"Okay, so how does talking to the corpses fit in... and what do you mean that they talk to you 'in a way'?"

Chris chuckled, "Yeah I know how that sounds, but what I mean is that I look in their file, which usually contains a picture of the person in life, and I force myself to think of them as still alive.

286

What they were like, how their voices might have sounded, how they carried themselves and such the like. Eventually I re-create them in my head as people, and then I can hold a conversation with them, and extrapolate what I think their answers will be."

"That's... kind of weird." I said.

Chris laughed, "Only 'kind of weird'?" I'd say it's far more severe than that. Here let me show you what I mean. I had this one person who had apparently died from a terrible stroke in his sleep. The thing was that he was relatively young, in his mid-forties, had no family history of stroke, didn't smoke and was supposed to have been an athlete in decent physical condition. Now, understand that a stroke is something that can be idiopathic, in other words it can just happen for no reason, but the idea of the stroke didn't sit well with me. I could see the guy's muscle tone and the volume of his lungs and couldn't wrap my head around the idea that this guy had thrown a blood clot or some such thing. Imagine my surprise when I opened up his brain and couldn't find the source of the stroke. His blood chemistry was clear and there was no report or indication of trauma to the head. I followed every typical cause of stroke and came up empty, so I started thinking, what if the cause of death wasn't a stroke? Now understand that the guy had clearly had a stroke from the amount of brain tissue that had apparently been destroyed by pre-mortem necrosis, but what if there another cause of death? Such that, as the man had been dying of his actual cause of death, it secondarily caused him to have a stroke just as he died?"

I couldn't help but interject, "Is that even possible?"

"Sure," Chris said matter-of-factly, "in fact there are several poisons that can make such things happen. The problem was that most of these are man-made compounds and show up on toxicology reports, and his blood work was clear. There are a couple of natural products that could have the same effect, but these would need to be injected directly into the bloodstream."

"Why is that a problem?" I asked.

"Mostly because injections leave puncture marks at the sight of the injection, not to mention signs of bruising that becomes very apparent post-mortem, because the blood that would normally circulate in and out of the tiny trauma ends up pooling and is very visible on the skin."

I nodded my understanding, so Chris continued, "I couldn't shake the sense that this was what happened, so I re-inspected the body for bruising and used a magnifying glass on all the bruises I could find. Nothing."

"So what did you do?"

I was about to give up and write the report as a death by natural causes, but it still just didn't sit right in my gut. I stepped back and pictured the guy as I believe he would be in life. The conversation was mostly about football and who had the best quarterback/receiver combination in the league. I pictured the guy sitting in the desk chair next to me and after "talking" to him for a while I noticed he wasn't able to sit comfortably in the chair. I asked him about it and he denied being uncomfortable, but he kept fidgeting in the chair. After a little more prodding on my part he admitted to having hemorrhoids."

I had been completely rapt in what Chris had been telling me right up until that point, but as soon as the word hemorrhoids came out of his mouth I was sure my friend was punking me. I rolled my eyes and started to get up from the table when Chris ordered, "Sit down!"

I froze, stunned. Chris never spoke like that to anyone, much less me, and I quickly sat back down in my chair. Chris' displeasure was evident in the frown on his face as he stared at me for a couple seconds before asking, "Where was I?"

"Hemorrhoids."

"Right! Hemorrhoids. So, the guy's fidgeting around in the chair complaining about his hemorrhoid problem and the 'eureka

288

moment' happens."

"The eureka moment?" I ask.

"Yes, exactly. I end the conversation, go back to the examination table, flip the body over and start looking where the 'sun don't shine.' I'm not sure what it was that clued my brain to make the guy fidget on the chair in our conversation, maybe it was the gut contents that I removed from his stomach, which was nothing but fast food, or maybe I had seen the hemorrhoids on my initial exam, but when I inspected the tiny arteries under the magnifying glass I found the puncture wound. It looked so much like an open rupture that hemorrhoids sometimes get that I had totally scanned over it without a second thought, but there it was. No bruising or any of the other signs of trauma that an injection site would normally have post-mortem."

I stared blankly at Chris before finding my voice, "Are you telling me that the guy was actually killed by a murderer who injected poison into his ass? This is your inspirational anecdote intended to help me?"

Chris smiled at me, "Think about it for a second and I'll tell you that a scraping of the man's skin around his mouth and nose had faint traces of a Chloroform derivative."

"Chloroform?" I knew about the chemical mostly from old spy novels and movies. It was a particularly dangerous compound that was one of the first used in surgical procedures to anesthetize a patient.

"Is that stuff still around?" I asked.

Chris shrugged, "Sure, but most doctors have abandoned it for something with far fewer side effects, or the risk of over-dosing the patient."

"So, who uses it these days?"

Chris said very seriously, "Mostly people who aren't concerned about the intended recipient waking up again."

I thought about what Chris was saying and asked, "So they

289

knocked the guy out with the Chloroform to make sure he didn't otherwise struggle or wake up while they injected the poison into his..." I suddenly didn't feel right about making light of an actual murder victim, despite the unusual circumstances. "...Before injecting him in an area that would likely be overlooked during an autopsy. That the idea?"

"Yep, pretty screwed–up, right?"

"Wouldn't the Chloroform be enough to indicate the murder?"

Chris shook his head, "You'd think so, but the body gives off a certain amount of Chloroform naturally as it decomposes, not specifically around the mouth and nose per se, but defense attorneys have a field day with our office if the only indication of foul play is the presence of Chloroform. In this case though, it was only one part of the explanation of how a man could be injected in that particular anatomical location without putting up any kind of struggle.

I shook my head both in astonishment at the brazen lack of empathy the victim's killers displayed to have performed such a cold act. I also had to wonder where Chris was going with this whole thing.

"So how did that case turn out?"

"Would you believe less than thirty minutes after I filed my report the NSA swooped in and confiscated all the files, photographs and recordings, as well as the victim's remains? I was also given standing orders to never speak of it again or I'd disappear as well."

I smiled, "And yet here you are blabbing all of it to me."

Chris smiled back and when he spoke again his words dripped with irony, "I am in the Russian territory of Nazran, Ingushetia and on the other side of the planet from those NSA guys, not to mention the fact that I am now believed to be dead while, in reality, I am a vampire telling the story to another vampire who also happens to be a Detective with the LAPD."

Chris let the inanity of the stuation he described linger in the air for a moment before finishing as he gave me that wolfish look of his again, "If the NSA wants to come and get me, then fuck 'em, they can come and get me."

My smile widened at that. It was classic Chris, just being Chris, but I still didn't get how it related to me.

"Great story bro, but how does it apply to our situation?"

"I think your brain is mentally locked in one position, specifically on the task of getting to Dimitri in order to have him reveal the location of the girls."

I nodded, "Sure, he's kind of our only link to them in this country."

"And there's my point, this little technique of mine was never something I would ever admit to while I was working for the LAPD. I mean, I really had no idea how true to life my re-enactments were, but as the 'conversation' evolved in my head, and I combined that with what I had already learned on the autopsy table and the victim's file, somehow my brain started formulating 'what if's' that I would never have come up with by concentrating only on what was right in front of me."

Chris pointed a finger at the top of my head, "That's what you need to do. Think sideways."

Well, I didn't have any other ideas, so I let out a frustrated sigh and asked, "How do I get started?"

"You've been focusing on Dimitri," Chris shrugged, "maybe if we were to grab one of his people?"

I interrupted, "Dimitri wouldn't make a trade, mostly because he treats his people like expendable assets." I thought about what I had just said and amended myself, "Well, he does likely have some people who are more important than others, like the giant that Alexei seems to be after, but we have even less intel on them than we do on Dimitri. Not to mention the fact that just because a person has value to Dimitri, it doesn't mean that he or she will know the information we need."

"Not worth a try?" he asked.

I shook my head, "A lot of risk just to gamble on the reward." I looked somberly at Chris, "not that it won't come to that before this is all over, but it's definitely not a best option."

"And you're sure that Dimitri wasn't hiding the girls at his offices?"

Again I shook my head, "It didn't feel right to me. I don't think he'd be keeping them in a locked office space while everyone around just went about their normal day. I mean it's possible, but if I were to make an educated guess, then I'd say he was keeping them in an isolated location, and away from the city... especially now that he knows we're here."

Chris took in a deep breath and let it out with a loud sigh, "Alright, so what do we know about why he needs the girls in the first place?"

Chris was switching the topics around and attacking the problem from different angles. I recognized the tactic as something I used to do as a Detective, so I didn't react badly to the abrupt change in subject.

"Initially, he was going to use the girl, Pha, as a bargaining chip against keeping William in line. We never really found out why he needed William precisely, but we do know that he had been psychologically programmed to attack Alexei."

"So there is something about Alexei that Dimitri is afraid of?"

I thought about the fight in Dimitri's office and how Alexei had matched blades with the ancient vampire. "Alexei would seem to be a potential threat to Dimitri if they were to have a one-on-one duel, but that doesn't explain going to the time, effort and expense that was put into William's abduction and subsequent brainwashing."

"Aha!" Chris raised a finger to the air in triumph, "so we know that Dimitri is afraid of something, and that he believes he needs William to fix the problem."

"Which is why he kept the girl alive after William's brainwashing was complete." I agreed.

Chris was getting excited thinking he had put something into motion, "So we need to figure out what it is that Dimitri is afraid of, and use it against him! Right?"

I inclined my head as I nodded, "That would certainly be useful information for us, and if Alexei were here I might be able to ask him the questions that could give us the answers, or at least send us in the right direction."

Chris' shoulders dropped and he deflated a little bit, "But, Alexei isn't here, I gotcha." Not to be dissuaded Chris immediately perked up again, "So what could William be preventing?"

"We don't know, Chris," frustration seeping into my voice, "it's something I'd hope Alexei would know, if he were here to talk to."

Chris waved his hands in front of him, "No, no. I mean, what is it that Dimitri wants to do, in general, that would be ruined by whatever he's afraid of?"

I thought about that for a moment, "You're saying that you think William was programmed to be more than some kind of bodyguard or assassin?"

"Exactly! What if the task William was intended to perform was to act as a kind of buffer against something that could alter or destroy Dimitri's plans."

It seemed impossible to me, "I'll admit that William is pretty impressive, but he's still only one man, and we're talking about Dimitri wanting to take over a huge amount of land. A territory larger than most countries." I looked away from Chris, despondent, "I just don't see how one man could make that much of a difference."

293

Chris asked, "So how is Dimitri planning on taking over the world?"

"Siberian territory," I corrected.

Chris waved off the correction, "Whatever, stay on topic."

I rolled my eyes but continued, "At this point he seems committed to contaminating the area with Dr. Whelan's biological weapon."

"And why would he do that?"

"You know full well why!" Anger filled my voice and I glared menacingly at Chris.

He only smiled back at me, "I think you're missing the point of this exercise, just go with it until you hit the 'Eureka' moment."

I growled, but said, "Because our kind are immune to bacteria and viruses, which makes the biological contamination of the territory more effective than any boundary line or border wall. The entire area would become a great big 'Hot Zone' for human beings and the contamination would keep the Russian government, or any other government, from entering and retaking the land."

"And why won't the government just lob some sort of missiles into the arena from a safe distance?"

"Because they need the non-organic resources that come from the area. Things like minerals, gold, diamonds, coal and oil."

"Won't they be contaminated too?" Chris wondered aloud.

"You can sterilize those things, while not taking anything away from their intended use."

Chris nodded with understanding, "So even if the government did manage to drive Dimitri and his people out they still couldn't go in and access the resources because the area would still be a biological Hot Zone."

"Right."

"There's a flaw."

"There is?"

"Sure, Dimitri can't possibly have enough skilled people to run all of the different operations simultaneously."

I nodded, "True, but remember what brought that crazy bastard Whelan to Dimitri in the first place?"

Chris eyes widened as he remembered, "The damn vaccine Whelan created from our blood that makes regular humans immune to all pathogens. It would make them immune to the biological contaminants that constitute the Hot Zone."

"And, as a vaccine, it is probably designed to only work for short periods of time, so anyone not a part of Dimitri's collective would eventually have to leave or risk dying from the contamination."

Chris thought for a moment before he asked his next question, "Do you think he was going to constantly drain William in order to get the raw materials for the vaccine?"

"No, William is huge to be sure, but I'm guessing that Dimitri would simply take small doses from his entire collective and use them as needed to make the vaccine."

"And then what? Just drop the biological equivalent of an atom bomb on Siberia?"

"No, even if the biologics were spread out by the wind, Siberia is still far too vast to simply bombard one area in the hopes for complete coverage. He'd need to..." I froze as the revelation began to wind itself together in my head.

Chris saw my face and said, "Is this where I yell 'Eureka'?"

I held up a hand and tried to keep the thoughts from swirling apart as I followed the latest topic of conversation, "He'd need to distribute the biologic over vast areas simultaneously before letting the wind finish the process."

"And that tells us what?" he questioned.

I looked up, eyes wide, "That he can't use bombs to deliver the biologics, any military planes capable of carrying such a payload would be seen as a threat and shot down before he could complete the runs necessary to cover the entire area."

"So what would he need?"

I nearly jumped out of my skin, and did jump out of my chair, slamming my fist on the table, as the answer came to me, "Air tanks!"

Chris jumped up as well and copied my exultation with the same exuberance, complete with accompanying fist slam on the table, "Yes! Air tanks!"

"Yes!" I fist pumped a couple times in victory and Chris started doing a touchdown dance just as our hostess came back into the room with another plate of food.

Chris walked over to her, put his arms on her shoulders and said, "Air tanks!" with celebratory gusto before planting an individual kiss on each of her cheeks.

The woman gave us a look as though she was certain we had lost our minds, before she carefully put the plate of food down, then turned and left without saying a word.

Chris was beaming as he watched her go, then walked back over to me and held his hand up for a high-five, "Air tanks!" he exclaimed as I slapped his raised palm in celebration. After that he just smiled and stayed quiet for about two whole seconds before he confessed, "I have no idea what's going on!"

"I know!" I said, my enthusiasm undiminished, "Chris, do you have internet out here in the sticks?"

Chris raised a small device from his pocket that I could see had a cable extending from it with a USB port, "I'm a supergeek. I always have access."

"Then get your computer Geek-boy," I laughed, "we got work to do!"

"Um..." Chris looked unsure, "....Eureka?!"

Chapter 32

It turned out the Internet was less difficult to attain than was a simple electrical outlet. Chris' laptop battery had run down to nothing as Alpha, Alexei and he had been rescuing me from Nightengale Industries, and the only compatible outlet for his charger was located on the gas powered generator we had stashed in the barn.

I was pacing in agitation as the laptop battery slowly absorbed electricity from the noisy generator and Chris took the opportunity to ask, "So, do you want to let me in on our magnificent discovery?"

"Remember back in Thailand when we found the area where they had tested the biologic?"

"Sure."

"The testing device looked like a small scuba tank and they had released the biologic as a gas into the area near the village." I reminded him.

"I remember, it had killed off everything in the area. Pretty disgusting really."

"The point is, the delivery system was basically an aerosol. That means Dimitri is probably going to deliver it the same way, just on a far more grand scale."

"So he's going to do what? Have his people walking around with industrial spray bottles on their backs, spraying down everything in their path like glorified pest control agents?"

I smiled, "I was thinking more along the lines of crop dusters and other small aircraft, customized to deliver the aerosol."

Chris checked the laptop's charge and then looked at me dubiously, "You think a few crop dusters could cover enough ground to blanket Siberia?"

I shrugged, "He'll need a hell of a lot more than a few, but yes."

Chris shot me a skewed glance, disbelieving my theory.

I elaborated, "You're used to seeing crop dusters on T.V. or in the movies, delivering their payload a few feet above the fields. That stuff they drop is heavy and falls straight down to the crops below. In this case we're talking an aerosol that will be released at altitude. It will trickle back down to earth, but not before being carried by the wind, mingling with the moisture in the clouds and eventually coming down as rain. It will descend hundreds, if not thousands of miles away from where it was released. It will also contaminate the water systems and be carried throughout the lands in the water supply."

Chris frowned, "But there will be no way of controlling the spread outside of Siberia. The contaminants will spread everywhere across the continent."

My face grew serious, "Chris, I don't think Dimitri is concerned about the collateral damage."

Chris' eyes widened slightly, "Holy shit."

We were silent after that as we waited for the laptop to gather enough electrical juice into its batteries to start working. The computer's start up chime set us back into motion and Chris accessed the Internet.

"So what am I doing?" he asked.

I took in a deep breath, and metaphorically jumped, "The air tanks that Dimitri would need to distribute the material have to be large enough to hold several cubic feet of aerosol, but still need to be small enough not to overweigh the small aircraft he is going to need to use, in order not to raise any military suspicion."

"So?"

"So that means he's going to need an enormous number of smaller air tanks to attach to the multitude of airplanes required for the job."

"How many tanks are we talking about?"

"Enough that storing them all is going to be an issue."

"Really?" A pang of worry entered into Chris' words, "the city has plenty of abandoned buildings and warehouses that he could use."

"True, but most of them are falling apart. If there is some kind of accident that releases the gas too soon and the people of the city start dying, then the government will find out before Dimitri is ready and his plan is shot to hell."

"Okay, so what am I looking for instead?"

"A warehouse sounds promising, but it would need to be isolated and away from the city."

Chris' fingers flew over the keys as he began his search, "Still pretty vague. Any way to narrow it down?"

"It would have to be warehouse built with a loading dock for the trucks that will be delivering the tanks. The tanks may not be huge on their own, but they are still heavy enough that, once stacked up on a pallet, they are going to weigh a ton."

"So any tilt-up box warehouse won't be enough to handle the deliveries, got it. Anything else?"

I stood behind Chris so I could see the laptop's screen, and placed my hands on his shoulders as I said, "He would need to be by an airport, probably a private one, where he could modify the planes and install the tanks."

Chris stopped typing, "Oh, that's good! There can't be that many private airports in this backwater burg."

"Exactly," I patted his shoulders, "my guess is Dimitri will be keeping the girls at whatever location he is using as his base of operations, which will also be the place serving as the initiation of his plans. It will be well guarded, isolated and have a ton of his people his working to get his plans together."

Chris resumed typing and chuckled, "Heh, eureka."

"Yep," I confirmed, "eureka."

It wasn't exactly a needle in a haystack search, but I could tell it wasn't going to be an instant gratification scenario either, as

Chris struggled with the computer searches. I didn't remember falling asleep on the floor, but almost two hours had magically passed when Chris kicked me awake. I noted the sun was near the horizon and the sky had begun to color with sunset, as I knelt to one side of the computer while Chris delivered the results of the search.

"Okay," Chris started, "as far as I can tell there are only two locations that are both functional airports and possess the warehouses that you said would be necessary."

"Only two?" I smiled at how narrow our search had become.

"More or less," Chris replied with less enthusiasm that I had been hoping for. "Look here," he indicated, pointing a finger at the screen, which had been split into two different windows. "Both of these locations currently have multiple aircraft of varying styles and are literally situated next door to a large grouping of warehouses that appear to have been used in the mining industry, but they were abandoned at some point within the last decade. It should be a simple enough task to clean them up for simple storage."

I nodded as I studied the screen, "Any recent activity?"

Chris shrugged, "Nothing dramatic on the outside, but it will be easier to tell for sure at night. If they leave the lights on, then we know that something is happening inside."

"So that's it?" I asked. "The girls are in either one of these two locations? No other possibilities?"

"Um..." Chris looked concerned, " Actually, there may be another possibility."

I could feel my spirits drop as I saw that Chris had found a flaw in the parameters of the search.

"How bad?" I asked, without truly wanting to hear the answer.

Chris turned back to the computer and sighed, "Pretty bad

actually."

His fingers flew over the keys again and video images switched from an industrial landscape to one of empty fields and pastures.

"When you mentioned crop dusters a thought occurred to me. Most of the people living out here in the sticks are either farmers or shepherds. Access to town is limited so, if they really had to, how do they get help or supplies quickly?"

"Don't tell me," I practically moaned, "they have what they need flown in?"

Chris nodded, "Igor was helpful to translate some of my questions I asked of our hostess, and it seems the rancher here, and his closest neighbors had worked together to construct a runway in the center of their properties. It's just a dirt road really, but it's enough for a small plane, equipped with the proper landing gear, to put down in case of an emergency. It's also centrally located enough that all the neighbors have to travel a similar distance to get to the landing strip. Apparently a lot of the farms, in the good old days of the Soviet Union, would deliver their goods to this central location, where they were loaded onto a plane. That was also when they would be given whatever supplies they were allotted under the communist system. After the fall of the Soviet Union the idea of either building or maintaining the existing runways grew from there."

"And this is a problem for us because...?"

Chris tapped a final key and the laptop screen flickered until an image of a wide pasture of what looked like little more than wild grasses came into view. In the center were a couple of warehouses that sat along what appeared to be a long and wide dirt road.

"What's this place?" I asked.

Chris shook his head, "Not sure really," Chris used the mouse pad to "zoom out" the image on the screen and I immediately noted that the area looked as if it had been constructed in multiple squares. The borders were simple roads or trails, likely used for moving farming equipment around, and those trails could still be seen despite the overgrowth of grasses. Each square was likely several acres across and completely enclosed the multiple warehouses. It instantly brought to mind a chessboard save for the four darkened warehouse buildings and long dark strip that was the runway.

"I don't see a flight tower or any other support equipment for a working airport."

Chris nodded, "I agree and I was about to cross it off my list as a potential place when I started thinking about how Dimitri would coordinate so many planes to take off simultaneously without anyone noticing? Better yet, if an unusual number of planes began landing at one of those other airports in order to get prepped for Dimitri's attack, wouldn't some aircraft controller take an interest?"

I shrugged, "Dimitri controls everything in this city. Maybe he just bribes them not to say anything?"

Chris nodded, "Maybe, but there's a chance that the locals wouldn't be the only ones to notice."

I finished Chris' thought, "And Dimitri can't risk taking that chance so far into his plans."

"Right, so what if he used a place like this? Full warehouse facilities and a private airstrip where his planes could take off."

"But the planes would still need to file a flight plan from wherever they originated. Even if they weren't truthful about their destinations, that would still be a lot of planes unaccounted for."

"Unless he didn't fly the planes in," Chris volunteered.

"Hmm?" I responded.

"Well, crop dusters are really light planes, so I thought why not just take the wings off and truck them in?"

I stared at Chris as he continued, "They could just deliver

302

the planes over time and store them in the warehouses next to the air tanks until it was time to go and no one would ever be the wiser."

I let out a frustrated grunt of air, "Damn, how common are these set ups around here?"

Chris' face dropped, "Dozens. I can weed some of them out, but it will take a few days of surveillance to see who and what is happening at each location."

"And that's time we don't have." I sighed. "You know, sometimes it would be nice just to get an answer the easy way."

Chris laughed, "As a former Medical Examiner, I can tell you there is no such thing. Every worthwhile clue is one that was discovered only once it had been dug out from under a pile of worthless shit."

I looked at Chris, one of my eyebrows askance, "You're not talking literally are you?"

"For the most part no," then Chris reconsidered, "but there was this one time when..."

"Never mind!" I interrupted and pinched the spot between my eyes that received so much of my attention, at least whenever I had a prolonged "serious" conversation with Chris. "So, all we can do is sit and..."

A draft swept into the room and delicious smells wafted in along with it, which served to shut me up mid-sentence. Chris turned hungrily toward the door beyond which our hostess was preparing the evening meal. I glanced outside and saw the sun setting even lower in the horizon and was saddened that my appetite had not returned, even for the real, home-cooked meal that had been prepared.

"Want me to start searching now?" Chris asked with what sounded like reluctance.

"Let's take a break. Why don't you grab the rest of the guys from the barn and I'll see if there's anything I can do to help our hostess."

Chris nodded, "Last I heard William was fetching water and I think Alpha went with him."

"What about Igor and Sasha?"

"Igor is busy on his cell phone doing his business thing and Sasha was chopping firewood, but they were both by the barn. I'll grab them."

We both stretched and walked from the room. As I approached the main house I could smell the cooking meat and felt my stomach roil in response. I should have been hungry and instead felt nauseous.

I strained to see through the kitchen window and my eyes locked on the stack of meat not yet on the fire as a pain pierced my guts and nearly forced me to the ground. I managed to stabilize myself and, concerned the lady of the house had seen me double over, I peered through the glass again. She was looking out the window, but not at me. I realized that she was staring, unblinking, out the window into the pasture with a worried look on her face. I turned and peered into the sunset to see the silhouettes of the sheep trotting in from the horizon along with the outline of the shepherd standing tall amongst them. I frowned, my pain now forgotten, as I watched the horizon, unsure of what had made the lady nervous, when a second figure came into view. Whoever was behind the shepherd was much larger and I could just make out the outline of a rifle in the waning light.

I immediately bolted for the barn yelling, "Gun!"

Instantly, Igor was off his cell phone and reaching for the weapons we had laid out on a table for cleaning. The sound of Sasha chopping wood halted abruptly and the young, shirtless man ran in from the back door of the barn, axe still in hand. Chris came around the far side of the barn where he had walked, likely in order to retrieve Sasha, and caught the hunting rifle that Igor tossed to him with fluid grace. Chris spun and immediately moved into a

304

position where he could use the sight to get a better look at what we were dealing with.

"Where's William and Alpha?" I shouted to Igor.

"They went to get water from the well a little while ago, but they should have been back by now!" Igor shouted back.

Damn, I thought. They were going to walk right into this, unless they had already been ambushed.

I turned to Chris, "Can you see anything?"

"Sun's not quite behind the horizon and it's screwing up my ability to see clearly through the scope. I can make out the gunman, but that's about it. Want me to take him?"

"Can you see the Shepherd? Does he look a prisoner or hostage?"

I could see the barrel of the rifle shift slightly as Chris aimed at the Shepherd, "I can only make out his silhouette, everything's going to be in shadow until the sun goes down completely, although he seems to be walking pretty casually."

The pair were around two hundred yards away and some of the sheep had already made their way ahead of the rest of the herd, funneling into the large pens on the property where they slept every night.

I shook my head, "Hold your fire, but keep the gunman in your sights, just in case."

"Got it."

I squinted my eyes to try to make out more detail on what was happening when the sounds of voices coming from the opposite direction made me pivot toward the noise. Alpha and William were walking up a small path carrying large plastic containers that were likely filled to capacity with water from the well.

"They've stopped!" Chris called out.

I turned and could see the figures facing Alpha and William, the gun man had raised his rifle up but hadn't aimed the

305

barrel at the rancher or in our direction.

Something small began to shift between the sheep that drew my attention. At first I thought it was one of the large dogs the rancher used to herd his flock, but soon realized it was something else.

"Chris!" I called out urgently, "put the gun down!" but Chris was looking through the sight as the sun dropped beneath the horizon and his eyes went wide as he suddenly could make out the faces of the figures in the distance.

"Holy shit!" Chris stammered out in surprise.

I turned to Alpha and William and saw that they had noticed the people in the distance as well. They too had both frozen, wide-eyed with shock, but it was William that began to tremble as his eyes turned from their unusual pinkish hue to one of dark blood red. Panic filled me, as the thought that some other mind-altering programming had just clicked on in the man, just as it had when he first realized who Alexei was. The water containers fell with a crash from his large hands, and he bolted toward the figures at a full sprint. Alpha made no move to stop him, but as I turned I could see the gunman take a surprised step back, raise the rifle to his shoulder in order to take aim at the oncoming William. The rancher noticed the maneuver, and immediately spun to grab the barrel of the rifle, forcing it upward as it fired. The sound of the shot echoed, but William made no indication that he had even heard it. The small figure milling its way between the remaining sheep stopped and watched as William charged forward. As soon as it stopped moving I could make out what, or better yet "who," it was. Emotion immediately rose and threatened to choke me with the lump it produced in my throat, as the small girl ran forward with a high pitched wail that erupted into tears. Pha ran with her hands held outstretched and her fingers grasping the air with every step, until William scooped her up and pulled her into his chest in a hug that looked as though it would crush every tiny bone in her

306

body. The girl cried fitfully into the giant's shoulder, but her sobs didn't quite cover the sounds of William's own emotional outpouring, as the big man fell to his knees and protectively folded his entire body around the child in his arms.

I hadn't realized that I had started walking toward the scene until I was standing next to the rancher, who was speaking the local language with the man that had accompanied him. The man was similarly dressed, but appeared older and larger than our man. The sight of Alpha and William was clearly not sitting well with the new arrival, as he glared at William and Pha, but the fatherly look of concern on his face seemed to be calming with every word our man was saying to him. Alpha was standing behind William and was beaming a bright smile at the scene, but in his eyes I could see the desperation to find out more about Lei. I also immediately recognized a similar dichotomy from my own emotions. I was overjoyed for the reunion happening in front of me, but I was simultaneously being torn apart with need to know Lei's fate.

Chapter 33

Eventually Pha's hysterical crying had turned to quiet sobs, and William stood while still holding her tightly in his arms, as he began walking toward the main house. The rancher nodded and suggested we all make our way inside to the meal that was waiting for us. I waved to Chris, Igor and Sasha, who were all still watching from the barn, to indicate that all was well as I pointed to the main house. Chris waved back and put his rifle down before heading over to the water containers and trying to lift them. He reluctantly called over to Igor and Sasha for help, and the other men quickly went to assist.

Once we were all inside the main house the hostess took over and made a big fuss over the rifleman that brought Pha to us, as if he was her long, lost relative, and then commanded rest of us to wash up before dinner in a voice that brooked no argument. I took the opportunity from the ensuing commotion to turn to the rancher and ask, "Who is your friend?"

"His land borders my own. We are neighbors, although there is enough pasture between the two of us that we rarely see each other."

I had promised myself that I would wait until after we ate before asking questions, but couldn't help myself, "And the girl?"

The rancher nodded, "He says she wandered out of the woods and onto his property last night starving and completely exhausted. He says she was very lucky not to have collapsed before his dog discovered her."

"Very lucky," I agreed, "how did he know to bring her here?"

"It was the only thing he could think to do. He speaks no English, but he knows it when he hears it."

"So?"

"So the girl was trying to talk to him in English, and I am

the only person he knows around here who also speaks it."

"That's the only reason?"

The rancher looked confused, but nodded and said, "As far as I know, yes."

There was a loud thump behind me and I turned to see Chris and the visiting rancher standing next to the water container they had just carried in. Both were out of breath from the effort and I absentmindedly remembered that William had been nonchalantly carrying a container in each hand when he returned to the ranch.

"You heard?" I asked.

Chris nodded, "Yep."

"What do you think?"

Chris smiled, "I'm buying it."

"Do you think that Dimitri let her go? Maybe to flush us out or something?"

Chris shot me a skeptical look, "So they let her go into the wilderness for who knows how long and, before getting eaten by wolves or bears, knew she'd end up on the doorstep of a friendly rancher who doesn't speak English, but knows someone who does, and that he would bring her to said English speaking person, all the while knowing that we had set up our operations at said English speaker's farm?"

Chris had run out of breath saying all of that, and he inhaled comically before continuing, "If that was their plan and, with all of the millions of things that could have gone wrong, it happened exactly as it was supposed to, then we might as well give up right now because they can see the future and mold it to their evil desires."

I smiled at Chris, "Well, when you put it like that, okay." I turned back to the rancher, "Do you think your friend can show us where he believes the girl came out of the forest?"

The rancher nodded and said, "I will ask," and walked from the room to prepare himself for dinner.

Chris tapped me on the shoulder, "After we eat I'll start narrowing the search to around this location and see if there are anything the satellites can see within a few miles of here that might fit the bill."

The meal consisted mostly of stewed mutton with potatoes and root vegetables, reminding me very much of a Hungarian Goulash, albeit with different spices. Also we had several loaves of bread that Igor and Sasha had retrieved from town earlier in the day. The hostess was constantly apologizing for not having baked the bread herself, despite the fact that her small wood-burning oven could never have handled the quantity necessary to feed the whole group. Water and beer, a brew the rancher made himself that wasn't half bad, if a bit yeasty for my taste, were provided and everyone tucked heartily into the food. William and Pha did not join us at the table, but William appeared and collected a loaf of bread and a large bowl of stew before retreating back to whatever bedroom he had claimed and where he had left his daughter. No one said anything, but everyone seemed to be on the same page, willing to give William and Pha some time alone. Regular conversation around the table was proving difficult as a result of the language restrictions, so the topic ultimately turned to planning.

"My friend will return to his own land tomorrow morning. He says you are welcome to accompany him and he will show you where he found the girl."

"Is there any way we could use the car and give him a ride home?" I asked, "we have little time to spare."

The rancher translated and the visitor shrugged his shoulders as if to say it was fine with him.

"How long do you think it will take us to get there?" I asked, still ignoring my food.

The rancher considered, "It is a day's walk, but that is a straight line from his land to mine. By car the road will wind around the forests and other natural barriers, so it is likely between three and four hours."

My heart sank. Four hours there, another hour or so to snoop around looking for a trail, and then another four hours back again. At least another day lost before we could even know where to begin.

Chris caught my expression and said with a cheery voice, "Hey, maybe we'll get lucky with the satellites?"

"Are they going to be able to see in the dark?" I asked.

Chris' voice dropped a little, "No, but if we find the right one, then they might have a bunch of lights on and people running around storing those air tanks of yours. I also might be able to tap into a feed from earlier in the day so we can see what was happening in the daylight."

Chris leaned over the table and whispered conspiratorially, "We have more to go on now than we had before, so cheer up."

He was right, and I knew it, but I could feel rage and a desperate need to do something active was building inside me to an unbearable level. I needed to act, I needed to do something more than all the cerebral investigating I had been doing. I was always better in the field getting my hands "dirty" as I metaphorically dug up my leads and followed them. It was taking every mental effort I could muster not to break down and simply scream my frustration into the night sky, so I simply clenched my fingers into a fist and focused on not smashing the table in front of me to splinters.

Alpha had been sitting silently the entire time like some great white ghost, but I thought I had caught him flash me a look of shock before he looked away and hid whatever it may have been. He set his plate aside and then rose from the table, excusing himself as he went. He was about to leave the room when he looked back and quietly said, "Steven, Chris, would you follow me please?"

Chris and I looked at each other, but quickly excused

311

ourselves before standing up from the table. In spite of the rage inside of me, I walked out of the farmhouse feeling a little bit the insensitive guest, for not offering to help clear and clean up first, but I made no atempt to deter from the direction Alpha was taking us as he exited the main house and headed for the barn.

None of us spoke as we walked and it wasn't until we were all inside the barn and Alpha had shut the large door that he decided to speak.

"Steven, what was your assessment of Dimitri's abilities?"

I shrugged, not sure where Alpha was going with this, "Hand to hand I suppose I'd have a pretty good chance against him. He's very fast, but I'm stronger; unfortunately, that means if he's armed with anything more than the skin on his knuckles, then I'm in trouble." Alpha seemed to process that as I asked the obvious question, "Why?"

"It would seem that, unless we can get Christopher a shot with his rifle that I will need to be the one who goes after Dimitri."

"What about William?" Chris asked.

Alpha nodded, "I had been hoping that William could hold off the bulk of Dimitri's people while I went after their leader, but I don't think we can count on William in the coming battle anymore."

Chris and I both remained silent, slightly shocked by the revelation.

"Why the hell not?" I asked abruptly.

Alpha made a face that conveyed disappointment but understanding, "He came for the child and, now that he has been reunited with her, I don't think he wants to put her or himself at risk again."

I couldn't help the surge of anger that bolted through me at those words, "But we were here to recover all of our people! We wouldn't balk at going after the girl if Lei had been returned to us!"

Alpha looked at me patiently, "You are not Lei's father, and

312

Lei is not an innocent nine year old girl."

I opened my mouth to protest, but Alpha cut me off, "Lei is an eighty-plus year old soldier, one of our people's Hunters, and with that title and responsibility comes the realization that, like any other soldier, casualties can occur."

Chris looked at me and volunteered, "You're not suggesting that we just leave her?"

Alpha's face turned from compassionate into intense as he looked from me to Chris, "Of course not!" I thought he might actually lunge for Chris, but he quickly calmed before saying, "I simply am saying that William is likely going to focus on protecting the child as opposed to going on the offensive with us. He is the only family that girl has now and she..."

Alpha's voice had trailed off, but despite how much I hated losing the human equivalent of a force of nature that William embodied in the coming fight, I understood his decision. I hated it, but I understood.

"So now you're wondering who can take Dimitri if you have to be the one on crowd control?"

Alpha nodded, "And there's also Alexei's relative Nicholas that we will have to worry about."

"He seem like a contender to you?" Chris asked.

Alpha shrugged his shoulders, "The history books certainly would say as much. His reputation is that of an extremely capable and dangerous warrior."

"So I should take him from a distance if possible?" Chris raised his hands as if holding his hunting rifle and looking down the barrel and through the sight.

Alpha nodded, "If opportunity presents itself, then that would certainly be a good choice."

Frustration that had been simmering inside me suddenly boiled over, "You both are talking as if we've found her already! Let me remind you that although we have more to go on than we

313

have had since we arrived in this God forsaken place, we haven't actually figured out where Lei is yet!"

Both Alpha and Chris' eyes went wide with surprise as I erupted at them, "I don't care about Dimitri, Nicholas, Siberia, Russia or even Alexei! All I care about is getting Lei back."

I was shaking with rage and my legs suddenly felt unstable beneath me, but I kept right on shouting, "If the two of you are just going to sit around and make stupid plans, then just give me the Goddamn guns and I will go to every fucking farm and kill anyone who even looks like they might be one of Dimitri's people until I find her!"

Chris and Alpha looked at each other, and then Alpha raised his hands before taking a step in my direction, "Steve, how long has it been since you dosed?"

I heard the words, but the meaning was lost on me as my rage continued to build. I couldn't believe Alpha was trying to change the subject on me. Didn't he know we were running out of time?

"We need to get the kid to tell us from where she escaped and if that means we have to drag her out into the forest and make her retrace her steps then that is what we should be doing!"

Chris backed away from me, "Okay let's assume for an instant that William doesn't rip us apart if we were to even look at the child cross-eyed, are you actually suggesting we force a nine year old girl back into harm's way?"

"Don't be ridiculous, we can protect her, she'll be safe with us," I insisted, "We're running out of time! We need to move!"

"And we will," Alpha's voice came from directly behind me, "but we will do this right and we will not endanger the child."

I spun, my hands already clenched into fists and my teeth barred in a snarl as I faced Alpha. He met my gaze with his own and I could feel the ancient confidence and power behind his cold stare. There was a time when Alpha and I had not exactly seen eye-to-eye. We have even fought in the past and, on every one of those occasions, the leader of our people had left me lying battered and broken. A part of me was screaming this fact in the back of my head, but the rage I was feeling overwhelmed the warning and pushed me forward.

I took a step toward Alpha and Alpha's face screwed up in a snarl of his own as he hollered, "No!" while pointing his index finger in my face.

I slapped the hand and finger out of my face and took another step forward as I focused on the hollow spot at Alpha's throat. From this distance if I struck first I could strike at Alpha's Adam's apple and shatter the bone and cartilage beneath. Even one as ancient as Alpha could suffocate as his pale blood was forced from the wound down into his lungs. I could do it too. I could kill him and then he wouldn't stand in the way of my finding Lei.

I felt my muscles tense as I planted my feet against the earth and readied myself for the strike when the sound of running footsteps behind me made me hesitate and back away. It was Chris, I had never even heard him leave, and now he was running back into the barn with a small duffle bag. The bag seemed familiar, but my focus returned back to Alpha and the threat he represented.

"They're all here!" Chris was calling out, his voice tinged with a slight panic "He's hasn't dosed since we arrived!"

"What?!" Alpha snarled and, in that moment of distraction, I launched myself forward with the web between my thumb and index finger of my right hand open and aimed directly for Alpha. Everything was in slow motion as his head turned back to me and his eyes again went wide in shock. He raised his hands to block the strike but I knew he was too late and I felt a smile spread across my face. Something moved in the periphery of my vision, something small and mostly in shadow, but I could still make out what it was. A chill burst from my core that was similar to the

315

sinking feeling one gets when going down the steep descent on a rollercoaster and I immediately let my hand fall from rigid to slack a millisecond before my strike made contact with Alpha. I still struck him hard in the throat but, with my hand loose, the impact did more damage to my hand and wrist than to Alpha. He gasped and choked a little afterward, but I think it was mostly shock and fear that I had struck him with what otherwise should have been a lethal shot. My wrist popped on impact, but I didn't notice the pain. My eyes were locked on Pha who stared at me as if I were some kind of wild animal there to rip everyone apart.

It was all I could do to stay on my feet, as I felt the weight of the stare coming from the girl. William was likely nearby but, as self-loathing threatened to overwhelm me and quickly began replacing the rage I had been feeling, I wouldn't have cared if the man squashed me where I stood. I just tried to kill Alpha, the leader of my people and the closest thing to a father I had ever had.

I sank down to my knees and put my face in my hands. I felt completely lost, confused and, for some reason, I couldn't remember where I was or what we were all doing here.

I felt a hand press into my shoulder and a calm voice whisper in my ear, "You're in the beginning stages of the heme-depletion and your Porphyria is taking control of you." It was Chris, kneeling next to me, and holding an EpiPen at the ready, "We need to get some medicine in you and I mean now."

I lowered my hands to look at him. His eyes were wary and I could tell he was ready to jump back and away if my reaction was anything but submissive. I only nodded and felt Chris jab the EpiPen into my leg. It made an audible pop and caused my head to swim briefly as the medicine made its way through my system and combined with the faulty red blood cells that my body had already created, which I was currently and foolishly trying to function on. My head began to clear and I suddenly realized I could take a deep breath where I had been practically hyperventilating before. The world seemed a little brighter and my anger disappeared. I was still worried about Lei, desperately worried, but I was once again in control of myself.

Slowly, ashamedly, I turned to look at Alpha. He gazed down at me between the strands of his long white hair that had flown out of place and were covering his face in the aftermath of my hitting him. His eyes were angry. Very angry, but like a petulant child who knew he had gone too far, I turned and walked over to him, awaiting his scorn.

I kept my eyes on my shoes as I stood in front of him, "Alpha, I..."

"Look at me," the anger in his voice stopped me cold, and it took an effort of will to break my gaze from the ground and raise my head up to meet his countenance. The second my eyes met his Alpha brought his arm up and slapped me hard on one side of my face. The blow staggered me and I had to take a step to regain my balance, but as soon as I had, I stepped back into place in front of Alpha with my head once again lowered.

"I said look at me!" Alpha's voice was even more angered than previously. My cheek was hot and the whole side of my head throbbing in rhythm with my accelerated heartbeat, but I raised my head again and faced Alpha.

"What were you thinking?!" Alpha practically screamed at me, "how could you be so reckless and irresponsible as to neglect your own dosing at a time like this?!"

"I was..." And Alpha cut off my words with another vicious slap to the side of my face. I didn't stagger, but the world did spin a bit at the force of the impact.

"SHUT UP!" Alpha bellowed and I complied as he continued, "You are the closest thing to family I have," and the words struck home harder than either of the blows he had given me as I felt my knees start to weaken, "but so is Lei, and God help me, but if we lose her as a result of your stupidity..."

The anger in Alpha's voice faded and was replaced by emotion I had never heard from him before. He opened his mouth to speak, but no words came. I frowned as a second attempt failed and he instead reached out with both arms and pulled me in close, hugging me fiercely, "Don't you ever put me in a position where I have to put you down, boy."

Initially I had thought he was going to hit me again, but when I registered what he was saying I lifted my arms and returned the embrace. Alpha had lived a long time, nearly six hundred years at this point, and he had lost scores of loved ones in that time. Losing people due to natural causes was bad enough, but when my kind lose ourselves to the condition we suffer, then it is the responsibility of the rest of us to put those people down like the mad dogs they have become. It is a horrible task when the person in question is just an acquaintance. When it is a loved one, it's more than devastating.

"I'm sorry, Alpha." I whispered, "I thought I could go longer between doses."

When Alpha spoke again his voice was hushed. He sounded confused and maybe frightened, "Why would you take such a risk?"

I sighed, "Because Dimitri has Lei and the Russian's don't believe in our modern methods. They still survive on raw blood like we used to. You know the effect that can have on us, especially on Lei. She's going to need the extra serum when we get her back."

Alpha let go of me and peered into my face. I could tell he could read the same fear on my face that he had just felt toward me. We were going to get Lei back, but what state would she be in when we did? Are we going to move heaven and earth, declare war on the Russian collective and risk our lives only to find she was neglected beyond the point of no return? Will she be so far into the madness of Porphyria that we... I would have to put her down as I had so many others?

I wouldn't survive that, and Alpha knew it, so he just sighed and nodded at me before asking, "All right. You know that we need you at your best if we are going to do this, right?"

I nodded, still ashamed.

"Okay then," Alpha continued, "how are you now?"

I shrugged, "In control, I guess."

Alpha scrutinized me, "Thinking clearly again? No more reckless impulses?"

Pha had come out of the shadows and stepped up to my side. She tugged at the hem of my jeans and I looked down in to her sweet face.

"Yes, sweetheart?"

In severely broken English she said, "Lei save me. She get me out." Tears welled in her eyes and for the second time I felt my legs start to give, partially at the thought that I had been willing to put this child in harm's way to get what I wanted, but also at the immense concern she felt toward the woman I love.

"You go kill bad guys and get bring her home?" Pha asked.

I don't know if it was her limited English that made her words so striking, it was disconcerting to hear such a small girl talk about killing so nonchalantly. I looked up to see Chris holding his sniper rifle and Alpha with his hands resting on the hilts of those unusual gothic-looking fighting knives of his, and I couldn't help but smile.

"Yes honey," I said as I nodded at my family, "that is exactly what we are going to do."

Chapter 34

"We have a hit!" Chris shouted from the main house as I collected the few things I was going to need for the coming trek through the forest.

I called back, "What?"

"The warehouse!" Chris answered, "the place they are keeping Lei, we have it on satellite!"

I dropped everything, running at full speed and into the main house, barely taking the time to make sure the door was open before bursting in.

When I reached the room where Chris had set up his computer Pha was sitting on a small chair and pointing at a place on the screen. Alpha and William were looking over her shoulder at the image on the screen and Chris was dancing around the room, still celebrating.

I had to squeeze in just to see past the wall that was made up of Alpha and William standing side-by-side, and was crest-fallen when I saw the spot the girl was pointing at. It was an earlier daylight video of just another farm in the countryside. Sure there was a warehouse and a long, straight dirt road that might possibly be used as a runway, but there were no planes, no cargo vans, no containers of air tanks nor any signs of life.

I turned away from the screen, "How can you tell this is the right place?"

Chris was still dancing around the room, as he said simply, "Pha says so."

I frowned, dubious of the word of a nine–year-old girl, who likely escaped from the wherever she had been held at night while pursued by monsters. I looked back at the screen, "And how does she know this is the right place?"

"Because of all the things considered, geographically, it makes the most sense, given where she was found."

I shook my head. I wanted to jump for joy, shout a battle cry, bolt out of the house and go running for the car, but I couldn't help being doubtful.

"I don't know Chris. A girl could get pretty turned around in the forest, even more so at night."

"See?" Pha called out, continuing to point at the screen. I turned and once again took in the image of the aerial view that the satellite was providing.

"Yes honey, I see it." I said, turning back to Chris, "What I don't see is any evidence that Lei is there, or any of Dimitri's people either, for that matter."

"No," Pha called out again, "See?"

Alpha looked up and stepped away so that I could get a better view. Once I moved in closer I saw that Pha's finger wasn't just pointing at the computer screen, but at a small dot that looked to be about fifty feet in front and to one side of the warehouse. I squinted my eyes, trying to determine what the spot might be. It had wheels, so the thought that it might be an old cart, or one of those really small cars that look more like toys than actual automobiles. What good one of those golf-cart type things would be doing out in farm country was beyond me. Whatever it had been, now it was clearly ruined. I could see pieces of metal shredded off of both of its the sides as it sat lopsided on the ground, making me think it was just some kind of wreck that had been abandoned.

"So, what is that and why re we interested?" I asked.

"That," Chris said triumphantly, "is a forklift."

It had been chilling to hear Pha tell us the story of how Lei had driven the forklift through the roll-up door of the warehouse, enabling Pha to get away while sacrificing her own freedom in the process. I doubt Lei had realized it at the time, but in letting the little girl get away, she may have just given us the means to get to her back as well. Chris reconfigured the satellite images on the

321

computer in order to give us a consistent live feed so that we could watch the location. gathering as much intel as we could before setting out.

"Now check this out," Chris announced as he switched the video from the earlier in the day feed, to the current live feed. Now the forklift couldn't be seen, but there were enough lights on and figures moving around to rival a shopping mall during the Christmas rush. Seeing the sheer volume of people was staggering, given that the place had looked more or less abandoned from the earlier feed that day.

Then we saw air tanks being rolled into view on carts, coming from one warehouse and going into another. The satellite imagery was too 'zoomed-out' to see what they were specifically doing with the canisters, or even tell why they were moving them, but given the general haste with which the people were working it seem like there was some kind of deadline in place.

As we watched the screen I heard Sasha call out from the other room, and Igor answering from just behind me. I turned, seeing him staring at the computer screen along with the rest of us, while he started dialing his cell phone.

"Important call?" I asked.

He only grunted his reply and then, begin speaking quickly in Russian to whomever he had been connected with on the other end. I watched Igor turn his back on us, and got the sense that something wasn't right about our "friend." I was about to follow Igor and try to get some answers from him, when the sound of a phone ringing came from the computer we were all watching.

All eyes turned to Chris expecting him to have performed some kind of goofy program, but he frowned and looked as perplexed as the rest of us. The ringing stopped, and after a brief pause it began again, but this time with an icon that had popped up in the corner of the screen. Hesitantly, Chris slid the cursor over to the icon and clicked on it, and the ringing silenced.

A window opened on the screen, and we all were graced with the image of Major Robert Larson's smiling face.

"Well, looks like the gang all there," the Major said with a chuckle as his eyes panned through the room.

"Larson? What the hell?" I stammered out.

Chris was a little more direct, "How are you doing this?"

Larson looked a bit indignant as his eyes locked on Chris, "Oh, come on Chris. You're an accomplished hacker, but do you really think your skills are on par with the criminals that work for our government?"

"You've been keeping tabs on us the whole time?" I asked, although I already knew the answer.

The major shrugged, "Mostly we were just watching your location, while monitoring whatever you were keeping under surveillance via the satellite connections on your computer."

"You have a tracker on my baby?" Chris turned to me, "I feel so violated."

"You need a hug?" I mocked.

Larson chimed in, "You boys can hug it out later, right now I only have a second to tell you that your surveillance video was seen by the "Big Brother team" at Langley, and that steps have already been taken in reaction to it."

And just like that the conversation turned dangerously serious.

"What steps?" I asked.

Larson shook his head, "Can't say, but I'm sure you remember what they're reaction was to the potential biological threat in Thailand."

I remembered that when the government received the location of Dr. Whelan's lab and the biological weapons he had been concocting within, the military started raining missiles down on the lab and planned to level the surrounding geography with a MOAB, the largest non-nuclear bomb ever created. The fact that there were villages of natives, as well as Lei, Chris and myself at ground zero didn't deter the decision to unload serious ordinance on top of us at all. Not even a little bit.

Chris turned to me, "Deja vu?"

"So the CIA is going to drop bombs on us again?" I accused.

"No," Larson stated confidently, "you're in Russian territory. The information will be passed to their Russian equivalent, and any decisions will be made by their people." Larson paused to consider, and then added, "I think our people will be offering some very strong recommendations as how to act, but ultimately the choice is going to be Russia's, at least from an official standpoint."

"What does that mean?" Chris asked.

"It means that if there are any indications that the biologic entity might already be in play, or if the Russian government doesn't act as the CIA would officially advise, then there's a chance that some more 'unofficial' steps will be taken to ensure the safety of the world."

I let out a disgusted sigh, "So the policy will be to advise, recommend a course of action to the Russian's, and assuming they don't act in the manner recommended, the CIA will just do what they want to do anyway?"

Larson smiled, "It's possible, but I can't say more than, it would be within character for something like that to happen. Welcome to the world of covert operations."

"Major..." I tried to take a breath to calm myself. I wasn't feeling the same kind of rage as I had before getting the dose of serum I needed, but there was still some residual desire to lash out at what was angering me, "Robert, Lei is still being held in that warehouse. How much time do we have?"

"I don't know my friend, and that's why I'm giving you the head's up. The wheels are going to move a lot slower than before, working through contacts and liaisons between our two governments, but the threat won't be ignored for the sake of politics for very long. You likely have between twenty-four and forty-eight hours, to get her out and become gone, and that's my best possible guess."

I nodded, "Any idea how the Russians will react?"

Larson considered the question, "The very same way our government did in our Thailand adventure. If they want to contain the problem they'll launch the missiles and enact a 'scorched-earth' protocol. If they want to try to make the biologic part of their own arsenal, they'll send in the troops. But I can't say for sure which decision they'll make. The boys at Langley will be pushing for the 'scorthed-earth' option, not only because they want to see the area contained, but because they also don't want Russia to gain access to such a potentially dangerous weapon, so..."

"Which," I added, "may be all the motivation the Russian government needs to try to take the weapon for their own use."

Larson nodded, "That would be a typical, if not an archaic, cold-war maneuver. But remember, even if they do send in the troops, there may still be missiles flying in anyway."

"Any chance you will be coming with the cavalry?" Chris asked hopefully.

Larson looked crestfallen as he replied, "I just can't say. Sorry."

I stood up straight, "All right, thanks for the warning, but we've got work to do."

Larson smiled a strained smile and nodded, "Understood. Good luck guys."

The video disconnected as Chris and I stared at the screen for an instant more, and then I put my hand on his shoulder and said, "C'mon, it's time to go."

Chapter 35

William watched as small day-packs were loaded into the trunk of Igor's car, and as various "thank you and goodbyes" were said all around. Alpha cast a glance his way, but William just stared back stoically, until Alpha broke his gaze and climbed into the front passenger seat. Chris and Steve loaded themselves into the rear seats, while Igor sat in the driver's seat getting ready to start the vehicle. Sasha had remained behind at the farmhouse, and was none too happy about it. The petite man was pacing and cursing in Russian at being left behind while the rancher's wife tried to console him. Eventually he simply sauntered off in a huff with a flurry of hand gestures and foot stomping.

William never moved until he watched the taillights of the vehicle disappear down the dirt road that had brought them to the ranch. When he finally returned to the main house he found Pha sitting quietly on the bed and, from her expression, William could easily tell she was troubled. No words were spoken, but the simple placement of a gentle hand on the small girl's shoulder spoke volumes.

Pha looked up at her adopted father, tears welling in her eyes as she spoke in Thai, "I thought I was going to be alone again. I was so scared because, even if I escaped, there are no alleys here to sleep in, no one speaks a language I understand, and there are no policemen or public 'safe houses' for me to run to."

William and nodded as he patiently listened to every word as Pha continued, "But father, now Lei is all alone." William frowned and started to rise from the bed, but Pha caught one of his fingers before he could walk away.

Pha bowed her head to William, "Please father. When they brought her to me I felt safe again. I felt like she would die before she would let anyone hurt me. She is the reason I am here, but now she is all alone."

William looked down at his hand and the grip Pha had on him. His eyes took in the little fingers that encircled his middle finger, as they held on tightly. His eyes traveled up that tiny arm to the face that looked back at him pleadingly. William sighed and gently pried the girl's fingers from around his own. He opened his mouth as if to say something, then thought better of it and simply shook his head, "No," before turning to walk from the room.

"Please help me save Lei," Pha called after him.

William froze, as the child's words seemed to echo in his mind. He inclined his head slightly back in Pha's direction, then angrily continued his walk away and into another area of the ranch house.

Chapter 36

Based on the satellite images that Chris had pulled up of the surrounding area, we were able to get Igor to drop the three of us off within a mile of the warehouse, while strategically placing a dense amount of forest between ourselves and our destination. Igor did not accompany us as the plan called for him to stay with the car in case we needed a backup getaway plan. The trek through the woods was a silent one, but not as a result of any kind of need for stealth. I think we were all too focused, or maybe just apprehensive, about whether or not the three of us were going to be able to pull off what seemed like an impossible rescue. Given the number of Dimitri's people we had seen on the satellite feed the odds were decidedly against us, and the chances would be better if we were able to sneak in and out without being detected. If we were exposed, then this would probably go down as a final, "blaze of glory" type of last stand attempt against overwhelming odds.

Once we arrived, Chris was going to have to study the landscape around the perimeter of the property to find a suitable location for setting up his sniper's nest. This location was also dependent on where Alpha, who was going to stand alone against the aforementioned onslaught of Dimitri's people, if it came to that, would decide he could have the best chance of holding out against such overwhelming numbers. His best bet would be similar to the tactic the Spartans used at Thermopylae. The Greeks used the natural landscape in order to pigeon-hole their opponents into a space that forced them to abandon the idea of attacking from multiple directions. The landscape the Spartans chose acted as a funnel so only a handful of enemies could be in the front line at one time, thereby limiting the number of opponents they had to fight at any given moment.

The task that fell to me was either finding Lei, killing Dimitri or both. Frankly, I didn't much stand a chance against

Dimitri in the first place, at least not in a fair fight. I had decided just after my escape from Dimitri's building in Nazran that, should it come to a standoff between the ancient Russian and myself, it wasn't going to be a fair fight, and I had prepared accordingly. The only unknown was Nicholas. The big man was a legendary warrior and military commander in his own right, and if he engaged me as I was fighting Dimitri, I wouldn't stand a chance, regardless of whether I brought my "sneaky toys" or not.

We reached the outskirts of the forest, staying within the tree line as we peered through binoculars at the warehouse in the distance. The sun was setting behind us, which further helped to shield our movements from observation, despite the fact that the whole place still looked as if it were abandoned and empty in the pre-sunset light.

"How long until nightfall?" I asked Chris, who had looked up the information before we had left the ranch house. Chris lowered his binoculars and checked his watch, "Just shy of an hour, why?"

"I'm thinking about doing some recon of the buildings to see if I can get a better idea of where they might be holding Lei."

"Didn't the child say she was in the main building?" Alpha volunteered, "in one of the office spaces?"

"Yes, but that was where they were before the escape attempt, I am guessing the have moved her to a place where they could keep her under a better form of lock and key."

Chris volunteered, "You're also assuming that they always wait for nightfall before they come out. The images we saw only showed one night's activity, and there's no way we can say for sure that there is any kind of a schedule they are sticking to."

I laughed, "You think they were all in there watching a movie that suddenly ended at sundown and they all went out for fresh air at once?"

Chris scowled at me, "I make the jokes around here, and in

329

any case, what I am trying to say is that we really don't know if that was something random on that particular night, or if it was a part of a regular routine. It's not as though they are going to burst into flames if they move into the daylight."

I agreed, but asked, "Don't you think it might be worth the risk?"

"There are four warehouses," Alpha noted, "and you think you can do a proper inspection of each, taking all the precautions necessary to keep us from being discovered and yourself protected, and still get back to us before sundown?"

I chuckled, "Well when you put it like that, no I don't think I could do that. What I can try to do is sneak up to each building, and at the very least look through a damn window. Maybe I'll find Lei, or more likely I'll just see where the majority of them are laying low before sundown. Who knows?"

Alpha was unconvinced, "If you are caught or killed, then this whole plan, which is unlikely to succeed in the first place, is ruined. Any chances of getting Lei back are over."

I shrugged, "Having a better understanding of what we are up against would increase our odds of grabbing Lei and getting us all out of here alive."

Chris just watched as Alpha looked at me, suddenly his expression dropped and his whole body drooped. I was about to ask if he were all right when he stiffened and seemed to recover completely. There was a new steely look in his eyes and a confidence in his demeanor as he nodded at me.

"Go," was all he said.

I frowned and turned to Chris who shrugged and then slid the bolt closed on his sniper rifle, effectively securing a round into the chamber. "I'll cover you from here as best I can, but you're on your own if you go around the buildings and out of my line of sight."

I gave Chris a quick salute to show that that I understood

330

him, and without another word, stood up and taking off as fast as I could for the closest building. No alarms or voices were raised as I reached my initial destination, so I gave myself a moment to recover from the sprint. Once I had my breath back under control I slowly worked my way round the building until I came to the first window. Grime and what seemed like years of weather damage covered the glass rendering it impossible to see through. No sound of anything stirring came from the interior and I would have bet it was empty. Still I made my way carefully to the next window, now scanning for any security systems that might have been in place. Seeing none, I stopped at the next window, this one equally opaque from the effects of time, but the lower left corner of the glass had a small circular break about the size of a silver dollar that I could put an eye to and peer through. Inside were rows upon rows upon rows of gas canisters. Each canister looked to be around six to seven feet long and must have weighed over two hundred pounds. They were arranged horizontally on pallets, how many pallets there were I couldn't easily count and didn't bother to try, but I did notice that each pallet held a neatly stacked set of twelve canisters. Given the weight and the type of aircraft that we had guessed they would be using I couldn't imagine how more than a single canister could be installed on such lightweight planes. Any more than that and the distance the plane could travel would be severely limited, assuming they'd be able to fly at all.

There were no office spaces or any places where Lei could have been secured, so I looked back to the trees where I knew Chris and Alpha were set up and flashed hand signals in an attempt to relay that I was about to move to the next building. My hope was that Chris would see me through his scope and get the idea.

I worked my way to the edge of the warehouse and quickly peered around the corner. Seeing no one, I bolted to the next building and assumed a position beneath a window similar to the position I had previously held at the first building.

This particular building looked like a central office, connected to another warehouse which reminded me of those self-storage places. The office space looked disheveled, as if a strong wind had blown through, scattering papers and tipping over desks as it went, but was otherwise unremarkable. I could see that the office had a large window on the far side of the room that appeared to be some kind of observation spot for the warehouse beyond. Moving further down the side of the building I found the door and checked to see if it was locked.

It wasn't.

Having seen that the office space was empty I made a quick decision that I knew was going to make Chris and Alpha extremely unhappy. As silently as possible, I opened the door and crept inside, smiling all the while as I could practically hear Chris begin to complain as he peered through the scope of his rifle.

***

"No, no, no!" Chris moaned as he watched Steve go through the door and close it behind him.

"What?" Alpha asked as he sat next to Chris with binoculars held up to his eyes. He had been scanning the surrounding area for any signs that Dimitri's people had been alerted to Steve's presence and wasn't watching Steve. That was Chris' job.

"Steve just went inside that second building," Chris said with a certain amount of disgust in his voice. "He's out of my line of sight and being an idiot again."

Alpha asked," Can you track him?"

"No," Chris said sarcastically, "and that would be because, as I mentioned, he moved out of my line of sight once he went inside the building."

Alpha bristled, but chose to ignore Chris' insolent tone as

332

he lowered the binoculars from his eyes, "Out of... Damn, what is he doing?"

Chris shook his head, "Gosh, I don't know. He didn't check with me before acting the fool."

Alpha turned his head to Chris, who was still looking through the scope of his rifle, and said with eerie calm, "You know, if anyone else talked to me the way you do I would probably tear them in half with my bare hands."

Chris didn't flinch or take his eye away from the scope's reticule for an instant as he replied with equal calm, "I seriously doubt it, but even if that's true, you wouldn't do that to me."

"No?"

"Nah, you know you love me."

"Excuse me?!?"

"Totally."

Alpha could feel his hands clenching into fists and his arms tighten, ready to strike, "You are not only obnoxious, but delusional as well."

"Nope, wrong on both counts."

Alpha inclined his head, his anger tempered slightly by Chris' confidence, "You seem very sure of yourself."

"Of course. You went through a hell of a lot of trouble to save me, despite being well aware of my colorful personality."

Alpha sneered, "We all make mistakes."

Chris chuckled at that, "Keep telling yourself that, but the truth is that Steve is basically my brother and you know it. That makes me family," Chris looked away from the scope for an instant to raise one eyebrow at Alpha, "which would also make us family, even if you hadn't turned me into one of your kind when you saved my life."

Alpha was silent as Chris went back to scanning the area, then he sighed and brought the binoculars up to his eyes, "You call me 'Daddy' even once, in conversation or in jest, and I swear I will rip your forked tongue out of your throat before stomping the rest of your head into the ground."

Chris was smiling ridiculously at Alpha's words, but only said, "Understood."

"Fine. Any sign of him?"

"No," Chris' voice suddenly sounded deflated. "As long as he remains in there, he's on his own."

***

As I moved through the office space toward the observation window I wondered how long I could leave Alpha and Chris alone in a high stress situation before Alpha tried to kill Chris. I'd have bet the "under" if the timeline were set at 30 minutes.

I stood to one side of the observation window and peered through to the space beyond, hoping that I would see Lei or get some indication of where she was being held. My breath caught in my chest as what I saw instantly brought back memories of the Pharmanetics corporation that Alpha, Chris and I had raided in Los Angeles more than two years ago.

The warehouse beyond the glass was simply a wide-open space that probably had been created to store multiple farm machines, and would have served well as an airplane hangar, given its expanse. Now, instead of machinery, there were scores of military cots arranged in long rows, and each with a human occupant of various ages and races, all of whom were tethered to an I.V. machine that branched out from a central line originating at a computer bank, in what served as the center of the room.

Memories of how we had liberated the people of my collective from similar captivity, when Dr. Whelan and the Pharmanetics corporation had assaulted and kidnapped as many of them as they could, flooded through me. Now Whelan was dead and Pharmanetics was out of business, but it seemed as if the

334

horror that had been created for my people had survived.

I scanned the cots closest to me and tried to make out the faces of the people lying on them. I could see that their skin was pock marked and discolored by what appeared to be the early to middle deterioration points of Porphyria. I realized that these people weren't being drained of their blood supply as my people had been. Instead, this was how Dimitri was sustaining his people without a ready source of blood and, apparently, it wasn't enough to help them recover full health... or perhaps that was the point? I couldn't be sure and I turned away from the window and shook my head at all of the new questions that began to run through my brain. Without realizing I had moved, I found myself working my way toward a second door that appeared as though it would open to the space beyond the observation window when my foot struck something in the shadows.

I looked down and yelped at the body that was lying on the floor in a pool of what looked like watered down blood. It was one of Dimitri's people, but not a pock-marked sufferer like those in the cots. This one was dressed all in black and looked perfectly healthy. No doubt the body was one of Dimitri's security people, one that was kept whole, healthy and fortified with blood as required, but what had killed him?

I grabbed one arm and noticed that the skin had cooled after death, indicating a significant amount of time had slipped by since the killing, and then I flipped the body over to find a gaping wound in the man's abdomen. Given the straightness of the cut he had clearly been killed by an edged weapon and thoughts of the battle between Alexei and Dimitri from earlier came to mind.

Then movement beyond the glass of the observation window caught my attention and I dropped to the floor, unable to avoid getting one pant leg saturated in the blood that had pooled there. I crawled over to get a better look through the window and instantly saw two men facing one another. Light glinted repeatedly from the objects they held in their hands and to my utter shock, I realized the smaller of the two men was Alexei and easily guessed that the much larger man was his uncle, Grand Duke Nicholas Nicholaevich.

My mind raced as I tried to make sense of what I was seeing. How the hell had Alexei found this place? Was he working with Dimitri and his uncle? Then I remembered Igor making a phone call after we found Pha at the farm...

"Damn," I growled and was about to look for a way inside when, without warning, there was the sound of the door behind me opening. I turned to see a group of men pushing their way into the room, only to stop in shock at the sight of me in the far corner.

The first man to register that I was standing there just stared at me, surprised and unsure of what he was seeing, as my own brain desperately tried to sort out the best course of action. And then the pregnant pause ended and, Alexei and Nicholas now completely forgotten, I ran forward with the barrel of my shotgun raised toward the group of men as I started squeezing the trigger.

Chapter 37

The first man through the door had just opened his mouth to shout a warning when the blast from my shotgun slammed him back and into the collection of others who had just made their way past the door's threshold. I kept firing into the stack of bodies as I continued toward the door in the hopes of driving the remainder back into the open, where Chris could pick them off. My plan was proven successful as I saw Dimitri's people outside begin twisting wildly from the impact of Chris' bullets as he shot them down.

So much for the "being sneaky" plan. I turned to look back to the observation glass to see a multitude of bodies rising ominously from the cots they had been lying on, rip the I.V. cords from their arms and start running for the door.

"Shit!" I bolted from the door and ran for the next warehouse, hoping that I could get to it before Dimitri's people caught up with me. Maybe I could lock myself inside, and with a little more luck maybe find Lei in there as well. I looked to the tree line where I had left Chris and Alpha to see Alpha running toward me, with one of his wicked and gothic looking knives in each hand as he closed the distance between us. Dimitri's people began pouring out of the building and were charging after me. I managed to reach into my pockets and push fresh cartridges into the shotgun with seconds to spare before nearly colliding with one of Dimitri's security guards. The man had been walking a perimeter when he saw me and reached for his sidearm. I raised the shotgun and fired, but the spread went wide of him and tore several small holes in the side of the warehouse wall behind him. The guard abandoned the idea of drawing his weapon and dove to the ground. I kept running and managed to reach him, landing a solid kick against his head without breaking stride, and continued my run for the entry door that was now visible, and my goal.

I expected to hear, or worse, feel the impact of return fire but none came. A small comfort, as I turned my head to see the mass of Dimitri's people practically on top of me. Wild, rage filled eyes locked on me, then shifted to one side and went wide with fear as Alpha flew past me at a full sprint and barreled into the oncoming horde of Dimitri's people. Bodies bent or bounced as Alpha pushed his way farther and farther into the throng until I could no longer see him in the crowd, but I could clearly hear the sounds of battle. Screeches and high pitched wails cut through the silence of the surroundings, as Alpha went into his dance of death, whirling his blades as they cut through flesh and bone alike. One of Dimitri's people suddenly broke away from the crowd that was now fully concentrated on Alpha and headed straight for me. I raised my shotgun but, before he could reach me, his body was thrown to the side as if he had been hit by an invisible car and he fell limply on the ground with a bullet hole clearly visible in his temple.

I raised an acknowledging wave to Chris before I continued toward the final warehouse knowing that, despite Alpha's best efforts to occupy the mass of Dimitri's people, some of them were going to follow me as I ran for the next building. I turned a corner of the structure and found the ruin of a roll-up door and felt the elation as I remembered Pha recounting how Lei had destroyed such a door with a forklift. I also realized that moving for the opening would once again take me out of Chris' line of sight, but I pumped harder with my legs, going faster and faster just to increase the distance between myself and any pursuers, scrambling for every additional extra second that I could devote to looking for Lei before I'd have to fight my way out again.

I leapt through the opening and landed on the concrete floor of the warehouse with my eyes darting around the darkened interior. I scanned the space as best I could as my eyes adjusted to the darkness, but immediately realized something was out of place and hanging from the ceiling above my head. I whipped my head around for a more complete understanding of what was above me, and the sight my eyes took in threatened to drop me where I stood.

Lei was hanging by her wrists and secured by chains a few feet off the floor. Her head dropped forward in what I prayed was just a sign of her being unconscious, and what was left of her clothes were, tattered, torn, and bloody, with all of her exposed skin blotched with purple bruises and covered in crusty, dried blood. Her hair covered her face, so I couldn't see if she were conscious or not, but she was as still as a corpse, with her body swaying slightly, as it dangled before me.

I wanted to scream, and likely would have, when a whir of something mechanical sounded and Lei's body was swiftly lifted to the ceiling, swinging precariously overhead and a voice called out to me.

"Is this what you have been looking for Mr. Jacobs?"

Dimitri Lagos' voice echoed in the expanse of the warehouse while I simply stared up in a panic at Lei. As difficult as it was to quell my need to see if there were any signs of life in her after the violent ascension, I looked past her body and studied her bonds. The chain was secured to a hook that connected to the cable of a winch system, and the control of that winch was clearly in Dimitri's hands, but as I looked around the warehouse I could see no signs of the man.

I heard a snarl and the sound of footsteps behind me and realized my precious few seconds of time were up. I whirled and screamed out all of my frustration and concern at the first of Dimitri's people to come through the ruin of the roll-up door after me, and I pulled the trigger of the shotgun. The shot tore through the closest one and also sent two more who were trailing close behind him to the ground, but more and more pushed through the opening. I had a very surreal moment at this point where my head was screaming at me to turn, run and get some distance between the horde pushing through the door and the spot where I was standing, but my body wasn't listening. Instead I began to walk forward as I ratcheted another cartridge into the chamber, firing again and again and again. I kept firing until I had used all of the shells the shotgun contained and then felt the quiet click of the falling firing pin as I tried to squeeze off yet another round, that simply wasn't there.

Despite the pile of bodies I had created both inside and just outside the opening, more of Dimitri's people started to pour in, emboldened by the lack of explosive shotgun fire. I tossed the shotgun away and realized I was still screaming fiercely at the bodies as they funneled in. All of the hand-to-hand training from Alpha and his hunters, which had continually been given to me throughout my long life, came back to me in a wave of pure instinct and reflex as I charged into the horde. I struck the first one in the throat and reveled in the feeling of bone shifting and breaking under the blow of my hand. I spun and kicked at the knee of another and heard the "pop-crunch" of the joint, first dislocating and then breaking beneath my shoe, as its owner dropped from the intense pain. I spun back in the opposite direction and wrapped my arm around the throat of another man before spinning us both back into the man with the ruined knee. I launched a palm strike with my free hand at his nose and it connected with yet another satisfying crunch as blood erupted out of the man's tear ducts while I continued my thrust as if to push the nasal bone fragments into the man's brain. I don't know if I was totally successful at that, but he collapsed limply with all the fight, if not the life, taken out of him. Another quick pivot and reversal of my body weight sent the man I still held trapped with my arm into a spin, while my free hand secured his head and neck, the violence of this move quickly broke the man's neck and I felt the strength instantly drop out of the man's arms and body.

I jumped back a few steps and then charged in again, my arms and hands seemingly lashing out under their own power as my body moved gracefully through the throng, avoiding the reaching hands and dodging under or around the bodies that threatened to smother me with their numbers. Each time my fist, palm or elbow struck its target I felt something breaking in my opponent, and eventually I began to find myself with greater distance and more time between the attacks. The problem was that there was less room to maneuver with a shrinking ring made up of the bodies that now littered the floor. My concentration was suddenly split between offensive strikes and dodging the obstacles on the floor and, as soon as I took my first misstep, I felt a "pop" in my chest.

Everything stopped.

I stood as motionless as a mannequin, as did all of Dimitri's people as well. My arms fell limply to my sides as I looked down in confusion at myself and saw that something very small and shiny protruded from between my ribs on the left side. My pale blood had begun leaking out of me where the thing penetrated me and then ran in a small rivulet down its length. I visually followed the metal until my eyes registered the hand-guard of a sword, and behind that, an old, spotted and gnarled looking hand. My brain didn't want to comprehend what it was seeing and it made my eyes track further up the hand, past the arm, to a face. There, set in a violent snarl, was the visage of Dimitri Lagos.

I frowned in confusion, and upon seeing my expression, Dimitri's lips curled into a smug smirk, before he twisted his sword blade sending my vision white with pain. Mercilessly he ripped the sword from my body and I fell flat to the ground, my arms too weak to break my fall as the concrete rose up and met my head with a crunch.

Chapter 38

Nicholas refused to take his eyes off Alexei, despite the battle that had begun in the adjacent room, and readied himself as he faced his nephew.

Alexei's voice remained deathly calm, "I have to admit, I never thought I get this chance."

Nicholas brandished his Shaska, swinging the sword in a horizontal cut to emphasize his words as he responded, "And what chance are you referring to exactly?"

"The chance that I could avenge your betrayal."

The intense look on Nicholas' face softened, "You know, then?"

Alexei only sighed, "I was there. How could I not know?"

Silence extended between the pair and, unwanted, the images of his uncle shooting, clubbing and stabbing Father Grigori to death, flashed behind Alexei's eyes.

Alexei shook his head, "I was never one to understand politics or comprehend how such devious acts could be perpetrated in the pursuit of power." Alexei mused, "It seems to me that only those who don't understand the ultimate repsonsibility that power brings along with it could ever covet such a burden."

Nicholas dropped his eyes and lowered his Shaska, "Our family was strong until your father took the throne."

Alexei's eyes immediately focused on his uncle, a frown furrowing his brow in confusion, "What?"

"It's true Alexei, your father couldn't admit he was unfit to lead and wouldn't reliquish his position. Even as everything crumbled all around him he still thought he knew best, covering his ineptitude with atrocities against the people. Atrocities that ultimately led to the creation of an even greater monster in the Bolsheviks."

Alexei's frown deepened even further, "What are you saying?"

Nicholas sighed with a weariness that Alexei had not expected, "I am sorry for what I did, but it was necessary. The war flowed in both directions but, if the Romanov family was going to take power again, then I couldn't allow someone as weak as your father to simply sit back on the throne once we had finished fighting to restore it."

Alexei's legs felt as though they were made of lead as a thought began to worm its way into his mind. Up to now Alexei had been pursuing his uncle because of his part in the brutal murder of his mentor, Grigori Rasputin, but that wasn't what Nicholas was apologizing for now, was it?

Alexei just stared at Nicholas as his uncle continued to bare his soul, "Removing your father wasn't enough. You, your mother, your siblings were all weak, meulling and incapable fools who would only worsen the situation. You all had to be taken..."

"Yakov Yuresev," Alexei managed to say, "the orders he received to execute us in that cellar... that was you?"

Realizing his mistake, Nicholas' head shot up, his eyes alert and his body tensed in what might have been an initial effort toward indignation, but then his face twisted into a sneer as he looked at Alexei and he raised his sword once more, "I see. Well, this is probably as it should be in the end. You, at least, deserve to know everything."

Alexei was silent as his eyes lingered on his uncle until a glint of light flickered off the Shaska in his uncle's hand.

"Whatever the issues you had with my father," Alexei's voice broke in sorrow, "we...my sisters and I...we all loved you."

Nicholas shook his head, "Alexei..."

Fury that Alexei had never felt before raged, "How could you?! Some of my sisters were little more than toddlers and you

343

had them shot! And you have the audacity to say the Bolsheviks were the monsters?!"

Now indignation did rise into Nicholas, "Don't you dare compare me to the ursurpers of our family. They…"

Alexei cut off his uncle, "Family?! You dare speak of family after what you have done?!"

Nicholas, seeing that there would be no stemming the tide of rage Alexei was in, raised his Shaska once more, "You cannot understand, but I do not expect as much. Your father was weak and, even with your gifts, you are your father's son."

Alexei fought to calm his breathing by concentrating on the knife in his hand, "And Father Grigori?"

"I gave him a choice and he chose to support your father," Nicholas chuckled. "I suspect he only made that choice because your father was little more than a puppet for the *Starets* to manipulate. In the end I think every idea your father had may have actually been Rasputin's."

Alexei's eyes dropped from his uncle's face to the Shaska, "That sword does not belong to you."

Nicholas looked to the Shashka, "The sword belongs to the leader who will…"

"The sword belonged to my Father!" Alexei interrupted, "and upon his death it passes to me."

Nicholas's face began to redden and darken his features, "Then perhaps you should come and take it." Nicholas pointed the Shashka at Alexei and spread his feet readying himself for battle.

Alexei raised his hunting knife and pointed it a Nicholas in a similar manner, "Come then 'Wolf-Killer' and let's see if you can finish what you started."

Nicholas immediately charged and swung the Shaska in an arcing overhead strike that would cleave Alexei's head vertically if it connected. Alexei twirled his knife around so that the dull side of the blade lay flush against his forearm, which gave him the added

344

leverage he would need absorb the force of the strike as he blocked and deflected his uncle's attack with the larger weapon. Sparks flew as the Shashka connected with Alexei's knife, but Alexei was unable to take advantage after Nicholas' powerful strike and had to go on the defensive a Nicholas followed through and used the momentum to immediately launch another slash at Alexei.

Forced to shift and pivot with each subsequent blow, Alexei could feel the unbelievable strength that the seven-foot Nicholas put behind each strike. He was completely on the defensive and desperately looked for a way to off balance his uncle in order to get inside his the larger man's sword range.

Alexei feigned a lunge to the right and tried to come in low, but Nicholas countered the maneuver as he shifted his weight onto his back foot and delivered a horizontal slash at Alexei's knees. Alexei was able to jump over the strike but, being in mid-air, he wasn't able to shift his body position around enough to avoid a follow-up thrust that missed piercing his side by millimeters. The edge of the Shaska did manage to score the flesh covering his ribs and the skin parted as the blade sliced cleanly through.

Alexei winced with the pain but kept his attention focused on his uncle's psotion and realized that the last thrust had overextended the giant's balance. Alexei flipped the knife around so that the blade was now forward in his hand as if it were a sword and attacked with a thrust of his arm in an upward arc so that the point initially traveled toward Nicholas' face before dipping back down and threatening his lower abdomen. Nicholas read the move and managed to avoid the lethal stab into his abdomen or pelvis but could not pull his forward leg back in time to avoid the knife plunging into the meaty part of his thigh.

Nicholas howled with the pain and, with one huge hand, grabbed Alexei's wrist before his could pull his blade free. Before Alexei could realize what was happening Nicholas pulled Alexei's wrist upward with a violent wrenching motion and Alexei's knife came out of Nicholas' thigh with a quick splash of blood. Alexei found himself off the ground, held dangling from Nicholas grip by his right wrist. Nicholas swung his right arm back in order to get his Shaska in position to run Alexei through, but with his left hand Alexei clawed at Nicholas's eyes, which caused the larger man to abandon his attack and drop Alexei. As soon as Alexei's feet touched the floor, he spun and launched a kick into his uncle's solar plexus with enough force to cripple a normal man. Instead of crumbling, the big man only grunted and bent over slightly from the tremendous impact, then the Shaska was again swinging toward Alexei.

When Alexei bolted back to extend the distance between the two of them, Nicholas held his position.

Nicholas looked at the sword, which was slightly wet with Alexei's blood from the slash that had connected along the ribs. Carefully he wiped one finger down its length until a large drop of Alexei's blood accumulated on his fingertip.

Alexei watched as his uncle ran the blood between his thumb and index finger and said mockingly, "Not the first time your family's blood was on my hands, is it Alexei?"

Alexei didn't answer and thrust his knife at Nicholas' chest in a wild and unrefined strike. Nicholas parried his attack and countered with one of his own. Alexei was too overextended to dodge or block the strike with his knife, so he was forced to deflect this strike with his bare hand, which he managed without losing his hand or fingers, although his the back of his left wrist was still lacerated.

Nicholas shifted his weight and, with his free hand, punched Alexei in the eye. Alexei could feel his head rock backward from the impact and he let his body go limp as he collapsed on the floor of the warehouse. Nicholas didn't relent and tried to finish Alexei where he lay on the ground, but Alexei rolled with the fall and had already regained his feet and the two collided with Alexei grabbing Nicholas's wrist and twisting it so the Shaska pointed out of harm's way. Nicholas must have had a similar idea because Alexei felt his uncle's iron grip synch around his right wrist again..

"You can't stay out of my range forever boy. The longer this goes on, the greater my advantage!" Nicholas said triumphantly as the two wrenched on each other's arms trying to simultaneously free themselves while also trying to shift into an advantageous position for the strike that would follow.

Then Nicholas, using his incredible strength pulled his sword arm free and reared the sword back, "So it ends!"

Alexei could see the angle that the sword was about to travel and realized the mistake.

"No we won't uncle," Alexei growled, "you shouldn't have let go of my wrist, I just killed you."

Nicholas hesitated for the merest moment at those words and Alexei flicked his knife out of the hand that Nicholas was holding and flipped it into the air toward his waiting free hand. The knife tumbled sideways in the air before slapping soundly into Alexei's palm, which shot forward and plunged the blade to the hilt into his uncle's abdomen and out the other side. Nicholas eyes went wide with shock and pain as he bent over at the waist and fell too his knees in response to the knife entering his body.

Alexei leaned in for added leverage as he twisted the blade in his uncle's guts, shooting pain through Nicholas, who dropped the Shaska as his arms went limp and fell to his sides. The sword hit the concrete floor with a "clang" as Alexei's felt the wet warmth of his uncle's blood cover his hand and run over his forearm as he held his uncle's mass in that kneeling position. Without removing the blade, Alexei stepped back and looked down on his uncle as Nicholas used the last of his strength to raise his head and spread an ironic smile at his nephew. Alexei didn't wait for any words that might have come and he wrenched the knife to one side with all his strength, cutting through his uncle's abdomen in a horizontal line until the knife burst out in a fountain of blood and gore. The nerves in Nicholas' body fired sending his form into a spasmodic tremor at the sheer enormity of damage caused by the wound and the giant immediately collapsed on the floor. Alexei looked down, ready to continue the battle, but his uncle's body seemed to deflate as more gore forced itself from his abdomen.

It was over. Alexei knew that no one, not even an ancient vampire could come back from so grevious a wound. Alexei slowly bent down and picked up his father's Shashka from where it had fallen and noticed clear droplets falling into the blood that was accumulating on the floor. At first he thought they were beads of sweat falling from his brow, but it was only a matter of moments before Alexei realized he was crying.

Chapter 39

Chris squeezed off the last round of his rifle and watched through the scope as the target's head whipped back from the projectile's impact, and fell to lie alongside the many others strewn around the ground.

Chris could see that Alpha was still doing his impression of a human wood-chipper on the collected mass of Dimitri's people, but the sheer numbers had begun to take its toll and he was losing ground. It was really an amazing sight to see how many of Dimitri's people had been within the confines of the various buildings, especially given how abandoned the entire area had looked, before Steve had set them all into motion with that first shotgun blast.

Out of bullets for the rifle and doing little good where he sat, Chris collected his side arms, as well as a hand full of extra loaded magazines, and was about to make a run for Alpha, when the forest came alive behind him. Figures wearing an unusual black camouflage pattern came toward him from where they had been hiding deeper in the woods. Chris was about let out a cry of shock, when a familiar voice shouted, "Now!"

The soldiers, armed with strange and somewhat antiquated looking rifles, ran past Chris and broke through the tree line. They then began forming into a line on the far side of the forest and started firing into the crowd of Dimitri's people. Dozens of bodies figures fell over but, despite the number of successful shots fired, the sheer mass of Dimitri's people made it seem as though the effect was mininmal at best in turning odds around.

Chris watched as the people attacking Alpha had their attention shift, and over a hundred sets of eyes turned toward the tree line and charged forward. The sheer mass of humanity that was coming at him was surreal and seemed overwhelming, but the familiar voice called out once more, "Here they come! Pick your targets and prepare to engage at close range!"

Several more rounds of gunfire exploded all around him and more bodies dropped as the mass came closer and closer before someone grabbed Chris' shoulder, causing him to let out a small yelp as he was tugged to his feet.

"You?!" Chris blurted out once he realized who he was looking at. Major Robert Larson smiled an ironic smile as he turned back to the still approaching mass of Dimitri's people, "Had to go loud, didn't you?"

"Wasn't the plan," Chris said weakly while desperately wanting to ask what, where, when and the how and why of Larson's appearance, but realized that none of the answers mattered, nor did he care.

"So what do we do now?" Chris asked.

Larson pulled out a pair of guns from holsters at his side as he shook his head, "I would have preferred to do this from a distance, with plenty of cover, but..."

Chris got the idea and he lifted his own guns up and clicked the barrels together, "Say the word."

Larson looked uneasily at Chris, "I don't suppose I could convince you to stay here?"

Chris' face dropped as if he was embarrassed, "Oh! Oh, sorry..."

Larson frowned, "Really?"

Chris smiled, "No," and he burst from the tree-line at a full sprint, guns raised as he ran toward the oncoming throng in the general direction where he thought Alpha was still fighting.

"Bring that shit to me!!!" Chris screamed as he fired with both weapons and bodies jerked and fell from the impact of the shots.

Chris could hear Larson screaming, "Shit! Cover him! Cover him!" as more bodies fell in front of him, cut down by the soldiers taking out Dimitri's people who were in his path before he could reach them. Suddenly, he was in the pack, shooting at any emaciated head that turned and locked onto him, as he continued to run through them. Surprisingly, most seemed to ignore him, their concentration focused on the soldiers behind him, or even still on Alpha in front of him, but enough of them had registered his presence that he had already expended the clips in the guns and had to reload.

At the push of a button the spent magazines dropped from his handguns and Chris quickly replaced them with fresh clips, when a cry went up by the tree line. It was a collective battle cry from the soldiers on the hill as they charged into the mass and met it head on. The sheer immensity of what was happening was almost more than Chris could take in, even if he had the time to comprehend it, which he didn't, as he had to shoot three more of Dimitri's people that suddenly seemed to realize he was kneeling amongst them. Everything was chaos now as black clad vampire collided with black camouflaged soldier, with the occasional sound of gunfire and the variety of screams, grunts and shouts adding a cumulative disorientation to the melee, which was threatening to overwhelm the thinking part of Chris' brain.

Forcing himself to not think, Chris took in a quick breath, set his feet and resumed his charge toward the last place he had seen Alpha. He gunned down more of Dimitri's people and didn't stop, even when the slides of his guns once again remained back and open, spent of their ammunition. The guns became blunt instruments within the close quarters where Chris now fought, and he pushed through the crowd until, almost as if he had crested a horizon, Alpha appeared in front of him. Strangely, his arrival had surprised both Alpha and his opponents because, for the first time since the fight began, the mass around Alpha seemed to hesitate.

Alpha was battered and bleeding from what looked like fingernail scratches that had dug deep channels into his face arms and legs. His clothes were tattered, but none of the marble white skin underneath appeared damaged as Alpha held his knives out in front of him, pale blood dripping down the blades, over his hands and halfway down his forearms.

Chris moved closer so the pair could stand back to back, "So what's the plan?" Chris asked, his voice half-panicked by how many were still surrounding them despite Larson's intervention.

Alpha chuckled, "We need to separate the group. Is that Larson up there?"

Chris' head swam, "I am going to assume for the time being that you just made an extremely good guess, but yes, Larson and a bunch of soldiers that seem to be following his orders."

Alpha nodded understanding, then yelled, "Reload!"

Alpha shot forward and began slicing the air with his blades. Chris dropped the clips and wriggled additional magazines from his pockets into the guns when Alpha ran past him yelling, "Shoot a path to the last warehouse Steve ran for, we can make a stand there!"

Chris surged forward, firing into the crowd and clearing a path, which Alpha widened, as they ran. Shouting as they went, Chris yelled, "We're going to be out of line of sight from Larson's people if we do this!"

"Yes! I know!" Alpha called back as he broke through the crowd and sprinted for the far side of the warehouse and the ruined roll-up door.

Chris shot the last of Dimitri's people standing between Alpha and him, grumbling, "Oh well, as long as you're aware of the situation."

Chapter 40

Have you ever had a dream, where you think you woke up but you can't get your body to respond? Or maybe one where you sort of wake up, but your head is so confused with whether you are still dreaming or just awake that you become completely and totally disorientated, having no idea what you are supposed to do? Or maybe there was a particular morning where you woke up, but were still so tired that you couldn't keep your eyes open, no matter how hard you tried to rouse yourself from sleep.

Well combine all three of those scenarios, and that was what I was feeling as my eyes fluttered in my attempt to stay conscious. All I could think was, "Sleep, bad. Eyes open..."

I knew I was alone, lying on a floor and it was cold. There was a strange sensation in my throat and chest, but as I couldn't really feel any pain, I tried moving and simply couldn't. I tried to take in a breath, but the air seemed to leak out of me, despite my trying to hold it in. I struggled to make sense of what was happening, ended up rolling onto my back and, through the haze of my vision, I could make out something hanging directly over me. Something inside me told me that the hanging thing was important, but my mind was swimming through a haze that I just couldn't seem to clear.

Something warm and wet struck my face and I blinked as it passed over my cheek and fell into my eye. It burned slightly and I tried to raise a hand to wipe it away when another drop struck me. I turned my head away as more droplets rained down from the sky and somehow I found the strength to raise a hand and wipe away some of the moisture.

I checked my fingers, prepared for the sight of blood, although I was uncertain why, and was surprised to find only damp fingers in my vision. Confused and seeing no indication of what had wet my face and fingers I placed my hand near my nose, but found no scent that would tell me what the liquid might be. More drops plunked down around me like a slowly starting rain and I wondered momentarily if there was a hole in the roof that was letting some rain in... but it hadn't been raining...

The idea of rainwater was appealing to me and I realized I was desperately thirsty. I somehow managed to lick my still damp hand and the salt that met my tongue sent a jolt into me. I dropped my hand to the floor, my only thought at how filthy my hand must be to make pure rainwater taste with such salinity.

My head rolled to the side and my eyes threatened to close again, and probably would have, if not for the sight of a tiny figure standing by an opening in the wall. It held very still, before running toward me, with its long hair flowing behind it as it approached and I searched my memories for who or what the figure might be. I felt the remaining air leave my lungs when I saw that it was Lei looking small and frail as she had on the day Alpha had introduced her to our collective, after rescuing her from her former life. I remembered the hard look on her face as she stared, unblinking, at everyone around her until her eyes fell on me and, as our eyes met, her defiant countenance slipped. In that moment I saw the frightened little girl that she really was and I swore to myself that I was going to make sure that nothing ever harmed her again.

Lei knelt next to me and placed her hands on my chest, which made me cough something wet up from deep inside myself. I managed to turn my head to keep from coughing anything at her and then felt my throat clear enough to talk.

"I love you," my voice was thin and weak, but I managed to get the words out in spite of how difficult it was to get any air. The effort made me realize that I was having trouble breathing and I forced myself, painfully, to take in as deep a breath as I could so I could say more. Lei's eyes went wide with surprise just as they had the first time I had said it to her when we were kids in the Nevada desert. I remembered how worried I had been that she would run from me after I confessed my feelings for her. I watched as her eyes filled with tears, same as they had before, and felt her push harder on my chest. It was painful and a pain that was unlike any I had ever felt before. Not so much that it was intense or excruciating, as it was an unusual sensation. It was like my chest was made of Velcro and the forced expansion as I drew breath was akin to ripping the two adhering pieces apart. It even sounded like that in my ears as I pulled more air in and was now able to hold it inside. It was an instinctive maneuver, but I realized that now the air was staying in me as opposed to leaking away and I felt my head begin to clear as the haze lifted from my sight.

I looked up at Lei's face again and realized that it wasn't Lei after all, but a small child that I didn't recognize. My thoughts suddenly came rushing back into me, and I looked upward at the ceiling and the object swinging overhead, remembering that this was where Lei was suspended. I turned back to the girl, her face jolting memories of where I was and what I was doing here.

"Pha?"

Chapter 41

"Right!" Chris screamed as he shot a final round from one of two his Berettas, all his extra ammunition for it now spent, "So what was the plan again?"

Alpha and Chris hadn't made it to the side of the warehouse where the roll-up door had been set in ruin as another, smaller group of Dimitri's people suddenly cut them off and sandwiched them between those chasing them from behind.

Alpha shouted back, "The plan is just to keep them all on us until Steve can either find Lei or kill Dimitri."

"Right," Chris agreed, "I'm a little unclear on what we're supposed to do after that?"

"Does it matter as long as Steve and Lei get away?"

Chris moaned, "Oh please don't tell me I fought my way to you just so you can get yourself killed Spartan-style."

Alpha laughed, "I did tell you to stay put."

"Yeah, but you know I never listen to you."

Chris flinched as one of Dimitri's people inched a little too close, so he threw the empty gun directly into the creeper's face. The solid grip struck hard and instantly split flesh, not in a mortal way or even an incapacitating injury, but painful enough to make the man retreat back to the safety of the group. Alpha frowned, "Now you're throwing your guns away?"

"Just one," Chris answered, "I have one more full clip for the other."

Chris could feel Alpha stiffen, "You know they're going to swarm us as soon as they see you're out of bullets?"

"Yep, so... on the count of three?"

"Agreed."

Chris took a deep breath, "All right. One..."

Movement from outside the circle of Dimitri's people caught Chris' eye. Someone was hurriedly walking over and calling out in their direction. Chris, feeling relief at the thought that Larson's people had finally reached them, squinted as he tried to make out who it was, only to have his stomach sink when he realized it was Dimitri Lagos.

"Oh crap," slipped from Chris' lips, making Alpha swivel his head to see what had interrupted the countdown.

"What is he carrying?" Alpha asked.

As Dimitri moved closer the sword in his hand and the blood that ran up his sleeve became evident and was a telling answer to Steve's fate.

"Oh no," Chris voice broke as he whispered the words and his head dropped while the air around him seemed to become very heavy, making it difficult to breathe.

Alpha remained stoic except for the gasp he took that indicated his surprise and horror at what the blood on the sword represented.

Dimitri called to his people in Russian, "What are you waiting for?! Take them!"

A multitude of heads swiveled from Dimitri and back to the pair in the center of their circle.

Even though he couldn't speak the language, at the sound of those words Chris raised his head and a snarl curled his lip, "Yeah, come get us you little fucking schoolgirls!"

Chris' hand whipped to his pocket, pulled out a fully loaded clip and slammed it home into magazine well before anyone, including Alpha, could fully register what had happened. The first shot was like a starting pistol that abruptly animated everyone to life, and suddenly their "dance" began again. Alpha lunged as Chris began shooting and Dimitri's people dodged around as they tried to close in.

Chris' final bullet blew cleanly through the forehead of another of Dimitri's people before the slide remained open and served as a beacon to the remaining two or three dozen zombies that he was out of bullets. They closed on him like the tide and forced him to the ground, pinning his arms and legs while the remainder went for Alpha. Chris could still make out Alpha's swirling form cutting down adversaries right and left until Dimitri walked behind one of his people, in this case a small anorexic looking woman, and pushed her bodily onto one of Alpha's blades. Though her bodyweight was slight it was enough to trap the blade and halt Alpha's momentum long enough for three more of Dimitri's people to grab onto the incapacitated arm. The remaining mass instantly saw the opening, and as a whole shoved their way in and tackled Alpha, pinning him to the ground in a fashion similar to the way Chris was pinned.

Dimitri sauntered around to the front of the pile, smiling triumphantly at the sight lying in front of his feet.

To Alpha he said, "All this for a girl?" he shook his head in either disappointment or disgust, "how did you ever manage to become the leader of the North American Collective?"

Alpha regarded Dimitri calmly, "It is exactly because I value every one of my people like family that we thrive."

Dimitri shook his head again, "No, that is exactly what makes you weak because it gives your enemies a target they can exploit," Dimitri inclined his head to Chris "just as I have done."

Having made his point, Dimitri lazily twirled his sword around a bit before walking over to the pile where Chris was pinned.

Inclining his head back to Alpha he asked, "One of your famed Hunters?"

Alpha did not respond, the same could not be said for Chris, "Goddamn right! You ugly, monkey sucking-!"

A fist from one of Dimitri's people slammed into Chris face and then covered his mouth, silencing him.

Dimitri looked perplexed and turned to Alpha for enlightenment, "My English must be slipping. Did... Was he about to call me a monkey-sucking... something or other?"

The inanity of the moment made Alpha blink with surprise as Dimitri considered the insult for another couple of seconds before he shuffled over next to Chris' head and kicked him squarely in the temple, rendering him unconscious.

The people holding Chris down let go and moved to surround their leader who turned back to Alpha, "All your people are precious to you? Well, despite what you think of me, I take care of my people as well."

Alpha's eyes glanced from one pock marked face to another as he took in the level of "care" that Dimitri seemed to be providing those that currently surrounded him.

"Ah, yes." Dimitri agreed as he followed Alpha's gaze, "my good friend Nicholas Nicholaevich wanted an army to command, so I provided him with people that were," Dimitri considered his next words, "less than what I would want fighting by my side."

Alpha looked at the mass of people holding him down and those by Dimitri's side when the realization came to him, "What have you done?"

"Ingushetia, the city of Nazran in particular, is a country of the disenfranchised and destitute. What greater service can I do for them than to give them purpose again?"

Alpha's memory of how his blood, given to Chris in a transfusion to save his life, had altered Chris' body chemistry on a genetic level and turned him into one his kind.

"You're turning regular humans into our kind? But that isn't possible on any kind of scale. Your blood..."

"Is now readily available thanks to the late Dr. Whelan's vaccine. It only takes a small sample of my blood to create enough vaccine to change these poor fools into beings like us."

Alpha shook his head, "But they're all dying of the Porphyria."

"Of course," Dimitri agreed, "once they have served their

359

purpose we will further restrict their source of sustenance until they kill themselves or simply die off. After all, we can't have a collection of simple, converted human waste sharing our victory with us. Until then, every commander needs pawns to lay on a blade for the cause of victory and I'd rather it be this collection of Nazran trash as opposed to my true bloods."

Alpha wasn't sure if it was because Dimitri was speaking in English that none of the people surrounding him reacted to what had just been said or if it was because most were too far gone in the throes of the Porphyria to understand anything more than instinct. Either way, Alpha could feel his anger flaring and he struggled against the multitude of hands holding him down, but Dimitri quickly walked over and placed the blade at Alpha's throat quelling his struggles.

"I'm going to give you one chance to live. Tell me where my property, the one you call William, is located and I'll let you and the girl go." He gestured to Chris' limp form and said, "I'll even throw in this insufferable fool for good measure."

Alpha took note of the few spots of pink blood that discolored the polished blade and fact that Dimitri hadn't included Steve in the equation.

Dimitri smirked, "What do you say."

Alpha looked Dimitri right in his eye and was about to answer him when a voice called out in Russian, "He says that you should go to hell, Bastard!"

Dimitri whirled, as did the heads of most of his people and were met by the sight of a figure so enormous that he seemed to fill the entire landscape with the sheer immensity of his size.

Alpha couldn't see past the mass of bodies, but knew that only one person in all of creation could cause the look of pure panic and fear in the eyes of everyone around him. In a loud voice Alpha called out, "Dimitri Lagos, may I introduce you to my friend William." Alpha then raised his voice to a bellow, "William, meet

360

Dimitri Lagos! The man who kidnapped your daughter!"

An eerie silence filled the air as the tip of Dimitri's sword swept away from Alpha's neck and gestured in the direction everyone was facing. Alpha could see Dimitri's hand shaking in the pregnant pause until a sound, like the roar of some great beast, exploded from beyond the circle of Dimitri's people. The cry was so full of rage and hate that its power seemed to shake the ground itself. Alpha felt the strength in the hands holding him down slacken as his captors desperately tried to rise from the ground where they pinned him. Alpha smiled as he realized they might have stood a chance if they had held their ground, but the chaos that ensued amongst Dimitri's people doomed them, as William rammed into them with bone splintering force, causing their bodies to either be crushed into the ground under his feet, or simply take flight into the air from the impact.

Dimitri shouted his orders, and the mass of his people seemed to generally rally at his words as they shifted toward William and then swarmed foward in an attempt to overwhelm the giant in a manner similar to the way they had overcome Alpha.

Then, from the other side of the melee, Alpha heard another sound, one that could only be someone cursing and, despite his unfamiliarity with the foreign dialect, Alexei's angry voice was easy to distinguish. Alpha could see Dimitri turn toward the sound, barking out more orders, causing a portion of the main group of Dimitri's people to separate and charge the second threat, only to find themselves being cut down, as Alexei advanced toward the spot where he and Chris lay recovering.

"Nicholas, Nicholas!" Dimitri had begun screaming as he backpedaled away from the fracas, desperately scanning the surrounding area for the big man.

Alexei made two great slashes with his Bowie knife in a crisscross pattern that practically bisected the closest of Dimitri's people before he turned to Dimitri and hissed, "My uncle will not be joining us!"

Alpha watched Dimitri's eyes go wide with emotion, as the words sank in. Dimitri cursed to himself under his breath, as he backpedalled in order to get behind a couple of his people.

Alpha knelt, retrieving his own knives from the ground, before standing and facing Dimitri. Noticing the movement Dimitri turned to face Alpha and raised his sword into an "on-guard" position.

Alpha held his knives in a ready position and chuckled, "Yes, this is probably how it should be."

The leaders of two vampire nations, from opposite sides of the world, faced each other, ignoring everything and everyone else around them.

Alpha raised up his knives and was about to step forward when Dimitri's other hand whipped out from behind his back holding a Colt's Python 2.5" barreled .357 Magnum snub-nosed revolver. Alpha froze, and Dimitri sneered at his American counterpart, "Yes, it probably is."

The sound of the shot overwhelmed the other sounds of battle, and Alpha felt the impact of the bullet shoving him back fiercely, as pain exploded into his chest. He hadn't actually realized he had been knocked from his feet, until the back of his head slammed down hard against the ground, making his vision swim.

A bellow of rage exploded from William's lungs at having seen Alpha fall and he turned toward Dimitri and charged him once again. At least four of Dimitri's people were still clinging to various parts of William's body, but he moved faster and faster toward the vampire as if he didn't notice them at all. Dimitri saw him coming and fired his revolver at him, but the bullet struck one of his own people, dislodging the man from William's shoulder where he had been clinging. Another shot rang out and blood exploded from William's opposite shoulder. William's body had jerked with the impact, but he never broke stride, continuing to close in on Dimitri's position. A third shot erupted and the bullet sliced through the flesh between William's shoulder and neck as the attempted headshot missed by mere inches. Still, there were arteries that ran through the area near the impact to make it a dangerous wound. No arterial spray erupted from the furrow the bullet created, but blood still began flowing copiously from the traumatized area.

William never even slowed.

Dimitri began to backpedal again, but as he turned he saw Alexei, hacking his way through the crowd and closing in from the other direction.

More of Dimitri's people climbed onto William's back, until nearly a dozen had some sort of grip on the big man until his steps were slowed and then finally halted. Realizing he would need to extricate himself from the clinging crowd, William began lashing out at the ones who held him, and so Dimitri chose the moment to turn and run.

Chapter 42

Dimitri had lived through many battles, some ended in victory and some in retreat, but he had lived through it all because he was able to tell how the tide of battle was turning and he was prepared to do whatever he needed to do to ensure his own survival. Now as he ran for the warehouse, he could clearly see the small combat unit that was decimating the remainder of his people who were not still engaged against the Romanov and William. Dimitri hated retreating, but common sense told him that it was time to leave and regroup. He had thousands more of his people that he could call upon to defend him, and all he had to do was make it back to the city where he would be safe. His plans would have to be put on hold after the army seized his cache' of biological weapons, but he still had the formulas, and there would always be those who would be willing to create new weapons for the right price.

All he had to do was get away with the girl Lei, and they all would just let him leave. He had exploited the American's weakness of sentimentality before, and there was no reason why it could not serve him again. Dimitri entered the warehouse, freezing in place when he saw only a puddle of blood where he had left the American, Steve Jacobs, lying dead. After running a person through with his sword, Dimitri expected death to follow. A sickening realization made his eyes dart to the ceiling, where he saw only the empty chains where his hostage had been suspended.

Desperately he scanned the warehouse and saw something move near the control switch for the winch that had raised Lei into the rafters. Quickly, and with his gun raised, he moved toward the spot, but found no sign of anything or anyone.

It was the slight sound of someone breathing in a slight, wet, wheezing series of breaths, which were apparently more noise than could be muffled that gave her away. Dimitri turned slowly toward a crate that had been discarded in the nearby corner, and cautiously approached. He stood on his toes to peer into the crate, but found it empty. Undaunted he continued around the large crate and placed one hand on an open side. With a grunt he flung the crate away and found Pha clinging to the unmoving form of Lei as she curled into the shadows that the corner had provided.

Dimitri raised the gun and pointed it at the child, but as he examined her face he didn't see the look of terror he had been expecting. Instead, the girl was smiling.

"Got you," Pha practically sang, in the way that children taunt each other. The confusion slowed time as Dimitri's brain tried to process the meaning behind the girl's words, and in that moment, Lei suddenly exploded from where she had been curled, her face a mask of rage as she snarled, flashing her teeth and leaping at Dimitri.

Dimitri's finger squeezed the trigger, but Lei had knocked his arm away before crashing into him, the force of her attack sent the bullet wide of its intended target and the gun flying from Dimitri's hand.

Lei bit down hard on his forearm, but released it as soon as she realized her attack hadn't reached the Ancient's throat. Dimitri tried to shift the point of his sword into a position for thrusting it through her, but the length of the blade and their bodies close proximity made it impossible. So, instead Dimitri began cutting with the edge of the blade where it had contacted Lei's torso. Feeling the edge ripping through her tattered clothes, Lei tried to shift into a position so she might grab Dimitri's sword arm, but lost her leverage on the man. Dimitri swung his free hand in an arc, catching Lei across her cheek with the back of his fist and the powerful blow knocked her away from him.

Dimitri scrambled to his feet, getting his sword into the ready position, as Lei rose to face him as well. He attacked with a series of wild slashes that served only to make Lei retreat farther and farther away, sometimes having to roll backwards to stay outside its reach. Feigning a final slash, Dimitri suddenly stopped and pivoted as Lei began her backward roll, and he suddenly bolted toward Pha, with the intention of scooping her up as a hostage. Lei screamed as she realized what Dimitri was going to do, and she stumbled awkwardly as she tried to come out of her roll to give chase, but there was no chance of her intercepting him before he could reach the girl.

Dimitri smiled to himself in triumph as the girl's silhouette came into view. He would get out of this yet, and he reached out with his free hand to grab the child, when in the dim lights of the shadows, he saw her spin and grab with both hands, onto something that was suspended close to her side. Something large moved in the shadows and there was a loud ratcheting sound that Dimitri recognized as he froze in surprise.

"Nyet!" Dimitri hissed in disbelief as the object levitated closer to him and emerged from the shadows of the corner. The barrel of a shotgun slowly oozed out from the darkness followed by its grip, trigger and finally the large, bloody hand holding it.

"Got you," Steve sang in the same manner that Pha had moments ago as he squeezed the trigger shooting Dimitri point blank in the chest. The old man flew back from the impact, as the 00 buckshot tore into his chest, shredding his body and leaving him supine on the floor of the warehouse.

Steve continued to emerge from the darkness as Dimitri flailed on the ground in agony. The ancient vampire managed to lift his head enough to see Steve stumble his way forward, the child Pha clutching his side and helping him move. Steve's left side was saturated with blood and his left arm hung lifelessly to one side, but his right arm held the shotgun with a strong and steady resolve. Pha was walking next to him, supporting some of his weight on his left side and, when he rotated the shotgun toward her, the child used both hands to ratchet the weapon into readiness

366

once again.

There was no preamble or witty remark as Steve repositioned the shotgun and fired into Dimitri's chest again. Blood exploded as the old man's body bucked from the impact.

Lei breathed a sigh of relief as she watched, noticing that Steve's face was no longer smiling. Instead he wore a look that was eerily similar to the one Alpha wore when facing down an enemy. The look was cold, emotionless and uncompromising.

Chapter 43

I held the shotgun in close to my body, guessing I only had one more cartridge available before I'd need to reload the magazine. Given my injuries, I had to make sure to end this with my next shot. I had let Pha participate up to this point partially because I needed her help, but also because I wanted her to be part of the destruction of the monster that had kidnapped her, forcing her to undergo so much pain and psychological uncertainty in her tiny life. Maybe knowing she had bested her tormentor would help stave off possible nightmares in the future, but there were some things that no child should have to see, so after Pha ratcheted the shotgun again I shifted my body to shield her from what was about to happen.

Leaning in close I said softly into her ear, "Look away, Pha."

She looked back up at me with eyes way too jaded for a child her age, but didn't argue as she turned her head and pressed her cheek into my side as I extended the barrel of the shotgun until the tip was just over a foot from Dimitri's head.

Dimitri's eyes rolled up in their sockets to look at me, as he registered what I was about to do. Somehow the ancient vampire managed, in spite of the massive trauma done to his chest, to curl his lips into a snarl flashing his teeth at me in one final defiant gesture.

I looked into eyes that had seen the rise and fall of empires, and I suddenly went cold inside as my finger hesitated on the trigger. I had a strange sensation run through me, making me feel like I was about to destroy some kind of antique or irreplaceable artifact. Then I realized that my eyes were locked with Dimitri's and I couldn't tear my gaze away. My body began to lose the adrenaline rush that it had been running on since I had pulled the trigger the first time, as pain and fatigue began to seep back in to me. I coughed and felt a bubbly foam come up from deep in my lungs and my legs started feeling unsteady. I heard Lei call out to me, but it was like hearing someone talking under water, as I had to shift my footing to keep from falling.

It was the sensation of Pha's arms hugging me tighter as I wobbled that brought my mind back to me. I blinked and suddenly I was looking down at the tiny figure clutching tightly at my side. She was such a strong little girl that a person could forget just how young and small she was. It was in those moments of vulnerability that children, who always want to push their individuality ever forward as they move toward adulthood, will do something to remind us just how much they are still the little ones who need adults to care, comfort and protect them.

My eyes began to fill with tears of sorrow and rage that someone, anyone, would use a child in such a manner as Dimitri had done. I locked eyes with Dimitri again and the ancient vampire's eyes widened with fear, as the only thought that ran through me now was that the "thing" lying on the floor at my feet should have been put down a millennia ago.

"Fuck you, old man," I said with a quiet rage as I pulled the trigger. Dimitri's head exploded as the shot pulped bone and brain, leaving only tatters of flesh and exposed vertebrae at the place on his neck where his head had been.

I stared down at what was left of Dimitri Lagos and wanted to spit on his corpse. Instead my legs gave out, and it was all I could do not to fall on top of Pha, or into the gore that I had created at my feet. Lei was at my side in an instant, and kept me from crashing down and further injuring myself. I honestly don't know where she got the strength, but it was all I could do to let myself fall into her embrace as she gripped me so very tightly.

"I think I have only one shot left in this thing." I said as the three of us held tightly to each other, "We really should go hide in our corner again, at least until Alpha comes for us."

Chapter 44

It only took about five minutes before I could hear the heavy footfalls of someone approaching. Not trusting my ability to distinguish friend from foe by the sound of their footsteps, I raised the barrel of the shotgun to cover the area in front of me. Lei and Pha were crouching behind my back in the shadows ready to move as needed, depending on what happened in the next couple of seconds.

Hiding behind the crates I couldn't see who it might have been that was walking around but, when the sound of the footsteps stopped, it wasn't difficult to figure out that they had stopped next to Dimitri's remains.

A voice called out in a heavy Russian accent, "Steve? Are you in here?"

Recognition hit in an instant and I called out, "Alexei? Is that you?

I could hear Alexei pivot toward the sound of my voice, "Da, my friend! Come out, we have won the day!"

"Friend of yours?" Lei asked.

I shrugged, "I think so. He's saved my life a couple days ago in any case." To Alexei I called out, "Are we clear?"

"Da!" I could hear Alexei begin walking toward me, "But come quickly. Your Alpha, William and Chris are all injured."

Upon hearing that her father, William, had been injured, Pha practically leapt from where she had been crouching and bolted out from her place in the shadows. Almost as soon as Pha disappeared around one side of the crate Alexei appeared, and immediately was kneeling at my side.

Lei tensed, "What do you mean Alpha is injured?"

Alexei didn't look up to face her, but instead gently pulled my shirt aside and inspected the wound that Dimitri had given me. With practiced movements Alexei's hand was in that weird messenger bag of his and removing some kind of pouch of herbs that looked like a giant tea bag. I yelped with pain as he unceremoniously pulled out the wad of my shirt that I had stuffed into the sword wound, immediately replacing it with the tea bag. Blood oozed momentarily saturating the bag, but once my blood mixed with whatever was in the bag it seemed to stop flowing out of me, not clotting exactly, as much as it just no longer leaked out from my body. By the time he was through, Lei was practically in a panic over Alpha, "What happened to Alpha?!" She insisted.

"He was shot in the chest." Alexei said simply and I could hear the intake of breath from Lei as she gasped. I might have gasped too, if I had been able.

I asked stoically, "Will he live?"

Alexei shook his head, "I don't know. They are working on him, but..."

I frowned, "Who is working on him?"

"My best guess would be American special forces, as there is an American in charge."

"An American, are you sure?"

Alexei nodded his head, "He seems to speak Russian fluently enough, but his accent is terrible."

"Imagine that," I said trying not to smile.

Alexei seemed to grow outraged, "Indeed, it is like listening to fingernails on a chalkboard, and my ears just want to bleed with the sound." He suddenly switched topics, "Do you think you can stand?"

Whatever he had stuck to my chest seemed to revive me, so with Lei under one arm and Alexei holding up the other, they got me to my feet. By the time we had made it outside we could see a helicopter flying in over the forest, to land where a group of black clad soldiers had gathered. Almost as soon as the helicopter had touched down the men lifted a trio of bodies on stretchers, loading them into the helicopter. Pha followed close behind one and was

371

hoisted up into the helicopter as well. I could see Chris, Alpha and William were all alive and being tended to by the soldiers that had loaded them on board.

I turned to Alexei, "You are absolutely sure they are in good hands?"

Alexei looked momentarily confused when another voice chimed in to say, "He can't, but I certainly can."

I tried to turn, but had to wait until Alexei helped both Lei and me stagger in a half circle, before I could see Major Robert Larson dressed in similar black combat fatigues and smiling broadly at me.

I didn't return the smile as I faced the man, "The last time my people were treated by regular medical personnel the results had been extraordinarily bad." Larson knew about the mass kidnapping and attempted genocide of my people after a Pharmaceutical company realized it could make billions from a medication derived from my people's blood.

Larson raised his hands up in supplication, "Easy Steve. These are all my people and I have full and total faith in them. They will act only in the best interests of your people. Besides," Larson looked around at the accumulation of bodies, many of whom had been brutally cleaved by Alpha's knives, smashed by William's fists or riddled with bullets from Chris' and my weapons, "I don't think I want to chance the consequences of betraying your trust."

It took all I had to unhook my arms from around Lei and Alexei, but I figured that when a person wants to say something imposing, he or she had better be standing under their own power. It looks a lot less impressive if someone is holding you up at the time you are trying to influence a person with your point.

"How is it you and the 'cavalry' are here, now?"

Larson smiled, "I warned you that the Russian government was aware of the warehouse and Dimitri's plans, didn't I?"

372

I looked at the soldiers milling around through the bodies and moving in groups into the warehouses, "They're not Russian."

Larson laughed, "Oh, hell no. The Russian's are probably still in the planning stages, but it won't be long until they show up, and by the time they get here all they will find is an empty space as barren as a parking lot."

"So who are these guys? C.I.A.?"

"Not exactly," Larson said, being deliberately cryptic, "Let's just say they are 'my' people."

I was beginning to understand and volunteered, "And because the Russian military was going to move in, maybe too late to stop what was happening, you brought in 'your' people to contain the situation, right?"

"Something like that, yes."

My legs started to wobble as my injuries began to overwhelm whatever Alexei had given me.

Larson watched me struggle, and before I could say anything else on the matter, he said, "There's room for you on the next helicopter."

I didn't like the change in topic and tried to dismiss it by quickly blurting out, "I'm fine." The effort must have unsettled my balance even more because Lei suddenly had one arm around my waist and a look on her face that conveyed she might kill me herself if I refused the medical care.

Larson stepped closer and peered at the wound, "That's a bad place to have a hole in your body that nature hadn't intended for you," he looked up to my face and shrugged, "not that there's such a thing as a good unintended hole, but that is right over a lung, and I'm not sure how your standing, much less breathing right now."

I made a feeble attempt at turning to Alexei to make introductions, but found only empty space, where Alexei had been.

"Alexei?" I asked out loud.

Lei's head moved from side to side, searching for him as well.

Larson had a surprised look on his face, then quickly reacted by speaking into some kind of communication device that hung around his neck. "All units check targets, we have an uncontained friendly on site." Larson turned back to me, "Was he the guy who was helping you out a second ago?"

I nodded my head, "He's been working alongside us since we got here."

"So he's on our side?" Larson asked.

I considered that, "I think so, but it would probably be better to think of him as someone who had a similar agenda. Helping us, in turn helped him achieve his own goals as well."

Larson nodded, but asked, "You have any idea what those goals might have been?"

"Seemed a personal thing between him and one of Dimitri's people called Nicholas." I gestured to one of the other warehouses where I had seen Alexei and Nicholas before the fighting began. "You should probably have your people look in that warehouse before the regular army guys get in there."

Larson looked skeptical, "You think it's more important than containing biological weapons of mass destruction?"

I shrugged, "You and you're team know about the W.M.D's and you're prepared for them. You don't know about what was going on in there."

Larson stared at me as the sound of another helicopter's blades could be heard coming in from over the forest.

"That bad?" he asked me and I could only sigh, looking down at my feet in reply. I was getting tired, and really didn't feel like talking anymore.

Lei answered for me, "Go see for yourself." I could hear the pain in her voice, as her will began to crack, and I realized that despite appearances, her own injuries were far more significant

374

than she had been showing.

"Is that helicopter for us?" I asked as I inclined my head in the helicopter's direction.

Larson looked behind him as the aircraft rolled into view, "It can be. I take it you've reconsidered? "

I nodded weakly.

I guess Larson couldn't resist, "You sure you want to trust me and my team?"

I looked up at him and found the strength to say over the pain that was seeping into me, "I trust you completely," before gesturing with my head at one of the more gruesome corpses on the ground, "because you understand the consequences of betraying my trust."

Larson smiled at me, turned and waved his arm at the helicopter as it landed. The moment it's landing gear hit the ground men jumped out with stretchers and their small cases that I guessed were medical bags. In seconds they had Lei and myself laid out and were inspecting each of us for whatever damage had been done.

Larson said, "Just relax, these guys have knit me up and put me back together more times than I care to remember. I'll see to the cleanup here."

Concern washed over me, not for myself but for what we were leaving behind here. "Major," I said as seriously as I could as my stretcher was lifted and I felt my body rise from the ground, "no one, not a government or an individual, should ever have access to the things in those warehouses."

Larson looked worried, "I have my orders Steve."

I let out a wet cough and my vision started to swirl, but I managed to shake my head and say, "Remember Bangkok?"

Larson's whole body seemed to freeze for a split second, before he recovered and said, "I have my orders." Then he gestured for his men to get us onto the helicopter. I wanted to plead with

375

him some more, but just didn't have the strength and instead simply watched as the helicopter grew larger in my field of vision as I was carried closer and closer to its lifesaving purpose.

The last thing I remember before passing out was Larson calling after me, "Trust me Steve, I'll take care of this!"

Chapter 45

Six months later.

I have to hand it to Larson and his team. Not only did they patch me up wonderfully, but Chris and Lei appeared to have come through their injuries with flying colors as well. Alpha on the other hand was in critical condition, or at least he was until William literally ripped him off of his life support and then disappeared with Pha and Alpha's body before any of Larson's people could stop him. Now, even after all this time, there had been no communication or sign from William, Alpha or Pha, but some small part of me knew that they were all right. After all, Alpha and William had been alive over six hundred years and must have learned some personal survival tricks in all that time. Still, it would have been good to hear something.

As for Lei, Chris and myself, we all headed back to Las Vegas and surrounded ourselves with our own kind. My people had all the medical personnel and education we would need to expedite our recoveries and rehab our bodies, but there were a few loose ends that needed to be tied up.

First of all, there was the issue of the business Lei and I had left behind. Once we felt up to it, we made a trip to our old office space and found an Eviction notice on the door. It wasn't a surprise. We had forgotten to leave an extended deposit with the landlord before we had left for Thailand to chase after Dr. Whelan, so the lease payment was grossly past due.

"Think they would lease it to us again?" Lei asked.

"Maybe, if we were to make good on the months we've missed, and leave a substantial deposit." A thought occurred to me, "Do we want to lease it again?"

Lei looked hurt by the question, "I really liked having a place to go every morning, and I liked it when we could help someone, you know, find their kid or something like that."

I nodded, "I do know, but there are other things we need to talk about before we can just set up shop again."

Chris tried the door and found it locked, "Is there anything in there you need?"

I looked at Lei with Chris' question in my eyes. She shook her head, "We never had a chance to clean up the mess we made when Dimitri and his people paid us a visit. I'm sure by this point the landlord has hocked anything valuable we had in there, just to pay for all the damages to his property ."

"So we can walk away?"

"If we have to, then yes." Lei sounded crestfallen, but she understood. With Alpha gone our people needed leadership, and the moment the question of who that was going to be was raised, all eyes had turned to me. I suppose it made sense. The people of our collective all looked at the Hunters as the people who ran things, even if it wasn't always the case, and with my being the unofficial leader of the Hunters everyone automatically guessed that I would fill the position. Frankly I would have preferred not to be the one in charge, because I had been living outside the collective for a very long time, and going back seemed stifling, but I had agreed to do it for the time needed until someone more appropriate could take over.

"So we'll walk away," Lei said regretfully, "and now what do we do?"

"Same thing we've always done. Protect our collective and search for those like us that may need our help."

Chris said soberly, "You know that means taking responsibility for those who have regressed into the ravages of the disease, right?"

Lei and I both nodded, saying in unison, "Same as before."

We were going to miss the life we had set up for ourselves. It had been rewarding, as Lei had stated, but the real purpose behind it was the tracking down of Whelan, killing him and

378

preventing anyone else from utilizing what the evil bastard had created. Now that all of that had been accomplished, a general lack of purpose washed over us and we just stood in front of our office building unsure of everything.

"What are you going to do Chris?" Lei asked.

"Me?" Chris sounded surprised to suddenly be part of the conversation. "Well," he chuckled, "I don't think there's a place for me with the L.A.P.D. as a medical examiner anymore."

"They'd be all the better to have you." I said.

Chris started to laugh, but then saw the look on my face and how serious my statement had been. He responded only with a quick nod before changing the subject, "I think I'm going to go to Disneyland."

Now I did laugh, "Oh really?"

"No, I'm serious. Haven't been there since I was a kid, and after I was shot and in the process of becoming..." Chris voice hesitated, "well, you know, all I could think about was, 'Why hadn't I ever gone back there?' I have all these memories of how much I loved the place, but I never made it back as an adult. Hell, I lived in Los Angeles for the entirety of my professional life and the amusement park was less than an hour away, so why had I never bothered? What was the reason? Did I think I was too old or something? Too jaded?" Chris paused in his rant, and I have to admit I was feeling more than a little guilty for laughing at him when he initially mentioned it.

Chris came out of his inner reflective moment and said triumphantly, "Well after everything I have seen, done and gone through in the past couple of years, I think it's time for me to get a little dose of that side of my life's potential. A little fill up of the magic that is held by the things that are good in life."

"And you think Disneyland will do that for you?" Lei asked and I detected a caution in her voice that I rarely ever heard.

Chris only shrugged, "It's possible I've romanticized the

379

place beyond what I am hoping for it to deliver, but it's a hell of a good place to start. If it is less than I need, then I'll move on to the next spot, wherever that might be, trying again and again until I get to a place where I am so full of the memories of why life is a blessing and worth living, that there will be no room for the negative things in my head anymore."

Lei and I were silent as Chris smiled at us. It was such a simple quest he had set for himself, and one that, for the most part, was highly irresponsible. Chris, although born a normal human, was now one of our kind. He was also a Hunter, trained by Alpha himself, and as such had a responsibility to the collective, to protect the group's interests... just the same as Lei and myself.

I walked to my office door, putting my hand on top of the Eviction notice sticker that had been adhered to it. There was nothing inside that really mattered. No unsolved case files, no photographs, no other memorabilia that need to be reclaimed. Just office supplies and old furniture, most of which had been in pretty rough shape after our initial tussle with Dimitri and his people when they had first came calling.

"Steve?" Lei's voice called out softly to me as I leaned against the building that represented our life together outside of the world to which we now had to return. "Are you all right?"

I sighed, "Yeah. I'm fine."

I inclined my head to see her looking at me with a worried expression in her eyes, and the moment my eyes fell on her, my heart quickened. Not an unusual reaction when one was looking at a woman as beautiful as Lei, but this was different from my usual awestruck, and often lustful response. For some reason my eyes looked past the more obvious and over-exaggerated aspects of her appearance, and the physical allure fell away, leaving a shining vision of her face, as it had been when we had first met as children. Some very, very old feelings of newness, uncertainty and potential discovery surfaced in me that I hadn't felt since that initial moment

380

so long ago. A small laugh escaped me, which made Lei frown in confusion before she asked, "Are you ready to go?"

"Go?" I repeated, and realized that I wasn't sure what, or where that meant...

...And then I did.

"Yes," I said confidently, as I push myself away from the door, "Yes, I am ready to go."

Lei smiled and nodded at me as she took my hand, but froze when I said, "You know if we left now we could be married by dinner."

Lei's voice caught as she realized what I was saying. "What?"

I shrugged, "It is Vegas after all. We could probably even get an Elvis impersonator to marry us and sing 'Love Me Tender' as the ceremony concludes."

"You want to take me to get married now? Just like that?" Lei said softly, more thinking about it out loud instead of asking.

"I think we've waited long enough, don't you?" I said in a confessional manner, "Look, we can do the whole grand ceremony and reception later. Make a real show of it. White dress, church, band, and anything else you might desire or imagine, but I don't want to wait even another second to make you my wife."

Lei just looked at me with a bewildered expression that made her even more adorable than usual.

I turned to Chris, "Feel like being my best man before you head out for the Magic Kingdom?"

Chris smiled but, before he could answer, Lei said again, "You want to marry me right now?"

"Yep," I said, then added, "assuming you'll still have me."

Lei didn't answer as quickly as I hoped and I felt a slight tremor in my legs as she just looked at me blankly. The unease didn't abate until I noticed tears welling in her eyes and, before the first one could fall, Lei jumped into my arms and kissed me.

We held the kiss, even as Chris began making "eww" noises through his wide smile that spoke of his true feelings on the matter. When we finally parted Lei wiped at her eyes and grew serious, "Steve, the collective. Our people…?"

I cut her off, "Have survived for decades with the rules that are in place. A couple of weeks, or months, isn't going to make that much of a difference."

Lei seemed unsure.

"Besides," I acquiesced, "We'll have our cell phones with us if there are any real emergencies, and we'll be close by, only a couple hours away, if we are truly needed."

Lei shook her head, "I don't have any clothes or..."

"Not a problem." I said quickly.

"Actually, that makes this even more interesting!" Chris got a quick slap on his shoulder for that one.

"Don't worry about any of that, I'll take care of everything. All you need to do is think about what you want to do for a honeymoon."

Lei looked skeptical, "We get to go on a honeymoon?"

"Disneyland's close," Chris volunteered.

Now it was Lei's turn to look aghast, "Me? Disneyland?"

"Why not?" Chris challenged.

"Because… it's my honeymoon!" Lei whined as if the answer was obvious.

"And?" Chris looked at her seriously, "are you trying to tell me you don't want to go?"

The smiles on their faces as they began to argue were endearing and I just sat back to watch the show. Listening to the banter, and the frivolity underneath the words was something that had been lacking in all three of us since we had returned home from Nazran. It filled me with hope, and I got the sense that despite the difficulties we were going to face in returning to our old lives, everything was going to be okay.

I turned one last time to the office door and noticed something small that had been wedged between the door and the door frame. I pulled the small piece of cardstock out and looked at it, expecting to see a flyer for pizza or some such thing. Instead, I found myself looking at a business card. The embossed logo was of a metallic, gold policeman's badge, just like I used to carry when I was with the LAPD. The word over the badge was "METRO" indicative of the Las Vegas Metropolitan Police Department, and the name on the badge read "Detective Angelo Dunn, Homicide." There were also phone and fax numbers, along with an e-mail address, printed in the lower right hand corner. I turned the card over and saw a few hand printed words on the back.

"If you ever return, please give me a call. - Angelo"

I knew Detective Dunn from the times when we had worked on some missing child investigations. I always thought he was a pretty decent guy and totally dedicated to his job. I felt he was one of the good guys that was always looking to make a difference wherever he could.

"...pretty little princess," Chris sang in a high mocking voice as my mind returned to the moment.

Lei looked as though she was about to start her retort, when she caught me looking at the card and asked, "What's that?"

"Nothing important for now," I made a mental note to call Detective Angelo, but not until after we got back from Disneyland or whatever it was that we were going to do. Lei and I were going to live for a very, very long time and we had earned the right to spend a little of it on ourselves.

Joining in the frivolity I said, "So? Anaheim?," and took Lei's hand in mine. She responded by leaning in and kissing me softly as we walked toward Chris' Hummer H2.

"Now you two can't be doing that the entire time we're at Disneyland okay?"

I looked down into Lei's beautiful face and said, "No promises Dopey."

"Hey!" Chris protested, "I never said I was going to be Dopey!

In unison, Lei and I both said, "Too late."

###

About the Author

Michael Weinberger graduated from University of Pacific after earning his undergraduate degree in Sports Medicine and then went on to the Los Angeles College of Chiropractic where he earned his Doctor of Chiropractic degree in 1993 at the age of 25. He returned home to Las Vegas and operated a successful chiropractic office until the fall of 2000 when a severe arm injury forced him to step away from his chosen profession. It was during his recovery that he began writing.

His first novel, "Blood Harvest: Book 1, The Hidden Amongst Us" won a 2012 Next Generation Indie Publishers Award for Regional Fiction.

His second novel and sequel "Madman's Monster: Book 2, The Hidden Amongst Us" won Best Book of 2013: Paranormal Genre', from the IndieReader Discovery Awards.

Michael Weinberger enjoys writing, archery, martial arts, deep-sea fishing, movies and is a self-confessed "foodie." He lives in Las Vegas with his wife and two daughters where, when not otherwise engaged, can usually be found shooting arrows into the garage from the custom archery bows he makes in his spare time.

Website: Weinbergerbooks.com
Facebook: MichaelWeinbergerBooks

Other works:
Published:
Blood Harvest: Book 1, The Hidden Amongst Us
Madman's Monster: Book 2, The Hidden Amongst Us
Rasputin's Prodigy: Book 3, The Hidden Amongst Us

Coming Soon:
Adult Fiction (High Fantasy): The Last Warden
Children's Picture Book: Oogie the Bear's Rainy Day Adventure